*A Rich Wife*

### *Alexandre pulled her gently to him and kissed her.*

Their lips touched, then pressed, exploring. The kiss took on a life of its own. Their bodies enfolded and found a rhythm. Their eyes were closed. The world did not exist.

Fredericka pulled her head back, pushed him away. He was flushed, his breath was coming fast. "I'm not experienced with kissing," she said, flustered. "Is it always like this?"

"Rarely," he said. "I'm sorry. I should have stopped myself, but..."

"I am glad that you didn't," she told him. "That was one of the things I was worried about. I was not sure if it was possible for you to feel—for someone—to feel that kind..."

He rescued her from having to say precisely what she meant. "Now you know it is possible," he said smiling at her. He had wondered the same thing himself. Now he felt confident. Confident, and a little surprised at his own response.

---

"A story of romance, separation, misunderstanding and the discovery of real love."
—*Sunday Oklahoman*

"Heartwarming." —*Chattanooga Times*

"Charming." —*Baltimore Sun*

# A Rich Wife

## Barbara Wyden

## WARNER BOOKS

A Warner Communications Company

WARNER BOOKS EDITION

This Warner Books Edition is published by arrangement with Macmillan
Publishing Company, 866 Third Avenue, New York, N.Y. 10022

Warner Books, Inc.
666 Fifth Avenue
New York, N.Y. 10103

 A Warner Communications Company

Printed in the United States of America

First Warner Books Printing: October, 1986

10 9 8 7 6 5 4 3 2 1

# Prologue

Madame Roussy's subscription dances, held in the blue-and-white ballroom of the Amsterdam Society, were a New York institution. Here it was that the children of New York's solidly rich and impeccably descended mingled with the newly rich and powerful to learn the two-step, the waltz, and the intricacies of the cotillion figures. Here that they polished their ballroom manners and—cautiously—practiced the art of flirtation.

This year there had been more fluttering and twittering among the girls in Fredericka's class than ever before. This year they would be dancing to a three-piece ensemble instead of the piano played by Madame Roussy's aunt, and the girls who up to now had worn their hair in braids down their back were permitted to put their hair up.

They were on the verge of life, on the verge of romance. It was almost more excitement than they could bear. Even Fredericka had been surprised to find herself looking forward to this October afternoon. Perhaps this year would be different.

But the only thing that was different for Fredericka was

her pinned-up braid secured by the huge taffeta bow. For her, things were the same as always, only worse. With the malice that Fredericka always seemed to evoke in her, Madame had chosen Willy Keiller, the shortest boy in the class, for Fredericka's first partner. Fredericka had sighed when she saw Madame whisper into Willy's ear and nod toward her.

As Willy put his white-gloved hand on his partner's back, he found himself all but smothered between her breasts, his vision blocked. Not even straining on tiptoe could he see over her shoulder. He was forced to peek around her to see where he was going. He struggled valiantly, a small tug piloting an ocean liner, but it was hopeless.

They collided with one couple. And then another. There was a soft tinkle of giggles, the hiccuping of repressed laughter.

Willy discarded all the elegancies of the waltz as taught by Madame Roussy and doggedly danced Fredericka the length of the ballroom and back. No turns, no swirls, no graceful reverses. Straining apart from each other, they concentrated on getting through.

Madame Roussy signaled the musicians and the waltz ended raggedly. All control had been lost by now. The laughter grew. Willy all but pushed Fredericka toward one of the gilt chairs lining the walls and retreated precipitously. Left alone, she sat isolated, miserable, her cheeks burning. If she could only leave. But she could not run away. She had to stay, trying to pretend that she did not mind. If only she could die right here and now, she thought. Or faint. But she had never fainted in her life.

*I don't have to sit here and be laughed at. I don't owe them that pleasure. Papa is paying for all this. Madame owes me courtesy. It would be stupid for me to stay.* That settled in her mind, a smile spread over Fredericka's face. The flush disappeared. She smoothed her taffeta skirt, crossed the floor, and approached the untypically flustered Madame

Roussy. Fredericka's head was high. There was a gleam in her eye. The laughter began to fade.

"I am going home now, Madame," she said and curtsied. Without waiting for a reply she walked out of the elegant little ballroom and across the hall to the cloakroom where Siddie was gossiping with the other maids.

"We are leaving now," she said. As she waited by the door with Siddie for the chauffeur to bring the car around, the music started again. Fredericka tapped her foot in time. *I really do like to dance,* she thought. *Perhaps some day...when I am older...perhaps...*

In bed that night she thought of Madame's face when she had told her that she was leaving. She smiled. And fell happily asleep.

# One

THE FORBESTAL BALL was in full swing when the Schumachers arrived shortly after eleven. They were one of the sights of Newport, Frederick Schumacher and his daughter. Handsome, courtly, amusing, and rich, Frederick was everything a man should be. As for his daughter, "a pity she wasn't born a boy," people said in smug charity.

There was nothing masculine about Fredericka. Her eyes grew as moist as the next woman's when a bride came floating down the aisle in a glory of white satin, or a baby, swaddled in heirloom lace, bawled at the christening font. But it was unlikely that she would ever figure as a radiant bride or proud mother herself.

The orchestra was playing and the room was filled with whirling couples as the pair made their entrance. Newport was out in full force. The Vanderbilts and the Berwynds, the Whitneys and the Tailers and the Van Alens. The great entrepreneurs and their haughty wives, the placid dowagers and the bohemian aunts, the glittering young crowd. Roses, planted for this one night, were trained up the walls of the ballroom to the frescoed ceiling with its clouds and cherubs.

Crystal chandeliers swayed in the ocean breeze coming through the French doors that opened onto the broad stone terrace.

"There he is, Papa," Fredericka said, tapping her father's arm gently with her fan and smiling as if she were commenting on the scene.

Alexandre de Granville was not dancing. He was standing, almost hidden by a palm, near one of the French doors.

It had been daylight still when Fredericka had stood before the mirror that covered one wall of her dressing room. For a full three minutes she gazed at herself. Then she sighed. She turned away and rang for Siddie.

"I'm ready," she said when her maid appeared. Siddie went into the bedroom and gathered up the gown of cloud-blue silk, light as ocean foam, that was spread out on the bed. Fredericka raised her arms and Siddie, scrambling up on a chair, settled the dress over her head without disturbing a hair.

"Lovely," Siddie said as she set about hooking the back. "Now, what shall it be? Your pearls? The aquamarines?"

Fredericka had brought all her jewelry to Newport except the diamond and sapphire parure Papa had given her when she turned sixteen. It was a pity in a way. The necklace would have been exactly right for the Worth gown. It had been an extravagant gift, even for Papa. The necklace alone with its pear-shaped diamond pendant would have sufficed for a princess's dowry. But the necklace and the tiara, the long dangling earrings and the bracelet were tucked away in the New York vault where they had been for years, ever since the day after her birthday.

"Don't you like your new jewels?" her father had asked a few days later. "I chose the sapphires myself. And the diamonds are the finest. Each of the first water."

"I love every piece of it," she told him. "It is absolutely gorgeous." But diamonds, Papa, she thought to herself, are not fitting for a girl of sixteen. She could not tell him this without hurting him. "I thought—they are so beautiful, really exquisite—I thought that I would save them . . ."

"Save them!" he had exclaimed. "I did not give them to you to squirrel away."

"For when I get married, Papa," she had explained. "You know what they say—something old, something new, something borrowed, something blue. They would be old and new and blue all at the same time. It would mean so much to me, Papa," she said hugging him. "Wearing them for the first time on my wedding day."

The sentimental explanation had satisfied Frederick. He was not aware that a proper bride would wear pearls on her wedding day. Or just possibly diamonds, pure and simple. But diamonds *and* sapphires seemed a bit—well, unchaste. Fredericka did not care. She would never be a proper bride. If indeed she ever were a bride. At sixteen she had thought it quite unlikely.

But tonight, ten years later, she thought it might be, just possibly might be, that by the time she was back in this room with Siddie helping her out of her dress she might be looking forward to being a bride. It was possible.

She turned slowly in front of the mirror, scrutinizing herself one more time. She nodded thoughtfully. The dress was one that Worth himself had designed for her in Paris last spring. It was as becoming as his genius could make it. She had thought it plain at the time, too muted, but the couturier had refused to alter it. He had been right, she thought.

Her hair had never looked better. Almost the golden rose color of polished copper, it was drawn back into an intricately looped Grecian knot. She had darkened her lashes to emphasize her pansy-blue eyes.

She had done what she could. The rest was in the hands of fate. No, she thought. It was not up to fate. It was simply a matter of whether her judgment had been correct.

What a way to approach marriage, she thought. Where are the delicious shivers, the flushed expectations and all the rest? I don't believe in them, she decided. Marriage is a contract like any other, and although I am a damned great virgin, I'm no ninny.

The young woman in the mirror stared back at her defiantly. There was a certain tightness about the corners of her mouth, a look of gritty challenge.

"Have you decided?" Siddie asked. She was standing in front of the open wall safe.

"Oh, the pearls I think." She bent slightly so the maid could clasp the three strands of fat, creamy pearls around her neck. She drew on a pair of long white kid gloves and stood quietly while Siddie fastened the pearl buttons with a small gold button hook.

Picking up her ostrich-plume fan, she walked slowly down the hall. She paused at the head of the curving staircase. Papa was waiting there below, staring out into the soft twilight. He looked splended as he always did in evening clothes. And very pleased with himself. She wondered how he would feel after he heard what she had to tell him.

"Come on," he urged. "We are going to be late." She followed him out onto the circular drive where the Rolls-Royce was waiting, gleaming ivory with golden brass fittings.

"There is something I have to talk to you about," she said, "before we get to the Marcys'."

"Of course, of course," he said expansively, holding her arm as she stepped up onto the running board and into the car. "But first I must tell you about Isabelle Wallace and the English ambassador. Did you hear what she did at her dinner last night? She seated that pompous ass Bishop Colford on her right and the ambassador on her left. On her left! Can you imagine! I made a point of staying on after the others left so I could tell her what I thought about it."

"That doesn't sound like Isabelle," Fredericka said. "I can't imagine how she came to do such a thing. The ambassador must have been puzzled. But what I wanted to talk to you about, Papa . . ."

"Wait, you haven't heard the half of it," he insisted. "I

told her 'My dear Isabelle,' I said, 'the ambassador represents not only the King and Queen, but the whole British
Empire. You don't insult a man like that.'

"And you know what she said to me?" he asked indignantly.
"She said 'Freddy'—God, I get furious when she calls me
that—'of course you are right, but dear Bishop Colford
represents God and all His angels.'

"I called on the ambassador this morning and let him
know that Isabelle tends to be a little silly at times." He
paused, then said with comfortable reflection, "I don't think
any real damage was done." In a final burst of indignation,
he snorted, "Angels indeed! What I would like to know is
what kind of nonsense Colford is filling her head with.

"I'm very disappointed in Isabelle," he concluded.

Fredericka turned her head to hide her smile. The beautiful widow Isabelle Wallace had made no bones about the
fact that she was counting on being the second Mrs. Frederick
Schumacher. Since she was as charming as she was determined, Fredericka thought that she might well succeed.

Suddenly Fredericka saw a way to turn the conversation to
the subject that was on her mind. "You know, Papa, I do
think that if Isabelle was married, her husband could easily
avert such blunders."

"There is no need to beat around the bush. I have made it
clear to Isabelle that while I am fond of her—really very
fond of her—I am not a man for marriage."

Fredericka pounced upon the opening. "But I am, Papa."

"You are what?"

"For marriage. That is what I want to talk to you about."

"Marriage? Who? You?"

"Who? You?" she mimicked with a nervous smile. "You
sound like an owl."

"Never mind what I sound like. Just tell me what this is
all about," he demanded. But Raymond, the chauffeur, had
already turned into the winding drive that led to the Marcys'
and the car was rolling along under the canopy of arching
oaks.

"It is too late now," she sighed. "We will have to wait until after dinner. We can talk on the way to the Forbestals'. It is very important, Papa," she emphasized. "You must speak to him tonight."

"Him!" Frederick exploded. "Who?"

His daughter did not answer. The car had stopped under the porte cochere and a footman had stepped forward to open the door. "We can talk later, Papa," she said over her shoulder.

It was almost three hours later when they left the Marcys' to join the rest of social Newport at the Forbestal ball. All over the elegant seaport town, members of other dinner parties were setting out for the Forbestal showplace on Bellevue Avenue. As soon as the car drew away from the house, Frederick picked up the speaking tube.

"Drive out along the ocean, Raymond," he ordered, "until I tell you to turn back.

"Now," he turned to Fredericka, "what is this all about if you please?"

"It is time I was married, Papa," Fredericka said softly. "I am twenty-six now. I should be married."

If Papa only knew how much she wanted to get married. How she writhed in bed on these balmy Newport nights. How she hungered for sex. But she could not speak of such feelings to Papa. If he were ever to dream of the mad ways she found to satisfy her body at night! Or the ways Alexandre drove her to ecstatic abandon. Only in her imagination, unfortunately. No, she could not speak of such things to Papa.

"Really, Papa," she repeated. "It is time I was married."

"Well yes, I agree," Frederick said judiciously. "A woman should be married. But you have time. There is no rush. And I must say I see no reason why we suddenly have to discuss the subject now in the car, on our way to a ball."

"Because you must speak to him tonight. When we get to the Forbestals'."

"Speak to whom?" Frederick was baffled. "In God's

name, what is this all about? It sounds like craziness. Who is this man?''

Fredericka was silent. The car rolled on in the dark. Finally she spoke.

"Alexandre de Granville."

Frederick leaned forward abruptly and turned to stare at his daughter. "You *are* crazy," he said slowly. "You must be."

This was more difficult, much more difficult, than she had thought it would be. And more painful. "Please, Papa. I have made up my mind. I want to marry him."

"Never!"

Fredericka looked at her father, her eyes suddenly a cold, stormy blue. "If you don't speak to him tonight, Papa, I will."

And she would, he thought. There was no doubt about that. Alexandre de Granville. He sighed and shook his head. Well, if she wants him, why not? Frederick was a man given to quick decisions. If it were not de Granville, it would be someone like him. Or worse. He was probably the best of a bad lot. And when Fredericka made up her mind, there was no denying her.

He capitulated. "I'll think about it," he said.

"There is no time to think," she informed him. "You must speak to him tonight. Kitty Parseval telephoned this afternoon. She is having an impromptu supper and dance for him. He is leaving in a few days. We must make our move now."

"We? Our move?" Frederick huffed imdignantly.

"Yes," his daughter told him. "Our move. It is to your interest as well as mine, you know." She paused and then she asked, "What kind of grandson do you think you would have had if I had married Webb Derwent?"

"You knew about him?" He was startled.

"Yes. And about that dreary Rutherford Selden too." She patted her father's hand. "I think you should tell Raymond to turn around now."

Frederick picked up the speaking tube again and directed the chauffeur to turn. He flicked off the light that illuminated the interior of the Rolls-Royce and, sitting back, he stared out into the night. A heavy orange moon was climbing up from the horizon. The car purred along almost silently. Father and daughter retreated into their own thoughts.

It was a damned shame, Frederick thought. A pretty woman could walk through life on rose petals, but a plain one—no matter how rich she was—had a hard row to hoe. And Fredericka was not pretty.

A woman who is six feet tall—and Fredericka was— might be described admiringly as statuesque if she were built along the willowy lines of a Gibson girl, but there was nothing willowy about Fredericka. Her curves were on the same generous scale as her height. And she had the Schumacher jaw, square and determined.

Sitting there, being driven through the night, Frederick pounded his knee with his fist. It was not fair. His daughter had everything. Brains. Money. Health.

Everything but beauty.

When Frederick had made up his mind to come East, Fredericka had been eleven and she had been motherless for ten of those years. Her life had been spent in mining camps and mining towns and the suite of rooms her father maintained at the Palace Hotel in San Francisco. She knew how to ride, pitch a tent, and play poker. She could handle a gun and, more than once, she had acted as her father's paymaster. It was a completely different world from the one she had encountered in New York.

It had been the right move at the right time for Frederick. He had realized that making a fortune was just the beginning. If he were to enjoy the power his wealth could generate, he had to be at the center. And the center was New York. He fitted into its lusty financial community as if he had been born to it. Wall Street was a man's world after his own heart and he flourished there.

But his daughter had had to make her own way slowly and painfully. He had enrolled her in Miss Caldwell's School for Young Ladies, which had been highly recommended. "She will meet the right crowd there," Bertie Sutphen, a J. P. Morgan associate, had told him. "She will make friends that she will have all her life."

Sutphen had been mistaken, although one could hardly fault the well-meaning banker. He had not set eyes on Fredericka. At eleven she towered over every other girl in school. Her language bore the stamp of mining camps and her clothes were a disaster. Schoolgirls tend to be appalling conservatives. Differences upset and confuse them—threaten them. Confronted by them, they withdraw into safe conformity like snails into their shells. The gentle daughters of the Fifth Avenue millionaires found this gawky adolescent heiress from the West disconcerting. And even worse. As one young miss murmured to another, "It's vulgar to be so big."

Fredericka had had everything to learn when she entered Miss Caldwell's. It had been a cruel and merciless—but successful—polishing. And she had survived, although despite Sutphen's optimism she had not made friends. Giggling in their tight little cliques, talking about parties to which she was not invited and boys whom she never met, her schoolmates never allowed her to become part of the group.

It might have been easier, Frederick thought, if he had left her with friends to grow up in San Francisco. He recognized that bringing her to New York had been like throwing her to the wolves. Women were killers, he mused. Vicious. Even little girls. When someone bigger than life came along, they were bound to try to nibble her down to size one way or another. There was no denying it, Fredericka had had a rough time of it. A lonely time. Nevertheless, he had done the right thing. She was rich and when he died—"If he died" was the way he phrased it to himself—

she would be extremely rich. She had to know how to handle this world.

When it was time for Fredericka to make her debut, she had insisted that it would be ridiculous. "As far as the world is concerned," she told Frederick, "I have been out for years. Ever since I walked out of Madame Roussy's. I am your hostess. I am invited to receptions and dinners with you. I am a part of society now. Not a dewy little deb. To present me to society is simply to say that you are ready to marry me off. I can't go through such a silly charade. People know that a girl of seventeen is marriageable. They don't have to be told."

She was quite correct. Frederick had been approached already. "Your daughter is a fine young woman," Walton Derwent had said one night at the club over brandy and cigars, coming to his point after fifteen minutes of chewing over the details of the house he was building uptown. So that was it. Frederick had been wondering why Derwent had sought him out that evening.

"Yes, Fredericka is a fine young woman," Derwent had repeated. "Healthy. Smart too. She will make a fine wife, a good mother."

Frederick nodded and drew on his cigar. It was an open secret that young Webb Derwent much preferred young men to young women. Everyone felt sorry for his parents, but Frederick did not feel sorry enough to sacrifice his daughter.

"Sorry, Walton," he had said brusquely. "My daughter needs a real man." He saw no point in allowing him to continue. He was mad as hell. It was damned impudent of the man to even hint that Frederick would consider such an alliance.

Then there had been Gordon Wymberley. Close to forty, Wymberley had run through two inherited fortunes and God only knew how many mistresses. What was certain was that he no longer had a penny to bless himself with.

"I'm a man of business like you," he had said to Frederick, lounging back comfortably. Frederick had listened,

stony-faced. "I'll come straight to the point. I am sure Miss
Fredericka is ready to receive me favorably," Wymberley
had concluded. "A man can tell when he has piqued a
woman's interest, don't you know?"

Frederick stared at Wymberley in disbelief. "No," he
had said finally, his voice thick with anger. "No. And stay
away from my daughter or I will shoot you."

The latest candidate had been Rutherford Selden. And
that had been two years ago. He might have made a mistake
there, Frederick thought. But at the time, he had thought he
was doing the right thing. Selden, a recent widower, was a
good enough looking man and came from a good family.
But he had no pluck or gumption. His wife had died in
childbirth, leaving a newborn infant and three other young
sons. Selden needed a mother for his brood.

It might have been a marriage for Fredericka. But he had
said no. He wanted something better for his girl. As it
turned out, nothing better had come along.

Frederick sighed. It was more like a groan. Fredericka
was twenty-six now. Getting on. All the girls in her class at
Miss Caldwell's were married by now, most of them were
already mothers. He slammed his fist onto his knee again.

"Don't, Papa," she said. "There is no reason to be so
miserable. We have to face facts. It is clear that the only
man who is going to marry me is a man who has to marry
for money. And if a man is going to marry me for my
money, I think I should do the choosing. I have made my
choice. Alexandre will be a good husband. He is strong and
healthy. He is very pleasant. And he is handsome, Papa.
Don't you agree?"

They had arrived. Raymond drew up under the columned
portico. A liveried footman opened the door. But Frederick
did not move. She put her hand over his. "Papa, it is a ball,
not a funeral. And if we succeed, I will be a happy
woman."

He nodded. "You may be right. I will do what I
can." And he stepped out of the automobile into the

flickering light of the Japanese lanterns strung along the portico.

Goddamnit, he thought. She is right.

But when he saw Alexandre de Granville standing alone in the ballroom, looking almost forlorn, he was not quite so sure. Goddamn foreigner, he thought.

# Two

Aʟᴇxᴀɴᴅʀᴇ Jᴏsᴇᴘʜ-Bᴇɴᴏîᴛ Lᴏᴜɪs Pɪᴇʀʀᴇ Hᴇᴄᴛᴏʀ ᴅᴇ Gʀᴀɴᴠɪʟʟᴇ had had only one goal in life for the past six months. This was one more goal than he had had in the rest of his twenty-four years, unless one accepted the pursuit of pleasure as a goal.

If he attained his present goal, he could afford to consider others. Or even revert to the pursuit of pleasure. But for the moment, his heart and mind, his total energy, his enormous charm, were concentrated on one objective. He had come to the United States to marry a rich American. So far, he had been unsuccessful.

In the early days, Alexandre reflected, young men had rushed off in pursuit of dragons or the Holy Grail. It was just as well that his goal was somewhat less exalted. If he recalled his lessons correctly, it took a saint to slay a dragon. And only those chaste in thought, word, and deed could hope to find the Grail.

What with one thing and another, neither sainthood nor the Holy Grail seemed within his grasp. And even if they were, he could not see that they would be of any use to him.

A rich wife, however—that was different. There was no questioning the utility of money, especially in vast sums.

"You come from a good family," Uncle Albert had said. "And you make a good appearance." The Baron de Granville sat behind the modest table covered with green baize that served him as a desk at Assurances Bruxbelges, the firm that had been founded by Alexandre's great-grandfather, Uncle Albert's own grandfather.

The Baron considered his nephew's quite extraordinary looks. Alexandre had green eyes. But they were not just green. They were the green of emeralds with topaz glints. His dark hair was glossy and his face just sun-touched enough that his eyes glowed like the jewels they resembled. Perhaps his lips were too full, but they hinted at a sensuality that, under the circumstances, could be considered an asset. Just under six feet, he was well built. And well mannered. Good stock, the Baron thought proudly, then frowned as he focused on the matter at hand.

"Your father," he said coldly, "was handsome too. But that was not enough. He was most unwise. As the younger brother he had the obligation to establish himself. We are not a rich family."

Alexandre lifted an eyebrow, so slightly that it might have passed detection, but his uncle, somewhat sensitive on the subject, noticed and repeated, "No, we are not a rich family. The firm is solid, but our growth has been slow and conservative. The profits do not permit personal extravagance, self-indulgence." His thin lips puckered as he uttered the last words, as if he were biting into a particularly sour lemon. "As you know, I live very carefully."

He paused. "Your father, I am sorry to say, did not. His income came from the firm—income, mind you, that he did not earn—income from shares that our father, your grandfather Joseph-Benoît, insisted he be given although he took no part in the business. 'Your brother,' my father told me, 'has nothing. No title. No estate. And no taste for our business. We must arrange for him a little income so that he has a base from which to leap, an island on which to stand while he surveys the sea of opportunity.' That income was frittered away.

"Your father never leaped, never explored the opportunities. He devoted himself to pleasure, to sports and gambling and, I fear, women. When your mother died, he plunged into utterly foolish extravagances. You are aware of his excesses. I will not depress you further by repeating them.

"By the end, as you have learned, he had sold everything—your mother's farmlands, her jewels, his horses, his paintings, his furniture, everything. And," Uncle Albert's voice dropped forbiddingly, "he sold his shares of Bruxbelges, the shares that our father had given him.

"So you, my boy, are penniless. I am sorry. And I regret that you will always have to remember that it is your father whom you have to thank for it. Rest his soul."

Alexandre suppressed a smile. His father, he was sure, was not resting his soul. Wherever he was, Pierre de Granville had undoubtedly gathered a circle of congenial companions with whom to embark upon eternity.

His uncle finally came to the point. "There is nothing for you here, my dear boy."

Alexandre started to get up. Had he been subjected to this sermonizing only to be told that "there is nothing for you here, my dear boy"? He had expected the offer of a minor clerical position where he would be at his uncle's beck and call and he had resolved to refuse it. He would rather starve. It would be a living death. He could see himself growing old, making never-ending entries in some musty ledger and suffering the pangs of a nagging pain just at the spot where his skull settled down onto his spine.

"I cannot ask my sons to give up their portions of the firm because of the folly of my younger brother," the baron continued, "especially since, like your father, you have never shown the least interest in Assurances Bruxbelges.

"So my plan is this." He paused and fitted his fingertip against each other in a judicial manner. "You must go to

America. To New York. I can arrange some introductions.
With your face and charm, you should be able to meet a
woman of good family—of wealth, that is. And marry her.
In that way, your future will be assured.

"No, no, don't interrupt." The baron raised his hand
admonishingly. "I will advance you a sum sufficient to take
care of your voyage and to maintain yourself for a year or
so. There will be no margin for extravagence, mind you. No
horses. No motor cars. No gambling. An above all," his
face grew even sterner, "no romantic liaisons. No little
cabaret singers like this Dita of yours. You must keep your
nose to the grindstone, as it were.

"You must look for the right woman, a woman of a
certain age, one who is close to giving up hope. Do you
understand? The young and lovely can contract advanta-
geous alliances easily."

Alexandre nodded. The notion was staggeringly unexpected. Never in this world would he have believed that he
would be sitting in Uncle Albert's office being advised to
seek his fortune in America, that fortune taking the form of
a rich wife.

"Well, what do you say?"

"It is an idea," Alexandre replied carefully. "I certainly
will consider it."

The Baron de Granville frowned. "There will be no
considering. If you want this chance, you must take it now.
If not, well, you are on your own. And in that case, I wish
you luck. You will need it."

Alexandre swallowed. "I see," he said. And he did.
Money had always been short, but when things grew strait-
ened, his father had always sold something—a racehorse, a
jeweled card case, a few hectares of farmland, a small
painting. Alexandre had never dreamed that one day there
would be nothing left to sell.

The shock of discovering himself penniless had unsettled
him almost as much as the shock six week ago of finding
his father dead in the library of their town house in Brussels.

The leather-bound volumes lining the walls had been sold recently, joining the heavy oriental carpets and the intricately carved library table. All had disappeared in the last few months. Alexandre had paid little attention to the gradual denuding of the library and the rest of the house. Truth to tell, he was home only to sleep. And not all that often. Dita, the singer at the Cabaret Louise, had agreed to move into the little apartment he had rented for her on rue Grand'homme. It would have been foolish to leave her there alone after he escorted her home in the dark hours of the morning.

There was little left in the library except the heavy draperies at the windows and the chair in which Pierre de Granville had sprawled, his jaw disconcertingly dropped like that of an idiot. A half-empty bottle of brandy was on the floor beside the chair. An apologetic note addressed to Alexandre was propped up on the mantel.

But that was all in the past. For the first time in his life, Alexandre was obliged to consider the future. His did not seem bright. He had a sketchy education, no money, and no way of earning a living.

"You are right, uncle. I have no choice. I accept your offer, and thank you heartily for giving me this opportunity."

"Not giving," Albert corrected his nephew. "This is a business transaction. A bit of a gamble perhaps, but I believe in hazarding small sums now and then. Venture capital, as it were." He cleared his throat. "Although it is a gamble, you are, after all, my own brother's child. The rate will be modest. Just two percent." He smiled thinly and added, "A month."

Modest? It was exorbitant. Not even the pawnbrokers charged that much. They, as Alexandre had reason to know, were content with a usurious one and a half percent—and claimed no kinship.

If he did not succeed in finding, wooing, and winning this hypothetical American heiress, he would be saddled with such a debt that he could never return to Brussels. Ah, that undoubtedly was what Uncle Albert had in mind.

Alexandre was not to present a challenge to his cousins Guy and Henri. He had been naive in expecting to be offered that dreaded clerkship. It was the last thing in the world his uncle would have proposed.

Alexandre wished to God that his own father, that charming irresponsible soul whom he missed bitterly, had just once sat him down and said, "It's a pity, my son, but I'm afraid you will have to prepare yourself to earn a living. The way I am spending money, there will be precious little left for you." But he could not blame his father. It was his own doing. He had been a jackass, a stupid boy who had refused to grow up.

He sighed and shook his head despondently.

"My dear boy, you must not worry about the debt," his uncle assured him. "When you are affianced, the payment can be arranged as part of the marriage contract. Your bride's family must settle a certain—and substantial—sum upon you at the time of marriage and agree to certain additional sums at appropriate junctures. The birth of a child, for instance. You will also insist upon a suitable position in a family enterprise. This will assure you a certain independence . . ." he interrupted himself. "We need not go into these details now. When the time comes, I will advise you."

"Yes, uncle. Thank you, uncle." The soul of generosity, the Baron de Granville. But there was nothing to do except take his offer and agree to pay the two percent.

Alexandre was no closer to marrying an heiress that August evening in Newport than the day he had arrived in New York. Uncle Albert's letters of introduction had produced a flurry of invitations to luncheons at various clubs and dinners in opulent brownstones and limestone mansions. But he had discovered that unless a man had experience to offer or capital to invest, his chances of being taken into any business were slim.

One banker had expressed interest in establishing a connection with Assurances Bruxbelges, but Alexandre's complete ignorance of insurance underwriting became so apparent in the exploratory conversations that the banker's interest had waned, although he had invited Alexandre home to meet his daughter, which, after all, Alexandre consoled himself, was what he was in New York for in the first place.

His pursuit of a rich bride, however, had been just as unproductive as his halfhearted pursuit of a suitable business position. He had met dozens of rich young women of good family. He had danced with them, ridden with them, criticized their watercolors, accompanied them to the opera and the theater, and when they fled New York for the summer, he had followed them to Newport.

July had gone by in a cheerful daze of sun and fog, of dinners and dances, of sailing and bathing, of fishing at the Gooseberry Island Club and playing tennis at the Casino. It had all been delightful. But the pretty and spirited creatures whom he pursued seemed to look upon him as more brother or playmate than suitor. The few who showed signs of romantic interest had, without exception, older brothers who would inherit, or fortunes too insignificant to provide the kind of settlement Alexandre—and his Uncle Albert—must insist upon.

Tonight, as he watched the dancers in the Forbestal ballroom, he was thinking desperately of what he should or could do when his money ran out, as it would within days. He had already notified the Bachelors Club that he would be giving up his rooms within the fortnight.

That afternoon he had returned to his rooms after playing tennis with the Parseval sisters and Harry Peckham. They had called it a day after two sets since Kitty insisted that she and Phoebe had to have a nap in order to look their stunning best that evening at the ball.

"It is the beginning of the real season," Kitty had told Alexandre. "You will see. July was nothing. The fun starts in August."

"What a shame," he had responded lightly, "that I will have to miss it."

"Miss it!" the girls exclaimed in unison.

"I fear so. My uncle wants me back in Brussels. He says it is time I went to work." It was the only excuse he could think of.

"You must tell him that you cannot possibly leave," Kitty said. "We will never forgive you if you leave now."

"Tell him that you have accepted engagements through the middle of September," added Phoebe, the quiet sister.

"And that's no lie. You must have," said Harry. "They work us bachelors like horses here. I am always glad to get back to Wall Street where I can relax."

"Don't! Don't!" exclaimed Alexandre. "When my uncle calls, I must obey." This was somewhat of an exaggeration, but what else could he say? That he had run out of money he had been lent in order to find and marry a rich American? Impossible.

Back at his rooms, he had bathed and stretched out on his bed where he lay staring at the ceiling. Everyone had been talking about the Forbestal ball. He must be in good form, rested so that he could appear fresh and interested until three or four in the morning—or even later. The invitation was for ten o'clock. By then the sea breeze should have cooled the air, but right now it was unbearably hot and sticky. The sun seemed to burn through the drawn blinds of the small bedroom.

His thoughts were going in circles. When he came to the end of his money, what then? Returning to Brussels, no matter what he told people, was out of the question. He owed his uncle all that money plus that blasted interest. He was not even sure he had enough money left to buy a ticket home. And where was home? His father's house belonged to strangers now. Under the circumstances his uncle certainly would not welcome him.

What would become of him?

It was too hot to think, too hot to worry. But he could not

stop. He should have listened more carefully to Uncle
Albert. He had advised him to look for a "woman of certain
age." He had warned that the young and lovely would look
higher for a husband than a penniless foreigner. But Alexandre
had pursued the young and lovely with never a thought for
their spinster aunts and ugly cousins, whom he should have
been courting.

Rolling over to a cooler part of the mattress, Alexandre
considered the women he could expect to see that evening:
the corseted dowagers, the aging, eccentric spinsters. He
threw his sweat-damp pillow on the floor and cursed the
heat.

It was hours later when he started up, his heart pounding
in response to some inner alarm. It was dark and quiet, as if
the whole world were slumbering. Had he slept the night
away? What would his cursed Uncle Albert say if he were to
learn that Alexandre had slept through a Newport ball
attended by some of the wealthiest women in America?

Turning on the light, he consulted his watch on the
dresser. Thank God. It was just past ten o'clock. He would
be more than fashionably late, but not disgracefully so.
Handsome bachelors were forgiven many sins.

In thirty minutes, he was shaved and dressed, ready to
leave. He inspected himself in the mirror. He looked almost
American. There was no reason why some wealthy woman
should not find him pleasing. He would simply have to
apply himself tonight. And if he succeeded? Well, his price
would be high. But it would not be as easy as he and Uncle
Albert had thought. Even with an eccentric maiden aunt or a
faded widow who longed for one last reprise of her youth,
there would be problems. All summer long Newporters had
been talking about Sylvester Tisdale's will, which provided
that if any of his descendants married a foreigner, his or her
share of his estate would be forfeited. Those who were
married to foreigners at the time of Tisdale's death had been
cut off with one dollar. There was a consensus among the
members of the community that Tisdale had been right.

Why should his money go to support dilettantish European sons-in-law?

The time when American millionaires had vied with each other to see who could buy the loftiest title for his daughter—even though that title might be accompanied by a weak-chinned and weak-minded holder—had passed. There were still marriages of rich American young women with great English titles, but these were more like alliances of great powers.

And Belgians, Alexandre had discovered, were even the wrong kind of foreigner. Americans seemed to look upon them as an inferior species of French. Alexandre had made a point of acting and looking as American as he could. He scrupulously tried to think as well as speak in English.

Turning away from the mirror, he shrugged his shoulders. All he could do was try. He had nothing to lose. Or, as he corrected himself cynically, it would be more correct to say that he had everything to lose. If he did not succeed tonight, that was it. He had lost his chance. And Uncle Albert had lost his little gamble.

He arrived at the ball feeling less assured than usual. He was ready to sell himself to the highest bidder. But he was not at all sure that there would even be a bidder. Suddenly he felt defeated. It was a strange sensation. He had barely enough strength to keep his shoulders from sagging, to keep smiling. He stationed himself by one of the French doors that opened onto the terrace to observe the guests and make his choice. Every minute counted now. There was so little time.

The Schumachers, he noted, had just made their entrance. That was strange, he thought. They were usually among the earlier arrivals. The orchestra fell silent and couples walked slowly off the floor, drifting onto the terrace and down the broad stone steps to the lawn where twin fountains were making their own melody. The women's pale dresses were like night-blooming flowers. Waiters were everywhere, bowing and offering champagne.

Suddenly Alexandre noticed that the Schumachers were looking in his direction. Are they looking at me? he wondered. Talking about me? No, that was most unlikely. Fredericka had unfurled her fan and behind the luxuriant ostrich plumes seemed to be speaking quite seriously with her father. No, it had nothing to do with him. He retreated to the shadows of the terrace.

It was cooler outside. He leaned on the balustrade looking out at the same heavy moon that Frederick had watched minutes earlier. It was high now, bright enough to cast shadows. Alexandre felt as if he might cry. Ridiculous. He had not cried since—he could not remember when or why—but his eyes were prickling with tears and he remembered the sensation. Tears for failure, for a wasted life, a foolish past, a hopeless future. You are feeling sorry for yourself, de Granville. And you are an ass.

He would go find Kitty. She would dispel his melancholy. But he did not move. If at this moment he had to smile or make a compliment or be amusing, he might make a fool of himself. As he thought this, his face fell. No, he would remain in the shadows and master this mood before the dancing started again.

"There he is, Papa," Fredericka told her father. "You must go speak to him."

"All right," Frederick sighed. "All right. But this is not how these things are done."

"How are they done, then?" Fredericka asked sharply. "By telepathy? Please, Papa. He is alone now. He may not be alone again all night. Ask him now. Please, Papa."

Frederick nodded. He had promised. If Fredericka wanted a poor, fortune-hunting Belgian for a husband, well then, he would see that she got him. And he would arrange matters, by God, so that the fellow would never deceive or grieve his daughter. He could do that for her. She had made her choice and if he did not welcome that choice, he at least accepted it.

If love did not come your way and you wanted it, the thing to do was go out and buy it. It was often better that way. You knew exactly what you were getting. You could set your own terms. It was clear from the very beginning who held the power. Frederick himself had entered into somewhat similar arrangements, although he would never have dreamed of formalizing them to the point of marriage. But things were different for men.

"All right, all right," he said. "I will ask him to come see me tomorrow." And he started across the floor.

"De Granville."

Alexandre spun around. "Good evening, Mr. Schumacher. It is a beautiful night, is it not?"

"Yes, yes," Frederick said, "I suppose it is." He hesitated and then went on uncomfortably, "I wanted to have a word with you, but this is not the time nor the place. Would it be convenient for you to come see me tomorrow morning?"

"I am at your disposal," Alexandre replied. "What time should I come?"

"I would suggest half past eleven o'clock. Unless you plan to dance the dawn in?"

"No, not I," said Alexandre, although until this moment he had expected to do that very thing. "Half past eleven is fine. I shall call on you," he consulted his watch, "in exactly twelve hours."

They returned to the ballroom, almost empty now except for a few gossiping groups half-hidden by clusters of palms and bay trees. Fredericka was sitting alone, her eyes on the two men crossing the floor.

She could feel her cheeks flushing. He was so attractive—the way he held himself, his walk, his knowing eyes, his smile, and those generous, full lips. How many nights she had pretended that those lips were pressing hers, caressing her body. The self-assured Miss Schumacher was reduced to schoolgirl confusion by the time her father and Alexandre stood before her, although no one could have divined it from her seemingly assured manner.

"The moonlight on the water is spectacular tonight. I think you should let me show it to you." Alexandre smiled at Fredericka. "A glass of champagne in the moonlight is the recommended way to begin a happy evening," he added.

A shiver ran down his back. He had a sense of being caught up by an irresistible force. It was as if this man and his daughter had read his mind and seized upon the desperate solution he had decided upon. Or was it simply fate that had stepped in and ordained his future?

"Moonlight and champange are a good start for many ventures," Fredericka said, accepting his arm. They went down the shallow stone stairs to the lawn where flickering torches lit their faces with a soft glow.

"You are coming to see my father tomorrow?" she asked.

"Yes, he suggested that I come just before noon."

"I asked him to talk to you. Perhaps you will be surprised. But I think that you are like me. Practical."

"You consider yourself practical?" he asked, in some amazement. Practical was not an adjective that any girl he knew would choose to describe herself.

"Oh yes, I am practical," Fredericka said calmly. "If you are like me, very tall and not very pretty, it is important to be practical. One is happier that way. I think you are practical too. And perhaps . . ." she paused and changed the subject. "Kitty Parseval tells me that you plan to return to Europe soon."

"News travels fast here," he laughed. "I only told her this afternoon. Yes, I am afraid I must leave within the fortnight."

"We must persuade you to stay longer."

"If only I could. But circumstances, not desire, dictate," he replied almost automatically.

They had reached the wall that separated the lawn from the rocky shore below. Alexandre beckoned to one of the hovering waiters who glided over with two glasses of champagne on a silver tray.

Fredericka turned to him and raised her glass slightly. "To the beginning of many new things," she said, looking straight at him with those remarkable blue eyes.

Alexandre felt shaky. It was a new experience for him, feeling at a loss with a woman. And such a very plain woman at that. Not attractive at all. But those eyes. They seemed to go right through him, to sense his unease.

"Many new things," he echoed and drained his glass. He tossed the empty glass over the wall and the sharp, tiny crash it made as it broke on the rocks below seemed to mark the end of something. And the beginning of something else. Nothing would ever be the same again.

Fredericka said nothing to his gesture, simply smiled, her eyes still searching his. Then she turned toward the water. They stood looking at the glittering moonlight spreading across the quiet ocean. Alexandre searched for something to say and then understood that silence would say more for him than any words.

What was this woman up to? And her father? He must be mistaken. Yet he had the very definite feeling that a proposal was being made. Of marriage? Impossible. Perhaps she had convinced her father to offer him a position. But why would she do that? No, it must be marriage. But that was unthinkable.

I cannot fathom these people, Alexandre thought desperately. It may simply be their manner of hospitality. But to ask one to call before noon on the day following a ball? The music had started again. They were alone under the midnight moon. "Shall we dance?" he asked, almost in a whisper. Fredericka nodded and they walked silently back to the house.

She turned to him with a kind of radiance as he clasped her waist. Spinning into the middle of the floor, he thought, she is more than she appears. She has magnificent eyes. And her hair is lovely. She even has a kind of grace, cultivation, although if anyone had challenged him to give proof of that grace, he would not have known what to say.

He stopped thinking and gave himself up to the dance.

# Three

ALEXANDRE WOKE with a sense of oppression. His head was heavy. His sleep had been plagued with nightmares. Then he remembered. The events of last night had been real. He groaned and swung his legs to the floor.

Sitting on the side of his bed, he reconstructed the night. Frederick Schumacher had said he wanted to talk to him. And Fredericka had hinted at—just what in the devil *had* she hinted at? There had been that business about being practical. That talk about beginnings. And what had possessed him to dash his empty champagne glass onto the rocks? Then they had danced. My God! All Newport must be talking. He had danced only with Fredericka, and when the Schumachers left they had swept him off with them, dropping him at the Bachelors Club and reminding him of the appointment for the morning.

Would he marry Fredericka Schumacher? Spend the rest of his life with her? Was this to be his fate? She had her good features, certainly. Those incredible eyes. That hair. But she was no beauty. She was taller than he was. And older. And on the heavy side.

But what was the alternative? He had no money. He was alone in a foreign country. No family to support him. No friends. The truth was that he was drowning and the Schumachers seemed—incredibly—to be throwing him a life preserver. He had no alternative.

He dressed carefully, more carefully than he had for the ball the night before. Knotting his tie, he wondered if he was a bit too formal for a morning call on a Sunday in August. But this was business. Whether it involved a proposal of marriage or an offer of a position, formality was in order.

He had never been inside the Schumachers' house. A fantasy of shingled gables and towers, it was an assemblage of exuberant and extravagent detail as overpowering as the Schumachers themselves. He was ushered directly into Frederick's study, an oval room no more than twenty feet in length, paneled in English walnut. Bars of light streamed through tall windows. He glimpsed slices of garden and ocean. The desk at one rounded end and the sofa facing it were shaped to conform to the room. There was a stock market ticker under a high glass dome beside the desk. Alexandre felt as if he had stepped into some vast dark egg and would have to peck his way out through the narrow apertures.

Fredericka had watched Alexandre's arrival from the third-floor landing. When the study door closed behind him, she had settled herself on the long porch facing the bay to wait, but not idly. The household account books were stacked in front of her.

Running two households on the lavish scale Frederick Schumacher enjoyed was like running a business and Fredericka handled the household funds as adroitly as any brokerage firm handled its customers' accounts. At the beginning of each year, Frederick gave her a lump sum based on the budget she had drawn up for him. "That's it," he always warned. "Don't come running to me for more." And she never had.

The idea of all that money lying uselessly in the bank until disbursed had appalled Fredericka from the very beginning. It seemed such a waste. Money held the same fascination for her that horses and cards held for others. It was the most absorbing game in the world. She read the financial journals with the same attention that other young women gave to romantic novels.

Ordinarily there was nothing she relished more than going over the accounts. She scrutinized each bill—and woe to the butcher, plumber, or wine merchant who tried to pad his. When the bills were paid and the books balanced, she would spend contented hours working out what to do with the funds remaining at her disposal. But today the ledgers failed to hold her attention. Time and again she found herself staring out across the bay, seeing nothing. She would force herself back to work only to have her thoughts wander in another five minutes.

It had seemed so simple, so logical at first, but now she saw it as reckless idiocy. One spring evening at the opera, her father had asked Sam Parseval about the young man who was chatting and laughing with his daughters.

"His name is de Granville. He's Belgian," Sam told him. "He had a note of introduction to Holcombe Fessenden and young Tim has been taking him around. He is a pleasant enough young fellow, but I suspect he's poorer than a church mouse. I told Kitty and Phoebe not to get too interested in him. They are neither of them cut out for the frugal life."

"You mean he is a fortune hunter!"

"I wouldn't go that far, but I don't suppose he would be averse to marrying money."

"Easy enough to find out," Frederick had said. "I'll write a few letters. Ask a few questions. We have to protect our girls."

"Oh, you don't have to worry about Kitty and Phoebe,"

Sam laughed. "They know what they want. And it's not an impoverished foreigner."

The rest of the opera was lost to Fredericka. Ever since he had appeared in New York, she had been charmed by Alexandre. She found him the most attractive and fascinating of the unattached young men who formed the supporting cast for New York's social whirl. It had been a wistful admiration. Short of a miracle, he would not look twice at her. But sitting in their box at the opera that night, she thought that perhaps there had been a miracle.

He was almost certainly a fortune hunter, she thought happily. And she had a fortune. She wanted a husband. He wanted a rich wife. It made sense when she thought about it. Marrying a man like Alexandre had been beyond her wildest dreams. But now it seemed possible.

She had studied her prey for months. He was intelligent, she had decided. And charming. So charming that he was invited everywhere. She sensed his bewilderment at his lack of romantic success. How was he to know that every banker and broker and businessman in New York knew or had guessed that he had little or no money and that they had informed their wives and daughters of this? The girls had responded by treating him as the dearest of playmates— someone who could be teased and cosseted as affectionately as a brother—but not as a possible husband.

There were times when Fredericka had grown impatient over the way he persisted in courting the most beautiful debutantes, the most fashionable belles, girls like Kitty and Phoebe Parseval. He was not using his head, she fretted. His obtuseness, she decided finally, was to his credit. There was an almost reckless gallantry in his refusal to stalk the easier quarry. The more she studied Alexandre, the more she wanted him. At night she fell asleep after imaginary scenes of passion. When her frantic fingers brought her release, she would gasp "I adore you" into the dark and pretend that he answered in a husky whispers, "And I adore you, my dearest."

In all probability she would have done nothing more than observe and dream if Kitty had not telephoned yesterday to announce that he was leaving. Fredericka had placed the receiver back on the hook, feeling as if a death sentence had been pronounced. He was leaving. She had lost her chance. Wasted half the summer in silly dreaming.

Her mind raced. Perhaps it was not too late. He must have run out of money. He certainly had not succeeded in capturing a rich wife. Hope flooded back. This was, she thought, the best possible moment to approach him—at the time of defeat. She had resolved to ask her father to speak to him that very night, at the Forbestal ball.

Now she was regretting yesterday's impulse. Such wanton foolishness. Why had Papa not stopped her? The whole idea was insane. What must he be thinking now, shut up in the study with Papa?

The fact that he was staying so long must be a good sign. She sighed impatiently. There she went again. She did not know her own mind, her own heart. Yes, it was foolishness, but it was what she wanted. To have this man for her own. And if she had to buy him? Well, what did that matter after all? What was money for?

The butler came out onto the porch. "I beg your pardon, Miss Fredericka. Would you like your lunch served here? Your father is having a sandwich upstairs while he changes to go sailing.'

Her heart stopped. He had left. That was her answer then. "Yes, Dietrich, you may serve my lunch here," she said.

She had let herself hope and that had been a mistake. She had thought that this might be different, but it was the same as it had always been. She was not attractive. Alexandre would not consider her—even with her fortune thrown into the bargain. Not even the Schumacher millions had been enough to entice him into doing what he had come to this country to do—marry money.

Her silly dream was over. She could just hear him telling

Kitty Parseval or Harry Peckham about the grostesque proposition that Frederick Schumacher had put to him. And Kitty's giggle. No, she was doing him an injustice. He was a gentleman. He would never say a word about the whole ludicrous business.

Even so, she could not face him again. He could not leave for Belgium soon enough to suit her. She would plead headaches or other indispositions and avoid all social engagements until he was safely on the high seas.

She rang for the maid to clear the table and turned to her account books again. She suspected that the gardener or one of his assistants was selling produce from the kitchen garden. If her suspicions were true—her mouth turned grim and she flipped through her ledgers, eager to find a scapegoat for her hurt.

As the door closed behind Alexandre, Frederick, not bothering to get up from his desk, commanded, "Sit down." Then with no preliminaries said, "I suppose you know why I asked you to come here this morning."

What to say? Should he venture? And then discover that he had made a bloody fool of himself? But what did it matter? This was his only chance. If it turned out that he was wrong, then—too bad. He would be no worse off than he had been yesterday.

"I hesitate," he said, "only because this is a delicate matter. Yet I do not know how to approach it except bluntly. I think you have asked me here in order to discuss the matter of—" he plunged recklessly ahead now, "the matter of your daughter's future."

"And your own," Frederick said. "You are correct. I am glad that you are not going to beat around the bush. Nor will I. First of all, there is a name for men like you. It is an unpleasant one. Fortune hunter."

Alexandre flushed. He started to speak, but Frederick raised his hand for silence. "When a young man of good looks and no obvious means of support spends his time chasing after the daughters of the richest men in New York instead of pursuing the business career that he gave as his reason for coming to this country, I make a point of finding out if he is what he represents himself to be. Your real goal was different. To marry a rich woman. What do you say to that?''

Alexandre sat forward. ''You are quite right,'' he said. Complete frankness, he decided, was his only hope. ''It seemed only sensible. When my father died in November of last year—he was a man of great charm, but very little foresight and no practicality—he had run through what money he had. And there was no place for me in the family firm.''

''So you decided to look for a rich wife in New York.''

''Exactly. Or rather my Uncle Albert decided that I should. Since I could think of no other avenue that would lead as directly to a position of comfort and security, I took his advice. I also took the money he offered to lend me at two percent a month.''

''Two percent!'' Frederick was shocked. ''A month! To his own nephew! What kind of man is this uncle of yours who sends you out looking for a rich wife instead of helping you get started in the world? Who charges you interest?''

''What kind of man?'' Alexandre responded. ''A shrewd businessman. Very frugal. Not at all like my father.'' He laughed. ''I'll tell you a story about my uncle that will help you understand him. His wedding gift to my Aunt Marita was a diamond necklace, the one extravagant gesture of his life. After the wedding night he took charge of the necklace. It was served as collateral for one venture after another. As far as I know, Aunt Marita has not worn it nor, I believe, seen it in the past quarter of a century. So you see,'' he smiled, ''for a man like that, it is only natural that he would charge me interest on the capital he advanced me.''

''For fortune hunting,'' Frederick said scornfully. The words echoed within Alexandre's skull. He had called himself a fortune hunter often enough. But the words had

never seemed so sordid as when Frederick pronounced
them. Up until this moment it had not seemed real. Miserably he told himself that he was not man enough to face up to
reality, even when confronted by the prospect of failure.

Frederick was equally uncomfortable. When he had opened
the interview he had not expected it to be much different
from buying Fredericka her motorcar or the sable coat he
had given her for Christmas, a matter of getting value for
his money. But this was more awkward than he had thought.
This time it was human flesh and blood he was acquiring for
her. A goddamned tricky business. He felt he was not
handling it as he should. He had been bluffing to a certain
extent when he had called Alexandre a fortune hunter.

The bluff had worked, though. Alexandre had admitted
that he was. But there was also the fact that he had made no
approach to Fredericka. It was his daughter who had taken
the initiative—or forced him to take it for her.

Frederick broke the silence. "It is not the way anyone I
know would have chosen to make his way in life. On the
other hand . . . If you live up to the bargain, it need not be a
dishonorable undertaking. If you do not," he said harshly,
"I will break you. Do you understand?"

Alexandre bowed his head.

"Another thing. I was informed of a liaison with a certain
Dita, a singer in a Brussels cabaret. An associate of mine on
the Continent . . ." he let his voice trail off. "I suppose this
is true?"

Alexandre inclined his head again.

"I do not object. As long as it is in the past. But I must
have your assurance that the affair is over. And that there
will be no similar episodes in the future."

"You have my word." Alexandre felt as if all initiative
was being drained from him. This man had taken command
of his life.

"Now, what do you propose to do with yourself?"
Frederick asked briskly, relieved to be turning to another
subject. "Have you any ideas?"

Alexandre looked at him blankly. Do? He would dance attendance upon his daughter. Forsaking all others. Wasn't that what they had just settled? Then he recovered his wits. "I was hoping that you would have a position for me. I know you do business overseas. I have talents that may be useful. I speak four languages, for instance."

Frederick nodded. He could use someone with a bit of polish. Alexandre would give an air to the office. That title might be a nice piece of window dressing too.

"What about the title? This Baron de Granville business," he asked. "Will you inherit it?"

"Not a chance in the world. It is not much of a title. It is very recent. My grandfather was the first to hold it. He had insured certain paintings that belonged to a member of the royal family. Some time later the gentleman reported that the paintings had been stolen. It was whispered that there had been no theft, that the paintings had been sold to pay certain debts. Grandfather ignored the gossip and paid up.

"In recognition of his discretion, the title was bestowed upon Grandfather. The title, mind you. Nothing more. No positions, no perquisites. My cousin Guy, Uncle Albert's elder son, will inherit it in due course along with," and now Alexandre grinned, "my uncle's undershirts with the embroidered coronets."

"Embroidered undershirts!" Frederick slapped his thigh with delight. Then he got back to business. "What kind of husband will you make my daughter?"

"A good one," Alexandre answered earnestly. "I will work to make her happy. I will be kind. Thoughtful. I will make her feel cherished. And I will give her children."

Frederick could not ask for more. But there was something that bothered him. "I cannot allow my grandchildren to be brought up as Papists."

What should he say? What could he say? Who could respect a man who denied his religion for money? "If Fredericka and I are not married in the Church," he said slowly, thinking aloud, "then it is as if we are not married in the eyes of God. We would be living in sin. Our children would be illegitimate. On the other hand, if we are married in the Church, then she must agree that our children be raised in my faith.''

"Nonsense," said Frederick. "Of course you will be married in the church. But in the Fifth Avenue Presbyterian Church. And if the Pope considers that you are living in sin, well, he is not the man I take him for. You will just have to get that Papist rigamarole out of your head.''

"That is impossible. It is part of me. I am not very religious, but I cannot turn my back on my Church. Nor do I believe you would want your daughter to marry a man whose convictions were so easily changed.''

"They would not excommunicate you or anything like that?" Frederick asked. "Anything that would cause notoriety?''

"They would certainly deplore it, but they would take no action,'' Alexandre replied, thinking of rotund Père Étienne, the priest of St. Hilaire, the village where he had spent his boyhood summers.

Alexandre had driven Dita out to St. Hilaire one Sunday. They had gone along the rutted country land bordering the fields that had been part of his mother's dowry and that his father had sold off hectare by hectare. He had halted his hired horse and carriage in front of the low stone farmhouse that had been his second home. He told Dita how he used to follow the farmer about and how proudly he had performed his chores—feeding the chickens, gathering eggs, filling the water troughs. Then they had driven back to the village to eat at its one café, Le Pèlerin.

Père Étienne had come trundling across the street to Le Pèlerin after the late mass, overjoyed to see Alexandre again. He had sat with them, accepted a glass of wine and then another, and congratulated Alexandre on his *jolie petite amie*. But Père Étienne who could accept a cabaret singer would have been shocked at the idea of Alexandre marrying a Protestant in a Protestant church.

\* \* \*

"Then we shall compromise," said Frederick. "You will be married in the Fifth Avenue Presbyterian Church and when the children come along, they can make up their own minds about religion. What do you say to that?"

"It seems a practical solution if you are not concerned," and Alexandre smiled, "that the Church will consider we are living in sin."

Frederick pursed his lips to keep from smiling. The Presbyterians would have something to say about that if the issue were ever raised. He could see Angus Buchan's scandalized face if it were put to him that a couple married by him in his church could be considered to be living in sin.

"No, I won't be concerned," he said, "but for God's sake, let's not tell Fredericka that she will be living in sin." He was startled to hear himself. His relationship with Alexandre had already taken on a certain masculine solidarity. It would be good to have another man in the family. He turned and pressed the panel behind his desk. It slid aside to reveal a bar. "I think we deserve a drink," he said. "Thirsty work, this talking."

The men sipped the whiskey and looked at each other with approval. The worst was over. The sun pierced the narrow windows brightening the oval study and the men sat in comfortable silence.

Frederick refilled their glasses. "We must decide just what we are drinking to. I am willing to wager that your Uncle Albert gave you orders about settlements and agreements and that sort of thing."

Alexandre stood up abruptly and looked out through one of the narrow windows, but he saw nothing. Now that it had come to the point, he could not bargain. He was not the shrewd negotiator who less than twenty-four hours ago had promised himself that he would come high. It had been sheer bravado. For a split second he considered saying that his uncle would handle the negotiations. But he could not. It would be too demeaning. Selling himself like a racehorse or a prize bull. The haggling over settlements. No. He shook his head. He could not. Would not.

He turned back to the room. "I do not want to bargain," he told Frederick, his face tense with enbarrassment. "You love your daughter. You will want her to live with dignity, not be continually reminded of the circumstances of the marriage. What I suggest is that you make a position in your business for me as I mentioned before. And that you pay me well for what I do. More than I will probably be worth.

"I do not ask for a settlement, nor for additional sums upon the birth of each child, something that my uncle suggested. No. All I ask is the chance to establish myself and to be able to maintain your daughter and our household in the style in which she lives now.

"She will not be happy, you see," he said spreading out his hands, "unless she feels that I am providing to the best of my ability. That I am accepting a husband's responsibilities. It would make her unhappy if the world judged her husband a parasite. And beyond that?" Alexandre shrugged. "I don't know. Perhaps there are important factors I have not thought of. But even so—whatever they are—the same consideration must rule. Fredericka must be able to respect me."

He turned and stared out the window again. His face was flushed under the tan. He wished he were anywhere but in this oval study. He wished none of this had ever happened. Why had he not begged Uncle Albert to make a place for him in the firm? No matter how lowly? He felt like bolting for the door, running down the stairs and out the great front door.

Frederick was making notes. The pen scratches were the only sound in the room. Finally he slapped his hand on the desk. "It's a deal!" he said exuberantly. "Here is what I'll do. One, I'll give the two of you a house. I have had my eye on a brownstone on Madison Avenue for some time now. Two, I will make you a generous allowance for your personal expenses for as long as you and Fredericka live together. Three, I will make a position for you. If you work hard, the sky's the limit. If you don't, I will be disappointed, but you are right. You must at least appear to be independent and able to support her. Your salary will enable you to maintain the standard to which she is accustomed.

"And finally, I will reimburse your uncle. But he will get no interest from me. I'll not have you paying it either."

"I promised," Alexandre protested.

"Don't argue with me." Frederick insisted. "I intend to let the man know exactly what I think of such shoddy business. Now," he concluded, "how does it strike you?"

"How does it strike me? My God!" Alexandre was overwhelmed. "You are more than generous. And you make me feel that you do not—" the words came hard, "you do not—despise me."

"I don't. I think I understand you. But don't mistake me," and he fixed Alexandre's eyes with his own, "if you make Fredericka unhappy, if you ever look at another woman, you will regret that you were born."

Alexandre recognized the ruthlessness that had enabled Frederick to build his enormous fortune. It frightened him. He had not known a man like this before. His uncle was a rabbity fussbudget compared with this man. Fredericka undoubtedly possessed the same relentless force. What was he getting himself into? I must not let them intimidate me, he thought.

"When I give my word, I keep it," he said coldly. "I told you I would make Fredericka a good husband. And I will."

"That's what I wanted to hear." He slapped Alexandre on the back. "Let's have another drink on that and then I must go. I promised Fessenden to go boating with him." Alexandre found himself being poured a fourth and then a fifth whiskey and listening to Frederick, now relaxed and in high good humor, reminisce about his early days in the Far West. Finally Frederick stood.

"I'll tell Fredericka about our talk. And we will expect

you tomorrow for dinner. It will be just a small group. A dozen friends or so. Come early so you two will have a chance to talk.'' He walked Alexandre to the door of the study, gave him a pat on the shoulder, and closing the door behind him, left him to let himself out.

Alone in the study, Frederick glanced at the notes he had made. He had handled it well, he congratulated himself. The title to the house on Madison Avenue would stay in his own name. Or he might put it in Fredericka's name. As for the position he was going to make for Alexandre, he had an idea that he would get his money's worth out of the man one way or another. He had to admit that he was a good fellow, even though he *was* a foreigner. He had a way about him. No doubt about that. He must go tell Fredericka that it was all settled.

But first he had to change. He went across the hall to his bedroom where his yachting flannels were laid out for him. ''I'll have a bite to eat before I leave,'' he told his valet. ''Have Dietrich send up a couple of ham sandwiches and some beer.''

Half an hour later he went downstairs in search of his daughter. He strolled out onto the porch looking pleased. ''Well, you have got yourself a husband,'' he announced cheerfully. ''And I don't know but that it just might work out.''

Fredericka stared at him and burst into tears.

# Four

ALEXANDRE WALKED BACK to the Bachelors Club, his head spinning, and only partly from Frederick's whiskey. At one point he stopped and pulled out his watch. Twenty-four hours ago he had been playing tennis and trying to conceal his desperation. Fourteen hours ago he had agreed to meet Frederick Schumacher. Two hours ago he had walked into the oval study. Now he was engaged.

He had pulled if off. Captured the heiress he had sought. Or, strickly speaking, she had captured him. What did it matter? He had been rescued.

It was unbelievable. He was engaged to marry Fredericka Schumacher, engaged the way a butler or an upstairs maid was engaged. Engaged to marry a woman he scarcely knew. He knew nothing about her except that she was rich—and that she must be lonely. Only a very lonely woman would resort to such an extreme.

He began to think of what would be involved. He and Fredericka were an unlikely couple. It would be up to him to quiet any malicious chatter. The world must be convined that it was a love match. He sighed. His new life would not

come cheap. But he would pay the price. Fredericka would
never have cause to regret her unconventional proposal. He
remembered how radiant she had been last night when he
had taken her in his arms on the dance floor. She was
always stiff and reserved in public. But he had elicited that
radiance. He could make her happy. It was his responsibility. He *would* make her happy. In his triumph and relief, his
heart was full of the noblest intentions.

As he neared the club, a florist's window caught his eye.
He looked at the wilting flowers on display. In the back of
the shop was a large ice box where the more expensive
blooms were kept fresh above blocks of ice. He cupped his
hands around his eyes to get a better view.

Fredericka's storm of tears had passed. She leaned her
elbows on the table and supported her head in her hands.
What was she going to do? How could she ever face the
man? She had made a terrible mistake. She felt worse, far
worse that she had an hour ago when she thought that
Alexandre had declined her father's proposal and walked
out of their house and out of her life.

She had not thought it through. Relationships could not
be plotted on balance sheets. All she had thought about was
how agreeable and exciting a lover Alexandre would be.
How blissful it would be to fall asleep in his arms after
lovemaking. And how madly passionate that lovemaking
would be. She had envisioned glittering dinner parties,
lively suppers with other couples, and receptions with
Alexandre as her husband and host. She had dreamed of
quiet little suppers, just the two of them. Of long walks in
the country. Of being able to say "Alexandre and I . . ."

But it would never be more than a dream, that kind of
intimacy. It would always be out of her reach. They would
always remain the buyer and the bought, the undesirable and
the desired. How could it be otherwise? She drew a deep
and steadying breath. She would write him a check, a
substantial one, and a note regretting her inability to go

through with the proposal her father had made. That was the way to handle it. The only way out.

As she started to draft the difficult message, Dietrich came out onto the porch, a florist's box in his hands. "For you, Miss Fredericka. Shall I open it?"

She nodded and Dietrich untied the ribbon and eased the lid off the long white box. Roses. Long-stemmed, tawny copper roses. She had never seen roses that color before. She opened the small envelope Dietrich handed her, her fingers suddenly clumsy.

"To our beginning. Devotedly, Alexandre."

She stared at the card thoughtfully. Perhaps it was going to be all right. Alexandre was practical. He had accepted the proposal. Now he was starting to play his role as fiancé. She was the one who was acting like a capricious virgin, like the inexperienced girl she was behind her mask of capability. It was up to her to match his behavior.

Frederick came into her sitting room early in the evening. "Feeling better now?" he asked. "Funny, your mother was the same way. Perhaps all women are. When they are happy the tears flow like Niagara."

"Do you really think it will work?"

"I don't see why not. I admit I was startled when you sprung it on me. But there is more to him than I thought. He has the right instincts." He patted her shoulder and started to leave. "I'm playing cards at the Nautilus Club tonight," he said. "Oh, and I almost forgot." He turned as he reached the door. "He is coming for dinner tomorrow night. I told him to come early so you two could talk."

"But Papa, we have ten people coming for dinner tomorrow."

"That's all right. Just ask someone else so we won't be thirteen at table.

"Ask Isabelle," he called over his shoulder as he went down the hall. "She's too stupid to be insulted at being asked at the last minute." Fredericka smiled. On no, Papa, Isabelle is too smart to be insulted when you ask her for dinner, she thought as she rang for Dietrich to instruct him about the change.

She dressed early for dinner the next night, letting Siddie arrange two of the tawny roses in her hair. Twitchy as a racehorse, she paced about the drawing room waiting for Alexandre. She sat down and arranged her skirt in a fan about her feet, then jumped up and walked restlessly about.

When Dietrich ushered Alexandre in, he came straight to her, grasping her hands as if he were indeed an eager lover who had been waiting all day for just this moment when they could be together. "You are wearing my roses," he said with pleasure. "They are almost the color of your hair. When I saw them yesterday, I knew you had to have them, but the shop was closed."

His green eyes sparkled as he told how he had found out where the florist lived and how he had coaxed him to leave the comfort of his Sunday rocking chair to open up the shop and sell him the roses. The anxiety and embarrassment with which she had been anticipating their meeting faded as he took command of the conversation. She could not take her eyes off him. He was so handsome. So masculine. She felt as if she had been transported to a different world where everything was new and exciting.

"There you are." Frederick strode in, seemingly having forgotten that he had arranged this time for them to be alone. "I've been thinking. I should announce your engagement here in Newport before we go back to the city. Nothing too elaborate. A small dinner party and a larger group after dinner for dancing."

"That would be lovely, Papa, but it may be difficult to arrange it in time. Perhaps it would be better to wait until we are in the city."

"Ridiculous. Didn't you tell me that the Parsevals were giving Alexandre a farewell party on the spur of the moment? He's not going anywhere now, so they don't have to give a party. *We'll* give one that evening. They can come here instead."

There was nothing to do but agree. Alexandre wondered privately how Kitty would react to having her party date usurped. And Fredericka sighed at the thought of having to break the news to her.

"That's settled then," Frederick said. "Now what about the wedding date? There's no point in putting it off. How long will it take you to get ready?" he asked his daughter.

"Months, Papa. There's so much to do. The invitations, my trousseau, planning the reception, the decorations, the flowers. We have to find a place to live and furnish it and . . ."

"I think we should set the date for October, the middle of October—that will give you nearly two months. Plenty of time."

"But, Papa . . ." she was objecting when the first guests were announced, putting an end to the conversation.

Fredericka performed her duties as hostess in a haze of happiness and incredulity. She could hardly believe that Alexandre was here, sitting by her side, smiling at her, paying her all those little flirtatious attentions she had observed men paying beautiful women. As dessert was served, Frederick stood.

"I have a happy announcement to make," he said. "I was going to wait, but I find now that I am among dear friends that I cannot keep a secret to myself until the formal engagement party."

The guests looked at each other and then at Frederick. Most eyes then flashed surreptitiously toward Isabelle, who appeared as baffled as anyone else. Fredericka had frozen in alarm. She, too, glanced at Isabelle, but only to note her reaction. She knew very well that Papa's announcement had nothing to do with Isabelle. But surely he could not mean to tell everyone about Alexandre? But there was no stopping him. She clutched the arm of her chair so tightly that her knuckles showed a painful white against her rosy skin. She could not look at Alexandre.

Pleased with the sensation he had created, Frederick

turned to Dietrich, who was standing at the sideboard.
"Dietrich, the occasion calls for the Pol Roger." In a lower
voice he added anxiously, "Do you have any on ice? I
should have checked earlier." The butler smiled reassuring-
ly. "We always have a dozen bottles on ice," he said.

Frederick parried the eager questions. "You must wait
until Dietrich has matters in hand," he told them, smiling
broadly. "This announcement demands champagne." Within minutes the glasses were filled and Frederick lifted his.
"I ask all of you here tonight, my good friends, to join me in
wishing happiness to my daughter Fredericka and my future
son-in-law Alexandre de Granville."

There was a stunned hush, and then a babble. Isabelle ran
around the table to kiss Fredericka and then Alexandre.
Dietrich poured more champagne and there was a flurry of
exclamations and congratulations.

The party broke up early. It was obvious that everyone
was longing to leave and spread the news. As the last couple
drove away, Frederick turned to his daughter and Alexandre.
"I'm sorry," he said, "but I could not keep it to myself.
You must forgive me. We will still have the party, of course.
But I have changed my mind about it. It will be the biggest
party of the season. A ball. We will give everybody something to talk about."

The couple looked at each other. It was a moment of
perfect understanding. Frederick Schumacher was incorrigi-
ble. He always had been and he always would be. He was
bustling about the drawing room pleased with the world and
with himself.

"Well, we made progress tonight," he said with satisfaction. "For all intents and purposes the engagement is
announced. As for the wedding date, I'll get Angus Buchan
on the telephone tomorrow and tell him to keep the church
free the second week of October. That's as good a time as
any, don't you think?"

Without waiting for a response, he continued, "We've
got a lot to do. You'd better get to bed. You young folks

need your rest." Before Alexandre was quite aware of what was happening, he found himself being ushered to the door. "Raymond will drive you home," Frederick said, shaking his hand vigorously. "We'll see you tomorrow."

Alexandre ran up the stairs to his rooms, went straight to the bureau, and took a small leather jewel case from under the neat piles of underwear. He spread its contents in front of him. It was a meager collection. A pair of mother-of-pearl cuff links, a set of pearl studs, a malachite signet ring. His mother's gold wedding ring. He caressed the smooth band with his finger and set it aside. A tiepin, gold with a small sapphire. That was it.

He took the cuff links and sapphire studs out of the shirt he was wearing. His father had given him the cuff links when he was seventeen. The sapphire studs—he shook his head—were nothing but paste, worth no more than colored glass. He examined the little collection and set the tiepin, the pearl studs, and the gold cuff links aside. After a moment he added the wedding ring.

In the morning he was pacing the uneven brick sidewalk outside the jeweler's when the shop opened for business. "How much would it cost to set this sapphire into a gold ring?"

The jeweler picked up the tiepin and examined its stone briefly with his loupe. "More than it is worth."

Alexandre drew the pearl studs from his breast pocket. "Can you set it surrounded by the pearls? Like this?" And he arranged the studs in a circle around the gem in the tiepin. "Still more than it is worth, but if you want it," the jeweler said, "I can do it for you. There is not enough gold in these pieces for a ring and a setting. I will have to add more. That will bring up the cost.

Alexandre put the gold cuff links on the counter. The man looked at them and brushed them aside. "Gold-filled," he said scornfully. Alexandre sighed and reached into his breast pocket again. "This should do it," he said as he handed his mother's wedding ring to the jeweler who looked at it, put it on his small scale, and read the inscription inside the band.

PIERRE—AMÉLIE, 1883

"You want to melt this down?" he asked curiously.

Alexandre scowled. "I do," he said, although he really wanted to snatch the ring back. It was all he had left that had belonged to his mother. "Can you have it ready by Friday?"

"Impossible, sir. Monday at the earliest." The jeweler looked at him sharply. "And what if the young lady says no? How will you feel then about melting down your mother's wedding ring? It is your mother's, isn't it?"

"I will come for the ring on Monday," Alexandre said curtly, ignoring the jeweler's questions.


The engagement was the sensation of the season. No one could understand how the romance had proceeded under their very noses without anyone suspecting. The Newport hostesses set themselves to entertaining in honor of the couple with the same fierce energy that their husbands and fathers displayed in the worlds of finance and business.

There were invitations for luncheons, teas, picnics, dinners, dances, tennis parties. Alexandre was always at Fredericka's side, charmingly attentive. But there was never time to talk. Not since Frederick had broken the news of their engagement had they been alone long enough to discuss anything but the weather or the party they were about to attend or had just attended.

Fredericka could not honestly blame it on the social whirl. It was her own doing. She could have arranged time for them to be together. But it meant having to face up to the fact that she had bought him, bought herself a fiancé, a husband. They had never discussed it, she and Alexandre, but it had to be brought out in the open. At least once. They had to talk about it. They had to get to know each other, to make plans for their future. She could not let Papa take charge of their lives as he seemed prepared to do.

"Siddie," she called to the maid who was pressing a gown for that evening in her dressing room. "Siddie, please ask Dietrich if he can spare someone to deliver a note to Mr. de Granville."

Siddie smiled. This was more like it. She had wondered at the cool distance these two kept from each other, just as she wondered how the courtship could have taken place without her knowledge. Every night in the servants' dining room, Siddie was put through an inquisition that made her feel as if she had been criminally inobservant.

Fredericka sat down at her desk, and on the heavy cream-colored letter paper that bore her monogram in gold she wrote two short lines. "Could we meet his afternoon? There is so much to discuss." She signed it "Sincerely, Fredericka." Alexandre's note with the roses had been signed "Devotedly." Should she have written the same? She did not dare. He might laugh. She tore up the note and took a fresh sheet of paper. This time she signed it simply "Fredericka."

His answer came within the hour. "I shall call on you at four," he wrote. "I look forward to our meeting." It was signed. "Your Alexandre." She traced his name with her fingertip. It was true. He would be hers. Her Alexandre.

It was a lovely afternoon. The great beech trees spread their branches, making pools of deep shadow on the lawn. Fredericka, carrying a lavishly frilled white organdy parasol that matched her dress, walked across the lawn, her hand resting on Alexandre's arm. She felt almost weak with happiness. He covered her hand with his.

"Where are you taking me?" he asked.

She lifted her parasol and pointed. "Over there. To the gazebo. I am the only one who ever uses it." It was a little trellised summer room covered with a tangle of wisteria. "Charming," he said.

After they had settled themselves discreetly side by side on the wicker settee, Alexandre reached into his pocket and took out a small box wrapped in heavy white paper and tied with blue velvet. He placed it in her hand and then clasped her hand with both of his. "It is small," he said, "but it represents the greatest promise I can make. I hope you understand."

She untied the velvet ribbon and carefully extracted a small box from the wrapping. A ring box? He was giving her a ring? She had been worrying about that. She was sure he did not have enough money for an engagement ring. And she wanted one. But it would have been impossibly awkward to give him the money to buy one. And she had not quite felt like buying one for herself. Her fingers trembled slightly as she pressed the clasp and opened the lid.

The jeweler had done well by him. The small pearls from the studs surrounded the sapphire which, raised on gold prongs, took on more importance than one would have thought possible.

"It is beautiful," she breathed. "Simply lovely. So delicate." And so insignificant, she thought to herself. But still, it was undoubtedly all he could afford. A proud gesture. She liked that. She looked into his eyes. "Thank you. I like it very much. And it is an original design."

"You have no idea how original," he said. "If you like it, may I put it on your finger?"

She nodded like a bashful child and he slipped the ring on the proper finger. "There. Now you have an engagement ring. Some day I hope I will be able to replace the stone with a larger one."

"Oh no, never!" she exclaimed. "It is perfect as it is. I would not want it changed. Ever!"

Her delight in the ring partly made up for the distress he had felt in having his mother's wedding ring melted down. Fredericka was holding her hand out, turning it this way and that, exclaiming again at the originality of the design the way other girls would turn their hands to catch the fire of a diamond and exclaim over the number of carats.

"I wish I could have given you a diamond," he said quietly.

"But why? I have diamonds. Dozens of them. I much prefer this. What did you mean," she asked, "when you said I had no idea how original it was?"

He was embarrassed. "Nothing really."

"Tell me," she insisted. "I want to know the story of my ring."

"It will make me feel like a bloody fool."

"That is all right," she said serencly. "I feel that way myself very often."

He took a deep breath. "Monday night," he started, "after your father surprised us by making the announcement, I noticed the others looking at your left hand. They wanted to see your ring. And you did not have one. I felt bad about that. But I have very little money. Barely enough to pay my bill at the club until..." he broke off, more embarrassed than before.

"I understand," she said matter-of-factly, "so how could you give me this ring?"

"The pearls are from a set of shirt studs and the sapphire was in my tiepin." His voice was tight. "I don't have very much. What I did have I had to sell after my father died."

Fredericka's eyes were soft. "So these were yours," she murmured. "You have worn them."

"Yes," he admitted, feeling relieved that he did not have to tell her about his mother's ring.

She studied the ring intently holding her hand out. "But what about the ring itself? The gold? There would not have been enough gold in those pieces for this band and the setting."

Did nothing escape her notice? "No," he said unwillingly. "There wasn't. I had to... it was my mother's wedding ring," he said. His face was stony in his effort to disguise his emotion.

"Alexandre!" It was the first time she had called him by name. "I shall never forget this." There were tears in her eyes. "It must have been very hard to melt down your mother's ring," she added softly, "for someone who is almost a stranger."

"I am sure my mother would say I had done the right thing," he said almost automatically. "And I hope that we will not remain strangers. I hope that we will be friends as well as lovers."

Lovers! She blushed. All her midnight imaginings were coming true, but instead of being greedy for pleasure as she was when alone in the dark, she felt shy and tremulous—a little frightened by what his words implied.

"I told your father that I would work hard to make you happy," he said looking deeply into her eyes. He had to convince her of his sincerity. "And I will. You will see."

"I will work hard too." There was a silence, then she went on, "I hope we—you, that is, will learn to love me, too." Her voice broke on the last words and she stared down at her hands and then looked at him pleadingly.

"You have been tormenting yourself," he said, suddenly sympathetic. "You must not. You have done me an honor. I have nothing to offer and yet you have chosen me. For myself." He could not lie to her, tell her that he loved her. Or promise that he would learn to love her. But he could make her feel better.

"I know your father had had offers for your hand. Fredericka Schumacher could have had any man she wanted. And you chose me. I remember that first night in the moonlight when you told me you were practical. I admired you for it."

She blushed again. It was not becoming to her, he thought.

"You are making it easy for me," she said, conscious of her reddened face "I wanted to see you today to tell you that there should be no falseness of any sort between us. I would like it if we could just accept the situation and put it behind us."

He stood and pulled her to her feet. "Look at me," he

said, his green eyes searching hers. "It is done. The situation is accepted. I refuse to think of it again. My sacred duty now is to make you—and me—happy. I promise you that. But you? What about you? Can you promise that too?" He felt it important to seize the initiative, to make a gesture that would be remembered. "Do you? Do you promise?"

"I promise," she whispered, looking down at her feet.

He pulled her gently to him and kissed her. He intended it simply as a kind of stamp upon their pact. Their lips touched, then pressed, exploring. The kiss took on a life of its own, prolonged itself. Their bodies enfolded and found a rhythm. Their eyes were closed. The world did not exist.

Fredericka pulled her head back, pushed him away. He was flushed, his breath was coming fast. "I'm not experienced with kissing," she said flustered. "Is it always like this?"

"Rarely," he said. "I'm sorry. I should have stopped myself, but . . ."

"I am glad that you didn't," she told him. "That was one of the things I was worried about. I was not sure if it was possible for you to feel—for someone—to feel that kind . . ."

He rescued her from having to say precisely what she meant. "Now you know it is possible," he said smiling at her. He had wondered the same thing himself. How would he ever bring himself to perform the marital duty? Would he, in fact, be able to perform at all? The acts of gallantry were easy enough. He had performed them all his life. But the physical act of love was different. Now he felt confident. Confident, and a little surprised at his own response.

Trying to collect himself, he brushed her hair back from her face. "Your hair is beautiful," he said softly. "I would like to take all the pins out one at a time and watch your hair tumble down your back."

"We really must talk," she said quickly. "There are plans to make. All sorts of things to discuss."

"I know," he said, continuing to pluck the pins out of her

hair, "but right now I discover that I cannot wait. I must see your hair loose this very moment. There," he ran his fingers through her hair. "No more pins. This is better. When I think that I will see it like this every night . . ." He lifted a strand to his lips.

Fredericka stiffened. "Dietrich is coming. He can't see me like this. I asked him to bring us some lemonade," she added in explanation. Alexandre looked over his shoulder. Dietrich was indeed approaching, a doll-like figure in the distance. "And why not?" he teased. "We are engaged to be married, are we not? What is that on your finger if not an engagement ring? Here, let me be your hairdresser."

He sat her down and drawing her hair back, divided it into three thick strands and quickly plaited it, securing the end with a hairpin that he bent to form a clasp. It reminded him of the lazy afternoons in the little apartment in Brussels when he used to plait Dita's luxuriant black hair. He smiled at the memory and leaned over to pick a trembling wisteria blossom. He tucked it in her braid. "There," he said, "you are all very prim and proper. Like a schoolgirl. Nothing like that passionate hussy I just held in my arms."

"What do you mean?" Fredericka started indignantly and then she saw his lips quiver. She smiled sheepishly. "I tend to take things too seriously."

Dietrich came up the steps of the little summer pavilion, a bit flushed and only partly from his long walk across the lawn. He set down the silver tray. Mint sprigs were floating in the crystal pitcher. A silver bowl held glistening shards of ice in which two glasses had been embedded. He indicated a silver flask. "The rum," he said.

"Thank you, Dietrich," Fredericka said, dismissing him. The butler inclined slightly and left. The couple, clutching each other's hands, watched him halfway across the wide lawn and then let their laughter bubble up.

The afternoon passed. The shadows were lengthening into dusk when they left the gazebo. It had not been so bad, thought Alexandre. He had enjoyed these few hours. Fredericka was easy to be with. Not at all the forbidding women he had imagined. They had talked about their childhoods. Both had been unhappy and lonely at times. Both had been motherless. It was a bond between them.

It was not the kind of flirtatious afternoon he might have spent if another girl, Kitty for instance, had been with him drinking rum-spiked lemonade under the wisteria, but there was something about it that had been very pleasant. He did not kiss Fredericka when he left, however. That first embrace had left him unexpectedly shaken.

# Five

I‌T WAS after four o'clock when a smiling Alexandre and Fredericka walked arm in arm under the canopy that led from the wide doors of the Fifth Avenue Presbyterian Church across the sidewalk to Fredericka's ivory Rolls-Royce waiting at the curb.

"Well, it's done," Alexandre said. "How do you feel, Madame de Granville?"

"A little shaky."

"I too."

They were silent during the drive to the house. When the car stopped, passersby formed a small crowd, watching the bride stand helpless in the bitter wind that whipped around the corners of Murray Hill until Raymond and Siddie could gather her veil and train. Then, linked by satin and tulle, the three went up the steps of the brownstone mansion, followed by Alexandre.

The musicians, hidden away in the conservatory, had started playing. The doors between the double drawing rooms had been opened to make one vast room. In the library a score of small round tables had been set up for those who preferred to sit and gossip. Dietrich was directing the small army of waiters with an almost Rooseveltian verve, exhorting them to do their best—and to keep their white gloves clean. To Fredericka's practiced eye, everything seemed under control.

As the couple took their places in front of the elaborate backdrop of orange blossoms and glossy greens that had been constructed in the drawing room, Dietrich hurried up to them with two glasses. "Drink this down and I'll pour you another," Alexandre said. He reached into the greenery behind them and, plucking a bottle of champagne from a silver cooler, refilled the glasses.

Fredericka looked at her husband of half an hour and raised her eyebrows.

"You will need a little champagne courage," he said, "if you are to keep smiling for the next two hours. When we finish that bottle, Dietrich will bring another."

"Two hours? No reception line lasts two hours."

"This one will. Your father is in it." She nodded ruefully and drained the second glass. Late afternoon turned into evening. The room grew hot with the crush of bodies. The fragrance of the orange blossoms mixed with cigar smoke and perfume was almost overpowering. The reception line lurched along at a pace irritating to everyone except Frederick, who insisted on chatting with everyone. As each guest escaped him, he was handed down the line from Fredericka to Alexandre to Isabelle Wallace to Harry Peckham, who had acted as best man, with graceful dispatch. Fredericka lost track of time and the faces blurred into a smiling haze. Finally the line dissolved into a few stragglers.

"That's enough," Isabelle said decisively. "Fredericka, it's time to cut the cake."

Isabelle had been a tower of strength this autumn. Fredericka had come to admire her tremendously. It was Isabelle who had encouraged her to veto her father's choice of an October wedding date.

"It won't do at all," Isabelle had agreed with her. "It is

undignified. And impossible. You have to order your trousseau, make the arrangements. You must speak to him.''

It had not been easy. Her father had shaken his head like
an angry bull, but eventually he had capitulated.

''All right. Have it your own way. But don't blame me if
he changes his mind before December,'' he had said. ''If
you take my advice, you will strike while the iron is hot.
Don't give him time to think it over. And don't give any of
those young beauties he used to escort a chance to meddle.
You could find yourself high and dry,'' he had said inelegantly.

''No. You are wrong, Papa,'' she had said. But she was
not so sure. She had watched Kitty flirting with Alexandre
all summer. There was a glint in her eyes when she looked
at him that went beyond friendship. It was well known that
Kitty could wrap her father around her little finger. All she
had to do was turn that pretty china-doll face toward him
and let her eyes fill with tears. Mr. Parseval could afford a
penniless son-in-law just as easily as Papa. But she refused
to worry. It was better to risk everything than start the
marriage in such unseemly haste.

It was somehow agreed, without ever being put into
words, that the wedding would take place in early December. Frederick now believed that he himself had set the date
in consultation with the Reverend Buchan of Fifth Avenue
Presbyterian.

Once that was settled, Isabelle had whisked her through
the city's luxury shops to select her trousseau. She had
installed her own seamstress on the fourth floor of the
Murray Hill house to produce delicately hand-stitched and
embroidered silk lingerie, lavish lace-trimmed gowns and
negligees, the basics of a bride's trousseau.

In her delicately critical manner, Isabelle had vetoed most
of Fredericka's own selections, steering her relentlessly to
softer colors and finer fabrics. ''No taffetas,'' she had
decreed. ''Too stiff. No brilliant colors. They're not for
you.'' Instead she directed saleswomen to show them bolts
of soft luxurious fabrics in bois-de-rose, pearl gray, mauve,

the softest of shades. A muted gray-green silk caught her eye. "That must have been dyed especially for you. We'll have your Worth gown copied in it."

Fredericka was dubious. It was such a drab color. And shockingly expensive. "Are you sure? It is so dear."

"You can afford it," Isabelle said dryly. "The Worth does all the right things for your figure and your complexion. It makes you look like a young duchess. And this silk is perfect for it."

Fredericka reddened with pleasure. "But it is so plain, that dress," she protested. "I told Monsieur Worth so, but he became quite cross and insisted that I must take it exactly as he designed it. And I did because I liked the color. He even told me how to dress my hair."

"In that lovely Grecian knot. That is how you must wear it on your wedding day."

"I had thought in a pompadour," Fredericka said hesitantly. "Siddie does it so well that way."

Isabelle simply closed her eyes and shook her head. She was too kind to tell Fredericka that it made her look like a washwoman. Only once did Isabelle relent when she saw Fredericka wistfully fingering a bolt of bright blue satin. "Blue," she said brightly, trying not to sneer at the glaring satin. "Of course. With your eyes."

"And with my diamond-and-sapphire parure."

Isabelle raised her eyebrows. "Diamonds and sapphires? I've never seen them."

"Papa gave it to me on my sixteenth birthday. Four pieces—a tiara, a necklace, earrings, and a bracelet."

"You never wear them." Isabelle was surprised.

"No, it was not suitable. Not for a girl of sixteen."

"I should say not." Perhaps Fredericka did have the basic elements of taste, Isabelle thought. She simply needed a little push in the right direction.

"And then when I was old enough to wear them, I didn't," Fredericka continued, "because I had told Papa that I wanted to wear them first on my wedding day."

"And you must." Diamonds and sapphires! Isabelle marveled at the young woman who had left them to sparkle unseen in a bank vault all these years. She would turn Fredericka into a glittering snow princess on her wedding day. As for that dreadful blue satin that she was still admiring, perhaps it could be used to line an evening cloak.

As Alexandre led his bride to the middle of the floor to open the dancing, she looked like a grave young queen. It was not simply the austere lines of her white satin gown and the magnificence of her jewels with their frosty fire. She had achieved a certain radiance, beyond beauty. There was an inner glow of joyous triumph that caused women to look more closely at her than they ever had before—and men to take a second look.

Isabelle took Frederick's arm. "You have given her a lovely wedding," she told him, "and a fine husband." He glared at her. "What do you mean—given?"

"You know exactly what I mean," she told him. "You are a good father. You are going to miss her."

He looked over at his daughter standing with her groom. Damn it. He *was* going to miss her. It had been the two of them against the world ever since her mother had died. He had been so proud of her, the way she had handled herself, run the house. Proud of her intelligence. And now as he looked at her, he was struck by her appearance. He had never seen her look so very attractive, never seen her look attractive at all for that matter. But today she was truly a beautiful bride.

He patted Isabelle's hand. "I have a lot to thank you for, my dear."

As Fredericka circled the floor in Alexandre's arms, her veil floating out from the tiara, she remembered another waltz, another dance floor, another partner, and wondered what had become of poor little Willy Keiller. His father had lost everything in the Panic of 1907. It was said that they had moved to Chicago. She hoped Willy had found himself a diminutive bride who would make him feel like a giant just as she had found the husband she had always dreamed of. Alexandre looked at her with concern. "There are tears in your eyes," he whispered. "What is it?"

"It's just that I cannot believe this is me. I feel like Cinderella the minute before midnight strikes. I am afraid to be so happy."

"Ah, but there will be no midnight," he assured her. "I will never let it be midnight for you." She smiled into his eyes with such happiness that it hurt him. If only he could feel the same toward her.

He looked around the room. He saw so many familiar faces. So many girls with whom he had flirted short months ago. He thought longingly of the carefree life he had led when he first arrived in New York—the skating parties, the mornings riding in the park or bicycling along the Hudson, the evenings at the theater and the opera, the dances and the late suppers. Suddenly he felt old. Midnight had struck for him.

Later, he found himself dancing with Kitty Parseval. "You are a sly fox," she accused him. "I never guessed. Not for one moment." He did not bother to respond. Kitty had said this so many times in the past few months that it was more of a greeting than a question. There was nothing he could say anyway.

He had been closer to Kitty than any of the other girls he had squired about, but theirs had been an innocent flirtation, nothing to warrant the tinge of jealousy he detected now. Or almost nothing.

"I want to hear all about your courtship," she insisted. "You have been so secretive. Perhaps we can meet sometime when you get back from your wedding trip. That is," she dimpled, "if she ever lets you off your leash."

"Is that the American concept of marriage?" he parried with a laugh. "In that case I do not believe that Fredericka and I will adopt it. Doesn't she look lovely?" he asked, looking across the room at his bride.

"Very nice," Kitty said without enthusiasm.

"When we are at home," he told her, "you must come to tea and perhaps Fredericka will tell you about our courtship. I believe it is the woman's prerogative," he smiled down at her.

He was grateful when the music stopped. She was a disturbing little minx. He made his way over to where Fredericka was standing with her father. She smiled at him. "I think we might leave now," she said.

There were no bridesmaids to troop giggling up the stairs after her, to help unpin her veil and try on the tiara in front of the mirror, to exclaim over the going-away suit laid out on the bed. No laughing girls to tease her about the night to come. Just Isabelle, who had insisted that Fredericka must have a bridal attendant and had appointed herself matron of honor in such a manner that no discussion was possible. Fredericka had found her presence deeply comforting.

She had never felt quite so alone in the world as when she had realized that she had no friends she could ask to be bridesmaids. Despite the luncheons and teas, the lectures and the musicales, the dinners and receptions that filled her days and nights, despite the countless acquaintances whose invitations she accepted and returned, she had no intimate women friends. Her school days had inflicted such pain that the child who had been snubbed and ignored still suffered from those old wounds and would not permit the woman to make herself vulnerable by reaching out for friendship. Fredericka had disciplined herself so ruggedly that she had come to believe that it did not matter. Until now. Isabelle, sensing this, had thoughtfully and warmly filled the void.

"You look elegant," Siddie said, stepping back and admiring her. Fredericka's going-away suit was of palest blue velvet—Isabelle's choice—with a sable collar and cuffs. White orchids were pinned to her sable muff. Isabelle kissed her. "You look ravishing," she said and left to wait with the others for Fredericka to descend the staircase.

Fredericka looked around her room. She would never

sleep here again. She had her own house now. And a husband. Everything was going to be different from now on. Better. Siddie handed her the wedding bouquet.

She came down the stairs slowly and paused on the landing. Isabelle was standing to one side in the hall below. She hurled the bouquet in her direction with all her strength. Isabelle flashed a startled smile at her as she caught it.

Holding hands, the couple raced for the automobile between rows of laughing guests who pelted them with rice. A swirl of snow came up out of the night and stung Fredericka's face. Minutes later she looked out into the December darkness to see where they were going. Not toward the docks where the great ocean liners waited, nor toward Grand Central. She turned to Alexandre. "Now will you tell me?" she asked. "Where are we going? I told Siddie to pack for every climate since you insisted on keeping our destination secret."

"Five more minutes," he replied. "You will know in five more minutes."

Snow had begun to frost the streets, coming down so heavily that the gaslights were only faint halos in the night. Raymond drew up before a brightly lit house, every window golden through the snow. She stared. It was their own house. The house she had been visiting almost daily supervising the refurbishing and furnishing. For the first time it looked like a home.

The door was opened with a flourish. "This is Walter." Alexandre introduced a dignified man in his fifties. "He comes highly recommended by Dietrich." A smiling woman wearing a crisp organdy apron over rustling black taffeta stood behind Walter. "And this is Anna. She is the parlor maid and she will act as your personal maid until Siddie moves in. And this," Alexandre said, "is Cook. Céleste Durand." Céleste stepped forward, an imposing figure in a brown cotton dress covered by a bibbed white apron that came down to her ankles.

Fredericka smiled and nodded to her new staff and then

Alexandre led her about the house. It had been transformed. Wood fires crackled in the drawing room and library. A coal fire glowed in the dining room. Fresh flowers everywhere. Lighted candles flickered in the tall candelabrum on the landing as they went up the stairs. Holding her hand, Alexandre pulled her through the bedroom dominated by a huge four-poster bed and through the door that opened into his dressing room. Beyond the dressing room was his den, a comfortable room with low leather chairs, heavy oriental rugs spread over the warm red carpet, and rows of shelves lining the walls waiting to be filled with books. The low table in front of the fire held silver chafing dishes over flickering blue flames. There was champagne in a cooler.

"A picnic supper," he announced with a brave flourish. He was nervous. Had her heart been set on a European tour or some sunny island? But this was all he could afford. Although Frederick, true to his word, was paying him a generous salary, he did not have enough money for the kind of honeymoon he imagined Fredericka would expect. And he had not been able to bring himself to ask his father-in-law-to-be to advance him money for a wedding trip. It was strange to be surrounded by so much luxury and yet feel so poor.

"What a marvelous idea!" Fredericka exclaimed. "No one will ever guess where we are."

He had to make sure that she understood. "It is where we are spending our honeymoon," he said. "Unless, that is, you dislike the idea." He looked at her searchingly, fearing that she might be thinking, "I did not marry a fortune hunter simply to stay home and save money."

"Dislike the idea!" she responded. "There is nothing you could have planned that would please me more. I have been looking forward so much to being in my own—I mean *our* own house." She was embarrassed by the slip. "Do open the wine," she urged hastily. "We must drink to our first night together in our own house."

\*        \*        \*

It was a curious wedding supper. They had become comfortable with each other. Alexandre was the playmate Fredericka had never had, the best friend she had always longed for. And he had become attached to her. She amazed him. He had never known a woman like this. Not flirtatious. Hard to know. She had erected a wall around herself that was difficult to penetrate. But when something interested her, her defenses disappeared and she glowed with enthusiasm.

He discovered that she was passionately interested in the world of finance. If she had not been so involved in her father's business affairs, in fact, he would have been lost. Frederick was much too impatient to go into details. "Ask Herbert about that," he would say. And Alexandre would go to the thin-lipped bookkeeper who had been with Frederick for years and knew his way through the labyrinth of deals and commitments. Herbert, however, could only speak in terms of profits and losses—he knew nothing of the negotiations that had brought them about. Frederick's right-hand man, Gwillim, was even less informative. Not that he was unwilling, but he knew very little beyond the day-to-day transactions. Frederick had never delegated responsibility nor shared his plans with anyone except his daughter.

Fredericka happily instructed Alexandre hour after hour until he came to see the world of finance as she did—a fascinating playground for those who dared risk its dangers. It was strange, he thought, that he had taken so little interest in Assurances Bruxbelges. Perhaps it was because Uncle Albert's approach to business had been so petti-fogging. The baron's preoccupation with minute details and safe profits had held little glamor for him.

The tutelage had not been one-sided. Alexandre, more by example than direction, had helped her be more at ease with people. The austere Miss Schumacher, once she relaxed, proved to have an infectious laugh and a bewitching smile that made people forget her plain features. "It must be love," the gossipers told each other. And once again they would revive their speculations about this unexpected alliance.

Now they sat comfortably across from each other at the end of their wedding day, their stocking feet propped on the table. It was a homey scene. His frockcoat and four-in-hand had been tossed on the tufted leather sofa along with her sable-trimmed jacket. The hours slipped by as they talked about the day. Bending forward to refill Fredericka's glass, Alexandre whistled softly.

"Do you realize we have finished two bottles of champagne?"

"Perhaps we should open a third," she said lazily.

"Do you want to?"

Suddenly they were self-conscious. They looked at each other. The fire was low, a bed of glowing coals with an occasional reminiscent spurt of flame.

"Why don't you put another log on the fire? I'll go change," she said standing up. "Then we might have a last glass of wine." He must not think that she was a reluctant virgin. "I will only be a few minutes." She picked up her jacket and padded out in her stocking feet.

He put a log on the dying fire and poked the coals until the flames sprang up again. God, he was tired. And there was work ahead. He went to his dressing room and took off his shirt. He splashed his face with cold water, then decided to shave. He owed Fredericka a smooth cheek on her wedding night. He turned on the hot water tap with a feeling of pride in the modern fittings of the house. Hot water at any hour. How his Uncle Albert would marvel—while criticizing the extravagance.

Fifteen minutes later he tied the sash of his new dressing gown of ribbed crimson silk. He yawned and hoped Fredericka would not be too long. The fire felt good.

Anna had been waiting in the bedroom. When Fredericka came in, she sprang to her feet. "I have your bath ready." A negligee of palest green satin embroidered with lilies of the valley and a matching gown were laid out on the bed. When she stepped out of the huge porcelain tub, Anna toweled her dry and slipped the gown over her head. She sat at her dressing table while Anna unwound the Grecian knot and brushed her hair smooth, letting it hang loose over her shoulders. Staring at herself in the mirror, she reminded herself of an overgrown schoolgirl. Certainly not a bride. And yet—she felt something. A kind of tremulous anticipation. She shrugged.

After she dismissed Anna, Fredericka turned off all but one light. Now it was up to Alexandre. She had done what she could. She wondered what he would think. If he would mention it. And if he did, what he would say.

It had been three weeks ago.

"Healthy as a horse," Dr. Godfrey had said heartily. Somewhat embarrassed by his choice of phrase, he went on hurriedly, "Your heart is superb, a good steady beat. Most young women in love tend to have a fluttering pulse," he teased.

She made no response. She sat there, enveloped in the scratchy white examining gown, making no move to get up and get dressed. "Well, that's it," he said. "You are fit as a fiddle. Not a thing to worry about. I shall be very surprised if I don't see you back here in a couple of months with some happy symptoms." Dr. Godfrey smiled and pushed his chair back from the desk.

Fredericka did not return the smile. She was twisting her hands, her face was red. "Doctor, I have to ask you something," she said in such a low voice that he had to lean forward to hear her.

I might have known, he sighed to himself. Probably ignorant as a baby. Frederick Schumacher was not the sort of man who would have imparted any sexual information to his daughter. He prepared himself for the inevitable question, but when it came, Fredericka's request shocked him.

"Doctor, I have heard that the wedding night . . ." She stopped and looked down at her hands. How could she ask

him? But she had made up her mind and she would. After
all she had done, this was no time to falter.

"Doctor," she began again, "I have heard that the
wedding night can be painful. I suppose that is true?"

Dr. Godfrey pursed his lips. "Well, yes, it can be
somewhat uncomfortable. But it is of no consequence, my
dear. Certainly nothing to dread. Pay no attention to the old
wives' tales. You may feel some discomfort at the moment
of, uh, insertion. But in a day or two, a night or two," he
said with a knowing and practiced twinkle, "the discomfort
completely disappears."

"I see. That is what I had surmised." She hesitated and
then plunged ahead once more. "Dr. Godfrey, I want to
avoid that discomfort. I do not want my wedding night
spoiled by pain. I have waited too long."

He looked at her quizzically. "I am afraid, my dear, that
it is woman's lot to suffer at certain times. But you truly
must not fear this. It is nothing more than momentary
discomfort."

"I do not fear it," she said, pulling the ties of the
examining gown tighter and retying them. "What I am
saying is that I do not want to feel any pain on my wedding
night."

He looked at her. She was as stubborn as her father. What
did she want him to do?

She told him. "I have read that if the hymen is cut before
the wedding night, there will be no pain at the time of . . ."
She searched for the word and produced it triumphantly.
"The time of insertion. And that is what I would like you to
do."

"Have you asked your father about this?" he asked,
recognizing it for a foolish question the momemt he had
uttered it.

"Of course not. It has nothing to do with Papa. I
considered doing it myself," she told him, "but I was
afraid that I might be too rough. Or not rough enough. You
know how difficult it is to inflict pain, I mean discomfort,"

she corrected herself pointedly, "upon oneself. So I decided to ask you."

"Mmmmh," he resorted to the noncommittal again. "I see. And when would you want this done?"

"Now," she said flatly.

"Is there any reason why you cannot do it today?" she asked as he remained silent. "Right now?"

Dr. Godfrey was dismayed at being asked to perform a surgical procedure that he had never even contemplated in all his years of practice, but what was he to do? "No," he sighed. "Not really. If you are positive that this is what you want."

"It is what I want."

"Very well," he said and pressed the buzzer on his desk. The nurse came in. "Miss Schumacher is . . ." He changed his mind and approached it differently. "Please prepare Miss Schumacher for a hymenotomy," he told her. "I will operate in ten minutes." The nurse stared at him. There was an awkward pause, then routine took over. "Will you come this way," she said.

Dr. Godfrey, scrubbed and gloved, entered the little examining room that doubled as a surgery. "There will be no pain," he said, "a little bleeding, but it will stop within minutes. Nurse, please secure Miss Schumacher's limbs."

The nurse strapped her feet to the stirrups, then pushed them apart. Fredericka felt helpless and angry. Why was he making such a production out of a simple procedure?

Crouched on his little stool between her legs, the doctor was hidden by the sheet over her knees. Fredericka heard the clink of metal as an instrument was withdrawn from the sterilizer.

"Steady now," he said. There was the unbelievable sensation of male fingers opening her genital lips. She was conscious of the silence, accented by the bubbling of the sterilizer. "I will remember this moment all the rest of my life," she thought.

Then there was movement. Sharp steel against the softest

flesh. She could feel the hot blood rushing down the cleft between her buttocks. The doctor stood and the nurse moved in. She sponged the blood away with pads of cool wet gauze.

"That's it," Dr. Godfrey said. "You can get dressed in twenty minutes. Lie there for now and relax until the bleeding stops." He patted her knee and left.

The nurse released the stirrups and as Fredericka closed her legs, she felt the hurt of raw flesh and opened them again. But it was bearable. And the thing was done. On her wedding night, there would be no blood, no raw flesh, no pain.

Alexandre must expect a virgin. Would he be shocked? It did not matter if he was. She did not need to tell him about this surgical deflowering. She had not only bought a husband, she had bought the freedom to do as she pleased, a freedom no married woman she knew enjoyed.

There was no turning back now. She went swiftly through Alexandre's dressing room into his den. The fire was burning briskly. A fresh bottle of champagne was in the cooler.

And Alexandre?

He was asleep.

She tiptoed over to his chair to be sure that he was not teasing her. No, he was asleep, with his head turned to one side, his arms lying relaxed on the arms of the chair, hands half curled like a child's. She stood looking at him. His face was pale against the crimson of his dressing gown. His lips curved as if his dream was a happy one. The long lashes against his cheeks made him look young and vulnerable. She turned away feeling that if she stared at him longer the intensity of her gaze might wake him. She covered him with the cashmere throw from the sofa and turned off the light.

A minute later she was in bed. It was almost two o'clock. She lifted her hand and looked at the wedding band that had joined her engagement ring. She smiled and yawned and turned off the light. It had been a long day. Tomorrow was time enough.

Sometime during the night she woke to discover that she was not alone. A back was fitted against her own as snugly as if it were a second half. The moment of consciousness was brief, her sleep so sound that it was like hearing the clock strike in the dark reaches of the night, a happening so natural that it would not be recalled in the morning unless there was reason for it to be brought to mind.

The gray December morning stretched on. The snow that had started the night before still came down. The world inside and out was quiet. Only in the basement kitchen where the coal stove radiated gusts of heat and a kettle was boiling was there any stir. Anna and Walter sat at the kitchen table drinking tea. Céleste had just punched down the dough she had set to rise early that morning and was shaping rolls.

"They may be expecting tea," Anna worried. "Perhaps I should take it up to them."

"I wouldn't," advised Walter. "You might be interrupting something." He smiled meaningfully.

"Oh go on. Not in the morning."

"The morning is best of all," he informed her. "Just you wait. You'll find out for yourself one of these years."

"That will be enough from you."

Fredericka woke slowly. She stretched and then paused in mid-yawn when she realized that Alexandre was in bed with her, curled in a ball like a giant hedgehog. For a startled second she wondered if last night's champagne could have blotted out the wedding night for which she had prepared so carefully. Then memory flooded in—Alexandre asleep by the fire, her momentary awakening sometime before dawn, and the warm, oddly comforting sensation of a back pressed to hers. She raised herself on her elbow to look at him.

He stirred, then uncurled and stretched. He opened his

eyes and looked at her. "My God, I'm thirsty," he said and padded half blindly into his dressing room. She heard the water running, the toilet flush with a grand roar. He came back carrying a glass of water. "Here," he handed it to her. She drank it, gulping it down as he returned to bed.

Now what? she wondered. Her dreams of marital intimacy had not gone this far. It had to be faced. She could not deny the need. She got up, clutching the strap of her nightgown that had slipped off her shoulder. There was heat coming up through the register in her bathroom. She stood over it, letting the hot air rise under her gown. She missed Siddie. Ever since she had come to New York, Siddie had been there in the morning to run her bath, brush her hair, help her dress. Never mind, she could manage. She washed her face until it glowed and brushed her hair smooth. She wondered what to do next. She could not stand over the hot air register for the rest of her life.

Alexandre lifted the covers. "Quick, get in," he said. "You must be frozen." Her nightgown slid up around her waist as she slipped between the sheets. She hastily tugged it down.

"Breakfast," he said. "What about breakfast?"

"Shall I ask them to bring it up here?"

"Yes, and quickly. Before the two of us starve to death."

The bell jangled in the kitchen. The three servants looked up at the board beside the kitchen door. "It's for me," Anna said and whisked off her coverall and tied on a starched white apron. She poured boiling water from the kettle into the teapot. "They'll be wanting tea, I'm sure," she said and started up the two flights of stairs to the bedroom.

"They'll be wanting me next," said Walter. He put on his coat, pulled down his cuffs, smoothed his hair back with his hands and sat down to wait. The bell jangled again. "What did I tell you?" He hurried upstairs.

Céleste looked at the clock. Almost twelve. The lovers

will be hungry, she thought. She started breaking eggs, separating the whites from the yolks.

"She wants you," Anna said, picking up a basket of kindling for the fireplace and darting upstairs again. Céleste nodded, checked the preparations she had under way, and slowly mounted the stairs.

The second floor hummed with activity. Baths were run, fires were lighted, the bed was made, curtains were opened. Walter, who was acting as Alexandre's valet, was shaving him in his dressing room when Céleste arrived to discuss breakfast with Fredericka. She made it clear that no discussion was needed.

"I have a compote of oranges and bananas. Eggs and ham, and chicken livers." She ticked the items off on her fingers. "I just put a pan of rolls in the oven. I will send Anna up with coffee immediately." She eyed the teapot with scorn.

When Alexandre emerged from his dressing room, the breakfast table was set in front of the bedroom fire. Fredericka, her hair pulled back in a simple knot, poured him coffee. He drained the cup and held it out to be refilled.

"This is the best coffee I have had since I came to this country."

"It is terribly strong."

He nodded approvingly. "I knew she was going to be a treasure. She comes from Lyons. They understand food there. There will be no weak coffee or floury sauces served in this house."

"She seems to have nothing against American ham and eggs," Fredericka said. "That's what we're having for breakfast." But when Walter arrived with the tray, the ham and eggs were not what she had expected. There was a cheese soufflé, miraculously puffed despite its journey from the basement kitchen. There were nearly transparent slices of ham arranged on a bed of watercress. There was a chafing dish containing chicken livers and mushrooms in an aromatic red wine sauce. There were hot rolls fresh from the oven wrapped in a damask napkin. There was a mound of butter curls on crushed ice and a dish of apricot preserves.

Alexandre surveyed the table. ''A promising beginning,'' he smiled.

''It is remarkable. And it took her no time at all. How did you manage to assemble a staff without my even suspecting? I expected to have to devote a couple of weeks to it after we returned from our honeymoon.'' Fredericka was as gravely formal as if she were discussing domestic matters with her father's butler.

''It was not easy. I can tell you that. We owe a lot to Dietrich, who seems to know all the right people in all the right kitchens,'' he replied, equally formal. ''I interviewed a dozen candidates at least. These three seemed to be the most agreeable and skilled. When our honeymoon is officially over, we can add another maid and a valet for me. And of course Siddie will be here.''

''We will need a chauffeur unless your valet understands motorcars.''

It was awkward, but what with discussing the servants, the food, and the weather—the snow showed no signs of letting up—they managed to get through breakfast without giving the slightest hint of what was on their minds.

She kept wondering how they would spend the rest of this first day of married life. Would they dress and descend to sit in the library? It was snowing too hard to go out. They could play cribbage or backgammon. She could spend an hour or two writing thank-you notes. Would he wait until evening before making love? Should she say anything about it? She rang for Anna to clear the breakfast things away.

As soon as Anna closed the door behind her, Alexandre sat at Fredericka's feet near the fire. ''I'm sorry I fell asleep last night,'' he said looking up at her. ''It was the last thing in the world I wanted to do. I was waiting for you—and then I woke up and it was four o'clock and I was very cold. I was going to sleep on the sofa, but I thought about the servants. What would they think? A quarrel on our wedding night?

Her laughter was strained. She sat looking into the fire. The silence fairly quivered with tension.

"Come," he said abruptly, standing and taking her hands. "We have been thinking about this far too long. It is time." The words carried an assurance he was far from feeling. But he had to reassure her somehow. What must she have thought when she found him asleep last night? Had she cried? He did not think so. Her morning face had not had the look of a woman who had cried herself to sleep. It was more likely that she had been angry. A sleeping lover was not what she had bargained for.

He was anxious. There was a chill at the base of his spine. Would he be able to do it? To deflower a woman who had been a virgin for too long? A woman who possessed neither beauty nor that special female seductiveness that excited him?

The room had a twilight feeling with the lamps lit against the falling snow outside. He led her to the bed and stretched out beside her, leaning on his elbow and looking into her now-timid blue eyes.

"Do you remember your promise?"

"Promise?" She was blushing and trying to evade his gaze.

"That day in the gazebo." He slowly untied the ribbons that fastened her negligee. "We promised each other that there would never be any idiotic embarrassment between us. And then we kissed. Like this," he lowered his lips to hers. Summoning up all his experience, he played the passionate lover with cool skill. He thrust his tongue deep into her mouth, noted her quick response and the tensing of her body. His caresses were practiced. Then, without his being conscious of the transition, he found himself no longer an observer, but a greedy lover, lost in the ebb and flow of passion. Finally he drew away and rolled off the bed. Fredericka lay there, feeling abandoned and, at the same time, apprehensive of what was to come. He shrugged out of his dressing gown and tossed it over a chair. He unbuttoned his pajama jacket and threw it on top of the dressing gown. Then he let the pajama bottoms drop.

He was so handsome, she thought, and clutched the negligee about her where he had opened it. What would he think when he saw her body? Perhaps he did not have to. People made love in the dark. They could make love under the covers.

"Let me take that off." He pulled her to her feet and slid the negligee off her shoulders and let it fall to the carpet. She did not think she could bear it. She was so big. He must find her ugly. He bent and picked up her nightgown by the hem, pulling it over her head.

"Ah!" he said. Nothing more. They were on the bed again. He was burrowing into her, his head between her breasts, his hand cupping first one and then the other as he kissed the nipples into hard peaks. She had never imagined anything like this. She moved under his weight. She pressed her legs together and writhed. Then she opened them wide.

He slid in. He was conscious of a momentary surprise, but the momentum of passion carried him past it into other more immediate surprises—the wealth of soft yielding flesh, the unexpected response, the cresting and the smooth slide down into exhausted peace.

They slept briefly, but he was aware even in his sleep of the woman beside him, those thighs that had gripped so eagerly, the breasts that had thrust like rose-topped Alps, the soft round belly, the great handfuls of buttocks. So much woman! Without opening his eyes he turned to her again. It was almost too much. He drew his hand up between her legs. He could feel her tremble as they parted. He thrust into the warm darkness and climbed to the crest again. And down, down. This time to oblivion.

Eventually Fredericka moved. He had collapsed upon her, his head on her breast. She had held him lovingly, stroking his hair, the smooth bareness of his back. One arm had gone to sleep long ago. As she eased out from under him, he half woke. "Dita," he mumbled. "Dita." And sank back into sleep again.

She was shocked out of her tender mood. Dita? Who was Dita? The softness faded from her face. Her lips pressed together. Well, what did she expect? He did not come to her without a past. But for a moment she hated him. She turned her back to him and stared out the window at the swirling snow. In time she fell asleep too.

It was evening when he woke. For a moment he did not know where he was or whose bed he was in.

He looked slowly around the room. It was half dark. The curtains were drawn. The only light came from a silk-shaded lamp beside a chaise longue. A woman was lying on it, propped up by pillows, her head bent over a book.

Fredericka.

Reality shattered the last remnants of sleep. That was his wife reclining there so quietly in the lamplight. The woman who had so unexpectedly and excitingly carried him to heights of passion he had never reached before.

He moved and she looked up. As he stretched and groaned comfortably, she came and sat beside him. He held out his hand. He was so relaxed that it took an effort to move.

"How long have I been sleeping?"

"Hours. It is after eight o'clock. You must be hungry."

"Famished," he said and sat up, then sank back again as he realized he was naked. Fredericka laughed and he joined in. How ridiculous to feel abashed. He was the man who had stripped in front of her earlier, proudly and consciously showing off his masculinity. But now there was a difference. Instead of the awkward virgin he had expected, he had found fire. He remembered his moment of surprise. This wife of his was evidently no virgin. But then why that initial timidity? That reluctance to expose her body.

She handed him his dressing gown. "Shall I order dinner—

or is it supper?—served up here? Or would you rather get
dressed and eat downstairs?"

"Here," he said. "I don't have the strength to get
dressed."

It was going to be very satisfying to run her own household,
Fredericka thought. She had more to learn than she had
expected, since Alexandre's tastes were so different from
Papa's. It was cozy, the two of them here all by themselves.
Making love and sleeping and doing just as they pleased.
Never before in her life had Fredericka spent an entire day
without getting dressed. That afternoon she had felt almost
wicked, lying in a hot bath fragrant with perfume while her
lover, her husband, slept in the next room.

She had explored her body, trying to experience it as he
had, feel it as he had, and been surprised to find herself
flopping like a fish as her body responded to stimulation.
Never in all her guilty, masturbating nights had she reached
such a strong climax.

Afterwards she had chosen another of her trousseau
negligees, this one with froths of soft lace at the cuffs. She
reached for the nightgown that went with it, then changed
her mind. She needed no nightgown. The robe was silky
smooth against her bare body newly sensitized to pleasure.

After dinner they sat in front of the fire in his den as they
had the previous night, feet up on the table. They drank
brandy instead of champagne tonight, relaxed and content
with life. But Fredericka was torn again between delight and
bitterness. Dita. It was foolish to wonder about this Dita.
She would ask him—that was best. There was no point in
waiting. This was the time.

"This afternoon, you half woke up once. Or perhaps you
were dreaming . . ." she hesitated. Was she wrong? She did
not care if she was. If she knew the truth, she could adjust
to it. But she had to know. She could not let herself be
tortured by her imagination.

"You said a name in your sleep. Dita. Who is Dita?"

My God! What had he done? What unconscionable cruelty had he committed? "Dita?" he said. "Dita?" Then his face brightened. "*Dina!* Not Dita. Dina. That must have been what I said. Dina," he repeated, hoping that his flash of inspiration was plausible.

He sat on the arm of her chair and kissed her lightly. "I might as well confess," he said, tracing the line of her lips with his finger, "that I have always thought Fredericka much too stiff a name for you. And a little masculine. When I think about you, I always think of you as Dina. Ever since the first afternoon we spent together." He bent down and kissed her again.

She put her hands on his shoulders, her great blue eyes so close to him that they looked like pools of liquid sapphire. She was smiling. "I have never had a nickname. All the other girls at school had them. I used to wish that someone would call me Rickie. Or even Freddie. But Dina is nicer. It is such a pretty name. But why Dina?" she asked. "It is not a nickname for Fredericka."

"But it is one for Diane, the goddess of the moon. She is tall like you, serene and beautiful."

"Beautiful!"

"My darling," he held her chin and turned her face toward him. "You are beautiful. Not pretty. But beautiful like a goddess. The way you walk with such dignity. The way you hold your head so high. I thought of you as Diane from the first evening when we stood watching the moon over the ocean. But Diane was too formal. So I created my own pet name for you. Dina.

"Dina de Granville. It suits you," he said.

"Yes, I like it. Dina de Granville. You must never call me Fredericka again. Not even in your sleep," she laughed.

He felt uneasy about his lie, but at least he had not hurt her. That was most important. And if his unconscious should play him another dirty trick like that, it would no longer be disastrous.

"Dina," he said again and ran his hand between her

breasts. She was incredibly enticing. He could not understand why he had not realized this before. Now he could not keep his hands off her body.

"Come," he whispered. "Let's go to bed." She stood and he stood behind her, his arms around her, holding her breasts. She untied the satin sash and he drew off her negligee. That body of hers! It seemed so immense and ungainly when clothed, but naked it was as voluptuous as any painted Venus. He had never dreamed that the consummation he had approached with so much anxiety would be so ecstatic. Nor that his bride would be so welcoming, so responsive.

He raised himself over her. "See what you do to me."

It was midnight. He listened to the clock strike twelve times. It took all his discipline to count the chimes. He was drained. Never in his life had he been so sated, felt so empty. It was an effort to move. All he wanted was to lie there next to that delicious, throbbing flesh.

But he had to move, had to speak. He had one more duty to perform before he could allow himself to sleep. He lifted his arm, circled her body and clasped her to him. "Dina, my darling Dina," he breathed into her ear. "I love you." As he let himself fall into sleep, he wondered if it were possible. Could he, of all unlikely things, really love her? It was more than he could think about now. He slept.

He was lying, she thought. Dita. Dina. I can tell the difference. But he was right. It was better to lie. He did not want me to be unhappy. She felt oddly comforted that he had forced himself to make his lie believable by that last murmured endearment. Whoever Dita was, she was not going to worry about her. Alexandre was hers now.

And there was something else. It was true that she had

always longed for a nickname. Dina. She savored it. Dina de Granville. It was both fashionable and romantic. Much more sophisticated than Kitty. She sighed contentedly and, in her turn, slept too.

# Six

In later years Dina and Alexandre looked back on their honeymoon as their own golden age when every hour was sweeter than the one before and the world far away and unregretted. When they eventually strolled down Madison Avenue to visit her father one Sunday afternoon just before Christmas, it seemed to Dina that she had been away far longer than the actual fortnight. The house struck her as gloomy and somewhat shabby after the bright elegance of her new home. The late-afternoon sun betrayed a film of dust on the furniture and the potted ferns drooped from lack of water.

"There is no fire!" she exclaimed as she entered the library. "Why are you sitting here without a fire?" Her sharpness covered her shock at seeing her father. His vitality seemed to have dimmed just as the house seemed to have faded.

"Has Dietrich been ill, Papa? This room is a disgrace." She flicked at a table with her handkerchief and picked up a brass bowl that held three cigar stubs. "I'll get rid of this," she said, wrinkling her nose, and left Alexandre alone with her father.

Her old rooms were immaculate as they had always been, the lace curtains crisply starched and the faint fragrance of lavender in the air. Siddie came hurrying in and threw up her hands in delight. "You look so happy!" the little maid exclaimed.

"I am. Happier than I ever dreamed of being," Dina replied in an uncharacteristic burst of feeling. "But I miss you. I want you to come to me as soon as you can.

"I'm ready now. I could come tomorrow."

"Good, Raymond can bring you and your trunk over after he has taken Papa downtown. I'm a little worried about Papa," she went on. "He doesn't look like himself."

"He's lonely. That's all," Siddie reassured her. "He misses you. He's not used to an empty house."

"Nor a dirty one," she said crisply. "I must have a talk with Dietrich." Her cheeks flushed in housewifely indignation. "I don't know what's gotten into him. He is letting the downstairs maid get away with murder. Everything is covered with dust."

"He does his best." Siddie defended the butler. "You forgot how much you used to do—planning the menus and doing the accounts and all that. Now Dietrich has to do it in addition to supervising the staff. Your father should have a housekeeper. Dietrich can't do it all."

Dina nodded thoughtfully. "Especially if you are coming to me."

"I must find a housekeeper for Papa," she told Alexandre that evening. "Dietrich can't run that house by himself."

"Your father needs more than a housekeeper. He needs..."

"A wife." She completed his sentence. "I know. You are absolutely right. He needs a wife." They looked at each other happily. Marriage, they had discovered, was truly blissful.

Nor did their delight in it end with their honeymoon. To

his surprise, Alexandre relished his new life as husband
and fledgling financier. He often wished his Uncle Albert
could see his office with its view of New York harbor. The
baron's baize-covered table and high-backed wooden chair
seemed even meaner compared to his own heavy mahogany
desk and leather-upholstered chair. But even more he wished
that his uncle could see the respect with which he was
treated.

All the right doors opened for Frederick Schumacher's
handsome son-in-law who was learning his way around the
financial district. It was as if he had been admitted to a
immensely congenial club. He had never been so close to
real power. It was exciting. The men who wielded it were
like giants. Or were they pirates? It did not matter. He
admired their audacity and daring. He could hardly believe
that he was, if not one of them, at least among them. He
marveled at his good fortune, at the same time feeling that it
was no more than he deserved.

And every evening there was that moment that still left
him breathless, when the door would open as he turned the
corner on Madison Avenue and Dina would be there, her
eyes glowing with pleasure. He no longer puzzled over
whether he loved her. He desired her and that was enough.
Desire wrought its own delightful confusions. Where once
he had seen vulgar overabundance, he now saw voluptuous
curves. Where once he had flinched at that strong jaw, he
now saw the soft features of love. He had never been as
captivated by anyone as by this amazing wife of his, never
been as close to anyone. She had become the best friend
that he had never had, the mother he had lost too early, the
mistress of his dreams. His wife. For the first time in his
life, he was conscious of being happy.

Dina had never let herself hope for more than that
Alexandre would play the devoted husband in public and be
conscientious about his marital obligations in private. That
he should love her seemed incredible. Impossible. And yet,
it might be. Hesitantly she allowed herself to believe it.

But occasionally when she woke during the lonely hour before dawn, doubt would creep in. She would listen to his breathing and wonder if he regretted the bargain, if beneath the ardor lay resentment, beneath the tenderness, scorn. The uncertainly would nag at her, spoiling the day until he came home again at night, his green eyes glinting with pleasure as he shrugged off his overcoat and embraced her, his lips warm and promising on hers.

Afterwards she would be angry with herself. He was hers. Why should she worry that he might be resentful as long as he lived up to his part of the bargain? And yet she did. She had not reckoned with love. She had not expected it. Now that she had experienced it, however, she felt she could not live without it. She could buy his services, but not his love. And if he did not love her? If he should stop loving her? The thought sent a chill through her.

Then she would be even angrier at her fearfulness. You have what you wanted, she told herself. More than you had hoped. And you are acting like a ninny, too cowardly to let yourself accept it.

As the weeks went by there were fewer awakenings in the dark hours. She abandoned herself to her love. Recklessly perhaps, but she intended to savor it all, not to dilute the emotion through timidity. She had been hurt before and lived through it. If she had to be hurt again, this at least was worth the pain.

Weeks before the wedding, Dina had relinquished her role as confidante and sounding board for Frederick. It would never do to have Alexandre feel that she was more competent than he. Once she had explained how Schumacher Enterprises operated and filled him in on the background of her father's present interests, they rarely discussed business together. It was better this way, she thought. He had to be able to respect himself, to feel that he had succeeded on his own.

But it left her with empty hours. The house ran smoothly with Walter at the helm and Céleste in the kitchen. It was

Isabelle who filled the void almost before Dina realized that it existed. Isabelle had grown fond of the younger woman, how fond she had not quite realized until one evening when she was dining with Frederick at Delmonico's after the theater.

"Can you explain why my daughter has suddenly insisted on changing her name?" he had asked testily.

"Women usually do when they marry," Isabelle said in willful misunderstanding.

"You know very well what I mean. This business of Dina. Insisting that she be called Dina."

"I agree with her. Frederick is a fine name for a man, but Fredericka is a little heavy for a woman. Names have their own magic, you know, Freddy. People grow to be like their names. Dina is elegant and feminine. Dina de Granville." She made it sound like poetry. "It becomes her."

"But why Dina? Where does it come from?" he grumbled.

"From her husband, of course. It's one of those pet names that every man and woman in love give each other. And they are in love." She sighed wistfully. "She is so happy I am almost jealous. She simply glows."

"She deserves to be happy," Frederick said. "It's a shame that she doesn't have the looks to match her brains. If she were just a little prettier, she would not have had to . . . had to . . . you know." He had long since confided the circumstances of the marriage to her. Despite his occasional criticisms of Isabelle's impetuous and sometimes imperious ways, he found her understanding and sympathetic.

"Freddy, you must be blind," she declared. "Where were your eyes on her wedding day? She was fabulously beautiful. Everyone said so." Isabelle herself had been astonished at the beauty Dina had shown as a bride. The exquisitely cut white satin and the fantastic jewels had done their part, but they were only the setting for the real jewel, the astonishingly beautiful bride. Love and excitement had coaxed her elusive beauty out of hiding.

"She looked exceptionally fine," he admitted. "You did

wonders with her. But then you are a wonderful woman."
He patted her hand.

The next morning as Isabelle drank her coffee, basking in
the sun that flooded through the bay window, her thoughts
were on Frederick. After the wedding she had thought that
he might abandon his resistance to marriage, but he had
resumed his old independent ways. It was a pity. He had the
makings of an excellent husband—at least, an excellent
husband for her—just as his daughter had the makings of a
beauty. Isabelle's mind flashed off on the new tangent. An
exceptional beauty, she mused. Dina was truly a diamond in
the rough. With polish, she could be superb.

She smiled. "I'll show Freddy," she decided, setting
down her coffee cup with a clink. Though not an easy one,
it was the kind of challenge she savored. Isabelle could coax
Dina into wearing the right clothes and doing her hair
becomingly, but the beauty had to come from within, from
her own confidence in being loved and admired. It meant
breaking through the defenses she had built up around
herself ever since she had been flung into the hostile world
of New York's rich and privileged young as an ungainly
adolescent. Isabelle understood the combination of unflinch-
ing courage and anguished timidity that made up Dina's
fortress. It was time she broke out of it.

Isabelle opened her campaign with a dinner party. She
had considered a dance, but Dina had been a wallflower at
too many dances for too many years. It was too much to
hope that she could break the pattern. No, a dinner was
safer.

Never had she agonized so over a guest list. Each name
was considered and reconsidered. It was a daring combination Isabelle was striving for—old New York and the new
New York, those people of brains and talent who were
turning the city into an intellectual capital and whom she
found far more stimulating than the financiers and businessmen with their pompous mien and grudging conversation.

Would they mix? If all went well, Dina would be the catalyst. She was something different. There were nights when Isabelle woke up and reached for her list, crossing off three names, adding two. It had to be perfect, a work of art.

"What are you planning to wear to my dinner party?" she asked Dina one afternoon.

"My maroon silk, the one with the draped overskirt."

Isabelle repressed a shudder. "But you wore that at the Fessendens' the other week," she objected. It was a dreadful dress, making the worst of Dina's weak points. "Let's look through your wardrobe. Why don't you wear one of your lovely trousseau gowns?"

Dina led the way upstairs and soon Siddie was bringing out one dress after another for Isabelle to scrutinize. "That's the one!" she exclaimed as Siddie held up a dark green satin with a daring décolletage. It was one that Isabelle had helped Dina choose. "I don't believe you've ever worn it."

"It's so plain. I need something more elaborate. My clothes should be beautiful, even if I'm not."

"This is beautiful. Even more stunning than I thought when we ordered it last fall. You will look marvelous in it." Isabelle smiled. "I think I will lend you my emeralds." She narrowed her eyes and studied Dina and then the green satin. "Yes, you will wear the emeralds," she said briskly. "And you will wear the dress for me."

It was impossible to refuse Isabelle. She was probably right. She always looked exquisite. She knew how to set off her delicate beauty. And it was true that whenever she wore something that Isabelle had suggested, Alexandre always complimented her.

After Isabelle left, Dina tried on the maroon dress and then the green satin. She studied herself carefully before the mirror. She had Siddie dress her hair in the elaborate pompadour that she favored and then made her take it down and arrange it in the Grecian knot she had worn on her wedding day. Finally she scowled. "The maroon is hideous," she told Siddie. "Pack it away. I won't be wearing it again."

Isabelle had been right. There was no use in trying to hide herself behind frills and furbelows. She should have understood that for herself. Hadn't she been wearing the plainest of all her ball gowns the night she danced with Alexandre at the Forbestals'? She tried on the green satin again. Yes, Isabelle was right.

Isabelle, standing at the head of the staircase to receive her guests, caught her breath when she saw Dina. She was like some fabulous flower rising from a green satin stem. The double row of emeralds clasped around her neck emphasized her opalescent skin. Her rose-gold hair was like a flame.

"You are ravishing," she whispered.

Dina seemed to grow even more luminous. "Exactly what I told her," Alexandre said. He kissed his wife's shoulder. "I have never seen her more beautiful."

The hum of conversation in the drawing room faltered and almost stopped as Isabelle led Dina in. Everyone focused on the lovely woman who stood there, a little shy but delighted with the sensation she was causing. It was only an instant. The conversational melody resumed, the comfortable deep voices of the men blending with the higher-pitched ones of the women.

Isabelle had composed the dinner table with the greatest of care, aiming for the tension that makes for good conversation and setting a stage on which she hoped the younger woman would shine. Reggie Hayes, the art critic whose weekly essays in *The World* made and broke painters' reputations, was at Dina's right. Brilliant, witty, and sometimes rather cruel, he would be his charming best with Dina, since Isabelle had told him that the de Granvilles were about to select paintings for their new house. It was an opportunity to reaffirm his position as the supreme arbiter of New York's art world.

"Mrs. Wallace tells me that you are looking for art for

your new home." Reggie was never one to beat about the bush. He prided himself on his disconcerting directness. "What school of painting interests you most? Have you a favorite period?"

Dina laughed. It was a guileless child's laugh, astonishing coming from this sophisticated woman, Reggie thought. "School?" she echoed. "I wouldn't know one school from another. Ask me about debentures and I might make sense, but painting?" She laughed again. "The other day I told Isabelle that we had to have a large picture on the north wall of the drawing room and a not-quite-so-large one to go over the fireplace. She was scandalized. 'You don't buy paintings by the yard like carpeting,' she told me. But what can you expect," Dina asked, "from someone like me who never saw an oil painting until she came East?"

"Never saw a painting? In what kind of wilderness did you live?" His tone was caustic. Had Isabelle misled him? Was she some bourgeois nothing who only looked so magnificent by chance?

Dina's face seemed to freeze and her beauty dimmed. She felt a little sick. Nothing had changed after all. The moment she let down her defenses, the whole world rushed to attack. Across the table Alexandre recognized her grim-jawed look. He could not let that supercilious little man with his pince-nez defeat his Dina.

He leaned forward. "My wife grew up in an American Garden of Eden," he told Hayes. "She had the kind of life I used to dream of as a schoolboy in Brussels when I read stories of the Wild West instead of doing my lessons. She was riding bareback like an Indian and sleeping beside the campfire at night when other children her age were having supper in the nursery and being taken for walks in the park."

Reggie looked at Dina with fresh curiosity. "I had no idea," he said. "I knew your father came from the West. But the wilderness! You were truly a child of the wilderness?"

"My mother died when I was a baby," she told him. "I

had an Indian squaw as a nursemaid. As soon as I was old enough my father used to take me with him when he went to mining camps. The wilderness was my school and Papa was my teacher. He taught me how to read and write around the campfire at night.''

She smiled across the table at her father. "I thought the whole world was ranches and mining camps and wilderness.''

"I had no idea," Reggie repeated. "It must have been dangerous.''

"No, not really. I had a gun," she said.

"A gun! When you were a child!"

"That's right.'' Frederick broke into the conversation. "You can't take anyone—man, woman, or child—out into the wilderness without their being able to protect themselves. My daughter was as good a shot as any man by the time she was eight," he said proudly.

."Did you ever shoot anyone?" Reggie asked.

Dina shook her head. "I did shoot a grizzly once.''

"A grizzly!'' She had captured the attention of the whole table. Her blue eyes were radiant now as she told stories of growing up among Indians and miners, stories she had never shared with anyone but Alexandre before, because no one had ever been interested. Reggie Hayes's skillful questioning drew one anecdote after another from her.

Alexandre smiled and relaxed. She was superb. He had the warm pride of creation. This was the woman who had been hidden inside the dour Fredericka Schumacher. And he had helped her emerge. She was magnificent. He felt sorry for all other men married to all other women. He caught his wife's eye and smiled again.

Isabelle sat back, listening and watching. Even Kitty Parseval, she noted, who had been rather pouty earlier in the evening, was entranced. As for Frederick, he was sitting there in amazement. She leaned toward him and murmured, "She's not only a beauty, she's enchanting.''

He looked at her in bewilderment. "I can't believe that is Fredericka.''

"It isn't," she told him smugly. "It's Dina. I told you that there can be magic in a name."

Dina woke late the next morning. Alexandre had left for the office hours ago. She had been vaguely conscious of his lips on her forehead and then had sunk back into her dreams. Now she looked sleepily around, a half smile on her lips. Fragments of last night trailed through her head like wisps of a delightful dream. She had never had a better time. People had liked her. They had found her fascinating. And beautiful. She had been beautiful. It had been like magic, but she knew that she had created the magic herself—with a nudge from Isabelle. Now she knew how the belles like Kitty Parseval felt. And—her sleepy smile deepened—Kitty had been there to witness her triumph. Dina stretched in delight.

Reggie Hayes had scared her at the beginning, but then he had softened. He had liked her. "I can't wait to guide you through the galleries and studios," he had said. "I trust you will permit me to be your guide. I want to see what you like. I have already made a wager with myself that you have impeccable taste. After all, a woman who knows how to dress as magnificently as you do must have an educated eye."

Dina had smiled without replying. It is Isabelle who has the educated eye, she thought. But I am learning. I will never wear maroon again. And tomorrow I will go through my whole wardrode with Siddie and try to learn more.

Her smile had been enough of a reply for Reggie. Under his carefully maintained poise, he was bubbling. She is a treasure, he thought. A real find. His reputation as a connoisseur would be seen to extend beyond the painted canvas to flesh and blood.

"May I call on you this week?" he asked. Dina smiled again and nodded. It would be a test, she thought. To choose an afternoon costume that this finicky, exacting man would approve. Yes, she would start to work tomorrow. An educated eye. That was what she must achieve.

And that painter. What was his name? Goddard. Jack Goddard. That was it. He had asked if he might paint her. She had thought him insincere, but his earnestness had finally convinced her. She smiled and stretched again. A painter wanted to paint her. Her. Dina de Granville.

She had refused of course. "I am flattered," she had said, "but I am far more interested in buying paintings than in sitting for one. Perhaps you would let me look at your work some time."

"Any time," he had said emphatically. "Any time at all. I'll show you my paintings. And those of my friends as well."

Dina stretched out her arm and rang for Siddie. She could not lie here all day dreaming like a foolish girl.

Over tea that afternoon Dina and Isabelle discussed the dinner party at length. Or, rather, Dina did. She went over each detail like a young girl after her first dance. Never before had she had a friend of her own sex in whom she could confide, with whom she could laugh and—as she was doing between sips of tea—endlessly analyze and speculate about every comment, every look, every nuance, both actual and imagined, of the dinner party.

"I had no idea you knew people like Jack Goddard and Reggie."

"Neither did your Papa. I think he was a bit taken aback at first, but he relished every minute of it. The truth is," Isabelle confided, "that I tend to keep my Newport friends separate from most of my New York friends. Last night was a gamble. Would the writers and painters mix with the bankers and businessmen? I think they did. And it was all because of you."

"Me!" Dina was delighted.

"You know it. Don't pretend you don't." Isabelle smiled affectionately at the younger woman. "I was proud of you.

So was Alexandre. He didn't take his eyes off you all night."

"It was the most wonderful night of my life," Dina sighed happily. "I was so happy on my wedding day that I cried. I could not believe it was happening to me. Last night was a little like that except that I did not feel like crying. All I wanted to do was smile. I loved everyone."

"And they loved you." Isabelle was triumphant. In one evening she seemed to have achieved what she had thought would take at least a winter-long campaign. As the days and weeks went by, her triumph was confirmed. Dina became the rage of New York—or, more correctly, of that small section of the upper crust that dictated the fashion. Jack Goddard was not the only artist who wanted to paint her. Nor was Reggie Hayes the only one who wanted to take her around and be seen with her.

The same young matrons who as schoolgirls had considered her gawky and vulgar now entreated her to join their charity committees, share their boxes at the opera, and grace their dinner tables. Their husbands who had once considered having to dance with the adolescent Fredericka as a hateful chore now urged their wives to entertain her.

There were still those who were mystified by the metamorphosis. "What do you see in that woman?" Flossie Winship asked her husband when he suggested they give a dinner party for the de Granvilles. "I've known her for ages. She's always been a dull lump of a thing."

"Dull? Lump?" Todd Winship was amazed. "I think she's absolutely splendid."

"I don't see what's so splendid about her."

"She's different. Not all the time talking about the servants or her dressmaker. You can talk to her. She gave me a very good tip. She's convinced this new income-tax amendment is going to pass. They'll be taxing everybody. Two or even three percent of our incomes. Washington has gone crazy. She says she has switched most of her portfolio into stocks that she expects to appreciate, but not generate much in the way of dividends. We have to start thinking in terms of sheltering our capital, she says.

"She's absolutely right, you know. I quoted her at our Monday meeting. Must say I didn't give her the credit, but I told the partners we ought to rethink our investment strategy. And they agreed with me, by God."

"If that's what you think is so marvelous," Flossie pouted. "Talking about money . . ."

"You have to admit that being able to talk sensibly about money with a beautiful woman is pretty remarkable."

Flossie pouted again, a trait that had once been charming, but now tended to make her look like a somewhat petulant simian. "That's probably all she can talk about."

"You're showing your claws," her husband chided. "Dina is more charitable. She told me that she and her husband had called on Jack Goddard to look at his paintings and had met that woman he lives with. I said that Jack was a fine fellow, but I supposed that he had felt uncomfortable being with a woman like that."

"I should think so." Flossie was all righteous indignation.

"Dina said that she had admired her. For her courage. I thought that was really splendid of her."

"Well, I don't. Imagine defending someone living in sin. She'll be defending adultery next." Flossie's father had maintained a mistress almost all his married life, a fact that Toddy thought might explain her unyielding moral stance.

"I don't know," he said slowly. "Dina says the woman is very sweet. I'd be interested in meeting her. I've never known anyone like that."

"I should hope not," Flossie said, achieving the righteous last word. Three weeks later, she was the proud hostess of a dinner party for the de Granvilles, confiding to her guests, "I've known Dina practically all my life. We were very close as girls at Miss Caldwell's School."

# Seven

ONCE DINA had tasted the heady pleasures of popularity and the delights of being considered a beauty, she shrugged it off. "It is not significant," she told Alexandre. "I am still the same person."

"No, no, no!" he exclaimed. "You are not. Before you did not know who you were. Now you have a sense of yourself and it has changed you. You are happy with yourself now."

"Perhaps. Thanks to you—and Isabelle," she agreed. "But what really matters is knowing that you love me. That's all I care about."

As winter turned into spring, it was considered quite a feat to lure the de Granvilles away from the quiet life they enjoyed together. The result was to make them even more sought after. Dina's interest was not in the world of society in which she had always been an outsider until her marriage, but in New York's art world, the painters and others, the creative souls who concerned themselves with beauty. She and Alexandre more often found themselves sitting on the floor eating spaghetti at the little house in Chelsea that Jack

[100]

Goddard shared with Holly, a somber-eyed sculptress who obviously adored him, than at fashionable dinner tables.

One evening Jack made a quick charcoal sketch of Dina that impressed Reggie Hayes so much that he asked permission to use it to illustrate his weekly essay. "I was looking for a subject and you have given it to me, dear boy. The art of portraiture. It begins with the sketch."

"And don't forget the educated eye," Dina teased him.

He bristled. "Of course, that is what separates the artist from the herd. He knows what he sees. He can tell good from bad. And the same with you, my dear Dina. I have known you how long now? Only a few months, but in that time I see your eye becoming ever sharper. You were looking absolutely splendid that first evening we dined at Isabelle's, but tonight you are even more ravishing. You have pared everything down to expose your happiness. Jack has caught it in his sketch."

"Jack," Alexandre interrupted Reggie. "Would you do a real portrait of Dina? I would like very much to have one."

Jack gave a wry smile. "She won't have it. I wanted to paint her the first time we met, but she said she was more interested in buying paintings than in posing for them."

Alexandre turned to her. "Do let Jack paint your portrait. For me. Reggie is right. You are superb these days."

She laughed. "If it will please you, then perhaps. If Jack has the time."

Jack leapt up. "I will always have time for you." He took her chin in his hand and studied her face, turning her head this way and that. "Yes, if I can catch her, it will be my masterpiece."

Reggie had to refrain from rubbing his hands together in delight. "I will postpone that particular column," he announced to the party, "until the portrait is finished. From sketch to portrait. It will be the definitive analysis of the art of the portrait."

*     *     *

Their happiest evenings, though, were the ones Dina and
Alexandre spent at home. Frederick usually dined with them
on Wednesdays. After dinner he would sit and talk business
with Alexandre. It was as if he had been waiting all these
years for a son to talk to. There were times when Dina felt
hurt that her father did not include her in the conversation,
but these were only fleeting twinges of regret. After all, she
herself had made the decision to break her ties to the
business. And the truth was that she was no longer as
interested in it as she used to be. Her world had broadened.

Isabelle accompanied Frederick more and more often on
Wednesdays, and the two women were as absorbed in their
own discussions as the men in theirs. When Dina looked back
at the days when she had thought Isabelle as just another
society hostess competing for the attention of her father and
babbling inanities in her fluting voice, she could not believe
this was the same woman. The Isabelle who had become her
friend was warm and thoughtful—and far from being inane.

"You used to frighten me," Dina confided one evening.
"Even when you were helping me with my trousseau and
being so kind, I was in awe of you. You were so elegant.
And frivolous. I did not know how to be one or the other.
You seem different now. Or perhaps it is just that we know
each other better."

"I still have my frivolous moments," Isabelle smiled,
"but it is a veneer. When a woman is alone, sometimes she
needs a mask to hide behind to diguise her vulnerability. I
chose frivolity for my mask. I may have made a mistake,"
she added thoughtfully.

Looking around the dining table one evening in May,
Dina was struck by how all four of them had changed. It
was not only Isabelle. Alexandre was different. No longer
the charming, aimless foreigner, no longer the reluctant and
luckless fortune hunter, he had established himself as Papa's
hardworking son-in-law and her devoted husband.

There was a little swagger to his walk that was new. It
endeared him to her even more, if that was possible. During

those bleak days last summer when he had come face to face with failure, there had been something of the lost soul about him, an inner sadness that belied his insouciant behavior. That had completely disappeared. Her father had changed, too. Or was it that *she* had changed? She saw him as a lonely man who refused to admit his loneliness, even to himself.

As for herself, she felt sorry for the woman she had been. Fearful yet proud. Awkward—and so very ignorant. It had been just as well, perhaps. If she had not been a misfit, not been so lonely, she would never have mustered the desperate courage to push Papa to put her proposal to Alexandre. She would never have been sitting calmly here tonight—and bubbling with joy within. She wondered if the others sensed her excitement.

Alexandre was telling her father and Isabelle about the wines he was putting down in the wine cellar that he had just constructed to his very exacting and detailed instructions.

"It takes time, you know," he had told Dina a few days earlier, "to assemble even a modestly distinguished cellar. When my father and my Uncle Albert were born, grandfather put down a cask of brandy for each of them—to be bottled on their twenty-fifth birthdays. It takes that long to age properly. I remember that first time my father allowed me to drink his. It was like gold and velvet. He put down a cask for me when I was born, but it had to be sold after his death to pay his debts. And it was almost ready for bottling. If we have a son, I want to carry on the tradition."

"In that case, I would advise you to order a cask without delay," she had said.

"All right. It won't hurt," he agreed. Then he caught his breath. "What? Do you mean . . ."

"I saw Dr. Godfrey today," she told him. "He says the baby should arrive very shortly after the first of the year. I think I knew it from the moment he was conceived. The very next morning, my body felt different. My breasts are larger already."

"Larger?" he said bemusedly. "And I haven't noticed?" He shook his head. "We are going to have a baby," he said in wonder. "Our own child. You are giving us a child."

"Don't forget that you helped," she laughed. But there had been tears behind the laughter. Tears of joy.

Now as she looked around the dinner table, she wanted to share her happiness. She caught Alexandre's eye. "I think we should tell them."

"Tell us what?" Isabelle asked. She looked at Dina sharply. "Oh! Perhaps I can guess."

"Guess *what?*" Frederick grumbled, annoyed that there was something he did not know.

"Momentous news," Alexandre said. "The fact is that I have just ordered a cask of brandy from France. In the de Granville family," he went on with a mock pompous air, "it has long been a tradition—a tradition that goes back all of two generations, I might add—to put down a cask of brandy at the birth of a son."

Frederick brought his hand down on the table, making the glasses jump and the silver jingle. "Goddamnit! You don't mean it! A son!" He jumped up and slapped Alexandre on the back. "This calls for a toast."

When the glasses were filled Frederick stood and proposed the toast. "To my grandson." He was beaming. Then he said, "I also have an announcement, one that calls for another toast."

"Isabelle?" Dina said softly looking at her friend. Isabelle nodded. "My baby will have such a beautiful grandmother," Dina said getting up to kiss Isabelle and her father.

"I'm so happy for Papa," she said in bed later that night. "If they are only half as happy as we are, their life will be wonderful."

"I hope that they will at least be happy enough," Alexandre said dryly, "that your father will let me act without having to ask his permission at every step."

She rose up on her elbow. "Is it really that bad?"

"No, not really." He traced his finger along her eyebrow. "But he does dig his heels in sometimes. To hear him talk, the old ways are the only ways."

"I've not paid any real attention to the business since we got married," she fretted. "Perhaps I should spend a few days downtown getting caught up with things."

"You have better things to do. You have a child to bear. Let your husband do the worrying about business." He threw the covers off and drew up her nightgown. "Let me kiss my son good night."

# Eight

THE SUN was shining as the wedding party emerged from the little Newport chapel. Isabelle and Frederick, smiling happily, posed for the photographers. They were a handsome couple—Frederick tall and stalwart; Isabelle almost fragile beside him, her eyes sparkling under a broad-brimmed leghorn wreathed in summer flowers.

Dina and Alexandre had served as their attendants, although Dina had hesitated. "The baby is beginning to show," she had worried.

"Only if you're looking for it," Isabelle had retorted. She was right. Dina's gown, cut in the Empire style as Isabelle had suggested, gave no hint of her secret.

It was a lazy summer like all the other summers she had spent in Newport, but there was an undertow of tragedy this year. Familiar faces were missing. When the *Titanic,* four days out of Southampton, had struck an iceberg in the April night, a heartbreaking number of Newport summer residents had gone down with her. The most celebrated was probably Colonel John Jacob Astor. Survivors reported that he had secured his young, pregnant bride a place in a lifeboat and, lighting a cigarette, stood alone on the deck watching the lifeboat vanish into the night. Within the hour the Colonel and some fifteen hundred others, including his acquaintance Benjamin Guggenheim, had gone down with the ship. Guggenheim had returned to his cabin when the last lifeboat pulled away, and changed into full evening dress. "If I must die, I will die like a gentleman," he had announced.

On the surface, little had changed as a result of the disaster. The balls were not quite so splended and the parties the slightest degree less ostentatious. But those men and women who had lost old friends and dear relatives were, many of them for the first time, reflecting upon the capriciousness of fate and the certainty of their own mortality.

It was this as much as anything else that had spurred Frederick into asking Isabelle to marry him. He had known so many of the victims. So many cold, cruel deaths. After all these years as a self-sufficient widower, he yearned now for the reassuring warmth of a wife by his side. He did not want to think about dying, but one thing he knew—he did not want to die alone. Isabelle would keep him from such dismal thoughts. Her gaiety and charm, that sharp mind of hers, would brighten and warm his life. Besides—he was willing to admit it now—he loved her.

It was the change in her own life that made Dina restive that summer in Newport. She was sought after as she never had been before, but compared to her new acquaintances in New York, the Newport colony seemed predictable and boring—even more boring than before, now that she had something to compare it to. As the weeks went by and her pregnancy became noticeable, life became even more tedious. Not only was she bored, but she had become a guest in what had been her own home. She had the same spacious rooms that had always been hers. Siddie was with her as always. But the reins of the household now rested in Isabelle's hands. She supervised the staff, invited the guests, and controlled expenditures. A sensitive woman, she was

considerate of Dina and had made no changes in the running
of the establishment, but Dina missed being in control.

The brightest spot of her summer had been immediately
after the wedding when she and Alexandre had spent a week
on Duck Island. One morning in New York as she had been
supervising the packing for Newport, she had turned to
Alexandre and said, "I've been thinking about the children." Her world was now focused on the baby she was
carrying and the others she was confident she would bear in
the future. "I don't want them to have to spend their
summers in Newport. I want them to have the freedom I had
as a child out west. To run around barefoot. To go out
without a nursemaid. To know how to cook an egg for
themselves. I want them to know what it is like to lead a
simple life and be close to nature."

"I suppose we could go to the mountains for a week or
two," he had said.

"That would be no better than Newport. Staying in a
hotel. Dressing for dinner. You know what I mean. Didn't
you enjoy those summers you used to spend on the farm in
St. Hilaire?"

"Ah yes," he smiled. "I did. I used to spend all winter
waiting for the summer."

"Our children could have that kind of life on Duck
Island."

"Duck Island! It's in the middle of the Atlantic!"

"It's only a few miles off the mainland and you know it.
Papa and I have sailed there often. It's a very special
place." She told him about it, her eyes dark blue with
remembered pleasures. The long sandy beaches. The fields
of daisies. The fishermen and their families. The ocean-
crisp air. "They could lead the simplest and healthiest kind
of life there in the summer," she concluded.

"Well? What do you think?" she asked after a minute.

Alexandre, whose attention had been on his wife's luminous eyes, had caught only a word or two. Summer on a
primitive island did not attract him, but he was so enchanted

by her enthusiasm, he did not want to dampen it. He stifled a sigh. "It may not be the way you remember it," he warned.

They arrived in the last light of the June evening on the creaking ferry that wallowed back and forth between island and mainland. Standing at the bow, they had seen the gray shingled houses clustered around the harbor. But by the time they had landed and climbed up the sandy track that led to the hotel on the bluff, the fog had rolled in and the harborside cluster of dwellings was invisible.

Morning brought a fresh breeze from the west and a washed blue sky. They set out to explore the island to find a spot where the might build a house overlooking the ocean. Instead they found an abandoned, silver-shingled house that seemed to be dreaming in the sun. Dina tugged at the door and walked into a low-ceilinged room with an enormous fireplace. Stairs as steep and narrow as a ladder twisted about the chimney to another room above. And that was all.

They ate their picnic lunch on the sun-warmed slab of granite that was the doorstep. "Is this primitive enough for you?" he asked. "Two rooms. No water. No stove. Just the fireplace?"

"A little too primitive," she laughed. "But we can add onto it. I know just what it needs. It is beautiful here. See how the wind blows across the field? The children can run loose here. We can go fishing and bathing. They will love it. I love it already."

No matter what they did to the house, he thought, the island would remain desolate and primitive. "I suppose it could be made habitable," he admitted. If she wanted it, there was no point in opposing her. It might be amusing for her to have this to think about while she was pregnant. And they might indeed spend a week or two here. But no more. He would die of boredom.

"You love it," he said kissing her. "That is what matters." He pulled her up from the doorstep. "Let's find out who owns it."

*       *       *

Duck Island was in the future and while she occupied
herself happily with plans for the little house, she longed for
the summer to be over and waited impatiently for the
weekends when Alexandre joined her.

In all his summers in Newport, Frederick had never gone
to New York more than once or twice during the season.
This year he showed no sign of going at all. "Why should
I?" he asked Isabelle. "I want to be with you." But
Alexandre, despite his father-in-law's encouragement to
take the summer off, had insisted on remaining in the city
and going to the office, leaving early on Fridays for the long
trip to Newport.

Frederick thought it nonsense. "Herbert and Gwillim can
manage," he told Alexandre. "They have for years. You
should do as I do. Settle things on the telephone. It is a
marvelous invention." He carefully refrained from pointing
out that when anything did require a decision, that decision
would always be made by him, not Alexandre.

It truly did not matter where Alexandre was in the lazy
summer months—except to him—and he persevered in his
punishing schedule. He had his reasons. Or rather, his
reason. It was Kitty Parseval, who did not bother to disguise
her interest in him. She even telephoned him.

"It is Miss Parseval calling Mr. Alexandre," Dietrich
would announce disapprovingly. Dina was always carefully
expressionless. Isabelle would raise her eyebrows and Frederick
would clear his throat. Alexandre would sigh, go to the
telephone, and gently refuse whatever invitation Kitty was
extending. "I know you wife does not feel up to much these
days," she would say with sweet malice. "I thought you
might like a game of tennis tomorrow morning. Or perhaps
you'd rather go sailing. I know Dina does not expect you to
spend the weekend in a rocking chair."

He could not fathom why she seemed so intent upon
captivating him. Last summer she had made it clear that she
enjoyed their flirtation, but was not interested in anything

beyond that. Anything like marriage, for instance. She must surely realize that he was happily married now and soon to be a father.

But Kitty kept up her pursuit. As soon as he and Dina settled into their chairs at the beach club, Kitty would appear. Playing with a beach ball. Running along the water's edge. Screaming daintily when a wave, in a last tired rush, dissolved over her ankles. Posturing gracefully as she gathered shells. She showed much more than her slim ankles. Her Roman-striped bathing dress with its long red silk stockings was brighter and shorter than any other on the beach. There were always eyes on Kitty, but it was Alexandre whose attention she courted.

One morning he turned his deck chair to face in the opposite direction. Dina looked up from her book. "You are bored with looking at the water?" she asked.

"I am bored with looking at Kitty make a spectacle of herself," Alexandre answered. Dina smiled and returned to her book.

He never knew what she thought. He had a feeling that she saw right through him, knew his every inner quiver. But what was there to see? To know? It was just as he said. He did not want to watch Kitty. Not because he was bored at her giddy showing off, but because he was finding himself dangerously attracted to her.

He could not deny it. She evoked a response in him. And she made him feel young. He had grown old over the winter. He was not even thirty, nowhere near thirty, and his life had fallen into place. His marriage. The house. The business. And now the baby coming. This was how it was and how it would be from now on.

It was a better life than he had hoped for, but security and luxury were no longer enough. He took them for granted now. Sometimes he tried to recapture the despair and fear he had felt less than a year ago, but he could not. All he knew was that he wanted more, needed more. And Kitty seemed to need him.

While Dina no longer did. Ah yes, she loved him. And he loved her. Or he supposed that he did. But marriage had given Dina confidence and love had given her beauty. She had become a personage. People sought her out. As for himself, everyone had always liked him, but he had never been the center of attention. She outshone him. Did that matter? He could not believe that it did. After all, he had helped her realize herself. And he was proud of it. But still and all, he did not feel comfortable in his secondary role.

The great appeal of summer nights in the city was that there were no demands made upon him. Occasionally he dined and played cards at the club with other summer bachelors, but usually he went home. He would read the newspaper as he sipped the two cocktails he allowed himself before dinner. After dinner he would ring for Céleste, ostensibly to discuss the menu for the following evening, but really for the pleasure of speaking French. They would deplore the American summer. The humidity, they agreed, was enervating. The heat insupportable. Somehow Alexandre felt more like himself after those prosaic chats with the cook.

Not the least of his summer pleasures was going to bed alone in the big four-poster with nothing to do but sleep. His lack of interest in sex was strange, he thought, especially after the wonderful intoxication of the early months. It was like a surfeit of cream. He felt himself drowning in it.

There were times when he could not believe it. Was this truly Alexandre Joseph-Benoît Louis Pierre Hector de Granville, recently a young man about Brussels, a devil-may-care fellow who played by night and slept by day, whose mistress had been the prettiest cabaret singer in all of Belgium? A man who was happy to spend the summer in the stifling city because it meant he could sleep alone? No wonder he felt old.

And he felt guilty. He was lying to himself. It was not true that he was no longer interested in sex. He was. But not with Dina. Since she had become pregnant, making love—thrusting up toward that secret place where his child was nested—made him uncomfortable. But lovemaking was his duty, a duty from which he was excused only by his absence.

During his solitary summer nights he often wondered if Kitty was still a virgin. Such a provocative girl must have had a certain amount of experience. But perhaps not. American girls were so free—and yet so chaste. One August night, so humid that one could hardly breathe, he found himself mulling over the probabilities of Kitty's virginity. There were rumbles of thunder in the distance, but the storm was too far away to relieve the oppressiveness. He lay in bed naked, thinking of the previous summer, of the day when he and Peckham and the Parseval girls had sailed across to Jamestown and picnicked on the rocks by the lighthouse. He and Kitty had wandered off by themselves to a sandy cove sheltered by rocks where Kitty had turned her heart-shaped face to him and asked, "Would you like to kiss me?"

Could this be innocence? Or was it provocation? "Very much," he had said. It was an innocent enough interlude. The other two had joined them within minutes. What would have happened if they had not? He sighed heavily and blotted the sweat off his body with the sheet. He remembered another August night when he had been lying on his bed at the Bachelors Club wondering what would become of him. Suicide had been floating at the edge of his mind. Tonight it was Kitty who preoccupied him.

He remembered how she had felt in his arms. Like a bird, her heart beating against his chest. Naked, she must be like a little porcelain figurine. He imagined how it would be to make love to such a delicate, feminine creature. To stroke her, excite her. To make her cry for more. His breath was coming faster. He reached for the sheet again, this time to absorb the glistening fountain of his sex.

A minute later, he was damply, deeply asleep.

* * *

"I miss you," he told Dina that weekend. "I want you with me. Would you feel deprived if you did not spend the rest of August in Newport?"

"Are you mad? I am bored to death here. I have had enough of Newport. Next year we will spend the summer on Duck Island."

This was a sensitive subject. She had spent days drawing plans for the remodeling of the little house and all summer she had been urging him to go to the island and get the work started. Just last weekend she had pointed out that if he did not go soon, the house would not be ready for next summer.

"Yes, yes," he said impatiently. "I understand. Perhaps I can get over there next week, but this weekend is impossible. It is already Saturday. I would not be able to get back to New York on Monday." And this weekend he had not even mentioned going to the island.

This was not the time to tell him that he was confusing his priorities, putting devotion to work and convenience ahead of her wishes. She could wait. It would be wiser. She had observed him watching Kitty and the even prettier girls among the new crop of debutantes. So slim and active they were. While she was growing heavier every day. She walked deliberately now, carefully balancing the new weight she carried. For the first time in her life, weight was a source of pride rather than shame. Nevertheless she did not want to give Alexandre any cause to look at her critically. No matter how extravagantly pleased he was about this new life inside her, she did not look attractive. Her body was swollen and her proportions could hardly be described as voluptuous. She did not want him to compare her to Kitty as she scampered along the beach or leaped to hit a tennis ball. Dina forced herself to gentleness and understanding.

She had felt a great tenderness for Alexandre that day at the beach club when he had turned his back on Kitty. She understood his move all too well. It was good of him. Honorable. There was no point, however, in letting things go too far.

She was more than ready to return to New York.

*     *     *

They lived like hermits that autumn, content with their isolation. There was no doubt but that Alexandre was looking forward to fatherhood. He studied the stretch marks on her stomach as if they were the parallels and meridians of a new world. He traced the large blue veins of her breasts, his eyes full of wonder. He caressed the hillock of her belly with tender hands and called it "my little son."

As the autumn deepened, Dina turned more and more inward. Nothing mattered but the life within her. She understood Alexandre's desire for a son, but she wanted a daughter. She had even chosen her name. Victoria. It was exactly what she would be. A victory. The triumph that she had once thought beyond her grasp. For years she had cried at christenings, grieving in the knowledge that she would never have a child herself because no man would marry her. But now—she would have Victoria. She would call her Vicky. But she kept all this to herself. There was no need to mention it.

She obeyed Dr. Godfrey's instructions as if they were graven in stone. She ate and slept and walked and contemplated the future. She spent hours resting on the chaise longue in front of the bedroom fire, staring into the flames as she planned her daughter's life. Hours went by in tender reveries. Vicky would be cherished as Dina had never been.

If she had seemed a grave young queen at her wedding, she was a medieval madonna, imperturable and assured, as she presided over their second Christmas. Alexandre found himself almost humble in the face of her quiet joy.

They had kept Christmas Eve for themselves. As they sat by the fire and admired the tree festooned with candy canes and spun glass ornaments, Alexandre put a slim rectangular package on the table beside her. Leaning over, he kissed her. "Merry Christmas, my darling. I wanted to give you my present when we were alone."

She felt it. It was a book, but of an odd size. "An art book?" she asked. She untied the ribbon and unfolded the

wrapping. It was a photograph album. She had given
Alexandre a camera and tripod for his birthday and he had
spent hours photographing her and Isabelle and Frederick
during the summer. She supposed the album contained a
collection of summer memories.

"Oh!" she gasped. "Oh!" He sat back, enjoying her
surprise. She leafed rapidly through the red morocco album
and then turned back to the first page. "I can't believe it. Is
it real?"

"As real as planks and nails and plaster and shingles can
make it."

It was a photograph of the house on Duck Island. The
little cottage now had an ell stretching toward the back just
as she had planned it. The original house was almost as they
had found it that June morning, but with a new roof and
windows and fresh paint on the trim. One photograph
showed brass andirons in the huge old fireplace holding
driftwood ready for a match.

"It is perfect, darling," she said softly. "But how—I did
not dare press you anymore. I thought—"

"I know," he said. "I know just what you thought. And I
let you go on thinking it. Otherwise, how could I surprise
you?" He told her of secret trips to the island, of the
workmen he had recruited and the simple furnishings he had
found. He was proud of what he had accomplished.

How wise she had been, Dina thought, to keep her
annoyance to herself last summer. How foolish it would
have been to confront him with her displeasure.

Frederick and Isabelle arrived Christmas morning, arms
full of presents to add to those already heaped under the
Christmas tree. The room was soon full of ribbons and
discarded wrapping paper and delighted exclamations. Isabelle
and Dina, their arms extended, compared twin bracelets,
one of emeralds, the other of sapphires. Isabelle had found a
delicate christening gown of Belgian lace for the baby.
Alexandre had been surprised when he opened a small box
and found a key inside.

"Is there a lock for this key?" he asked.

Frederick drew him to the window. A gleaming Packard was parked in front of the house. "Something to go with your new status," he said. Alexandre was surprised that his impending fatherhood was being so richly rewarded, but he accepted the automobile as he had accepted so much from Frederick—with a bow and a smile.

After the Christmas goose and plum pudding, Dina showed the photographs of the island house to her father. He was perplexed. "I can't understand why you want to go way out there. It's a godforsaken spot. No one there. Nothing to do. We have plenty of room in Newport. You can have the whole third floor if you want. There'll be plenty of room for the baby and his nurse. I can't believe you want to spend a summer on Duck Island."

Alexandre silently agreed. Dina's passion for the island baffled him. He had watched her poring over the photograph album the night before with a dreamy smile. Nothing could have made her happier than that collection of photographs. But the idea of spending every summer on that desolate island for the rest of his life! No, he would not. He could not. Next summer perhaps. The quiet would be good for Dina and the baby. They could spend a couple of weeks in the little house and then go back to Newport.

And after that? He would worry when the time came. No one could foresee the future.

Frederick cleared his throat. "There is one more present." He drew an envelope from his breast pocket and handed it to Alexandre. Dina drew in her breath. Papa would not do anything so crude as to give him money? Or would he? She bit her lip.

The envelope was unsealed. Alexandre drew out a sheet of paper. Unfolding it, he discovered that it was blank except for the engraved letterhead. He was smiling in a politely confused manner when the wording of the letterhead suddenly registered. His eyes widened. He handed it to Dina.

"SCHUMACHER & DE GRANVILLE," she read. "Schumacher & de Granville! Oh, Papa!"

Frederick beamed. "It's only right. You have more than pulled your weight this year," he said turning to Alexandre. "The father of my grandchild should have a position of some stature. And an automobile to match the position," he added with a pleased chuckle.

Overcome, Alexandre stammered his thanks to Frederick and then turned to Dina with a questioning look. "No, I didn't know," she said in response to the look. "I did not even suspect." He recovered himself, shook Frederick's hand and kissed Isabelle. "I can't tell you how much this means to me."

"I know," Frederick patted him on the shoulder. "I know."

Dina was touched. Papa could have given him nothing that would have meant more. Dear Alexandre was so set upon making good. He worked like a donkey. But she knew without Papa having to tell her that he did not have a business head. He was fascinated by the mechanics of buying and selling. He viewed it as a marvelous game and kept complicated charts, but that was his problem. He did not understand that the real game was in the negotiating and the ability to outthink others, that the buying and selling were truly mechanical. And even if he had understood, he still would have been a lamb among the wolves of the financial district. For Alexandre believed that in games one had to play fair, to be a good sport. He did not understand that there were some rules that called for lip service only. And she loved him for it.

It was the best of all Christmases, Dina remarked that evening when they were alone. Alexandre agreed. He had been accepted. His father-in-law no longer had reservations about him. That had been the message of the new letterhead.

And I damn well should be accepted, he thought. I've worked like a galley slave. Done everything I said I would. Even given him a grandchild.

"I must write my uncle on the new stationery," he said. "Perhaps seeing it in print—Schumacher & de Granville—will convince him that I'm not wasting my life as an idle ne'er-do-well."

His uncle seemed to find it difficult to believe his happy-go-lucky nephew had become a loving husband and hardworking businessman. When Alexandre had written that they were expecting a child, his uncle had replied that he hoped Alexandre now regretted not having paid attention to his advice about insisting on a marriage contract with a clause calling for additional sums at the birth of each child.

"I suppose, however," he had written at that time, "that like your father you are pursuing your own headstrong, pleasure-bent way, ignoring the considerations that could secure your future."

He had been stung by the letter. He resolved that his uncle would have reason to view him more appreciatively in the future."

"I wish we could convince him to visit us," Dina said. "He would be so proud if he could see what you do."

"Impossible. We have tried. There is no more we can do." Dina had written months ago to invite his aunt and uncle to visit New York and meet their nephew's new family. The baron had replied rather frostily that it was impossible for him to leave for any extended period. Alexandre thought privately that his uncle's refusal probably stemmed from Frederick's vehement indignation over the interest the baron had expected Alexandre to pay on the money he had advanced him. Frederick had written an extremely moralistic letter on the subject. The baron could take little pleasure in the prospect of meeting him in person.

Isabelle and Frederick were also getting ready for bed. "It was a thoughtful gesture, Freddy. Making Alexandre part of the firm," Isabelle said. Her reflection smiled at him from the mirror of her dressing table where she sat taking the pins out of her hair.

"Alexandre is a fine fellow," he said, "good company. But he's no businessman. He believes everything he hears. He never wonders why people tell him things or what they expect to gain as a result. Did you notice that he did not even ask if I was going to make him a partner?"

"But you did, didn't you?" she asked in some puzzlement. "Isn't Schumacher & de Granville the new name of the firm?"

"Absolutely. The new name. And that is the new letterhead. And that is all. He has no more share of the business today than he had yesterday."

"Then I don't understand," she said. "Why do it at all?"

"Pride, I suppose. I am going to have a grandchild. I hope he will want to go into the business when the time comes. It won't hurt the world to start getting accustomed to his name."

"Poor Alexandre," Isabelle murmured to her reflection in the mirror.

"Poor Alexandre, nothing. He is sleek as a cat," her husband retorted. "Look at him. A fine house. A fine position. Plenty of money. A baby on the way. When I think of the frightened puppy he was a year ago! He's done all right for himself.

"Mind you," he added. "I like him. They've made a better match of it than I expected."

Isabelle nodded. "Dina is a happy woman. Like me."

He sat heavily on the edge of the bed and scuffed off his slippers. "I tell you—if anything ever happens to me she will have to take over. She is worth ten of him. I'm sure she has no illusions about his business sense. If she were a man she'd show Wall Street a thing or two. And if anything ever happens to me, she may have to."

"Nothing is going to happen to you, Freddy dear," Isabelle said sliding into bed beside him. "I won't let it." He patted her cheek, but he was not so sure. He was getting on, approaching the biblical three score and ten. He could not expect much more, he thought as he settled down in bed and pulled the blankets over his shoulders.

Dina stayed in her serene baby-centered cocoon through the holidays and into the New Year. The only flash of annoyance she experienced was caused by Kitty Parseval. As she was waving good-bye to Alexandre one morning a hansom cab swerved over to the curb. Kitty leaned out and called, "Let me give you a lift. I'm going downtown." Dina had not heard his reply, but she saw him tip his hat and continue on his way. That evening she asked why he had not accepted Kitty's offer of a ride.

"How can you ask?" he said with a grimace. "It would have taken forever and been chatter, chatter, chatter all the way."

"I wonder what she was doing in the neighborhood so early in the day." Alexandre had a shrewd idea that she had been in the neighborhood for one reason only—lying in wait to offer him a ride. But he was not going to voice his suspicion.

Nor was Dina, who shared the same suspicion. Let sleeping dogs lie, she thought. But she was sudddenly impatient with being pregnant. She wanted to get it over with. She had had enough of dreaming about the future. It was time for the future to present itself.

A few days later on a brilliant and bitterly cold January morning, the future arrived. Not without pain. After several hours of labor, she had looked at Dr. Godfrey and smiled tiredly.

"You find something amusing?" he asked her.

"I was thinking of the time I saw you before I got married. Do you remember?

"I remember," he said, holding her wrist and taking her pulse.

"You were speaking of a slight discomfort then. I was just wondering what you would call this." Her face crumpled as she spoke and sweat stood out on her forehead. She groaned and bore down with all her strength. And that, it turned out, was that. The baby was born.

She heard the doctor's voice as if from a distance, so lost was she in fatigue now that her work was done. "A girl, a beautiful little girl. And absolutely perfect," he was saying. For a confused moment, she thought she was dreaming. Dr. Godfrey would never relax so far as to call a baby absolutely perfect . . . "Her name is Victoria," she whispered into the dream. But it must be reality. A baby was crying. She smiled wanly at the sound. She had her daughter.

The nurse showed her a red-faced little being with wisps of wet hair. She folded back the receiving blanket so Dina could see the baby's tiny bowed legs and the bloody umbilical stump. "She is absolutely perfect," the nurse gushed. "In every detail. A beautiful baby."

Dina peered tiredly at the infant. "Beautiful?" she said faintly. "She seems ugly to me." They wheeled her back to her room. The sun was streaming through the windows and somewhere in what seemed to be another dimension, the nurse was still chattering about the baby. She lay in the narrow bed, limp in defeat. She had let herself hope. And this was what she got. The baby had looked like nothing she had ever seen before. A grotesque little creature. It was better to face facts immediately, not delude oneself. She fell asleep, disappointed.

Alexandre was sitting beside her bed when she woke and the room was full of flowers. He smoothed her hair back from her face when she opened her eyes and kissed her. His smile was twisted. "You are all right," he said. "I was so worried. If anything had happened to you . . ." he broke off and kissed her hands.

"Did you see it?" she asked.

"We're awake, are we?" The nurse bustled in before he could answer. "How is our little mother?" She thrust a thermometer into Dina's mouth and took her pulse. Alexandre made a face behind the nurse's back. "Well, we're just fine," she said, shaking down the thermometer.

There was a stir in the corridor outside. A student nurse in a starched blue uniform and voluminous white apron poked her head inside the door. "The babies are on the floor," she said. "Visitors must leave." She rushed on to the next room. "Babies on the floor!" They heard her spread the alarm.

Alexandre kissed her. "I'll be back tonight. You have a good visit with our little beauty."

Beauty? Dina smiled up at him, timid hope in her eyes. "Here's our little darling," the nurse announced.

Dina held the small bundle stiffly. She looked down at it. The baby's face was concealed by the pink blanket. Slowly she folded it back. Her eyes widened. It was true. The baby was lovely. Not ugly at all. What had possessed her to think she was ugly?

She touched the baby's nose and chin. She examined the tiny perfect hands and feet. She traced the exquisite little ears with her fingers. She folded the pink blanket about her again and kissed her head with its faint halo of wispy hair.

"Victoria," she whispered. "Oh, Vicky."

# Nine

WHEN FREDERICK's new Rolls-Royce drew up in front of the house on a sparkling June afternoon in 1914, Walter ran down the steps with Alexandre's suitcases. His trunk had been taken down to the Cunard pier the day before.

Dina followed. She was wearing a dove-gray costume that set off her burnished hair and, instead of a hat, a veil caught up at the back with a cluster of silk flowers in the same gray. "Let other women walk about looking like mushrooms in those heavy broad-brimmed hats," she told Isabelle, "I refuse to." She had achieved a look all her own in the last two years, a mixture of dignity and enchantment. She had no idea that her bearing and the unerring sense of style she had developed made other women feel vaguely shabby, but it did.

She stood on the sidewalk smoothing her gloves and waiting for Alexandre, who could not tear himself away from Vicky. She was adorable, prettier every day. Finally he kissed her one last time and put her down. She lifted her thumb to her mouth and stared solemnly at him with great sea-colored eyes.

"Come on, come on!" Frederick commanded. "The *Lusitania* waits for no man." As the car drew away from the curb, Frederick turned to Alexandre. "I hope the lid stays on until you get back. Europe is going to hell in a hand basket."

"Oh Freddy, do stop talking about war. It's so depressing and you are worrying Dina."

"There's no reason for her to worry," he said. "Alexandre is going to Belgium. It's neutral. He'll be safe no matter what."

All journeys, the storytellers say, start with just one step. The first step of Alexandre's journey was taken one evening at the dark end of winter. The de Granvilles were giving one of their coveted small dinner parties. There was only one topic on everyone's mind that evening and everyone felt qualified to discuss it—the European situation. The Kaiser had made another of his saber-rattling pronouncements and sent a fresh shiver down Europe's collective back. Reggie Hayes stated in a tone of absolute certainty that there was bound to be war in Europe within the year. Americans, he was saying, should start raising money to bring Europe's artists to New York.

"We must get them out of cannon range if we are to save civilization," he proclaimed.

"That is a splendid idea, Reggie," Dina interrupted him in mid-speech, "and we must discuss it seriously, but not at the dinner table. Perhaps tomorrow at tea. Please, no more war talk tonight. It is too dismal."

"But Reggie is right," Alexandre said somberly. "War is closer than most people think. You are right too, my dear. There are more cheerful subjects." And the conversation turned to the heart surgery that the amazing Dr. Carrel had just performed upon a dog. "They will be operating on human hearts next," Harry Peckham said. "I wonder if he can mend broken ones," a woman laughed. And the Kaiser and his threats were forgotten.

*      *      *

"Reggie *is* right, you know." Alexandre was lying in bed later that evening waiting for Dina to join him. "Someone should do something about helping artists to get out of Europe."

"All it takes is money," she said absently, pulling her hair back and securing it with a ribbon at the nape of her neck.

"A ball! An artists' ball!" He was suddenly excited. "And a midnight auction. If we auction off paintings and sculptures, the artists should get a share of the proceeds. We can't ask them to donate what may be their only sale in months. Let's say they keep half," he was jotting down notes as he spoke. "That should be fair. If people start bidding, that will push the prices way up. And it's good publicity. I suspect that every painter we know would sacrifice a year of his life for a little recognition."

He was silent as he jotted down ideas. Finally he put the paper aside. "I think it will work," he said. "I'll put Reggie to work setting up committees tomorrow."

Dina slipped off her creamy satin wrapper and stood smiling at him. "Are you sure you don't want to start tonight?"

"I have something more important to do tonight," he laughed and held out his arms.

The room was warm, but the flush on the faces of the elegantly dressed men and women who thronged about the auctioneer's stand at the Artists' Ball was caused by excitement and pleasure.

"I have been bid eight hundred dollars for this landscape by James Rowett, one of this country's most promising young artists. Who will bid one thousand?" Alexandre looked out into the crowd.

"One thousand," shrilled a woman's voice. "One thousand one hundred," came another voice. "I bid five thousand dollars." The commanding voice belonged to Mrs. Abner Campbell Marcy, the celebrated Newport hostess.

Alexandre smiled triumphantly. "Going...going...gone," he intoned, "for the sum of five thousand dollars, this fine landscape by James Rowett. And this ends our auction. I congratulate all of you on your dedication to the arts. We have exceeded our goal by seven thousand dollars tonight. We have raised fifty-seven thousand dollars. Half of this sum will be used to bring artists from war-threatened Europe to this country where they can work in peace. The other half goes to our own painters and sculptors whose works were auctioned here tonight. It should help them buy a lot of paint and canvas—not to mention an occasional bottle of wine."

He nodded to the orchestra leader and the catchy rhythm of "Alexander's Ragtime Band" set the cream of New York society bobbing happily around the room. Alexandre made his way to the table in a far corner where Dina, wearing white satin beaded in jungle colors, was sitting with her father and Isabelle. "You were wonderful, darling," she told him as he kissed her and sat down.

"Congratulations," rumbled Frederick. "I don't know how you did it, but you got more money out of this crowd tonight without their seeming to feel it than I thought possible. Fifty-seven thousand dollars! I wouldn't have believed it."

"But even more remarkable," Isabelle broke in, "is how Alexandre coped with all the artistic and social prima donnas. He managed to convince each and every one of them that they were the most important figure of the evening. I don't know how you did it," she told him. "And everything went so smoothly. Not a slip."

"Organization," he said. "I have discovered that if I have any talent, it is the very dull one of organization. I don't understand it, but there it is. And also," he smiled broadly, "I have charm. Or so I am told."

Frederick guffawed. "That you do."

Alexandre took Dina's hand. "Come, one dance. I have been working all night. I am ready to play." But they had not circled the floor once when the orchestra broke into the strains of "Auld Lang Syne."

"Ah, too late. I am the victim of my own organization. I told them to play 'Auld Lang Syne' twenty minutes after the last piece was auctioned off. I don't want anyone to have time for second thoughts."

He stationed himself near the door as the subscribers to the Artists' Ball streamed out, stopping to shake his hand and congratulate him as they left. Dina watched him proudly. People are looking at him with different eyes tonight, she thought. He is no longer just Papa's charming son-in-law. He is in no one's shadow now. He is a force in society. He pulled together a fabulous evening in record time and pleased everyone. Look at them, they are basking in the warmth of their philanthropy.

"It was wonderful," she summed up the evening with a happy sigh an hour later as she poured the hot chocolate that Céleste had left for them. "Perfect. You could not have improved on a single thing.

"Now, aren't you coming to bed? It's late."

"Not quite yet. This latest tirade by the Kasier is disturbing. He seems bent on war. I want to finish reading the text," Alexandre replied.

"You really think there will be a war?" Dina asked.

"Almost certainly. I remember—before my father died— some German wrote a book that sent a shiver down everyone's spine. Even I was aware of it. He said that war was a biological necessity and that Germany had only two choices. It could fight to exert its power over the world. Or accept downfall."

"Biological necessity! What nonsense! Thank goodness we have an ocean between us," she said comfortably. "We don't need to be concerned about these European quarrels." As she said this she realized that she had only the vaguest idea of how the European political ferment might affect Schumacher & de Granville. Neither her father nor Alexandre talked business with her anymore. She did not miss it. In fact, she spent surprisingly little time plotting her own investments these days. Her life was centered on her daughter and her husband. They were enough, she thought. And yet, she felt a little twinge. It had been a long time since she had had the satisfaction of sinking her teeth into a real problem.

"But I *am* concerned," he said stiffly. "I worry about my uncle."

"Your uncle!" she exclaimed in disbelief. "You worry about that man!"

"He is my uncle," Alexandre said simply. "And now that I have a family of my own, somehow I feel closer to him. And the fact is," he said, "that if there is a war, and I think there will be one, things will go badly for my country. Ever since I can remember, whenever the German General Staff has indulged itself in threats, it has pointed out that Belgium is the backdoor to France. Neutrality means nothing to them."

Dina yawned. "In that case," she said sleepily, "you must write and say that we want him and your Aunt Marita to spend this summer with us." Alexandre's concern seemed out of character. He always took things so lightly. But of course he was a European. That explained it, she supposed. She kept forgetting that he was a foreigner.

Three weeks later Alexandre came running up the stairs, taking them two at a time, and burst into the nursery where she was watching Vicky waving her spoon about as she tried to feed herself.

"My uncle," he sputtered. "That man is so stiff-backed!" He was both indignant and resentful. "Let me read this to you. Just listen . . .

" 'My dear nephew,' he begins, 'I am touched by your concern, but I fear that you have become so Americanized that you have forgotten that our country's neutrality is guaranteed in perpetuity and that Germany is one of the guarantors.

" 'I might add that the Kaiser would never declare war on King Albert, who is his own flesh and blood, being related as every schoolboy knows through Leopold I, Queen Victoria's most beloved uncle. With such a close blood relationship, the Kaiser would never make a move that would endanger Belgium. Nor would he disregard our sacred neutrality.' "

Alexandre threw the letter down on the nursery table. "He goes on like that. Refuses to face reality. Well, that is it. The stubborn old idiot. There is no more one can do."

He was as frustrated as he was angry. "Why could he not agree at least to come for a visit?" he sputtered. "He could go home if the situation calmed down. It is not as if I had suggested that he go to the Congo and camp out in the jungle."

A few days later on the way home from the theater, Dina brought up the subject that had been on her mind all evening. "Darling," she said, "forgive me, but you look so shabby. You must have some new evening clothes made. That hat," she gestured toward the silk topper he was holding on his knee, "should be thrown out. It's green with age."

"I did not realize I looked so disreputable," he said stiffly.

"Well, you do. Even Papa mentioned it the other day. He told me to give you the name of his tailor and shirtmaker." She paused and then pounced again. "How would you feel if I went around in threadbare skirts and tattered shirtwaists and coats that were almost worn through at the elbows?"

"Embarrassed," he said bitterly. "It would show the world that I could not provide for my wife, which happens to be the truth. Fortunately she can provide for herself. I suppose you are concerned lest people think you are not generous enough to me."

Dina was stung. "I happen to know exactly what Papa gives you. You could order two dozen suits and not even feel it. But you don't spend a penny. I pay for everything. The house, the servants, even your precious wine cellar." She talked herself into a fury. "I would really like to know what you do with your money. I suppose I shall find out that you are keeping a mistress," she finished spitefully.

He leaned forward and slid open the glass partition separating them from the chauffeur. "Pull up at the corner, Burns." As the car drew toward the curb, Alexandre jumped out and closed the door so gently that she knew he was longing to slam it.

She was in bed when he came home hours later. She heard him come up the stairs almost stealthily. She saw a line of light under his dressing-room door. She waited for him to come in. Then the light went out. A door closed. He was going to sleep in his den.

The rebuff added fuel to the anger. She slammed her fist into the pillow. That bastard! Running away from her. Did he have a mistress? Had she hit on the truth? It did not seem possible. Where would he find the time? But what did he do with his money? He spent nothing. Could it be that he was waiting until he had accumulated enough capital to leave her? Could that be it? In the predawn, she was ready to believe it.

She was not going to lie there and let him get away with it. She flung off the covers and stormed into the den. He was lying on the sofa, his hands behind his head. He looked up at her inquiringly.

"You bastard!" she shrieked. "I'm surprised you dare come back to this house. But of course . . . I should have known . . . You're too miserly to spend money for a hotel room." She stood glaring down at him, her face red and her hair unkempt.

She looks like a fishwife, he thought scornfully. And then he sprang to his feet. "Money! Money! Money! That's all

you think about. All you care about. It runs in your veins.
Money!'' He spat the word out.

"I'm not the one who sold myself for money," she
sneered. Her nightgown had slipped off one shoulder and
her rosy breast was exposed. She could have been naked for
all he cared.

"You are a bitch. A bloody bitch," he said slowly, his
eyes as cold as the inner depths of an iceberg. "How would
you like to have to pay every day, every day over and over
for the rest of your life for a bargain you made when you
were desperate?" Each word dripped bitter regret, cold
poison.

"Every goddamned day I wake up knowing that I must
say and do only what will please you. And I have done it.
And done it until my soul is sick. I have lived up to the
bargain I made—except for this matter of not dressing
fashionably enough to please my lady's taste. And I have
never once complained."

"Complain!" she exploded. "What have you to complain
of? I am the one who can complain, except that I made up
my mind that I never would, never would make you feel
embarrassed about the situation even—" and now she took
a deep breath, "even when I found that your idea of a
honeymoon was to stay home in the house my father gave
us, waited on by the servants whose wages I pay."

Even in her hot fury, she felt a twinge of guilt. Their
honeymoon had been the most wonderful time of her life.
But the guilt vanished in the triumph of seeing him flinch. It
was extraordinarily satisfying. She had never permitted
herself to lose her temper before. She enjoyed the feeling of
being out of control, of spitting out venomous accusations
without even caring if the were true.

There was a half-second of silence and then he attacked
on another front. "I have always wondered where you spent
your first honeymoon," he said icily.

"What do you mean?"

"You were certainly no virgin when I got you," he

sneered. He had been surprised that his bride was not a virgin, but he did not consider it important and would never have mentioned it ordinarily. He was sure the explanation would be bitterly embarrassing. Undoubtedly a matter of one desperate, sad occasion when she had gone to bed with someone who was probably unsuitable. Or possibly suitable, but who had declined the honor of marrying the heavyset Miss Schumacher. Having hurled this accusation, he too was caught up in the frenzy of saying whatever came into his mind—as long as it would hurt. And he had an unerring sense of what would truly hurt.

"It was probably your father, the only man you really love," he snarled.

It was too grotesque. Too obscene. The harsh vulgarity. The unthinkable act. She stared at him, her eyes and mouth open. "My father! You are loathsome. Loathsome European scum. Here to sell yourself for money and then, when you have enough, run back to Europe with it."

She was so angry that it was hard to get the words out. She stopped for a moment looking at him with horror and breathing heavily. She fought to get control of herself.

"I see no reason for you to stay any longer," she said coldly. "I will give you whatever amount you want and you can go home." Her anger broke through the dam again. "Back home to your Dita," she shouted, her eyes blazing. "If the little whore is still waiting for you."

It was his turn to be speechless.

"You know about Dita!"

"You lied from the very first day. I never want to see you again." She left the room, slamming the door behind her with a mighty crash.

She paced up and down the bedroom. He had not followed her. She had thought he might, if only to continue the fight. But the minutes passed. He did not come in. The house was silent. She was damned if she was going to lose any more sleep over that bastard. She went to bed. And to sleep. But it was a sleep full of agonizing dreams interrupted by fearful awakenings.

By morning she was no longer angry, but forlorn as an orphan. What had possessed her? What did it matter what he did with his money? He was her beloved Alexandre. Her husband who had changed her life and made her happy. Given her a beautiful daughter. What if his collars were frayed? What if he was tightfisted? What did it matter? And she was the one who had told him it was ridiculous for him to spend his salary on the household expenses. "I have so much," she had said. "I'll take care of the house." And then she had reproached him for it! She must have been crazy last night.

But, and misery washed over her again, what if he really had a mistress? Then what would she do? If he had been keeping a mistress, probably all New York knew about it and was laughing at her. She moaned.

How could he? She set her jaw. No one could laugh at Dina de Granville. And with that, she burst into tears.

What *would* become of Dina de Granville, the fashionable young matron? Without Alexandre she was nothing but homely Fredericka Schumacher, her father's housekeeper. And even that role was closed to her now that Papa had married Isabelle. Her life was ruined, and it was all her own fault.

She had never cried like this in her life. Great howls of agony. She had spoiled everything. It was like ripping the wings off a butterfly. Handsome, gallant Alexandre. So ready to laugh. So loving. So passionate. So sensitive. What had she wanted? A puppet? A fashion plate? She had gone too far. Her body shook with gasping sobs. Her eyes and nose were running. It was difficult to breathe. She felt feverish. And abandoned.

A strong hand lifted her head from the damp pillow and smoothed her tangled hair back from her face. The hand grasped her shoulder and pulled her around so that she lay on her back. Her face was scrubbed gently with a wet wash cloth.

"There, there," he was saying. "Enough of that, my little love." There was another application of the washcloth. Her hair was smoothed back again. "Here, blow," he commanded. Obediently she blew into the huge white handkerchief. "Again," he said.

He bent down and kissed her forehead. She turned her head. She did not want him to see her flushed and swollen face. "Dina, Dina," he said, his voice catching. "What are you doing to yourself? My little love. My little darling."

She could not believe it. Alexandre? So kind? After what she had said? She opened her eyes and looked at him. He looked dreadful. His face was drawn, haggard, his eyes sunken. He looked old, even ill.

"Will you forgive me?" he asked.

She sat up in bed and put her arms around him. "It is for you to forgive me. I don't know what got into me."

"No, no," he said, holding her and patting her back the way he patted Vicky when she cried. "You were right. It is . . . It was . . . I don't know how to tell you. My uncle," he finished helplessly.

This made no sense. She drew back and stared at him. "Your uncle?"

"The interest. Your father paid my uncle the money he lent me to come to New York, but he refused to pay the interest. He said it was immoral.

"But your father does not understand our European parsimony. We are all peasants at heart. We want enough gold to bury under the house so that we can survive disaster when it comes. We know that it will come.

"And I had promised. I could not break my word. So I have been paying him back. Ever since the summer before Vicky was born. Sending him every penny that I could the first of the month. And I have been putting money aside to repay your father too. It was my debt. I cannot accept his paying it. I should have told you. It was my stupid pride that stopped me.''

He had walked the streets last night. His first flash of anger had dissipated in minutes. He recognized that what he had been telling himself was virtue was anything but. He reproached himself for the way he had repaid generosity and trust with selfishness and secrecy. Why had he wanted to keep his project of repaying his debts to himself? Because there was nothing else he could call his own except those debts? But he had forfeited the right to that kind of pride long ago on the Sunday when he and Frederick had discussed the financial basis of the marriage.

Dina would have understood how he felt and agreed that he must do it. But the matter of repaying Frederick with the very money Frederick paid him? What kind of gesture was that? A mean one. Dina would not have understood it. Tramping along the night streets, head down, hands in his pockets, he realized how much his foolish gesture would hurt Frederick. And insult him. Finally he turned toward home. He would tell Dina what a self-righteous prig he had been.

The house was still when he let himself in. Upstairs the bedroom door was closed. He laid his hand on the knob, but could not bring himself to turn it. If he walked in and she refused to speak to him, what then? Perhaps she had locked the door. He did not want to turn the knob and find out. He would wait until morning.

He stretched out on the sofa in his den, covering himself with the same cashmere throw she had put over him when he had fallen asleep on their wedding night. The memory shamed him. Was it his fate to keep disappointing her?

He was staring miserably into the dark when Dina burst in. He could not believe the accusations he had flung at her. It was gutter fighting. After she stormed out of the room, it was clear to him that he would have to leave. She would not be able to tolerate the sight of him after this night. But where would he go? What would he do? The thought of never seeing her again, never seeing Vicky again, made him physically sick. He rushed to the bathroom.

Afterwards he crept up the stairs to the nursery and stood watching Vicky sleep until the sky started to lighten and he left so the nurse would not find him there. As he came down the stairs he heard Dina crying. Her great wrenching sobs tore at him. Perhaps she still cared, he thought not quite daring to hope. But even if she did not, he could not let her go on crying like that.

Now he was crying himself. It was impossible to tell her what hell he had been through in these few hours, but he tried. She held him as he had held her minutes earlier. "My darling," she was crooning, "you are talking nonsense. Of course you had to pay your debt to your uncle. Tell me you forgive me. The last thing I ever want to do is hurt you. And when I think of all those things I said!"

He took a deep breath. "Shall we forgive each other?" he asked with the beginnings of a tremulous smile. They spent the day talking. There were so many things they had never dared tell each other before. So many hurt feelings that had been concealed. So many questions that had gone unasked.

"We must never do this again," she said finally.

"You are right. Once is enough for a lifetime. No more fights," he assented.

"Oh, we can fight. What I meant was that we must never cast these things up at each other again. They are too hurtful. And it is not fair." As she spoke, her old insecurities vanished. She felt a new and comforting sense of peace. Alexandre truly loved her. He would not have been so agonized if he did not.

"Have you heard from your uncle lately?" Dina asked. It was a chilly night toward the end of May. They were sitting by the library fire. The newspapers were in a heap beside his chair. He had just thrown them down, declaring that the mess in Europe was worse than ever.

"Last week. Nothing of interest. The weather—it has been wet. His health—it is excellent. The business—he cannot complain. That is new. He usually complains. My cousins—they are doing well. His vacation—they plan to spend August in Ostend as they have for the last thirty years. Nothing new."

"I think you should go see him," she said. "Letters are not enough to keep people close. Why don't you go to Brussels this summer? It may be easier to persuade them to come visit us once you are there. And if not, you will know that you have done your best."

"I would like that," he said slowly. "Very much. What about you? Will you come with me?"

"I would love to, but Vicky is really too young to travel. And I don't want to leave her. Even for a month. No, you go alone. I will take Vicky to the island while you are away."

Now, finally, he was on his way. It was a gala sailing. The *Lusitania* was sparkling in the sun, her four raked funnels bedecked with streamers of flags. There was a frenzy of activity on the dock, with fashionably dressed passengers arriving with friends and relatives. Stevedores shouted and cursed as the last of the cargo was loaded. Liveried messengers delivered bouquets and baskets of fruit. Porters strained with valises and balanced hat boxes.

On board the bustle was only somewhat more restrained. Ladies were posing on the grand staircase of the first-class salon for the society photographers. Bon-voyage parties were spilling out of the cabins into the passageways. Little clusters of passengers were leaning over the rail, calling to friends in the crowd below.

Frederick took them in tow, showing off the ship as if he had built her himself. "The Cunarders are the best liners in the world," he boasted. "Blue-riband vessels, all of them."

Isabelle and Dina smiled at each other. "Next he is going to tell us how the *Lusitania* carried the gold that stopped the Panic of 1907," Dina whispered.

"I know. I know," Isabelle said with mock despair.

It was a cheerful little sailing party. Frederick had long ago forgotten his indignation over the baron's insistence that Alexandre pay interest on his loan. He was full of enthusiasm at the prospect of playing host to him. He charged Alexandre not to fail in his mission of bringing his aunt and uncle back with him. "We will have some grand parties for them," he said. "A baron. He should make a splash."

After the last good-bye, the last embrace, when Dina was standing on the pier waving and smiling, slightly chilled by the later afternoon breeze off the water, she felt a pang of abandonment. Even though she had urged Alexandre to make the trip, she had felt at the very moment of urging that she was putting an end to a very special period of happiness. That she was making a mistake in letting her conscience triumph over her love. Or was it love that was triumphing over selfishness? It was right that he go. They would never forgive themselves if he did not and the Germans, by some unlikely chance, swept over Belgium. Nor would she forgive herself if this turned out to be the end of their happiness together.

Maudlin foolishness, she scolded herself. It was nothing but a combination of fatigue and letdown from the passions of last night. Their lovemaking had taken on a new dimension. Their caresses had been sweetly clinging. They had made love long and slowly, and then erupted into a crescendo that had left them both exhausted. They had achieved an aching intimacy as if trying to bridge the days that would separate them. Even in their sleep they had clung together, waking still damp with passion to the June morning.

Her father's voice broke in on her thoughts. "What brings you here, Sam?" Sam Parseval, his wife, and Phoebe had just approached them. "We have been seeing Kitty off," he said, "and giving her all sorts of advice. At least her mother has. Kitty is spending the rest of the season in London with her fiancé's family."

"It is not announced yet," Mrs. Parseval said. "It was a very sudden romance. We want to be sure she knows her own mind. If she still wants to marry him at the end of the summer, we will announce the engagement."

"How romantic," Isabelle said politely.

Dina said nothing. Kitty would be on board the *Lusitania* with Alexandre. Had he known she was sailing? Of course not. He would have mentioned it. Or would he?

# Ten

NEW YORK'S skyscrapers had sunk into the ocean before Alexandre loosened his grip on the rail. His hands were cold, his body stiff. The deck was deserted. It was the bleak moment just before dark descends. He shivered and turned to seek the warmth of his cabin.

He was hungry, but he did not want to face the dining salon. God knows who would be sharing his table. He had not taken time to arrange this with the purser earlier. He decided to eat in his cabin. "Something simple," he told the waiter who, accordingly, suggested starting with caviar and champagne to be followed with rack of lamb and a claret.

Half an hour later, he was sitting back in the comfortable armchair scooping up gobs of caviar with toast triangles and reading *Trent's Last Case*, which Isabelle had given him for the voyage. After a few minutes he put the book down and gave himself up to the luxury of being alone. He felt like a man who had been running for a very long time and finally stopped. He felt tired but peaceful. It was a good feeling. Standing on deck that afternoon, waving good-bye to Dina and the others, he had felt as if he had escaped. But from what? He had been heartsore at leaving Dina and Vicky.

He ate slowly and contentedly. When he finished he lit a cigar, poured himself a brandy, and picked up the book again.

Some time later he woke with a start. The knocking that had wakened him was repeated. He stood up and retied the sash of his dressing gown. Still groggy, he cursed what he thought was the waiter coming to collect his dishes, but then he remembered that the man had come and gone hours ago. He glanced at his pocket watch on the table. It was nearly midnight. Probably some drunk too befuddled to be able to read his cabin number, Alexandre thought disdainfully.

He opened the door. Kitty Parseval, in a cloud of pink chiffon and perfume, smiled up at him.

"Kitty!" For a moment he wondered if it was a dream. There had been times when he had dreamed of her. But this was no dream. This was Kitty, very much in the flesh.

"May I come in?" she asked, wriggling past him.

"What in the world are you doing here?" he asked, looking down at her as she perched on the arm of the chair and arranged the drifts of chiffon about her.

"I'm on my way to London to visit Bucky's family. Buckingham Milraven-Peake," she explained. "My fiancé. Or almost. I'm as good as engaged. Practically as good as married."

"That is wonderful. I'm delighted for you."

"You are? I hoped you would be gallant enough to say that you were heartbroken."

"You are a minx," he laughed. "Now tell me, how did you know I was on board?"

"I've known for ages that you were sailing on the *Lusitania,*" she said airily. "There are no secrets in New York. I told the purser that we would like to sit together in the dining salon. You can imagine how I felt," she said half-indignantly, "when you didn't appear."

"So we are sitting together, are we? Who else is at the table?"

"No one else. I said that since I was secretly engaged to be married and you were married, neither of us was inclined to be social. We would keep each other company."

"A table for two. I don't care whether you are half engaged or not. People are going to talk. They will talk anyway if someone saw you coming here at this hour."

"No one saw me. I just came to see why you were not at dinner. I thought you might have been avoiding me."

"Good God, how could I be avoiding someone I didn't know was here? The truth is that I did not feel like making conversation with a lot of strangers. I had an excellent dinner by myself."

"You see," she crowed triumphantly. "You won't have to make conversation with a lot of strangers. Just me."

He sighed. "We'll see. But now I want to get some sleep. Off with you."

She made a little face and got up. "Wait," he said. "Let me take a look first." He peered out the door. "All right, the coast is clear."

"Good night, Alexandre," she said demurely, then reached up and drew his head down to hers. She kissed him on the lips, a curiously sweet kiss, almost childlike. She patted his cheek and was out the door. Seconds later he realized he was still holding the door open. So much for a quiet night at sea, he thought as he got into bed five minutes later.

Kitty was good company. The next day they walked their mile around the deck before retreating to their chairs in a sheltered corner. They read. They chatted. They looked idly out to sea. Alexandre dozed. They ate at their table for two. And after dinner they drifted into the ballroom.

"You will not lack for dancing partners," he said. "You are the prettiest girl on board."

"Then you must dance with the prettiest girl on board," she replied, drawing him onto the floor. She was wearing a low-cut black dress that set off her pale skin and blonde hair. She was an enticing mixture of innocence and devilishness, he thought, holding her in his arms.

She looked up at him. "What shall we do afterwards?"

"Afterwards?"

"I was hoping you would ask me to have a brandy with you in your cabin. A nightcap."

A nightcap? He did not want to seem prudish. The best thing was to be natural. After all, he was practically like an older brother to her and Phoebe, he told himself.

"Why not? We can keep the door open. That will satisfy the proprieties."

"Alexandre! I am not going to sit in your cabin with the door open so that every curious biddy can peer in and see me drinking brandy. That would really cause talk. You go to your cabin and I will join you. I promise no on will see me." She shrugged out of his arms as if it had been decided that they would leave then and there. He followed her off the dance floor.

Fifteen minutes later there was a tap on his door. Kitty was wrapped in a huge Spanish shawl, covering her from head to foot. She laughed. "Do you like my disguise?"

He poured her a brandy and offered her a cigarette. He opened the conversation with what he had decided was a safe subject—intimate, friendly, and yet emphasizing that she was practically engaged. "Tell me about this Englishman who has swept you off your feet. I suppose you are madly in love with him."

"You idiot!" she blazed.

Taken aback, he set down his cigar and said, "What do you mean by that?"

"Do you know why I'm marrying Bucky?" she demanded. "To get away from you and from thinking about you all the time. I have been in love with you ever since that first summer in Newport."

His careful brotherly facade was suddenly shattered. "With me?"

"Yes, with you. If I had had any idea that you were

courting Fredericka—well, you never would have married her. Daddy warned me against getting too fond of you. He said that you had next to no money and that with my tastes it would be better if I married a man of means. But he would have given in eventually. He always does. My mistake was that I thought there was plenty of time.

"I made such a fool of myself after you were married," she said dismally. "When I think of how I chased after you . . . But truly, I could not believe you were in love with her.

"Are you?" she asked suddenly.

"Of course I am. Devotedly. She is a wonderful woman."

She looked at him silently.

"And we have an adorable little girl," he stumbled on awkwardly. She said nothing and he could think of nothing more to say. She picked up her glass and swallowed the brandy in two gulps. They sat looking at each other.

"It's getting late. I think you should leave," he said uncomfortably. She bent her head in agreement and after a moment stood up and reached for her shawl. Alex was settling it about her shoulders when she looked up at him forlornly. Her eyes were clouded with tears.

"Kitty," he said tenderly, "don't. I'm not worth it. Let's forget what you said. It's just that you are overwrought. I can understand that. It is a big step you are planning to take. To get married and live in a foreign country. I know exactly what it means. But it will be all right. I am sure your Bucky will make you happy. As Dina has made me happy."

"But I don't love him," she burst out. "The only reason I am going to marry him," her voice was strained in an attempt to repress her sobs, "is because I can't bear being in New York and seeing you with your wife."

"Kitty, Kitty," he said, putting his arms around her. She was so fragile, it seemed as if she might break under the burden of her emotion. "Stop it. You don't mean it."

"Yes, I do," she sobbed and, putting her head on his

chest, gave in to her tears. He held her saying, "There, there, Now stop. Please stop. Your eyes will get all red. Kitty dear, do stop it." He found himself sitting in the armchair with her on his lap. He tried to blot her tears away with his handkerchief.

"There, that's better," he said as the tears subsided. She flung her arms around his neck and suddenly the fragile body was irresistible. His hand roamed over her curves—compact little hips, a tiny waist, and breasts that he cupped gently within his palms. She lifted her face to his. Was she a virgin? he wondered frantically. His hands explored, sliding gently between her legs as she moved in pleasure.

When he woke in the morning, Kitty had disappeared. There was no trace of her. No cigarettes in the ashtray, no brandy glass. Could he have dreamed it? No, there was a fragrance in the air, just a hint of her perfume. A blonde hair on the pillow. It was no dream. What should he do now?

He rang for breakfast. He would take his cue from Kitty. As he shaved he examined his face. Had it changed? It was strange. He felt no guilt, but he had betrayed Dina.

His hand holding the straight-edge razor remained in the air as he considered this. Yes, he supposed he had. But she was far away and he was here. More to the point, Kitty was here. Dina need never know.

He had no intention of letting this become serious. She was adorable—so rosy and delicate—yet not frail. "Am I hurting you?" he had whispered last night. "No, no," she had gasped. "Don't stop." He smiled and resumed shaving. He felt very good about himself this morning.

A week later he stood at the rail as the *Lusitania* was maneuvered into the harbor at Le Havre. Kitty had disembarked at Southampton where the Milraven-Peakes had turned out to welcome her. She had been pale, but he was sure that a night's sleep would restore her to pink-and-white normalcy. He felt on top of the world. There was nothing like an ocean voyage, he reflected, to ease the transition between one world and another.

# Eleven

ALEXANDRE ALMOST FAILED to recognize his uncle at the railroad station in Brussels. He seemed smaller, slighter—and he was smiling.

"Ah, you have put on a little weight," the baron greeted him. "That is good." It was true. In the last year or so he had thickened, just slightly, through the middle. On the *Lusitania* he had found himself sucking in his stomach when he was with Kitty.

It was good to be back in Brussels—the food, the language, the very age of everything. It was home, this city he had once considered the epitome of dullness. In his reserved manner, his uncle seemed pleased with him. Alexandre had developed a sense of family, he told his wife in the privacy of their bedroom, as this trip bore witness. He had also developed a sense of responsibility, demonstrated by the way—in defiance of the express wish of his wealthy father-in-law—he had paid the interest on his loan in full. "Blood will tell," the baron remarked with sublime illogic.

July slipped by. Alexandre canceled his return reservations on the *Lusitania* and made fresh ones for the first week

of August. He wrote Dina that he was extending his stay
because he had not been able so far to persuade his uncle to
leave Brussels.

What he did not write was that convincing the baron to
come to New York seemed less urgent now that he was in
Belgium—nowhere near as important as it had been on the
other side of the Atlantic. True, there had been that nasty
business of the assassination of Sarajevo that had taken
place the day he arrived, but it seemed just another pointless
tragedy, typical of the Balkans.

When his uncle suggested that he accompany them to
Ostend for a little sea air before leaving, he accepted
happily. Everything was so peaceful in Brussels and the
summer so golden that a few days at the fashionable resort
seemed an ideal way to wind up his vacation.

But the world seemed to have spun in double time, and
within hours everything had changed. Even as the little
family party traveled the short distance from Brussels to
Ostend, the Serbian affair had become the fulcrum on which
all Europe was balanced. When they arrived at the resort,
they learned that Austria had bombarded Belgrade. There
was talk of a German ultimatum if the King of the Belgians
insisted upon maintaining his country's neutrality.

It was the last Wednesday in July, their second day in
Ostend.

Alexandre and his uncle were sitting at the Café de la
Mer, whiling away the time before they had to make up
their minds where to dine. The sky was brilliant, building
up to another of that summer's spectacular sunsets. Sail-
boats were tacking their way back to the harbor. The two
men were silent, comfortable with each other as they had
never been in earlier times.

Alexandre watched the promenaders, without really seeing
them. It had been a mistake, he told himself, to come to
Ostend. He had known it the instant he had heard the news
about the German ultimatum. He cursed himself for having

lost sight of the essential. He had fallen into the same trap
as his uncle, believing only what he wanted to believe.

He wondered how to open the subject of New York again.
The last time he had mentioned it, his uncle had been
impatient. "I thought by now," he had said sharply, "that
you were over that American hysteria. You can see for
yourself that this is not a country preparing for war." That
had been all too obvious, but he had not pointed out the flaw
in his uncle's logic or pressed the matter. It was easier to
drift.

A harsh voice dominated the café terrace, shaking him
out of his self-reproach. "If we Germans don't assume the
leadership of the world, then civilization is doomed," it
proclaimed. "The English think only of their trade. The
French—they are of no account, a decadent race. The
Russians are barely civilized. No, only Germany can pre-
vent Europe from slipping back into the Dark Ages."

Alexandre twisted slightly to look at the speaker. He was
a handsome man, aristocratic, with finely chiseled features. "An attaché at the German Ministry," his uncle
murmured.

"A very diplomatic fellow," Alexandre commented. "Uncle, I must ask you again. It means a great deal to me. You
are all the family I have. There is little time left. The
Germans are going to invade Belgium. If not today, then
tomorrow, next week.

"Come to New York," he urged. "If I am wrong and this
is simply a scare launched for political purposes, you can
return in October. Or after the first of the year. You will find
a warm welcome in New York. I can promise you that.

"There is another thing," he went on. "If Germany
crosses our borders, you will be able to do more for
Belgium from the outside than as a civilian in an occupied
country." He was mildly surprised to hear himself speak of
"our" borders. He had come to think of himself as American.

The baron fitted a cigarette into his jade holder. His lean

face was expressionless. The cigarette had burned down to the holder before he spoke.

"Perhaps you are right," he said slowly. "It may be that the best service I can render my king and my country is to give them two fewer civilians to feed."

Alexandre let out his breath. He had succeeded. "I think you are right," he said matter-of-factly. As the two men left the café, they passed the table where the German attaché was still holding forth on Germany's mission of saving Europe from itself.

"Barbarians," the baron said when they were at a discreet distance.

Aunt Marita did not take kindly to the announcement that they must leave Ostend practically the moment they had arrived. It was the high point of her year. Not even Alexandre's descriptions of the balls and yachting parties of the Newport summer and the excitement and glitter of New York's autumn season mollified her. She had a thousand objections.

"They will laugh at my English," she declared.

"They will find your accent charming," Alexandre assured her.

"My clothes . . ." she began.

"Are extremely elegant," he finished. "You will be the envy of New York."

"We will be refugees."

"You will be treasured guests," he said embracing her.

She sighed and turned to the trunks that were being wheeled back into their suite. But there was no way of hurrying her with her packing. It took her almost three days, despite the baron's fond but exasperated chidings. She clung to Ostend and its pleasures as a periwinkle to a rock. But finally the trunks were strapped and dispatched to the station.

The train to Brussels was more crowded than one might have expected on a Sunday morning. Normally reticent burghers stood in the corridors outside their first-class compartments exchanging rumors, each more dire than the last.

"The French have no ammunition. They will be forced to capitulate within forty-eight hours if the Germans attack," a well-groomed man declared. Another swore that he had it from someone "in a position to know" that King Albert had suffered a heart attack during the night. The rumor that worried these solid businessmen most was that the Germans would take over all businesses and banks and that Belgians in management positions would be replaced by Germans.

Guy was startled to see two cabs draw up in front of the house that Sunday evening, one with his parents and Alexandre, the other with their luggage. He put down the oily rag with which he was cleaning his rifle in the salon—something he never would have been doing if his mother had been there—and covered the disassembled parts with a cloth before going to greet them.

The three travelers had grave faces. The *affiches* posted outside the railroad station had proclaimed the German invasion of Luxembourg. The threat of war was suddenly very real and much too close.

Marita glanced at the cloth on the table. "What's that doing here?" she exclaimed and picked it up. Undernearth lay the parts of Guy's rifle.

"What are you doing with that?" she shrieked in dismay.

"I'm cleaning it, *maman*. I'm leaving tomorrow. For the army," he told her. "They came to the house Friday night and handed us our orders. Everyone is being called in. Henri left yesterday."

His mother looked at him and then at her husband. "I cannot believe it. It must be a dream," she declared. "You drag me back from Ostend saying we must go to America immediately. Henri has left for the army without saying good-bye. Guy is oiling his rifle. But there is no war." There were bewildered tears in her eyes. "Why must I leave home?"

"Trust me, my dear," her husband said gently. "It is

better. You saw the *affiches*. The Germans are in Luxembourg.
They will not respect our neutrality. You do not want to be
in Brussels when the Germans march in. It will soon be
over. We will be back by the New Year. In the meantime
you will have the trip to New York that you have dreamed
of.''

But when his wife left the room, the baron shook his
head. ''Unbelievable,'' he said. ''We are neutral. How can
we mobilize? And who is the enemy? No one has shot at
us.'' He sounded old and querulous, almost as bewildered as
his wife. ''Why, just the other day,'' he said, ''I read in the
paper that the German minister said that Belgium has
nothing to fear from Germany.''

''Words, Papa,'' Guy said. ''It is just as you told *maman*.
If the Germans are in Luxembourg tonight, where do you
think they will be tomorrow? It may be too late even now for
you to leave,'' he told his father. ''There is no doubt but
that the Germans will march through our country from the
Meuse to the North Sea, no matter what we say or do. And
that means we will fight.''

''You and Alexandre sound like hysterical women,'' the
baron said regaining his normal acerbity. ''If the Germans
cross our borders—and I do not believe that they will, but if
they do—they will not be able to pass Liège. Our forts on
the Meuse are impregnable.''

His son shrugged his shoulders. ''With modern artillery
anything is possible.''

A little more than two weeks later, the Germans blasted
the last of Liège's twelve guardian forts and occupied the
city. There had been no defense against the enormous
German siege guns.

Days before Liège fell, Alexandre had convinced his
uncle to leave the city for St. Hilaire, the village where he
had spent his childhood summers. It was impossible to
reach Le Havre. They had waited too long. The roads
between Brussels and the French border were choked with
refugees and dust as people, horses, cattle, carts, and a

sprinkling of motorcars pushed toward the border. His uncle agreed that the rural backwater of St. Hilaire would be safer than the capital.

Alexandre breathed a sigh of relief when his aunt and uncle were finally established in the village. Brussels surrendered without a whisper of protest four days after the Germans had taken Liège, thus sparing itself the shelling and destruction Liège had suffered. For three long days the city's boulevards echoed to the thudding tramp of the Germans. They burned the Belgian flags and flew the German Eagle from their standards. The king and a few thousand troops, all that remained of Belgium's ill-prepared army, had retreated toward the coast where they held a few square miles of salt marsh, their backs to the sea.

A handful of German soldiers were quartered at Le Pèlerin, the café in St. Hilaire, but Père Étienne, rounder and rosier than ever, assured the baron and Alexandre that they were behaving absolutely correctly. Civilians had nothing to fear.

But Père Étienne did not foresee the evening when a sniper would fire on the Germans at the checkpoint outside the village. One soldier was killed, another wounded. The Germans retaliated. Every man, woman, and child was commanded to gather in the small square in front of Le Pèlerin. The soldiers searched every dwelling and barn, thrust bayonets into the hay to detect anyone who had hoped to hide, looted the houses, and set fire to the barns. Then they turned their attention to the villagers waiting in the square.

They lined them up—the men on one side, the women on the other facing each other—and methodically raked the rows with machine gun fire until no one was left standing. The dead were left where they fell: two hundred and twenty-three corpses.

When word reached Brussels, Alexandre, who had returned to watch over the house until he could find a way to return to New York, was slow to believe it. There had been other atrocity stories, other villages where lives had been taken in revenge for sniping if one was to believe the rumors.

He tried to sort fact from rumor, but the few facts that he was able to establish were so chilling that the rumors became believable. He remembered that his father had said that terror was every bit as vital a weapon as guns in war. "And cheaper too," he had said. It was possible that the rumors about St. Hilaire were true. He must find out for himself.

During the humiliating three days the Germans had paraded through Brussels he had stayed inside. He still thought it wise to be inconspicuous, and searched through the house until he found a worn pair of trousers and a blue workman's jacket. He appropriated a beret from Henri's wardrobe and set out to walk to St. Hilaire, a matter of some fourteen kilometers.

It was late afternoon when he swung along the rutted country road that led into the village. There was an ominous quiet. No voices in the fields. No groups of three or four making their way home. Once in the village, he stopped and retched in horror. The bodies were still there, crumpled on the ground in front of Le Pèlerin. It had been no rumor. Birds were darting and pecking at the corpses. There were signs that small animals had been at work. A gaunt collie lying in a pool of dust snarled at him as he approached, but was too weak to rise. His master must be lying here, Alexandre thought. A few distracted hens scurried about pecking and clucking. And that was all.

He went along the rows searching but could not find the bodies of his uncle or aunt. Nor that of Père Étienne. Occasionally he would put his hand on the shoulder of a corpse and turn it to see the face, then shudder at what he saw. Could it be that they had spared the baron and his wife? Spared the priest?

There was no one to tell him. Only the dying dog, the chattering magpies, the hens. He walked to the farmhouse where his uncle and aunt had been staying. It had been

ransacked. Feathers were all over the house from the feath-
erbeds that had been slit. The crockery had been smashed,
the simple furniture broken. The cows, the poultry, even the
rabbits in the hutch had been killed.

He walked to the next village, another crossroads like St.
Hilaire. A man there told him that the peasants had been
stealing over to the village after dark each night to bury their
neighbors. "We are burying them in the fields," he said.
"It does not matter. There will be no one to harvest the
wheat."

"The priest?" Alexandre asked.

"Dead."

"My aunt and uncle, the Baron de Graville. They were
staying in a farmhouse outside the village." His statement
was an anxious query.

"There were no exceptions."

He went back to St. Hilaire, to the wheat fields outside
the village. He followed a path of trampled wheat and came
upon the burying place. The rich earth was freshly turned.
The dead were buried, the man had told him, three and four
together. On each small communal mound lay a sheaf of
wheat tied in the shape of a cross.

He stood there, his head bowed in grief. He made the
sign of the cross and said a short prayer for them that he
remembered from his catechism days.

As he left, he met a group of men and women pulling a
two-wheeled cart full of bodies. An arm hung over the side.
Shovels were lying on top of the corpses. The peasants
stared at him suspiciously. He asked if they knew in which
grave the Baron de Granville and his wife had been buried.
They shook their heads and went on, a grim cortege melting
into the dark of the wheat field as he watched.

He sat on the ground, his back against a tree, considering
his next step. He should return to Brussels. His clothes and
money were there. Before he left, he had buried his money
in the pots of palms and ferns in his aunt's conservatory, just
in case. Brussels was occupied, but the Germans would not

molest an American. But he was not an American, he reminded himself. He was a Belgian, as the papers he carried testified—an able-bodied man of military age. He had lost sight of this. He had considered himself a privileged observer. If he should be stopped and questioned, the consequences could be dire.

He sighed. Sitting on the ground, staring up into the sky at the stars showing themselves between the poplars lining the road, he thought of his wife and daughter. Of the house on Madison Avenue. Of Frederick and Isabelle. He thought of Kitty. None of them seemed real. This was real. His country, under the heel of the invader. His country. His king. His duty was clear.

Equally real was his sense that he had helped kill his aunt and uncle. If he had not urged them to retreat to St. Hilaire, they would be alive and well in Brussels instead of in an anonymous grave in a wheat field. He was to blame for their death. If he had been firm, they would have been safe in New York a month ago. And he would be safe in Dina's arms right now.

He got up stiffly. A decision of sorts had been taken. He would stay. What he would do, he did not know yet, but he would expiate his guilt for these deaths. He had let himself be seduced by the delights of irresponsibility. He had reveled in his uncle's approval. It had been a selfish few weeks, a kind of return to childhood. Now he had to pay for it.

As he tramped along the road that led to the highway, he heard shots now and again in the distance. Snipers? Poachers? Germans? Suddenly he was afraid. He had heard how the Germans treated prisoners. If they were lucky, they were shot, but most were sent to Germany to work at hard labor.

He became more cautious as he went along. He stopped in deep shadows, sheltered from the moonlight, and listened carefully for footsteps and voices. Once, in a panic, he thought he heard the sound of deep breathing close to him, but there was no one there. As he listened, his heart thudding in his ears, there was nothing except the cranky chirp of birds disturbed in their sleep.

Dawn found him slipping along the streets of Brussels making his way toward his uncle's house. There were German soldiers at all the main intersections. He avoided the boulevards and dodged about the back streets. The street he turned into was familiar. He had been here often in the old days. He passed the courtyard behind the iron-gated entrance that led to the little apartment he had rented for Dita. He smiled briefly through his fatigue at the memory of those rollicking days when he used to spend his evenings at the cabaret where she sang and then go home with her to the little nest under the roof where life was so delightful.

The distance and the sleepless night were taking their toll. He was putting one foot in front of the other almost in a trance. Was Dita still there? he wondered. It would be good to crawl into that familiar bed and sleep until it was dark again.

He snapped his fingers. He was being stupid. How could he be sure she would welcome him after all this time? Or that she would be alone? That was most unlikely. No, he had to keep going. It would be easier now that it was daylight. He would be taken for a laborer on his way to work.

In the next street the shutters were being rolled back from a café. A couple of men, obviously regular patrons, were waiting outside. He took his place with them. They exchanged quiet greetings and lapsed into silence until their coffee was pushed across the counter. They were better dressed than he. Perhaps this was not a café for workingmen. One man was staring at his feet. He glanced down. He was wearing custom-made brown-and-white leather shoes, dusty and scratched from his long walk, but hardly the *sabots* of the unshaven worker he seemed to be. If asked, he thought feverishly, he could say they were hand-me-downs from his employer. He swallowed his coffee, put the money on the counter, and left. No one stopped him. In less than an hour he let himself into the de Granville house.

Everything was as he had left it the day before. There was a ham in the larder, which he attacked with the aid of a bottle of white wine. There was no bread. He wondered where the cook was.

He did not have to wonder long. He heard her determined footsteps in the hall and she came into the kitchen holding a loaf of fresh bread like a marshal's baton. "They have even put the clocks on German time," she announced. "Who can live like that?"

He told her what he had found in St. Hilaire.

She crossed herself. "The poor baron. Poor madame. I will clean the house and put the covers on the furniture. And then I will go to my sister's."

"Where does your sister live?"

"In Antwerp."

"And how do you expect to get there?"

"I do not know. I will walk if necessary. I cannot stay here. The baron and madame are dead. Their sons are in the army. And you? You will not be here long."

"No," he agreed. "I will not be here long."

The next morning he woke in a fever of energy. He must go to the office. It had been closed for too long. Assurances Bruxbelges could not disintegrate just because there was a war on. He must do what he could to preserve the business.

In the sunlight his fears of the day before seemed ludicrous. The nightmare of St. Hilaire and his panicky escape back to the city were behind him now. Fatigue made one see terrors that did not exist. He was dressed in his most formal business suit, his gold watch chain threaded across his waistcoat. It seemed odd, his going to set things in order at Assurances Bruxbelges. Not all that long ago he had dreaded the possibility that his uncle might offer him a position there. His horizons had been very limited in those days. He

felt confident now that he could make whatever decisions
were required.

The green baize-covered table was still in the same place.
He sat in his uncle's chair and started going through his
papers.

# Twelve

ALEXANDRE GROANED. He did not understand a thing. He was simply turning page after page in the ledgers, flipping through his uncle's correspondence files. It might as well have been Greek. If someone had asked him what had to be done next, he could only have shrugged his shoulders.

He stiffened. The door was opening. Germans? No, they would stalk in as if they owned the place. A head poked around the door. He relaxed. It was Wim, the elderly clerk dating from his grandfather's time. Wim slipped into the room, closing the door behind him. He stood there shaking his head.

"You should not be here, monsieur."

"No?" Alexandre asked. "And why not, my friend?"

"The Germans," he explained. "They will send you to prison. Or Germany. Or—" and he drew his hand across his throat.

"I am leaving," Alexandre reassured him, "but first I wanted to see that everything was in order here. It seemed wrong not to try to do something. Although I am not at all

sure what should be done," he confessed. "But what about
you, Wim? Why are you here?"

"I came for the files," the old man said. "I told your
uncle that I would bury them among the azalaes if anything
happened."

So his uncle had taken the threat of war more seriously
than he had let it be known. He had made plans to protect
his business and his clients. It was more than he had done
for himself.

"I will help you. What should we take?"

The stoop-shouldered clerk darted about, pulling files
from cabinets, stacking ledgers on the floor. "There," he
said finally. "That should suffice."

"But will happen to them? If we bury them, who will
know where they are?"

"I will take care of everything," Wim said, "except for
this." He darted to the back of the table, gestured for
Alexandre to stand, and then seized the arm of his uncle's
chair. He twisted it sharply and it came loose in his hands.
He tilted the arm and a bright chain of glitter slid out of a
hollow less than an inch in diameter that had been bored
into the arm. "Here," he said triumphantly. "Here it is. I
know *Monsieur le Baron* would want you to have it."

Aunt Marita's diamond necklace! He had never seen it.
But this had to be it. A brilliant dazzle of light among the
ledgers and files. "You must take it with you," Wim said.
"Take it with you and keep it safe."

Alexandre ran it through his fingers, a sparkling rivulet.
A fortune. He was embarrassed when tears rose in his eyes.
Poor Aunt Marita. How she would have loved to show off
her necklace, show how dearly cherished she was. Had she
known where it was kept? he wondered. Hidden in the arm
of this old chair? The left arm, the one closest to his uncle's
heart.

"You had better go now," the clerk said. "I will take
care of matters here. I will come to the house tonight after
dark. It won't take long. And then, if I may repeat myself,

you should leave. Especially now that you have the responsibility.'' And he nodded toward the necklace.

Alexandre waited in the shrubbery at the side of the house for long hours that night. He was dressed much as he had been for the journey to St. Hilaire, although he had substituted a pair of stout boots for the brown-and-white sport shoes. He dug two holes among the azaleas while he waited. Safe graves for his uncle's records. It had been easy work. But Wim did not come. Had something happened to the old man? Had he been stopped at some checkpoint? Or had he decided it was not safe to come tonight? There was no way of telling. At three o'clock in the morning he decided to wait no longer. The old clerk had given him good advice. Get out of Brussels. He would take it. He was not likely to get any that was better.

He slipped out of the garden into the street. Aunt Marita's diamonds were hidden in a chunk of sausage that he had hollowed out earlier. The sausage and half a loaf of dark bread were wrapped in a kerchief. No one would confiscate a refugee's pathetic hoard of bread and sausage. He could think of no safer way to carry the necklace. He walked along in the still dark of the morning wondering where he would be twenty-four hours from then.

# Thirteen

ISABELLE PLACED the receiver back on the hook and rejoined Frederick on the broad porch overlooking the bay. It was a heavy July afternoon with an occasional threatening rumble of thunder in the distance. They had been playing a lazy game of cribbage while they waited for Dina and Vicky to return from Bobby Prentice's third birthday party.

Isabelle hoped the storm would hold off until the party was over. The Prentice grandparents had hired a circus for the event, an extravagance even by Newport standards. Earlier in the day red-and-gold circus wagons pulled by white horses had rolled down Bellevue Avenue followed by three elephants and half a dozen cavorting clowns. It would be a shame if rain spoiled the children's fun.

"That was Eugenia," she told her husband. "Back from London and full of her trip."

"Full of gossip, you mean."

"She couldn't wait to let me know what a scandal Alexandre and Kitty created on the *Lusitania*. She said she only mentioned it so I would not be too shocked if someone who had nothing better to do than mind other people's business should bring it up. I felt like telling her that at least a dozen of her friends had beaten her with the news.''

"But you didn't."

"I just laughed and said wasn't it ridiculous the way people jumped to conclusions. I told her that Alexandre had met Kitty's fiancé briefly at Southampton and thought he was most agreeable. But no matter what I say, it's not going to stop the talk.'' She sighed.

"Let them talk," he grunted. "They'll get tired of chewing over the same old fat one of these days.''

"Do you think Dina knows? She seems so calm. She went off smiling this afternoon as if there was nothing on her mind but watching Vicky have a good time. Is it possible she hasn't heard?''

"I'll wager you a yard of pearls that she was one of the first to know,'' he said.

Frederick was right. Dina knew. She had known long before the first insidious questions were asked, long before the first sidelong glances were cast. She had known ever since that June afternoon when they had met the Parsevals on the Cunard dock and learned that Kitty was also sailing on the *Lusitania*. There had always been something between Kitty and Alexandre. It was like a fire waiting to be lit. And Kitty was sure to strike the match.

The delightedly scandalized whispers that had filtered back to New York proved her correct. The news arrived so swiftly that one might have thought it had been carried by the sea winds. And now that each transatlantic liner was crowded with the rich and fashionable who had cut short their stays abroad because of the threatening political situation, the gossip was reaching a crescendo.

There were moments when Dina believed her heart was actually breaking. At night she hurled her tear-soaked pillows to the floor and then lay awake until sleep overcame her shortly before dawn and erased her misery for a few hours. But no one knew of her heartache or the sleepless nights and the tears. Only Siddie who changed the tear-stained pillows every morning and spent her spare time taking in her mistress's dresses as Dina grew slimmer and paler. To the world, Dina de Granville seemed as poised and gracious as ever. No one had the satisfaction of seeing her flinch.

That is what they want, she thought as she joined the score of women gathered at little tables under the shade of a great oak on the Prentice grounds. They want to draw blood. They are peering at me as if I were an insect under a microscope.

The light buzz of conversation died down as she walked toward them. What are they waiting for? she wondered. And then Flossie Winship, done up in ruffles and flounces as if she were sixteen, said in her piercing voice, "I understand that Kitty Parseval crossed on the *Lusitania* with your husband."

It was a challenge, and unprecedentedly rude. The hush intensified as the women waited for Dina's reply. The children's voices and circus music a few hundred feet away emphasized the silence. One of the clowns came cartwheeling around the table followed by a troupe of laughing youngsters. Dina was barely aware of him. A surge of anger swept over her. She took a deep breath and smiled. They would get no satisfaction from her.

"I thought you knew that, Flossie," she said kindly. "Yes, we all saw them off last month. Alexandre and I thought it very courageous of Kitty to make the crossing alone to meet her fiancé's family. I understand from Alexandre that they are distinguished and extremely pleasant. And that Kitty seems to be truly in love."

Flossie pressed her lips together. She had been sure that Dina would be shaken. She had expected at the very least to have the pleasure of seeing her tremble and flush. She had hoped to bring tears to her eyes.

"They all tell the same story," she complained to her

husband that night. "When Lydia Pendlestone asked Isabelle about it, she said practically the same thing."

"Probably because it is the truth," Todd Winship said with some irritation. "I do not understand what you women are so excited about. I'm sure the whole thing is a misunderstanding." No man who was married to Dina de Granville, Todd was convinced, would even consider being unfaithful.

"Men!" Flossie said petulantly. "You just don't understand."

But she had a moment of doubt. Dina's aplomb was disconcerting, almost enough to make her believe the gossip was wrong. But it could not be. Kitty had been seen slipping out of Alexandre's cabin at a scandalous hour according to no less an authority than Mrs. Fish Alwynne-Armstrong, who had been returning to her cabin with Mr. Alwynne-Armstrong after playing bridge into the wee hours. "She was wrapped in a Spanish shawl and her face was covered, but I know Kitty Parseval when I see her," Flossie's old schoolmate Lucy Alwynne-Armstong had stated.

Dina smiled and chatted her way through the afternoon with the regal grace of a swan. No one was going to know that she was heartsore. But that night after dinner when she was finally alone in the suite of rooms that had been hers ever since Frederick had built the Newport place, her composure deserted her.

How could he do it? How could Alexandre subject her to the prying of women like Flossie Winship? She paced her bedroom, striding back and forth, her negligee switching from side to side and her fists clenched, alternating between rage and anguish.

Rage at Alexandre for being unfaithful: If he had to be unfaithful, why could he not at least have been discreet? Anguish that he should have deceived her. She had trusted him. Loved him. She had believed that he loved her. She was deeply wounded.

She stopped and stared out at the bay, glittering in the moonlight, without seeing it. "You pay for everything,"

she said aloud. "And as bargains go," she went on thoughtfully, "I did not do so badly. I am someone now. Dina de
Granville. I have a position in society that many people
envy, one I never thought I would have. I am considered
beautiful. I never dreamed of that. And I have a daughter, a
wonderful child. I had *never* dared hope for that." She
nodded and in that moment she began to come to terms with
Alexandre's infidelity.

Even so, the strain wore on her. There was a tinge of
fragility about her that was new. When Reggie Hayes arrived
in Newport to spend a few days with them, he was struck by
this new dimension to her beauty.

"Dina, you are ravishing this summer!" he exclaimed.
"If I didn't know, I would suspect you had taken a lover."
The instant the words left his mouth, he was stricken. He
took off his pince-nez and rubbed the bridge of his nose to
disguise his embarrassment. How could he have made such
a faux pas? Dina must believe he was referring to the vulgar
gossip that had been titillating New York and Newport for
the past fortnight.

"Now *that,* I am afraid, would really cause talk, Reggie
dear." She smiled and patted his hand.

"I'm sorry. That was dreadfully tactless of me," he said.
"But you do look marvelous. You *must* let Jack Goddard
paint your portrait. After all, you promised you would sit
for him. Why not now? You have never been more dazzling."

"You are a master of flattery," she laughed. They had
wandered down to the wisteria-covered gazebo. Dina was
wearing a linen dress that echoed the deep lilac of the flower
clusters and deepened the blue of her eyes to violet. Even
by the harsh light of a summer afternoon, she was beautiful.
The new fragility had brought a heart-catching quality to her
looks.

"I am serious," he protested. "It would be a shame if
you did not sit for your portrait."

"Well, perhaps I will," she said thoughtfully. "I do have
the time now."

"It would be good for Jack. In more ways than one." He hesitated and then went on. "You may have heard that Holly has married."

"Married? You mean not to—"

"Not to Jack," he confirmed. "It seems that she tired of the bohemian life and went back to Muncie to marry her childhood sweetheart who presumably had no idea of the life she was leading in New York."

Reggie carefully refrained from mentioning that Holly's departure had been triggered by one too many of Jack's little flirtations and that it had been Holly's money that had paid the rent on the little house in Chelsea and allowed Jack to paint without worrying about where his next meal was coming from. Now it was important that Jack secure a large commission. A portrait of Dina de Granville could catapult him to fame and assure his future. Reggie enjoyed playing God.

Dina smiled. "I see you are up to one of your good deeds again. Of course I'll sit for him." It is not a bad idea, she thought. She had promised Alexandre that she would let Jack paint her portrait. It would be a surprise for him when he returned.

"Splendid!" Reggie was beaming. "I'll go by his studio first thing next week and tell him he must start immediately before you change your mind. Should he come to Newport?"

"No, that's not necessary. I am planning to be in New York," she said quickly. She had made the decision that instant. Why stay in Newport? It had always bored her and this summer she found it actually disagreeable. She and Vicky would go home. She was longing to be her own mistress again. Considerate as Isabelle was, she was a guest in her father's house. This was no longer her home. Her home was the bright and charming house on Madison Avenue. She would go back, sit for her portrait, and then take Vicky to the island for a couple of carefree weeks at the end of August.

*    *    *

"You're doing it again," Jack shouted. "You're looking positively grim. I want you pensive and romantic. Is that too much to ask?"

"It is when your bones ache as much as mine do," Dina told him. "All I can think about is how uncomfortable I am. That's hardly romantic."

"Keep the pose," he growled, "and think of something romantic." He continued painting.

The dining room had been turned into a temporary studio. The furniture was pushed against the walls, the carpet rolled up, and the draperies taken down to let the light pour in. The model's dais and Jack's easel dominated the room. Dina was standing on the dais, one hand on an ornate balustrade, a prop Jack had brought along one day and bolted to the dais. Her head was turned just slightly, looking into the distance. It was hard work. And Jack was a hard taskmaster. The gallant and amusing dinner companion was distant and abrupt standing at his easel.

Finally he put down his brush and rubbed his forehead, leaving a smear of paint across it. "That's it. I'm through."

"Thank goodness!" she exclaimed. "I can't wait to get out of this dress."

Jack had gone through her entire wardrobe, choosing and discarding until he had finally settled on the cloud-blue ball gown she had worn the night she had first danced with Alexandre. His eyes had brightened when Siddie brought it out.

"That's it," he said. "Put it on and let me see you."

"But it's much too large," Dina had protested. "I have lost weight since I last wore it."

"Never mind. Try it on for me," he commanded. Ten minutes later, as she modeled it for him, he nodded. "Yes, that's it. Have it taken in for tomorrow."

The long afternoons of posing provided her time for thought. She thought about herself and how she had changed. The young woman who had worn this dress to the ball that

long ago August night in Newport had been all rough edges
and gritty determination. The determination was still there,
but silken now.

She thought about Alexandre. Without bitterness or sadness. His infidelity no longer loomed as a major tragedy. He
would be home one of these days. At heart he was a
domestic soul. He was likely to walk in the door any day
now with his uncle and aunt, laughing and proud to be
showing them his home. They would take up their life
together again. She would say nothing about Kitty. There
were some things that were best ignored.

This forgiving train of thought was shattered one Monday
afternoon. Walter came into the makeshift studio. Jack
stiffened. Dina frowned. The staff had been given strict
instructions not to interrupt the sittings.

"Excuse me," Walter said, "but I thought you would
want to know." He was carrying the early editions of the
evening papers. "They have declared war. The Germans
have invaded Belgium." He showed them the threatening
black headlines.

Dina shivered despite the heat. So Alexandre had been
right. It was war. And he was in the middle of it. Instead of
rescuing his aunt and uncle from the threat of war, he
himself had been caught in it.

"War," she said dully. "War."

"I am sure your husband is safe," Jack said. "They are
not going to harm American citizens."

"Yes, I am sure he is fine," she replied automatically,
despite the cold fear that had invaded her.

After this, when Dina thought of Alexandre, a series of
questions arose in her mind. He must have known that war
would be declared. Why had he not come home? She had
convinced herself that his affair with Kitty had been simply
a shipboard fling, but perhaps not. Had he actually chosen
to stay abroad rather than come home to her and Vicky?

As the days passed, however, she thought most of all about Jack. He was an emphatic masculine presence. She imagined herself in his arms. She dreamed of him in her bed. As she stood on the dais looking into the vacant distance, she thought of love. Of long nights. Twisting bodies. The delight and the peace of passion satisfied.

Jack seemed completely oblivious of her except as an object that must be transferred onto canvas. He said nothing except for issuing an occasional curt order—"Keep your head up . . . Don't move . . . Relax, your arm is too stiff." He treated her as cavalierly as he would any professional model. Possessed by his painting, he worked furiously, cursing when the light changed and faded at the end of the day.

He had not even permitted her to see the portrait. "Not yet," he had said after the first sitting. "Not yet," he had repeated at the end of the first week. And so she had stopped asking.

Today Dina could hardly wait to get out of the Worth gown and into something looser and less constraining. The sapphire-and-diamond necklace and tiara seemed to grow heavier by the minute. It had been sultry all day—humid and hot as only New York could be. Now as she stepped down from the dais, snatching the tiara from her head and shrugging her shoulders to get the stiffness out, Jack said quietly, "Don't you want to see it?"

He took her hand and led her to the front of the huge easel. She stared at the canvas.

"Well?" he said finally.

"It's frightening. You know me better than I know myself. I see things in that face. Feelings. It's frightening the way you have caught my feelings."

"Frightening?"

"Frightening that someone knows me so well. I see my whole life in that face."

It was true. It was all there. The grittiness of the young

woman who had schooled herself to survive in a hostile environment. There was her pride, her independence, her strength, and her longing for love. At the same time, it was the quintessential portrait of the society woman, all poise and dignity.

"How could you know me so well?" she asked wonderingly.

"Because I have watched that face for months," he said. "For years. You know how long I have wanted to paint you. Ever since the first night I saw you at Isabelle's dinner party in that green dress. You were like an exotic flower. The glitter of emeralds against your skin. Your eyes. Your hair. That was all I saw at first. Your beauty. Then when I watched you during dinner, I saw one emotion after another as you responded to everyone and everything—each carefully hidden behind a composed face and smile. But I caught them. It is the painter's eyes. Ever since then, I have wanted to capture them on canvas. Wondered if I *could* capture them."

She studied the portrait for several minutes and then turned back to him. "You have succeeded. And you must forgive me. I have not thanked you. It is beautiful. I think it is a masterpiece. I did not expect anything so powerful."

"Neither did I, although I hoped. Reggie was right. He said it would be my best work. And it is."

She felt a sense of loss. She was going to miss these afternoons in the makeshift studio, tedious and uncomfortable as they had been. She was going to miss her daydreams of passion and romance. She was going to miss Jack.

"You look exhausted," she said. He was pale and drawn. It was understandable. He had been working every afternoon as if pursued by demons. "Please stay for dinner. I will change and then we can have cocktails—Walter makes a very good Orange Blossom. And then a leisurely dinner. Unless you have another engagement?"

"No, no engagement. You are right," he said wearily. "I am tired."

"Then you will stay. We will celebrate the completion of your masterpiece."

"I hope my bath is ready, Siddie," Dina said as she entered her bedroom. "Quickly, please help me off with this dress. And the gloves. Everything is sticking to me. I can't bear it another minute." She tossed the sapphire-and-diamond tiara on the bed and started unscrewing the heavy dangling earrings without waiting for Siddie.

"There is a letter," Siddie said, not moving to undress her.

"A letter!" A letter from Alexandre? Her heart leaped. It was a large official envelope with a State Deparment imprint. She caught her breath. Could he be dead? Was this the notification? She tore it open. There was a note that the enclosed letter had been forwarded from Brussels to Washington in the diplomatic pouch at Mr. de Granville's request and was now being forwarded to her.

Dina's hands trembled as she opened the second envelope addressed in Alexandre's distinctive script. Eight pages. She scanned them hurriedly, then read them slowly.

He related what had happened at St. Hilaire so graphically that she could feel the horror and emptiness that had greeted him. He continued:

You can understand, my dearest, how much at fault I feel. If I had been more forceful, Uncle Albert and Aunt Marita would be alive and in New York today instead of lying in a field outside St. Hilaire. You will understand, I am sure, that I cannot leave now. The Germans must not be allowed to overrun all of Europe.

I plan to leave Brussels on foot tonight and make my way somehow to Paris where I am confident I will be able to join the fight against Germany in some useful capacity. I long to see you and Vicky, but I would not be worthy of you if I shirked this obligation. Nor can I live with myself if I do not avenge the deaths of my aunt and uncle . . .

\* \* \*

"Ah!" she exclaimed scornfully as she threw the last page of the letter down. "What does he think he can do?"

She rang for Siddie, who had retreated discreetly. "He is well, Siddie. He is trying to reach Paris and join the French in the fight against Germany

"And now, if you don't get me out of this dress, I shall get into the tub with it on." She tapped her foot as Siddie unhooked and unbuttoned and finally slid the dress over her head. Her eyes were glittering. Paris, indeed! she was thinking. What naiveté. Did he believe he was going to defeat the Germans single-handedly? And what about me? And Vicky? She felt abandoned and betrayed, but most of all angry.

The glitter in her eyes turned to tears a moment later. "Alexandre, why are you leaving me?" she called out in her heart. And then she stiffened again. "Let him lead his foolish life. I will lead mine."

Dina floated into the drawing room in a tea gown of foam-green chiffon that fluttered around her as she moved. She was magnificent, Jack thought. Despite the heat and the fatigue of posing, she looked as if she had spent the afternoon resting.

"It is so warm, I think we should have our cocktails in the garden," she said. She led the way to the walled garden behind the house. Ivy climbed the walls. A small fountain splashed softly in the center. The sun had left and the garden was green and cool.

As they settled back in the ornate scrollwork chairs by the fountain and Walter served their drinks, they were silent. The cool peace of the garden was restful. "I am sorry it is finished." Jack broke the silence. "I shall miss our afternoons together."

"I shall miss them too."

Dusk fell and deepened into darkness. Walter hovered at the doorway from time to time. Dinner was ready, but he did not feel he could interrupt the two shadowy figures whose murmuring conversation rose and fell almost like the splashing of the fountain.

He descended to the kitchen. "They're still talking," he reported to Céleste.

"You must tell them that dinner is ready." The cook was upset. It was not like Madame de Granville to be inconsiderate. If she did not bring her guest to the table soon, dinner would be ruined. Céleste's proper French soul could not accept that.

"But they are talking," he protested.

"They can talk at the table," Céleste replied sharply. "Go light the candles. Make a little noise. It is time to serve dinner."

The table had been set in the library since the dining room had been turned into a studio. Walter lit the candles and then touched a match to the two gas lanterns that illuminated the garden.

Dina looked up, her eyes dazed by the sudden light. "Oh, Walter. Is dinner ready? Before you serve, please open a bottle of champagne—the Pol Roger that my father gave us. We are celebrating the completion of my portrait."

"Champagne," Walter announced dramatically as he went through the kitchen on his way to the wine cellar. "They will not finish dinner before midnight."

Nor did they. Sometime during their hours in the evening garden, all barriers between Dina and Jack had fallen. There was an ease between them, an ease laced with excitement that they both found intoxicating. Suddenly, in a pause, the library clock struck a single note.

"Half past what?" Dina asked idly. Jack looked up. "Half past nothing. It is one o'clock in the morning."

"One o'clock!" She was startled. "But I didn't hear it strike twelve. Or even eleven."

"Nor I," he smiled.

She smiled back. "I don't care. This has been the

pleasantest evening I have spent in a long time. I wish it didn't have to end."

He leaned forward and put his hand over hers. "I wish the same thing." He did not know whether he was going too far or not. His introduction to the gilded society of New York was fairly recent. He owed it to Reggie Hayes who had decided that he had a talent worth watching and had brought him to the notice of a select handful of art patrons.

He had never dreamed that one day he would paint the famous Dina de Granville, much less that he would dine alone with her—the two of them at a candle-lit table overlooking a dark summer garden, mysterious in the glow of lanterns.

"One o'clock," Dina said softly. "I suppose it is too late." She hestiated and looked at him.

He stood up. "Much too late," he said. "You must forgive me for staying so long. I had no idea of the time."

"That is not quite what I meant," she said. She stood now and took his hand. "I was thinking that you . . . that we . . ." She drew him through the house into the spacious center hall and stopped at the foot of the staircase. She looked at him, her blue eyes almost black with intensity. "Is it too late?" she asked.

Suddenly he understood, and cursed himself for his slowness. She was in his arms, that magnificent body straining against his. She broke away. "I think perhaps it is not too late at all," she laughed. Her laugh was husky with passion. She reached for his hand again and started up the stairs.

He hesitated. "Wait," he said. "What about—"

"My maid?" she finished his question for him. "Before I joined you for cocktails, I told her not to wait up for me."

Later, sauntering home through the quiet predawn streets, his hands in his pockets, Jack gave a shrug, then smiled. "Let's see what happens," he told himself.

# Fourteen

Dina PULLED a towel over her bare breasts. The sun was hot in the sandy hollow of the dune. They had made love hungrily and quickly. Jack was different from Alexandre. Less subtle. But she was in the mood for his lusty simplicity. The strains that had built up in her over the summer had disappeared. If she were a cat, she would have purred.

Jack stretched and got up. "It's like paradise, this island." He peered over the beach grass that protected their sandy nest. "Not a soul in sight. Not even a fishing boat. Let's take a dip and wash this sand off."

They joined hands and raced down the dune, across the smooth beach and into the water. Dina gasped at the first impact and then dove through the shallow waves as they rolled in, frolicking like a mermaid. Jack watched her and then retreated to the beach. Minutes later when she looked around for him, he was sitting on a rock with his sketching book. She let the waves carry her to shore and started to walk toward him. He lifted his hand. "Wait," he said. "Stand there. Just as you are." She laughed at him and ran to their hiding place in the dunes.

When, sun-dried and dressed, she joined him carrying the picnic basket, Jack retrieved the bottle of wine he had buried in the wet sand at the water's edge. They ate with hungry relish. Pouring the last of the wine, Jack asked, "Why wouldn't you let me sketch you?"

"You can sketch me all you want, but not naked."

"You surprise me," he said. "You are not like that in bed."

"That's different. I don't want to talk about it. I'm not going to do it."

He shrugged. "It's not important." He leaned over and kissed her.

They had been on the island for almost a week. It had seemed the logical retreat for two lovers. A place where they could be together without fear of scandal. No one in her circle would dream of spending time on this primitive island. They might anchor their yacht in the little harbor for a picnic lunch, but no one would wander more than a few hundred feet down the road. They were as alone as if they truly were in paradise. It was a delicious bit of stolen time for Dina.

For Jack, too. He had been dubious about committing himself to going to the island with Vicky and Siddie. His concept of a romantic tryst did not include a small child and an elderly maid. But the thought of having Dina to himself overcame his hesitation. Practicality also played a part. He was now assured of having a rich patron. But a rich wife would be even better. He had heard the gossip about Alexandre and Kitty Parseval. Anything was possible.

The days went by in sunny simplicity. They went clamming and picked blueberries. They built sand castles on the beach and gathered shells and pebbles. Vicky found her Uncle Jack diverting. He made strange animals for her out of shells and bits of driftwood. He gave her colored chalk and paper so that she could draw pictures, too. One day he painted a miniature picture of the house that he promised to frame when he got back to New York so that Vicky could hang it in her dollhouse.

It was a productive time for Jack. One afternoon he laid his work out on the long wooden porch table—charcoal sketches and watercolors, a few oils. Dina and Vicky bending over a tidal pool. Dina and Vicky collecting shells. Dina standing looking out to sea. Dina holding the blue chicory that matched her eyes. Dina lying half asleep on the beach.

"You have worked hard," she said as she looked at the pictures with him. "I love the watercolor of Vicky with her shell collection."

"This is my favorite." He indicated a rough sketch showing her poised to dive through an oncoming wave. It was obvious that she was naked, although only her back and arms were visible.

She snatched it from the table. "I told you I didn't want to be sketched naked. And I certainly don't want this where Vicky can see it." She was angry.

"Dina, my love," he protested laughingly. "No one could ever tell it is you. It could be anyone who is half-mermaid."

"But I know who it is," she said. She ripped it in half.

"I'm sorry you're upset. It's not worth quarreling over," he said. "It's just a sketch. What I really want to do before we leave is paint you by the fire some night. Just you and the firelight."

"Why not tonight then? We don't have many more days here." She sighed. "I hate to think of going back to New York, but Papa and Isabelle plan to reopen their house early in September and I should be there."

"Will you really? Pose for me tonight?"

"Of course," she said affectionately. "What do you want me to wear?"

"Nothing. I just want the firelight on that marvelous skin, all glowing and warm."

"No, not in the nude," she said sharply.

He laughed. "I thought it was worth a try."

His persistence grated on her. Did he honestly believe he could coax her to do something that she felt instinctively was unwise? Or was it that painters had one-track minds? She made no comment, but asked, "How about my red-and-blue striped skirt and a shirtwaist?"

He looked at her, his eyes half-closed. "The skirt, yes. But no shirtwaist. Wear your blue sweater. And this." He snatched a blue-checked cloth from a table. "Here." He draped it around her shoulders. "Wear it as a shawl. And I want your hair down."

That night he was no longer the lover, but the imperious tyrant who had painted her portrait. His mind was no longer on her, but on his painting. He lit the driftwood fire, moved a high-backed wooden chair to the side of the fireplace. He ran his hands through her hair to tousle it, arranged the shawl, sat her down, and went to work.

He was all concentration, standing at the easel, painting by the light of an oil lamp. He interrupted his work only to throw more driftwood on the fire from time to time. The house was quiet except for the creaks and sighs an old house gives as it settles for the night.

The hours went by silently. Dina sat motionless, but her head was whirling. What would happen when they were back in New York? It had been a wonderful interlude. She had needed to make love lustily and often. She felt at peace with her body now, and she had put Alexandre out of her mind. But what next?

She did not love Jack. She was not sure she even liked him. But there was something—she could not put her finger on it—something about him. He was not a man she could love. But he was a man who could arouse her. Amuse her. What more did she want?

Nothing more, she decided. Not even that. It was time to end the relationship. He had filled a need, but she no longer needed or wanted him. Nor did she think he needed or

wanted her. Her money, yes. She had always known that—
and understood. She would pay him handsomely for the
portrait. That would take care of his feelings.

It had been a wonderful secret holiday—and a very
satisfying private revenge on Alexandre. But it was over. Or
almost. A few more days of sun and passion and then she
must leave—and so must Jack. But in different directions.
She would return to Newport and spend a few days there.
And once she was back in the city, she would make it clear
that the affair was over.


"Dina! Dina!" His voice interrupted her thoughts. "Are
you asleep or have you turned to stone?"

She was startled. She had been so deep in reverie she had
forgotten where she was and what she was doing. "Are you
through?" she asked confusedly. She had no idea how long
she had been sitting there.

"Through!" he said triumphantly. He was excited, exhil-
arated as he often was when his work had gone well. She
got up a bit stiffly and went-to look at the picture. She did
not know what she had expected, but she knew it wasn't
this. This was a wanton, sitting and dreaming by the fire. In
her face was the expression of the wild satisfactions of love.
A primitive woman, warmed by her shawl and the flickering
fire, a woman whose life was passion. And yes, she
recognized that woman. It was the wild, surging side of her
soul that was suppressed everywhere except in the bedroom.

She was confused. Her thoughts tonight had been so cold.
How had he caught that current of desire? He was a great
painter, she thought. One had to respect his talent. His
genius.

"Come walk on the beach for a while," he urged. "I
can't possibly sleep yet. I'm too wound up. Look at the
moon. It is almost as bright as day."

"I'm too sleepy to walk on the beach," she said. "Even
on a night like this. You go. Perhaps you will find a

mermaid to paint.'' She kissed him and went up the narrow
stairs that wound around the chimney, to bed.

When he returned from his walk she was asleep, her hair
spread across the pillow, the curve of her hip and the long
length of her legs outlined by the sheet. The moon was still
so bright that every detail of the room was distinct; even the
little jar of field flowers she had gathered that afternoon.

He caught his breath. ''Marvelous,'' he whispered.

He spent the rest of the night painting her as she slept. He
was like a madman, working faster and surer than ever
before. Each brush stroke was perfect. When he finished he
felt as if he had run a marathon. He was sweating and
exhausted. But he had done it. He had captured her. He was
satisfied with his night's work.

He then fell into bed as the first pink streak of day
appeared on the horizon.

In their last few days together, Jack worked like a man
possessed. He could not get enough of Dina. His every
waking moment was spent committing her to canvas. Each
picture was more gripping than the one before. He called his
favorite ''Dina in the Wind.'' She was in the windswept
meadow in front of the house, her fabulous hair streaming
behind her as she stood looking out to sea like a ship's
figurehead.

At sunset he would slump into a chair and fall asleep until
Dina roused him to eat. After dinner he would stumble up
the narrow stairs and collapse onto his bed. There was no
more lovemaking. His passion had taken a different direction. ''Only four more days . . . three more days,'' he would
mutter. ''It's not enough.'' The next morning he would be
up at dawn, ready to work.

Dina came out of an erotic dream in which her body was
tensed in a long arc of delight to find the dream was real.
Jack was lying beside her, caressing her with practiced

strokes. She exploded in a climax of pleasure that subsided slowly into shuddering little aftershocks. Finally she opened her eyes. "What a wonderful way to say good morning." She smiled, and then sat up in bed as if someone had flung cold water on her.

Jack was painting her! How could he! To make love and then leap to his easel. It was cold, heartless.

"What are you doing?" she asked icily. "Stop it. This minute."

He came back to the bed. The sun-bleached hairs on his tanned chest brushed her breasts as he bent over her.

"Let me, Dina," he said huskily. His eyes were only an inch from hers. "You must. This has been the most exciting time of my life. And it is coming to an end. This is the Dina I dream of. That lovely glowing creamy skin. Those curves. Let me paint her. Let me have her."

He slipped into bed beside her, caressing her as he spoke. Once again she was lost in a sweet erotic delirium. Later, she pulled the sheet up over herself and sighed. "I must get up. Vicky will be awake soon."

"No. Not yet. I need you. Take that sheet away. Give me another hour." He was painting as he spoke.

"No. Vicky will be awake any minute now. She must not find you in my bedroom. And she must not see that picture. Please, Jack," she said urgently, "do hurry and put all your gear in your room. This minute. And I mean it." She sprang out of bed.

Dina spent the last morning with Vicky on the beach. Mother and daughter, both wearing wide-brimmed hats to shade them from the sun, were gathering treasures—bits of colored glass washed smooth by the tumbling waves, colored pebbles and shells. "We're going to Newport tomorrow to see grandpapa Frederick and grandmama Isabelle," Dina said. "This is our last day on the island."

"Is Uncle Jack going too?"

"No, dear. Not with us. He has to go to the city and paint more pictures."

"Good," said Vicky. "I like my papa best."

Dina knelt and hugged her daughter. "So do I, dear. So do I."

Jack spent the morning packing his gear. He hummed as he worked. These two weeks had been far more successful than he had ever dared hope. He picked up a thick portfolio of sketches and watercolors and went through them slowly. He could not suppress his smile. There were many that Dina had never seen. He lingered over a pencil sketch—so finely drawn it might have been an etching—of Dina, naked, sleeping in their sandy nest in the dunes after lovemaking. It was not just a naked woman. It was a woman fulfilled and momentarily drained by love. No other interpretation was possible.

And then there were the large canvases. All of them equally revealing. Dina asleep, her body spread in relaxed abandon. Dina nude in the tumbled bed. And the wanton Dina by the fire.

His smile was cold now. "It's not over yet, my dear," he said out loud. He had sensed her withdrawal from him. But she was not going to withdraw. Oh no. Quite the contrary, he told himself. If she tried, she would regret it. No matter what happened, he thought happily, his future was assured.

"And Uncle Jack painted a picture. Just for me. For my dollhouse. He's going to frame it. Like mama's picture." Vicky chattered away precociously at the Newport breakfast table happily telling her grandparents about her island vacation.

Dina's heart sunk. Vicky had started talking over the summer, much to the pride of her grandfather, but she had not dreamed that her daughter possessed such narrative ability.

Isabelle smiled and spoke before Frederick could say anything. "That was very kind of him. I think your dollhouse does need pictures. I have a miniature of my mother—a very tiny picture—that was painted when she was a little girl just like you. It is just the right size for your dollhouse. If you like it, you can hang it over your dolls' fireplace. We can look at it after breakfast.''

She turned to Dina. ''Speaking of portraits, you have not told us about yours. Were you satisfied with it?''

''Extremely. I begin to think he is a genius. Wait until you see it. I shall be very interested in your opinion.''

Later that morning when her nursemaid had taken Vicky to the beach and Frederick had gone off to play golf, Isabelle knocked on the open door of Dina's sitting room. ''May I come in?''

''Of course, Isabelle. Anytime.''

Isabelle sat down in an apricot silk-covered armchair. ''I am embarrassed, but I must ask you. Jack Goddard was on the island with you?''

Dina nodded.

''Staying with you?''

''Yes, he was, but you must not make a scandal of it. He was on the island painting. I had told him that I was going there with Vicky and I think—well, I don't really know . . .'' She hesitated. ''Did you know that he and Holly have separated and that Holly is now married?''

Isabelle shook her head.

''I gather from Reggie that it was very recent,'' Dina continued. ''Jack did not say a word about it when he was painting me, but I did sense he was very lonely. He did not tell me he planned to go to the island, but I do think he went expecting to run into me. A bit like a lost puppy. He was not very subtle.'' Dina smiled at Isabelle and wondered how convincing she sounded.

''We ran into him one day when we were watching the fishing boats come in with their catch. I asked him to have dinner with us that night. And then I thought it was a shame for him to stay in that pokey hotel when I had plenty of room. After all, Siddie was there. And Vicky. He accepted

immediately. And he did some exquisite sketches and watercolors of Vicky," she told Isabelle. "Let me show you."

She took a portfolio from the table and drew out three
sketches of Vicky—wading at the water's edge, building a
sand castle, looking at a starfish in the palm of her hand.
Then she showed Isabelle a watercolor of herself and Vicky,
all sunlight and sand and romantic femininity. An enchanting child in a sunbonnet holding onto her mother's hand.

Isabelle nodded. "Interesting. There is a whole new
feeling in those sketches. And the watercolor is superb. He
has developed tremendously. I am more eager than ever to
see your portrait. I gather you were pleased with it."

Dina looked straight at her friend. "I was awed by it. He
is immensely talented. You should be proud of yourself for
having discovered him."

"I hope . . ." Isabelle began. "That is—I hate to sound
like a prude and a stepmother—but his being there—I hope
it did not compromise you in any way. He is very gifted,
yes, but—"

"Oh, Isabelle!" Dina laughed and hugged her friend.
"Don't be a goose. You don't think that Siddie would allow
even the semblance of something improper. No, we saw a
lot of him, but it was mainly because he wanted models—
and there Vicky and I were. He sketched Siddie too. See?"
She pulled out another drawing. "And the islanders. I would
not be surprised if he did not have a show next year
comprised entirely of weather-worn fishermen and their nets
and boats and lobster traps.

"I must confess, I was rather glad when we left. In fact, I
had planned to go back to New York, but I did not look
forward to traveling with Jack so I came back here instead."

"And we are delighted that you did." Isabelle smiled and
got up. "Forgive me. I have been in Newport too long this
summer. I'm starting to think like the gossips. I must hurry
now. I promised to join your father at the club for lunch."

As Isabelle walked down the hall, she was thoughtful.
She hoped Dina had been discreet.

# Fifteen

THE ROAD TO PARIS was longer than Alexandre had
expected. Belgium was now overrun with Germans intent on
the same destination, and his countrymen and women—
although their king and the remnants of his army had been
pushed into a few square miles of sand and marsh with their
back to the sea—were doing their best to hold back the
gray-clad hordes. Bridges were destroyed. Roads were barri-
caded. Foodstuffs were hidden. Telephone lines were cut.

Even the refugees unwittingly did their part. The roads
leading to France were choked with women and children
and old men whose villages had been burned or shelled.
There were women pulling little carts loaded with their
household goods, older sisters carrying weary toddlers on
their backs, old men stumping along with the aid of a cane.
When the German columns came, they scattered to the
ditches alongside the roads. Time and time again the troops
had to halt while a clot of refugees was cleared from the
road.

Since the Germans shot every man of military age on
sight on the premise that he was a soldier out of uniform,

Alexandre traveled by night, bypassing the towns and making his way from village to village. He was dependent on the trust and good hearts of farm wives for food. Some would sell him a bit of sausage and a chunk of peasant bread to eat on the road. Others would conceal him in a hayloft or a shed and bring him a hot meal with whispered instructions to hurry and be on his way. There was always the chance that a German patrol might check the house, and the reprisals for hiding a man of military age were brutal and prompt.

So he progressed, sleeping in concealment during the day, traveling by night. The Germans were ahead of him and behind him. Every day in his hiding places, he heard the sound of tramping feet, the whinnying of horses, the creaking of wagon wheels as troops and munitions advanced inexorably toward France. Often he caught sight of the field-gray stream of soldiers.

At night he found himself part of an army of other fugitive shadows, young and not-so-young men wanting to make their way to France. There was little camaraderie among the shadows. Life had changed too rapidly in the last few weeks. Who was a friend? Who a foe? Who was a spy? It was better not to confide in anyone. Alexandre felt it best to avoid his fellow refugees altogether. Aunt Marita's diamonds were in his pocket, wrapped in a rag that had once been a sock. He had long since eaten the chunk of hollowed-out sausage in which he had concealed the necklace when he left Brussels. If anyone were to suspect he carried such a treasure, he would not have it—or his life—for long. He had heard whispers of thieves who preyed on helpless refugees, taking whatever treasures and money they carried with them. It was safer to travel alone.

For the past two days he had been skirting German encampments. Now he was at the front. The crackle and blast of high explosives filled the air. Once he reached the French side, he had decided to strike out for Amiens where he could get a train for Paris. But how was he to get across that deadly zone between the two armies?

He would have to cross under cover of darkness, he decided, but he could as easily stumble into the Germans in their field gray as into the French in their blue and scarlet. That evening as he set out, he came upon a group of refugees making camp for the night. A woman hailed him. "Tomorrow we will be behind French lines. Just one more night."

"Where do you plan to cross?" he asked.

"Down the road a bit," she replied. "They told us in the village that there is a track hidden by hedgerows between two fields. They say that people cross over all the time."

"Good luck," Alexandre said and left them behind in the dark.

A track between hedgerows. That should not be hard to find. But there were hedgerows between all the fields he passed as he strode along. It seemed hopeless, but then he came upon it. A couple of planks over a ditch, and beyond that a path concealed by bushes on both sides where the earth had been beaten down by many feet.

The night was quiet. He started out, encouraged by the thought that by morning he would be behind the Allied lines. Less than half an hour later, the sky lit up with bursting shells. He knew the pattern. The big German guns would boom for hours to soften the way for the German attack at dawn. The Allied guns would reply, trying to knock out the German gun positions. The shell bursts were uncomfortably close. He must be in no-man's-land, that perilous territory between the attackers and the defenders.

The path stopped at the edge of a deeply rutted road. He had no idea of which way to turn. As he stood trying to decide, he heard the sound of a motor and, as a shell burst overhead, he saw an ambulance, a cross painted on its back, a few dozen meters to the right. He approached cautiously. There was a figure slumped over the wheel.

"*Qu'y a-t-il?*" he asked. "What's the matter?"

The driver stirred. "*Blessé. Blessé.* I'm wounded," he muttered. It was an English voice.

"Can I help you?" Alexandre switched to English. "Where are you wounded?"

"My arm," he replied. "I can't drive. A shell fragment got me. And there are six wounded men in the back."

Alexandre opened the door. The driver's khaki sleeve was soaked in blood. He eased the young man out of his military tunic and made a rough tourniquet with his web belt, then got behind the wheel. "Where to?" he asked.

"The field hospital."

"And where is the field hospital?"

"Straight ahead." The man's voice was weak. "Just behind the lines."

Alexandre stopped the ambulance in front of a white tent with a red cross on its side. He helped the orderlies unload the wounded. "The driver is wounded, too," he told the British doctor who was directing the operation. "He has lost a lot of blood."

"The driver! Damn it! We've no one left to drive."

"I will if you tell me where to go," Alexandre offered.

"Where to go!" the doctor asked in weary astonishment. "Where have you been? Who are you?"

"A Belgian refugee, captain. Headed for Paris to offer my services against the Germans.

"I did not expect to find English troops here," he added.

"This is our sector. The French have deployed their troops farther east," the doctor explained briefly. "Very well, we can use you. Go back the way you came until you reach a white post beside the road. Our men are collecting the wounded and bringing them there. All you have to do is load up and bring them back."

He shuttled back and forth over the rutted road all that night. A foggy gray day dawned and he saw that he had been driving through a devastated countryside. The trees were blasted. The wheat fields on either side of the road had been churned into mud and were full of shell craters.

The fighting continued until late afternoon when he heard
the German bugles signaling a cease-fire. It was dark again
when the last of the wounded were delivered to the field
hospital. All the cots were full. Now men were simply
placed on tarpaulins on the bare ground.

"You lost some good men," Alexandre told the doctor
who was still on duty. "The wounded had to wait for hours
because I could only take six in the ambulance. Some could
not wait that long. You need more ambulances."

"Of course we need ambulances, damn it!" the doctor
barked. "We're lucky to have this one. I commandeered it
in Boulogne. And now we have no driver. The young man
you brought in is not going to drive for a long time."

He peered sharply at Alexandre through fatigue-reddened
eyes. "What about you? You say you want to fight the
Germans. You can fight them here. No need to go to Paris
for that. We need you. Tomorrow night it will be the same
thing again. More dead. More wounded. But there will be
no one to drive them back if you leave. We will have to use
horses and wagons. And the waits will be even longer."

"I'm sorry, sir," Alexandre replied, "but I must go to
Paris. As soon as I've had a few hours sleep, I'm heading
for Amiens and a train."

The doctor laughed harshly. "Amiens! By the time you
get there it may be in German hands."

"Then I must go cross-country." He could smell defeat
and retreat in the air here. If he died here, Dina would never
know what had happened to him. At the thought of his wife,
his heart twisted in anguish. She was so dear to him—and
so far away. He had to reach Paris. He could write to her
from there. And in Paris he could find a spot where he was
needed just as much as he was needed here.

"I understand the need," he said, "but I cannot fulfill it
for you. There are other demands on me. If Amiens is out
of the question, I shall continue to make my way on foot. I
have come this far. I can go farther."

"You're a damned fool," the doctor said wearily. "You

can't outwalk this war. The Germans will be in Paris before you ever each it. No matter." He clapped Alexandre on the shoulder. "Go over to the mess tent and have a hot meal. Tell them I sent you. And then come back here. You can sleep in the ambulance."

The doctor was correct. The Germans were already between Alexandre and Paris. Only by making a wide detour was he able to avoid them. An elderly peasant bringing vegetables to Les Halles, Paris's central market, had given him a ride on the back of his wagon for the last twenty kilometers of his journey. When they arrived at Les Halles, Alexandre spent his last few centimes on a bowl of soup. It was just enough to make him realize how desperately hungry he was. It was four o'clock in the morning and the great market was bustling. Alexandre leaned against one of the stalls. He had reached his destination, but he had not thought about what he would do once he had arrived. Just getting here had absorbed all his energies, mental and physical. He decided to go to the small hotel where his father had always stayed in Paris. They knew him well enough that they might overlook his appearance—especially in a country at war.

It was much too early, however, so he hung around the market, watching the wagons being unloaded and the storekeepers and restaurant owners buying their day's supplies. Half the market was dark. The war had cut off supplies and most of what was available was going to the army. He overheard buyers grumbling about the shortages and high prices, but to him, with his gnawing hunger, it seemed like luxurious abundance.

Finally he started walking, and an hour later presented himself with a certain degree of trepidation at the small hotel just off the Champs-Élysées. Earlier, catching a glimpse of himself in a window, he had looked around to see who the disreputable character was before he realized that the hollow-eyed, unshaven spectre was himself. Fortunately, Lucien, the hotel manager, was still there. He was white-haired now and a trifle stooped, but Alexandre recognized him immediately.

Lucien drew himself up and flared his nostrils as Alexandre came slowly across the lobby to the desk. Then there was a flash of recognition. "Monsieur Alexandre!" the old man exclaimed. "It is truly you!"

"It is truly I," he replied, "but I shall not feel like myself until I have bathed and eaten and slept. And changed these clothes. Lucien, I need new clothes from top to toe. Can you manage to outfit me while I sleep?"

Lucien's face froze. "Have no fear," Alexandre reassured him. "I am penniless at the moment, but tomorrow I shall be in funds. For old time's sake, I hope you will trust me."

The manager shook his head slowly. "It is impossible. We are full up. I suggest you try elsewhere." He turned to go in his office.

"Lucien, for God's sake! Look!" Alexandre dug into his pocket and pulled out the grubby sock that held the necklace. He undid the knot and the necklace slid out, glittering coldly on the counter. Lucien stared. He picked it up and examined several of the larger diamonds carefully. "It is real," he said in quiet amazement.

"It is real. I promise you that," Alexandre said, the chill of his voice exceeding that of the manager's. "Now, is there room for me here? Or do I go to the Ritz?"

"Of course, of course," the old man said, obsequious now. "You understand, I have to be careful."

Alexandre followed him up the marble staircase to the first floor. Lucien opened the door to a room overlooking the courtyard. "This was your father's favorite."

"Yes, I remember it." He felt as if he had entered another world, one that he had forgotten existed. The room was spotless. A round table and two chairs were placed before the window. The bed was neatly made with the bolster at the head and a comforter folded at the foot. The bathroom glistened white.

"This is fine," he said. "Now Lucien, I beg you. Send someone out to buy me clothes. Everything. And I need food. I am famished."

An hour later he was bathed and shaved. The chambermaid brought him cold chicken and a glass of wine. "Monsieur Lucien says that is all for now. If you eat more, he says, you may not feel well." He got into bed after devouring the chicken and washing it down with the wine.

Twelve hours later he opened his eyes. Disoriented at first, he soon remembered where he was. It was dark. He had no idea of the time. Turning on the light, he found that Lucien had fulfilled his commissions. The wardrobe door was open and inside hung a dark suit and an overcoat. On the chest, underwear and shirts were displayed. A dressing gown was laid ready on the chair beside the bed. And a bill for the purchases was folded on a tray on the bedside table. The filthy rags he had arrived in were nowhere to be seen.

The necklace! He panicked. He leaped out of bed, shrugged himself into the dressing gown, and rang the bell. "Where are my clothes?" he demanded when the chambermaid appeared.

She looked around her. "They are here. On the chest. In the wardrobe." She was bewildered.

"My old clothes!" he shouted. "The clothes I was wearing this morning when I arrived."

She looked blank. "I don't know. Perhaps they are in the wardrobe too.

He searched furiously through the drawers of the chest. He flipped through the new clothes hanging in the wardrobe, looked in the bathroom, even looked under the bed. He found nothing. "Send Lucien to me this moment," he commanded.

"Monsieur Lucien has gone home," she said. "It is almost midnight. He will be here tomorrow at eight o'clock."

"Did he leave a message for me? Is there anything in the safe for me?"

She was convinced that she was dealing with a madman.

She backed out of the room. "I do not know, monsieur. I will look, monsieur. Excuse me, monsieur."

He sat on the edge of the bed. That slippery snake Lucien. He had stolen the necklace. And why not? He had made it easy for him. Had dangled it before his eyes and then fallen dead asleep. He groaned.

Slowly, tiredly, he got dressed in his new clothes. Lucien, damn his eyes, had done a good job. Everything fit. The underwear. The shirt. Even the trouser legs were the correct length. He went down to the lobby, light-headed with shock and hunger. The night man was on duty at the desk.

"I believe you have a package in the safe for me. Monsieur Alexandre de Granville."

"I will look, monsieur." The man disappeared into the office. In a few minutes he reappeared, shaking his head. "No, monsieur. There is nothing."

"A man's sock," insisted Alexandre. "A dirty sock."

The desk clerk looked at him. Was he drunk? Or crazy? A dirty sock in the safe? "I assure you," he said stiffly, "there are no socks in the safe. And nothing bearing your name."

Alexandre turned on his heel. So that was that. Lucien had taken advantage of him. And tomorrow he would be out on the sidewalk, no doubt about that. He felt slightly dizzy for a moment and steadied himself by holding onto the back of a chair.

He faced the clerk again. "I may have been mistaken," he said. "I will straighten things out with Lucien in the morning. In the meantime I am hungry. I will have an *entrecôte*, a salad, cheese. A bottle of burgundy. And bread. Lots of bread."

The desk clerk nodded distractedly. Anything to be rid of this madman. "Immediately, monsieur."

"And brandy," Alexandre said. "A bottle of brandy."

*        *        *

Alexandre awoke to a persistent knocking. Someone was at the door. He sat up and his head spun. He lay down again and called, "Come in." It was Lucien, spruce and smiling.

"Good morning, monsieur. Ah, you look more like yourself this morning," he said, "but a little—a little under the weather."

"A little the worse for drink," Alexandre confirmed.

"You need coffee." Lucien rang the bell. He caught sight of the brandy bottle. "Ah," he said. "I understand. But a drop of brandy in your coffee will do wonders. You will see."

Alexandre ignored this. "Lucien," he plunged in. "Yesterday I showed you a necklace. When I woke up last night the necklace was gone. I suppose you have an explanation." I'll throttle you if you don't, he thought, and was momentarily surprised by his own viciousness.

"The necklace?" Lucien smiled and reached in his pocket. "Do not worry. I have it. I found it in your clothes." He shook his head in dismay at the thought of those clothes.

"I took the liberty of showing it to a jeweler friend of mine," he said. "It looked valuable, but I am no expert. And I cannot afford to make a mistake. He said that these are indeed diamonds. Excellent stones." He held the necklace out to Alexandre.

Weak with relief, Alexandre collapsed into the armchair. "Thank God! That necklace is all I have in the world."

"It is enough," Lucien said briefly. "Where do you plan to take it?"

"My father used to go to Durand."

"I remember. But he has left. He did not want to wait for the Germans to capture Paris. My friend's shop is around the corner on the Faubourg St. Honoré. He indicated that he would be interested. Diamonds are in demand now. So many people turned their assets into diamonds before leaving Paris that they are more precious than ever. You might try him."

Undoubtedly Lucien would get a rake-off, Alexandre thought. But why not? He could easily have denied that I

had ever shown him the necklace. Who would believe me?
"Good," he said. "I will pay a call on him this morning.

"And when I come back, if you will have the bill ready, I
will settle my account," he said coldly.

Lucien bowed. "I will appreciate that."

That morning he sold one of the smallest diamonds in his
Aunt Marita's necklace. Stuffing the proceeds in his pockets, he went apartment-hunting. There were hundreds of
empty apartments in Paris, he discovered. The fearful had
fled to relatives in the country or to the south where they
hoped to wait out the war.

He found a spacious apartment in the old Faubourg St.
Germain, on the rue du Bac just two blocks from the Seine.
It was larger than he needed, but its serene proportions and
handsome furnishings convinced him to look no further. The
concierge recommended a maid who would come in for a
few hours a day. There was a famous restaurant around the
corner and a congenial café on the boulevard.

His father had had many friends in the aristocratic Parisian
quarter. He should call on them, he thought. They would be
able to advise him where he could do the most good in this
war. But for tonight he was going back to the hotel. The
necklace was now safe in a bank vault. And his anger at
Lucien had dissolved. The poor old man, he thought. I
came in off the street looking like a tramp. Smelling like
one, probably. I can't really blame him.

The next day he took possession of the apartment. The
formalities concluded, he walked through the rooms, moving a chair here and a table there, making it home. Dina
would like this, he thought. He stiffened. He must write to
her immediately. He had no idea if his last letter, which he
had left at the American legation in Brussels with a request
that it be sent in the diplomatic pouch, had arrived. If not,
what must she be thinking? He knew that he must write.

He would go to a café and ask for a pen and writing
paper. But when he went out and settled himself in the café
on the boulevard, he was at a loss for words. He scribbled a

few lines, telling her that he had arrived safely after a
fatiguing and frightening journey and that he missed her and
longed for her. Then he put down his pen.

How could he tell her that he had just rented an elegant
apartment in Paris? He had written her that he was staying
in Europe to fight the Germans and avenge the deaths of his
aunt and uncle. One hardly needed an apartment for that.
He wrote a few more lines explaining that he was still
recovering from crossing half of France and Belgium on
foot. He would write in more detail shortly.

He folded the letter and sealed the envelope. He signaled
the waiter and ordered another *café crème*. At the moment
Dina seemed very far away. His life in America seemed
unreal. He settled back in his chair and watched the passersby
on the boulevard. He felt completely at home here in Paris.

# Sixteen

THERE WAS a glitter in the Parisian air that autumn of 1914. A kind of gallant tension. It was both sad and wonderful.

The city had almost fallen to the Germans shortly before Alexandre had arrived. They had advanced to within thirty miles of the Arc de Triomphe. Unless fresh troops could be sent to the front, the hobnailed boots of the German legions would tramp up the Champs-Élysées.

The troops were available, but there was no transport. It was the taxi drivers of Paris who had turned the tide. Answering the call to arms, they had deposited their passengers at the nearest corners and reported to the military governor of Paris, General Joseph Gallieni. Six thousand French soldiers were rushed to the front by the taxi brigade between darkness and dawn, and the German advance was stemmed. This gave an illusion of victory that infused Parisians with both pride and confidence, the latter little justified, although few understood this at the moment.

To Alexandre, Paris was almost its old self despite the shuttered shops and the streets quiet as country lanes. Even

the drawing rooms of the Faubourg St. Germain that he had
frequented with his father in former years seemed unchanged.
He rapidly became a favorite. Not only was he charming,
almost as charming as his father had been, he was that most
desirable of creatures, a presentable extra man. And young—
in a society whose young men had disappeared into the
army.

It was in an old mansion on the rue de Grenelle that he
first became aware of the misery in which most Belgian
refugees found themselves. His hostess, splendid in a gown
of aubergine taffeta that was unmistakably by Worth, described a sad episode that she had witnessed that day.

"I was leaving Lanvin's after a fitting and a woman was
there on the sidewalk tugging at people's sleeves," Madame
Courtois related. "There was a little girl hanging onto her
skirt. I couldn't understand a word she was saying. Caroline,
my sister-in-law who spent several years in Belgium when
her husband was at the embassy there, said she was speaking Flemish, but she could not understand her either.

"We gave the poor thing some money. I felt so sorry for
her. A refugee, obviously. Heaven knows if she even has a
roof over her head."

"But what can one do?" asked an elegant dowager whose
décolletage was accented with a triple strand of huge creamy
pearls. "One cannot adopt every penniless refugee."

"Isn't there a shelter for these poor people? Where do
they stay?" Alexandre asked.

"I believe there is a shelter," an elderly gentleman
replied. "But there are hundreds of these refugees. A dozen
shelters could not begin to house them. I understand that the
miserable creatures haunt the railroad stations. Even sleep
on the floors at night."

Alexandre thought of all the refugees he had seen clog-
ging the roads during his flight from Belgium. His heart
went out to them. The next day he went to the Gare du
Nord. Rail traffic was practically at a standstill except for
military transport, but the station was crowded. Women and

children were lying on straw spread on the floor. Others wandered along the platforms, lost and bewildered.

He approached several of them, asking where they had come from and how long they had been there. The women stammered out horrifying stories while their children stood by with vacant eyes. Some of them were clearly ill and all were hungry and frightened.

The last of the dozen or so women he spoke with seemed less daunted by her plight. The baby in her arms was clean, although pale and pinched. "What part of Belgium do you come from?" he asked.

"Kortrijk, sir. My husband is in the army. I thought to find safety in France with my children but I fear it was a mistake. I do not speak French, only Flemish, so I cannot find work. Nor can the other women here. Without work I cannot pay for lodgings. Or even for food for my children much longer."

"Children? Where are the others?"

She pointed to two little girls huddled together on a thin scattering of straw.

"Come," he said impulsively. "Tonight you and the children will stay with me."

She scowled at him. "Choose someone else for your games," she said grimly. "I am an honest woman."

"No, no!" He was horrified at her misunderstanding. "Nothing like that. You don't understand. I am a refugee, too. More fortunate than most. I simply want to help you. You have nothing to worry about."

"Your wife is with you?"

"No, my wife is in the United States, but I assure you, I simply want to help."

She was not convinced. "What do you want of me?" she asked suspiciously. Never in her experience, nor in that of her peasant forebears, had anyone offered something for nothing. There was a catch somewhere.

"Nothing, nothing at all. My idea was to feed you and the children, give you a chance to bathe and wash your clothes, and let you have a bed for the night. That certainly would be better than staying here.''

She looked around, hesitated, and then agreed. "I will look at your place. If it is as you say, perhaps I will stay.''

"Good. No matter what you decide, I hope you will stay for a meal at least. I'm sure the baby could use some warm milk. And perhaps a little soup.''

"A hot meal?'' she considered briefly, then called her daughters. "Janine. Lisette. Come here.'' She brushed off the wisps of straw clinging to their clothes, and they followed Alexandre out to the street. "If you touch my children,'' she threatened him as he held the door of the taxi for her, "I will make you sorry.''

"No one is going to hurt your children,'' he said, impatient now. "Come, the sooner we are home, the sooner the children can eat.''

He did not know what he had expected. Certainly not this. Gratitude, perhaps. Thankfulness. Even surprise. But not suspicion. Not threats. It had simply been a whim, a desire to make life a little more pleasant for one woman and her children. As the taxi made its way across the Seine, he cursed himself for being a fool. No wonder this woman is suspicious. What am I trying to do? Pretend I am a fairy godfather? Change their lives for one day to make myself feel good? And then what? Send them back to the station in a taxi?

The taxi stopped and put an end to his bitter musings. He led the woman and the two little girls through the iron gates into the courtyard. It was pretty, with yellow chrysanthemums blooming in ornamental pots and a large plane tree in the center encircled by a bench.

He pointed to the windows of his apartment. "I live there,'' he said. "Just one flight up.''

"I will look at it,'' she said. She turned to the older girl. "Janine, you sit here with Lisette. On that bench. Wait for me.'' Then she followed him into the house and up the stairs.

Holding the baby in her arms, she stood in the foyer and looked around. "Let me show you the kitchen." She followed silently. The maid, Thérèse, was busy at the stove.

"Thérèse, will you show—" he turned to the woman. "I'm sorry. I don't know your name."

"Lucie. Lucie Soerbijk."

"Will you show Madame Soerbijk the guest room? And the bathroom. She and her children may be staying tonight."

When she returned with Thérèse, the cloud had left her face. "It is a pleasant apartment," she said. "I thank you for your invitation." She looked at him squarely. "You can understand why I did not trust you. But Thérèse tells me you are an honest man. I still don't understand why you are doing this."

He shrugged. "Perhaps it is because I hope someone would do the same for my wife and daughter if they were in a similar situation."

That afternoon his apartment was far from the serene refuge it had been. Baths were taken. Clothes were washed. Thérèse went marketing and returned with two laden string bags. A stewing hen was put to simmer in a large pot with carrots and leeks. That night incredible amounts of soup thick with vegetables and chunks of chicken were consumed. The children, half intoxicated by the warmth and the food, feel asleep at the table.

Once they were put to bed, Alexandre sat down to talk with Lucie Soerbijk. Although she was almost as sleepy as the children had been from the food and the glass of wine Alexandre had insisted she have, she was attentive and responsive.

He learned from her that there was a handful of private organizations that offered food and shelter to the refugees, but that they were overwhelmed. "And, of course, they favor the French refugees. It's only natural," she had added. She had taken a ball of thread from her skirt pocket and was working with a needle as she talked.

"What is that you are doing?"

"Making lace. This will be a collar. I have sold several of them on the street. Enough to take the children to the public baths one day. And to buy myself a coffee at the café."

She was a survivor, he thought. Even without a roof over her head and only the railroad station for shelter, she was making lace collars to earn a few centimes. How could he send this woman back to the station? It was no place for her, or for the children. He had to find a way to help them with something more than a hot meal and a bed for the night. But how?

"You need to sleep," he said at last. "Tomorrow I will try to think of something for you and your children. I don't know what, but I will," he said with determination.

He could not get to sleep that night. The women he had seen in the railroad station had shocked him—decent women having to sleep in a railroad station, their children filthy and hungry and cold. What could be done for them? Where could he send this little family?

Why send them anywhere? he thought suddenly. I can help them as well as anyone. Perhaps better. I at least speak Flemish. And I have money. Excited, Alexandre got up and started planning.

He rummaged through the apartment looking for paper so he could jot down his ideas. Finally he found a pad of coarse paper in the kitchen, settled himself at the table in front of the sink, and started writing. He would provide a shelter—not just for Lucie Soerbijk and her children, but for several families. He would organize it so that some women could work and others could care for the children, do the shopping and cooking.

Finding work might be a problem, he worried. Thérèse had told him that many families who fled Paris when it seemed that the Germans were about to capture it had left their household help behind. As a consequence hundreds of domestics were searching for work. The Flemish women from Belgium, who could not even speak French, would have no chance of finding employment.

Lace! That's the answer, he thought. There was always a market for Belgian lace. His own Vicky's christening gown had been made of Belgian lace. Brides wore lace. There were lace tablecloths and lace curtains. His favorite of all of Dina's negligees had lace dripping from the cuffs. No one was exporting lace from Belgium now because of the German occupation. If the women in his shelter could make lace, there should be a market for it in New York. Dina would know.

He leaned back in the wooden kitchen chair. Dina. It was almost as if she were there in that pale lavender negligee with the lace spilling from the sleeves, her hair loose, falling down her back. And those blue eyes looking at him with love. If only it were true. If only she were sitting across this kitchen table from him, planning this shelter with him.

It was three o'clock in the morning and he felt more alive than he had in all the months since he had left New York. Now there was something important he had to do. He pushed aside the sheets of paper he had filled and reached for a fresh sheet. He had to write to Dina. He was suddenly eager to share his excitement with her.

"It was like an excursion into hell," he concluded at the end of an hour and fifteen closely written pages:

First you see the flags and then you hear the drums and the trumpets sounding. And then the guns and the shells bursting. You see the blood and the pain, the wounded and the dead. Villages burned and shelled. Women and children homeless.

Many of those women and children made the same hard march that I did and are now in Paris, homeless and penniless. I have decided to establish a shelter for some of them. Once it is a going concern, I plan to offer my services to the Volunteer Ambulance Corps.

During the short time I have been in Paris, I have found that the French are not eager for my services as a fighting man. By the time their red tape was untangled, I would be a graybeard. But several Americans have formed the Volunteer Ambulance Corps, which supplies ambulances and drivers to the French. That one dreadful night at the front I learned how important ambulance drivers are. I suspect I will be more useful driving than in the trenches.

I expect to be ready to volunteer in a matter of months. First I must establish the shelter and—this is very important— find a way of helping these women earn money.

He considered telling her about his Aunt Marita's necklace, but decided against it. It was wartime. Letters would be censored. Better that no one knew he had a fortune in diamonds. He went on:

Many of them are skilled lace makers. Lucie Soerbijk, a refugee who has been living in the Gare du Nord for the past month with her three children and who seems to be a most capable woman, says it is something the peasant women do to earn a little extra money when their work is finished. I think this may be the answer. I would be most grateful if you—and perhaps Isabelle—would find out if there is a market for such lace in New York. If you could let me know what would sell most easily, I will be able to advise the women.

I miss you and Vicky very much . . .

He brushed the back of his hand across his eyes. Tears blurred the words in front of him. He did miss them desperately. He felt miserably homesick. It had been so long since he had felt close to Dina. Now that he was sharing his experiences and plans with her, he missed her bitterly.

He dipped his pen in the ink and started to write that he had changed his mind. He would not volunteer for the ambulance corps, but would be home as soon as he possibly could get there. He put the pen down. How could he? After all his lofty phrases? After swearing that he must fight the Germans to avenge the deaths of his aunt and uncle? How could he show himself to be all talk and no action? Dina would scorn him. He had trapped himself.

He took up the pen again and finished the letter with a promise to write regularly and a plea for her to write with news of herself and Vicky now that she had his address.

His plans took shape. He rented an empty tenement with twenty small apartments, most of them only one room each. The building lacked most conveniences, but it had the advantage of being empty. And it was not far from the Gare du Nord.

In the meantime he had found temporary lodgings for Lucie Soerbijk and her children. He stopped by one afternoon and said, "I have something to show you. It's just a short walk from here."

"Janine, you watch the baby. Lisette, you be quiet," she commanded and picked up her shawl. Five minutes later they were standing in front of an empty building on the rue Maubeuge.

"What do you think?" he asked.

She was bewildered. "I don't understand."

"I have rented it. I am going to turn it into a home for twenty Belgian women with children. There are twenty apartments. They are very small but they will be better than the railroad station."

She stared at him. He must be a mad millionaire. "It is a miracle," she said carefully. "If it is true."

"It will be true," he assured her, "if you will help me. I want you to choose the women who will live here. They must have small children. And, if possible, they must know how to make lace. I think I can find a market for lace and that will help them earn a little money. Will you do this for me?"

She did not bother to answer. "There's Annette Kop," she said. "And Marthe, Marie-Thérèse, and—oh yes, I can find women who can make lace. There is no problem. There are all too many of us.''

Readying the ancient tenement was a far greater undertaking than he had expected. He was involved in a hundred negotiations—and found them fascinating. With money and charm, he discovered, almost any problem could be solved. He exerted every last bit of his charm to induce the bureaucrats to process the necessary red tape for renovations and repairs. He offered double pay to the elderly painters and carpenters who were in great demand now that all the young men had gone to war. And he paid stall keepers at the flea market prices that became a legend for secondhand tables and chairs. Slowly things fell into place, and shortly after the beginning of the new year the building was habitable. There was still much to be done, but they were all things that could be dealt with in time. Right now, Paris was cold and wet. His little group of refugee families could wait no longer.

Alexandre felt like the Pied Piper as he set off from the Gare du Nord one afternoon with sixty women and children trooping at his heels. He turned a corner and led them along the rue Maubeuge. A few minutes later he stopped in front of the shabby building. He turned and faced his followers. ''Your new home,'' he said and waved them through the door.

As each woman took possession of an apartment and herded her children in before her, he felt an immense satisfaction. When he finally tore himself away from the house that afternoon, he walked home to his apartment on the other side of the Seine in a daze of triumph. ''Twenty families,'' he kept thinking. ''Twenty families who have a place to live and food to eat.'' He had saved lives. It was a marvelous feeling. If only Dina had been there to share it with him.

# Seventeen

IN LATE January Alexandre presented himself at the headquarters of the Volunteer Ambulance Corps on the Place de la Concorde. When he requested to be sent to the front as an ambulance driver, Ned Buswell, the head of V.A.C., shook his head: "I'd be a fool to send you off to the front. We have more eager young drivers than we have ambulances. And not enough competent headquarters staff.

"Not that our drivers are all that competent," he fumed. "I was at the front yesterday," he told Alexandre, "and what did I see but one of our new ambulances right up on the firing line. Parked next to a French battery. I went down there posthaste and asked the young fool what he thought he was doing.

"You know what he told me? 'I wanted to see how they handled these big guns.' Well, I sent him back to his post with a blistering reprimand. Later I made time to point out that the German guns were bound to center in on that French battery sooner or later and that he could have been blown to pieces. His ambulance, too. And if he was killed, I said, all that would happen is that the French would shrug and say that another reckless young American had thrown away his life and lost an ambulance for nothing.

" 'But if you lose your life in the performance of duty,' I said, 'the French will pay you every honor at their command. How would you rather die? As a fool? Or a hero?'

"He looked pretty sheepish and admitted to preferring a hero's death."

Buswell shook his head and smiled. "He's a good lad, but I tell you there are times when I feel more like a nursemaid than a hard-headed businessman doing his part to make the world safe for democracy."

"If you take me on," Alexandre assured him, "I can promise you that I'll stay at my post. I drove an ambulance one night in Flanders. I know what it means to the wounded."

"You're too valuable to send to the front. I need you right here," Buswell insisted. "You speak French, which is more than the rest of us do. I need someone to act as liaison with the French and handle all the nasty, niggling problems that arise every ten minutes." He grinned at the younger man. "Not the great adventure you were hoping for, hmph? Once we're better organized, I'll see that you get to the front if that's what you want."

This suited Alexandre well enough. He had no romantic illusions about being at the front. He had seen the trenches and the barbed wire, and the awful carnage wrought by distant cannons. He had watched the wounded die. In that one night at the front, he had seen enough to be content to be needed more at headquarters than in the field.

He buckled down to his job of liaison with enthusiastic energy. "You should think about going into diplomacy once this war's over," Buswell complimented him. "The French tell me that things are going much better now that you have taken over."

Alexandre was relieved. By this time he wanted nothing more than to stay in Paris. One dismal morning as he was crossing the Champs-Élysées on his way to the V.A.C. and cursing the weather, he had heard his name.

"Alexandre! Alexandre!" As he turned, a soft hand was laid on his arm and a familiar face smiled up at him.

"Kitty! Whatever are you doing here?"

"Working," she said. "One doesn't come to Paris just to shop these days."

"Working? What do you mean?"

"I'm with the Red Cross. I'm on my way there right now."

He tucked her hand under his arm. "I'm with the V.A.C. and that's where I'm bound. It's in the same building. How long have you been in Paris?"

"Almost three months."

"And I haven't run into you before!" he marveled. "Unbelievable!" She smiled. She had seen him going in and out of the V.A.C. headquarters a dozen times, but had taken care he did not see her. She had no intention of renewing the shipboard romance. She was married now. What did she want with a penniless lover?

As the weeks went by, however, she came to realize that he was far from penniless. She could not imagine where his money came from. Dina certainly could not be giving him so generous an allowance—not to lead a bachelor's life in Paris. But he had money, Kitty could tell. He was dressed in the height of fashion. And she heard he had rented the apartment of the old Comte de Perrine. He did have money; there was no doubt about it.

For a time she thought he must be romantically involved. Why else should he be staying in Paris? If the woman was wealthy, that would explain everything. But asking around with delicately disguised curiosity, she found no hint of a woman in his life. His interests revolved around a houseful of refugees for whom he had made himself responsible and his work at the ambulance corps. His social life seemed confined to dinner parties given by the staid old aristocrats of the Faubourg St. Germain. Considering all this, Kitty had decided to try to renew their romance.

*     *     *

Alexandre shook his head. "I can't imagine why we never ran into each other before. How was your stay with the Milraven-Peakes? Did you come here straight from England? Is your sister with you?"

"Stop! Stop!" She held up her hand. "I can't answer everything at once," she laughed. "And I am late as it is. Perhaps we could have dinner together some night?"

"That's a splendid idea. What about tonight? Are you free?"

"If I were not, I would make myself free," she said softly. "I'll give you my address." She pulled a small notebook from her handbag, scribbled a few words in it, and tore out the page. "Here. I'm staying with a Mrs. Constable, a friend of my mother-in-law. I'll expect you this evening at eight o'clock." She slipped through the door and disappeared into the bustling Red Cross office.

Alexandre looked across the table in the dimly lit restaurant near the Place de l'Étoile. "Did I understand you to say that Mrs. Constable was a friend of your *mother-in-law?*"

She made a little face. "And the dullest woman imaginable."

"Then you are married?" His face reflected his disbelief.

She held out her hand. An enormous rose-cut diamond in an old-fashioned setting was accompanied by a plain gold band. "Bucky was called up. He loved me," she said in a matter-of-fact voice. "What could I do? He was going to war. He might never come back.

"We were married in the little stone church in their village and then we went to Scotland for our wedding trip. Just five days, thank goodness. I nearly froze to death.

"When we got back, Bucky had to join his regiment. He had one leave. We spent it in London. It was lovely," she said wistfully. "We went dancing every night. I met some of the other officers in the regiment. They were all charming. And then he was off to France."

"Why didn't you return to New York?" he asked.

"Papa wanted me to. But I couldn't see living at home as

a married woman whose husband was at war. I wouldn't be able to do anything. And his family wanted me to stay with them.'' She wrinkled her nose prettily. ''You have no idea how worthy they are. They do good things for people and talk about their responsibility to the villagers. I would have spent all my time carrying soup to sick old ladies and arranging flowers.

''They live in the country most of the year. They only use their house in London in the spring and early summer. It's all too dismal for words. So I decided to come to Paris. But Paris isn't much fun either,'' she concluded disconsolately. ''In fact, it's a bore.''

''Your problem is that you've been cooped up with that Mrs. Constable. You should be with someone closer to your own age. Isn't there someone at the Red Cross you could share an apartment with?''

He was preparing a defensive position. It was one thing to have dinner with Kitty, but quite another to be expected to squire her around. He had no urge to resume their shipboard fling. As he watched her across the table with her little flirtatious moues and movements, he wondered how he could have been so strongly attracted to her. The china-doll prettiness was still there, but he had Dina in his mind. Dina with her elegance and her openness, her generosity, and her heart-stopping beauty. He was proud that he had been the one who had brought out that beauty. Sometimes he felt like a sculptor who had been confronted by a clumsy block of marble and, little by little, had revealed the beauty it held. But Dina was no marble woman. Kitty might be a china doll, but Dina was flesh and blood.

During his musing he lost track of what Kitty was saying. There was a silence. ''I beg your pardon. I didn't hear . . .'' he apologized.

''I said that you seemed to be taking it well.'' Kitty had decided to make her move.

He lifted an eyebrow. ''Taking *what* well? Your sudden appearance?''

She wore an expression of soft concern. "No, Jack and Dina."

"I don't know what you're talking about."

"Oh ... well ... in that case ... and I'm sure it's nothing." She fidgeted in mock embarrassment.

"What is nothing?"

"Nothing. Nothing at all. I shouldn't have said anything. It's probably just gossip. Although ..."

"Well, out with it. What is this precious gossip of yours?" he asked with more than a tinge of exasperation.

"Nothing." She hesitated and then said very seriously, "It's just that I heard that they were spending a great deal of time together. Alone."

Listening to her, he grinned to himself. What a mischiefmaker she was. As if he would believe for one minute that Dina and Jack Goddard were having an affair. He would not be surprised if Jack had made some overtures. After all, Dina was a most appealing woman. But he knew she would never encourage him.

"Jack and Holly are good friends of ours," he told her. "We have always spent a lot of time together. And Jack painted Dina's portrait a few months ago. That's probably what started the gossip."

"Then *that's* why he was on the island!" she exclaimed. "Painting her portrait. All perfectly innocent. I'll have to write my sister. You see, Phoebe wrote me that Todd and Flossie had seen them at a distance one day when they sailed over to the island for a picnic. You know how Flossie is always peering through her binoculars hoping to see something scandalous."

"Oh, Flossie." He managed to dismiss her with a shrug, but suddenly he felt ill. On the island? Dina had written that Jack had painted her in their dining room on Madison Avenue. On the island? He could feel the blood drain from his face. There were beads of sweat on his forehead. Dina and Jack? It was true then. For a moment he felt as if he were going to disgrace himself, to get sick right there at the

table. And then a wave of anger washed over him. That
bitch! Cuckolding him! And how long had that been going
on? His fists were clenched.

"Let's get out of here," he said abruptly. "There's a
little nightclub around the corner. I think you will like it."

"I'm sure I will," she purred. "I'm already beginning to
change my mind about Paris." She leaned across the table
and drew her finger along the line of his jaw, looking up at
him from under her lashes. He took her hand and kissed it.
If Dina could not be faithful, why should he? So all New
York was gossiping about his wife. He'd give them something to gossip about. And let Dina see how she liked it.

It was late when they left the nightclub, but Alexandre
did not want to call an end to the night. Not yet. He was not
ready to be alone with his thoughts. His arm was around
Kitty's shoulders. He bent down and kissed her. "Let me
show you my part of Paris," he proposed. "Unless you are
tired."

"Tired! I'm too happy to be tired," she said and returned
his kiss. Things were going better than she had hoped. He
would soon be eating out of her hand. She was even more
strongly attracted to him than she had been before. He was
definitely more physically appealing than Bucky, although
she did not regret her choice of a husband for a moment.

Despite her dismissal of the Milraven-Peake way of life as
dismal, she looked forward to playing her role as Bucky's
wife. To playing Lady Bountiful to the tenants who lived on
their country estate, to being a personage in the village and
the country. She happily anticipated the yearly splurge of
the London season with the balls and the theater, the
Trooping of the Colour and Ascot. And the fabulous wardrobe that was part of it all. It was a good life and after the
war, as Bucky's wife, she would have an important part in
it.

In the meantime she was not ready to play the part of the
dutiful daughter-in-law sitting around waiting for her husband to come back from the wars. She would go to Paris,

she had decided, and volunteer her services to the Red
Cross. There was always the chance that Bucky would get a
leave and join her for a few days. And if not, well, Paris
was Paris.

But Paris had been a disappointment. She had not been
able to avoid living with Mrs. Constable. Bucky's mother
had been so solicitous of her welfare and insistent that she
live as befitted a Milraven-Peake that there had been no
resisting it. It was even worse than she had feared. She had
never led such a cloistered life. Her days were spent with
other women at the Red Cross and she came home to dinner,
served early out of consideration for the elderly maid, and a
few games of Patience before bed. Tonight with Alexandre's
arm around her, she felt reckless. Who would ever know if
she had an affair with Alexandre? Certainly not Bucky or his
family. And they were the only ones who mattered.

They walked hand in hand through the night streets, empty
except for an occasional policeman pedaling by on a bicy-
cle. It was dark. The lights of Paris had been dimmed to a
subdued glow this first winter of the war. When they
reached the Seine, it was a darkly glistening ribbon. They
leaned against the parapet of the Pont Royal, watching the
swirls of the current.

"I talked about myself all during dinner," she said.
"What about you? Did you manage to convince your uncle
that he should leave Brussels?"

He told her the story of St. Hilaire. It was good to be able
to talk about it. Writing to Dina had helped, but having
Kitty at his side, reacting with horror and soft sympathy,
was even better. "It is unbelievable," he said. "They are
all dead. My uncle and my aunt. My cousins."

"Your cousins?"

"Yes, Guy and Henri. The last day I was in Brussels, I
walked home from my uncle's office and on one corner I
saw people reading notices that had been posted on a wall.
I went over to see what was going on. They were lists."

His voice grew husky. "Lists of soldiers, Belgian soldiers who had been killed in action. Both Guy and Henri were among them."

"Then you have inherited your uncle's fortune?" she asked.

"Fortune!" he scoffed. "There is none. Everything was in his business. And the Germans have taken control of everything. If there is any money they will take it all."

That was not it then, she thought. Where had his money come from? She shivered.

"I'm sorry," he said. "I've been thoughtless. Keeping you out in the night air and burdening you with my story. My apartment is very close. I will light a fire and give you a brandy."

She leaned her head against his shoulder. "Do you remember what happened the last time you gave me a brandy?"

Alexandre awoke the next morning to see Kitty wrapped in his dressing gown, its skirts dragging the floor, bringing in his breakfast tray. "Your maid was not even surprised to see me," she said. "What kind of bachelor life have you been leading here all by yourself?"

"The celibate life of a monk," he assured her, sitting up in bed as she poured hot milk into his coffee. "Thérèse is probably reassured that I am normal." He broke a roll apart and slathered it with strawberry preserves. "What about Mrs. Constable? She must be out of her wits with worry that you did not come home last night."

"I doubt it," she said. "She does not leave her bedroom before eleven. She will simply think that I have gone to the Red Cross as usual."

He swung his legs to the floor. "We have to move you out of there. What are you going to tell her?"

She dimpled. "Could I say that a very dear friend has offered to share his apartment with me?"

"I wouldn't advise phrasing it quite that way," he said dryly.

"Of course not. I was simply joking. I certainly don't want to cause a scandal that will get back to Bucky's family. I will just say that you and your wife have invited me to stay with you. You made a good impression on her last night."

By midafternoon the move had been accomplished. "Mrs. de Granville is one of my oldest friends," Kitty told Mrs. Constable. "She's the daughter of Frederick Schumacher. You may have heard of him.

"I shall miss you," she said insincerely, "but I feel that I have already imposed on you too much."

It had been enough for Mrs. Constable. She did not dream of asking to meet Mrs. de Granville. Truth to tell, Kitty, restless and fretful, had been a difficult guest. The elderly matron was happy to turn her over to her American friends.

And so it began. Paris was miserable that winter of 1915. For weeks on end, the sun hid behind heavy gray clouds. The fogs were damp and bone-chilling. Rain gave way to snow, and snow to rain. The war news was worrying. But Alexandre was oblivious to it all. It was Paris, and he was in love. Although sometimes he wondered. It was more like being intoxicated, he thought. Kitty was like champagne. All sparkle.

They frequented the smoky *boîtes* of Montmartre, the nightclubs with husky-voiced singers. They went to the dance halls where the tango had become the rage. They would come out into the night almost dizzy with the sexuality of the beat and make their way back to the apartment where Kitty would put a tango record on the phonograph and they would dance until Alexandre finally lowered her to the floor and the record spun while the needle whined in empty grooves.

They went to the opera and the theater. They sat for hours over brandy in small cafés late at night. They went riding in

the Bois de Boulogne on chilly gray Sunday mornings and
then rushed back to a lunch of bread and cheese and wine,
toasting themselves beside the ornate porcelain stove that
heated the bedroom and later tumbling into bed full of wine
and desire.

They denied themselves nothing. And when Kitty discovered
the source of Alexandre's money, there was no end to her
extravagance. He had had no intention of telling her, but she
had teased it out of him one night.

"A necklace!" she had exclaimed, sitting straight up in
bed, her cheeks pink with excitement. "A diamond necklace! Oh Alexandre, do let me see it." And the next day he
had taken it out of the vault and brought it home wrapped in
his handkerchief and stuffed in a pocket like a schoolboy's
hoard of sweets.

She had run it through her fingers, looking carefully at
each stone. "They are so big," she said. "It must be worth
a fortune!"

"According to the jeweler, each one is flawless," he said.
"I would expect no less from my Uncle Albert."

"Such a shame that you have to break it up."

He shrugged. "One must eat."

Kitty looked at the glitter in her cupped hands and
smiled.

He still spent most of the day working diligently at the
ambulance corps, although Kitty had dropped her Red Cross
work. Several times a week he visited the house on the rue
Maubeuge. It was a noisy house with children's voices
echoing from floor to floor, but a happy house.

And a busy one. Dina had found a shop in New York that
had promised to buy all the lace the group could make, and
Alexandre was sending regular shipments to them by the
executives of the V.A.C. who crossed and recrossed the
Atlantic as if it were a mere river as they went about their
work of fund-raising and buying ambulances. The little
project was bringing in enough so that each woman had

pocket money to spend on small necessities for herself and her children. It had done wonders for their morale. He was convinced that the house and its inhabitants were well worth the diamonds he had spent.

In truth, compared to what Kitty was spending, the house on the rue Maubeuge was only a minor drain. Sometimes he felt that she would never have enough of anything. Sam Parseval had encouraged his favorite daughter to believe that she should have anything she desired. And Alexandre was discovering that her desires were wide-ranging. She was insatiable.

She had descended upon the salons of the great Parisian couturiers as if she were trying single-handedly to make up to them for all the wealthy American clients who had been kept away by the war. Alexandre teased her that they laid a red carpet down the center of the rue de la Paix when they heard she was coming.

It was a fact that Jean Worth himself came out into the gray-carpeted salon to discuss her needs. One whole diamond had gone to settle her account at the House of Worth. And then there were Lanvin and Collot, Paquin and Poiret. At each house she was welcomed with the smiles and bows accorded a favored client.

Her whims were almost as expensive as the wardrobe she was accumulating, but Alexandre found them enchanting. When they awoke one morning to find every lamppost and tree limb covered with snow, Kitty declared, "I feel like playing Marie Antoinette. Today we shall picnic in the snow at Versailles."

While Alexandre searched for a taxi with enough gasoline to make the trip, Kitty sent Thérèse out to buy the picnic lunch. A combination of French *luxe* and American simplicity, her menu ranged from truffle-stuffed foie gras to little sausages to be toasted over a fire to a chocolate torte. All to be accompanied by Roederer's Cristal.

They left the taxi in the great cobblestoned stable yard of Versailles and walked around the palace and down the long central avenue to the Apollo Basin. Theirs were the only footprints in the snow. Kitty skipped along carefully balancing the chocolate torte while Alexandre and the taxi driver struggled along behind carrying the rest of the food, the champagne bottles, and wood for the fire—the driver muttering about the insanity of people who chose to eat outdoors in the middle of winter.

The foie gras was gobbled with greedy enjoyment and washed down with great gulps of champagne. The sausages were grilled over the fire that Alexandre had built despite his misgivings. "Fires must be forbidden on these grounds," he worried. "We'll be thrown in prison."

Kitty had laughed. "Who will throw us in prison? The guards are all in the army. We can do whatever we please."

As they sat by the pool snuggled in their furs with a red fox lap robe around their legs, drinking champagne in the snow, the memory of the day and night he had spent at the front in Flanders flashed into his mind. The wounded lying on tarpaulins on the bare ground, the young men in the trenches. He imagined he could feel their accusing eyes on him. And then he thought of Lucie Soerbijk. He was glad that sensible woman with the level gaze could not see him now.

He had come to think of money as something that was there to be spent, just as wine was to be drunk, but he could not help realizing that he had spent enough on this capricious winter picnic to support the little Belgian colony for a month. There was something shameful about such extravagant indulgence, but the truth was he was not ashamed. He was enjoying every minute of it and the best part was looking ahead to the pleasures that waited him once they were back in Paris. When Kitty was indulged in her whims, it seemed to spark her passion. She became as impetuous and imaginative in bed as she was in her pursuit of other pleasures.

He took her to rue Maubeuge one day, sure that she would share his enthusiasm for what had been accomplished. He

was as proud of this house as he had been of the house on
Madison Avenue. Perhaps even prouder. The women had
scrubbed and scoured until every surface gleamed. There
was always a great kettle of soup simmering on the back of
the stove, filling the air with its warm fragrance. And
everywhere, there were children. For him it had the feel of
the home he had longed for as a child, full of warmth and
love.

The visit had not been a success. Wrapped in her furs, her
face delicately made up, her hair fresh from the hands of the
coiffeur, enveloped in a cloud of Worth's *Je Reviens,* Kitty
was a hothouse orchid. The Belgians in their long skirts
covered by aprons, their hair severely pulled back, their
faces innocent of makeup, looked at her with shy discomfort. Kitty barely glanced at them as she was introduced.

He showed her the communal dining room and the kitch-
en and took her upstairs to the workroom where other
women were busily making lace and chatting. She drew her
furs closer around her and said nothing, even when he
introduced her to Lucie Soerbijk, who smiled and bobbed a
half curtsy. Kitty looked at her distantly as if she were some
strange specimen. Hurt, Alexandre cut the visit short.

"My God!" he exploded as he helped her into the
waiting taxi, "you might at least have smiled. And said
something about how hard everybody works."

Kitty looked petulant. "I don't see what you think is so
wonderful. All those drab women. And those noisy children. Packed together like sardines. And that Soerbijk
woman you keep talking about. She's just a flat-faced
peasant. She has no style. A nobody."

He stiffened. "She is a woman whose husband is fighting
for his country and his king, whose home has been destroyed,
and who made the same hazardous trip on foot that I
did—except that she did it with three children, one of them
just a few months old. She's a remarkable woman.

"And when I see what she is doing here—do you understand," he asked passionately, "what it means to manage a community of nearly two dozen little households? And supervise this little lace-making business?"

"Yes, yes, it is very worthy, I'm sure." She nestled into her furs and sighed. "Let's get out of here. I've never seen such a depressing neighborhood. I think you should take me to lunch at the Tour d'Argent to make up for this awful morning."

"Poor Kitty." He relented and patted her cheek. "You're right. You don't belong here." He leaned forward and directed the driver to the Tour d'Argent.

He was abstracted during lunch. He kept thinking of Dina. There would have been no barrier between her and these women. She would have recognized their courage. She would have appreciated the warm, homey atmosphere. Dina would have hugged the toddlers and asked the older children how their French lessons were progressing. She would have told them about her own little girl. And she would have admired the lace the women were making.

He made an attempt at conversation. "What did you think about their lace? It is selling quite well in New York. We have had two orders for bridal veils this month."

"It's quite nice, that lace," Kitty said thoughtfully. "You know, I didn't think about it while I was there, but why don't you ask them to make a few yards of lace for me. I could use it to trim my summer petticoats."

"That's a wonderful idea," he said enthusiastically. "I should have thought of it myself. There must be dozens of women like you in Paris who would buy their lace."

She looked at him with exasperation. "I didn't say you should buy it for me. I think they should do it for nothing. After all, look at all you have done for them."

"No," he said quietly. "I couldn't ask that. They would do it, of course, but I would not take advantage of them that way. I'm surprised you would consider it."

Kitty's face froze. For a second she looked pinched and mean. "I'm not going to sit here and listen to you lecture," she snapped. "You should have asked your wonderful Lucie Soerbijk to lunch with you." She put down her napkin and swept out of the elegant restaurant.

He followed her. "What's the matter? Where are you going?"

"I'm bored, that's what's the matter," she said, her porcelain-pretty face as hard as if it were truly porcelain. "I'm going to Paquin's. At least there they are pleasant."

"They're pleasant because you spend a fortune with them," he said coldly. "I hope you enjoy your afternoon." He saw her into a taxi and returned to the table. The waiter was standing there indecisively, not knowing what to do. "Monsieur is leaving?" he asked.

"No, monsieur is staying." But halfway through the meal, he put down his fork. He thought of Kitty, her pretty little face set in hurt defiance. He was no longer outraged by her callousness. She was what she was—and he was drawn to her despite her selfishness. He would go comfort her, coax her into laughter—and bed.

Ten minutes later he walked into the ivory and gilt salon on the couturier. Paquin's head *vendeuse* came to greet him. "Madame is in the fitting room," she murmured. "I will tell her you are here."

"No," he said smiling, "I want to surprise her."

"But you must not—" she said hurriedly. Before she could finish he had gone through the tall paneled double doors that led to the fitting rooms and stopped outside a half-open door.

"I adore it," he heard Kitty say, "but it is really too dear."

"Ah, but it is so becoming," the saleswoman said. "You know, Paquin had you in mind when he created this design. It is cut to show off your tiny waist and your *poitrine*."

"And it does," a strange voice said, a male voice. "You must order it, my dear. De Granville will spring for it. It makes you look like a sophisticated shepherdess."

"And what does a sophisticated shepherdess look like?" he heard her demand coquettishly.

"Oh, a bit like a naughty minx. And you are the naughtiest little minx I have ever run across."

Alexandre turned on his heel and made his way down the hall. The *vendeuse* was still standing in the middle of the salon, wringing her hands. "I decided not to surprise Madame," he told her and winked. It seemed the appropriate gesture.

When he returned to the apartment that evening, Kitty was all smiles. Her eyes were warm again. He recognized the look. It signified that she had made love long and well.

"Did you enjoy your afternoon at Paquin's?" he asked politely.

"Immensely! But I know you are going to act like an old bear when you hear what I spent."

"That would hardly be gallant when I know that you are only trying to delight me." His eyes were cold, but all Kitty saw was his smile.

"You are a dear." She stood on tiptoe to kiss him. "I will thank you properly tonight," she promised.

Much later that night as Kitty slipped out of his arms and he turned on his side to sleep, he thought, The little bitch. How often has she betrayed me? And with how many men? He gave a mental shrug. What did it really matter? She was tantalizing and delightful in bed. What more did he want?

He wanted more. His cynicism was purely defensive. He was hurt and shamed by her betrayal. At the same time he realized that he, too, was unfaithful in a way. He was going through the motions of a devoted lover, but the fact was that Kitty bored him dreadfully. Once he had thought her the champagne of his life. Now he realized that champagne in excess led to headaches.

Their life together changed almost imperceptibly. He began spending more time at the V.A.C. and at the house on rue Maubeuge. And Kitty was more and more often away during the day, giving only vague explanations of her whereabouts.

He now saw her as imperious and spoiled rather than enchanting and beguiling. Even his passionate desire for her subsided. He often pretended that it was Dina in his arms, not Kitty—and wished with all his heart that his pretense were true. But there was nothing he could do. There was no way of getting rid of Kitty, even if she was sleeping with half of Paris. He had made her his responsibility.

As for Dina, even though her letters were pleasant enough, he was convinced she would never allow him back in her life. Buswell had cautioned him that his affair with Kitty was known in New York. "They are abuzz with it back home, my boy," he had said. "I told everyone that I had no knowledge of it." That had been an act of staunch friendship, but he was sure that Dina knew the truth. There were times now when he wished that he had never set eyes on Kitty.

What he never suspected was that Kitty, too, was beset by secret feelings. What had begun as a vague concern had escalated into terror. For the first time in her life she was up against a situation that she could not charm or cajole away. She lay awake nights analyzing the alternatives and night by night she grew more terrified. She felt as trapped as any rat, in a trap of her own making.

She was pregnant—and she had no idea who the father might be. Was it Alexandre or Rémy? Or Paul? Or possibly Luc, although she had only slept with him once?

She had nowhere to turn. Alexandre was firmly married even though his wife was an ocean away and seemed unconcerned about their affair. For Dina knew about it. All of New York knew about it. Sam Parseval had written his daughter warning her not to consider returning to New York unless she was accompanied by her husband. The letter had been a heartbreaking mixture of worry and pain that his beloved Kitty had made herself a target for gossip. But his message was clear. She would not be welcome. Nor could

she turn to Bucky's family. They knew full well that she had
not seen Bucky in months.

She had decided she would go to some provincial French
city under an assumed name to have the baby. Then she
would put the infant up for adoption or put it into an
orphanage, whichever seemed more practical. But then
what? Bucky was her only hope. If she could have the baby
with no one knowing, then she would rush back to his
family, grateful for the haven. But how could she keep this a
secret for seven months? How was she to explain her
disappearance?

Money—and she always breathed a sigh of relief when
she thought of it—would be no problem. She would sell the
expensive clothes Alexandre had given her. The furs should
bring a good sum. She had already broached the subject to
her favorite saleswoman at Worth's, saying that she was
bored with some of her clothes and would like to sell them.
The saleswoman had indicated that she was quite used to
dealing with such delicate matters.

But one spring day there was what Kitty considered a
miracle: a telegram from the War Office. Bucky had been
wounded and gassed and was being invalided home. She
turned white as she read it, her hands shook, and she felt
faint at the shock of deliverance. As Thérèse helped her to a
chair and ran for a glass of water, Kitty permitted herself a
smile of triumph. She had her passport to escape.

She would go to Bucky. He was alive. His war was over.
He needed her. And she needed him. No matter how weak
he was, how ill, how incapacitated, there would be a joyful
reunion that would produce a joyous result. And if the baby
were to arrive a little early, who would be surprised? A
woman whose husband had been wounded and gassed must
be under a terrible strain. That would explain everything.

Kitty and Alexandre were going to the opera that evening,
and Kitty had been looking forward to wearing the scarlet
dress with a fishtail train that Lanvin had just finished for

her. Now she asked Thérèse to bring her luggage from the storeroom. There was no time to waste. By the time the maid returned with the bags, Kitty was dressed—dressed as Thérèse had never seen her before. She was wearing a sturdy tweed skirt with a plain silk shirtwaist and a heathery wool cardigan. Her shoes were sensibly low-heeled. They were all part of the trousseau she had assembled so rapidly the past summer for her short honeymoon in Scotland.

The bags filled rapidly as Kitty pulled things from drawers and hangers and Thérèse folded and packed. Thérèse was perplexed. Why was she packing these clothes? Walking skirts, heavy sweaters, woolen underwear, and stockings. Why was she not taking her pretty things?

Kitty went into the little room that she used as a clothes closet. The chic tailleurs and evening dresses that Alexandre had given her hung in rows. She looked at them longingly, but shook her head. She would have no use for them. The evening dresses, perhaps. If Bucky got well and the war ended. But how could she possibly explain them to Bucky or his family? What would a war wife working for the Red Cross be doing with such a luxurious wardrobe? It was not just a matter of money. If was the life those clothes represented.

She fingered the scarlet silk of the new Lanvin. It was the most alluring dress she had ever owned. But it was out of the question. Besides, in a matter of weeks it would no longer fit her.

She went to the telephone and called the saleswoman at Worth's. "I would like you to come immediately," she said. "It is an emergency." When she arrived, Kitty took her into the little room and gestured to the clothes. "I must sell these. All of them," she said. "My husband is wounded and I must go to him."

"But Monsieur de Granville," the woman began tactlessly.

"Forget Monsieur de Granville," Kitty said impatiently. "I must sell these. Can you do it for me? I will give you a ten percent commission."

The saleswoman looked around appraisingly at the little suits and afternoon dresses. At the evening gowns. The coats. The chic hats. One side of the room was taken up by Kitty's furs. An everyday black seal. A sable. An ermine evening cape. A small fortune had been spent on these clothes, she thought.

"You are free to sell them?" she asked cautiously.

"Of course," Kitty snapped.

"I will not be able to get even half of what they cost," she said. "You must understand that. If you still want to sell them, I will be glad to do it for you."

This was no time to haggle. "All right," Kitty agreed, "but you must take everything with you now. Immediately. I will have a taxi called for you."

"And where shall I send the money?"

"To Worth's in London, of course. That is why I chose you. It should be possible for you to get the money there one way or another."

The woman nodded. "It will not be easy, but it can be done."

Half an hour later, the little room was empty.

When Alexandre came home, Kitty's luggage was piled in the hall. Her traveling coat and an umbrella were on a chair. He was startled, not the least by Kitty in her tweedy costume.

"What's going on?"

"It's Bucky." She showed him the telegram. "He's been wounded. And gassed."

"But why must you rush off? What can you possibly do? If he's been gassed, his lungs are probably shot. He may not be able to speak or—" he hesitated, "or do anything."

Kitty looked at him. "My place is with my husband," she said abruptly, her face newly stern. "My taxi will be here shortly. Will you go to the station with me?"

\*      \*      \*

He walked back to the apartment after seeing Kitty off. It was raining, but he welcomed it. He felt in need of a cleansing. It had been hard to disguise his relief at her departure. But yet—now that she had left on the first leg of her roundabout route to London, he felt lonely. Suddenly and bitterly lonely. And angry at himself.

He had fallen into the kind of life his father had led, not even considering that the pursuit of pleasure had not been particularly rewarding for his father. It had led to a lonely death in an empty room with only a bottle of brandy for companionship and courage. He had left nothing to his son but a humble note of apology. That charming, spirited man with a score of friends had deserved more from life. But you had to earn it, Alexandre told himself.

Tears mingled with the rain on his cheeks. For the first time he felt sorry for his father. Poor, foolish man.

And for the first time he understood how secure he had become in Dina's love, secure enough to rebel against it like a spoiled child who was never satisfied. Who was he to have criticized Kitty? Even to himself? He was as spoiled as she was. Tramping along beside the Seine, his head bent against the rain, he realized how deeply he loved Dina. Would he ever see her again? He thought not. He had burned his bridges behind him. There was no going back. What a fool he had been. He felt physically ill.

The apartment was cold and unwelcoming. He shivered in his wet clothes. There was no comfort here for him. He wandered into Kitty's wardrobe room. There was nothing left. Just empty hangers and the lingering scent of *Je Reviens*. He thought of all the diamonds taken from Aunt Marita's necklace to buy those luxurious costumes.

Aunt Marita's necklace. It was a necklace no longer, simply a handful of stones. He must have been mad. With the money he could have rented several houses, provided shelter for a hundred refugees and their children. He sat down, his elbows on his knees, his head in his hands. His life was ruined, and he had ruined it himself. He had lost his wife and his daughter. His shoulders shook.

The next morning he walked into Ned Buswell's office at the ambulance corps. "I've had enough of Paris," he declared. "I want to go to the front. If you can send me with an ambulance, fine. If not, I'll volunteer as an orderly in the French medical corps."

Ned looked at him keenly. Alexandre was haggard, his voice hoarse. Little Kitty must have shown her claws, he thought. He clapped Alexandre on the shoulder. "If that's what you want, I can send you to the front four days from now."

# Eighteen

THE DAY BEFORE Alexandre left for the front, he paid a visit to Lucie Soerbijk. They sat at the table in the large kitchen. She poured him a cup of the bitter chicory brew that served as a substitute for coffee and waited to hear what was on his mind. His face was strained and his attitude formal. She was worried. Was he going to tell her that he could no longer provide for them? Had that haughty blonde bitch stripped him of everything before leaving him?

He placed a thick envelope and a small package that was securely wrapped and tied on the table. He adjusted his tie nervously. All his former jauntiness and verve had disappeared. He handed her the envelope.

"This is for you. I have left enough money to run the house for the next few months. I will be back in Paris from time to time, but just in case——" His voice trailed off. "I've also given you the name and address of the man who heads the Ambulance Corps, Mr. Edward Buswell. When you have enough lace made, take it to him. He will see that it gets to New York and that you get your money.

"The package is something else." He picked it up. It was

small. It fit in the palm of his hand. "Something personal. And valuable. Will you keep it safe for me?" He hesitated. "And if, by chance, you should hear that I am not coming back—"

She crossed herself. "No, no. Do not say that."

"In wartime, no one knows. So, if you will, please take care of this for me. And if one day Mr. Buswell should tell you that I will not be coming back, please open it. I have left written instructions—in Flemish—inside about what to do with the contents. I know that I can trust you." He leaned back now, somewhat relaxed. "Will you do this for me?"

"Whatever you ask, I will do," she said firmly. "Any one of us would be grateful for a chance to be of service to you."


The summer went by like a bad dream. At the front, Alexandre made no friends. He had no time. Except for the few hours when he fell onto his cot like a dead man, he was shuttling the wounded from the trenches to the field hospital and sometimes to civilian and military hospitals well behind the lines. He spent his days and nights alone with his groaning cargo of wounded except for an occasional dinner with the French colonel in charge of the field hospital, Jean-Luc Chandon. Alexandre looked forward to these evenings. They ate well and drank better in the colonel's quarters. Chandon was cynical and witty, eminently civilized. He had no illusions that he was fighting a war to end all wars.

"That is nonsense," he said, holding his wine glass against the candlelight. "What we are doing is fighting the barbarians, trying to push back the darkness. They will probably win," the colonel said bleakly, "because they have nothing to lose."

Alexandre disagreed. "We will win, and for just that reason. We have everything to lose."

*    *    *

Autumn with its cold and damp brought coughs that turned
into pneumonia, scratches that developed into raging infec-
tions, diarrhea that escalated into dysentery. No one was
immune. Alexandre had a hacking cough that shook his
body and left him exhausted, but when Colonel Chandon
ordered him to Paris on leave, he refused. He manned the
ambulance night and day. Occasionally he slept while waiting for the wounded to be loaded into the back, his head
cradled in his arms on the steering wheel. The whole thing
was like a dream. There was no end to it. Back and forth,
back and forth, with his load of the wounded, the dying,
and—too often—the dead. Sometimes he thought he was
driving the same men trip after trip.

His cough was worse and he had a fever, but there was
nothing to do except go on. He drove like a madman, intent
on getting the wounded to the medics as fast as possible. He
was in a race with death. And death seemed to be winning.
One night he reached the field hospital hardly realizing he
was there. One of the doctors, unshaven, his smock spattered
with blood, opened the door. "You had better come with
me, my friend."

"No, I cannot let death win," Alexandre mumbled,
suddenly so deeply tired he could barely speak.

"Come with me. I will help you fight death," the doctor
said. He took Alexandre's arm. "Come." Alexandre tried
to pull away, but he had no strength. His vision blurred. He
toppled sideways into the doctor's arms.

When Colonel Chandon left the operating table that day,
the doctor told him that Alexandre had collapsed. "Our
Alexandre was talking to death," he reported. "I think he
may be closer to death than he knew."

Alexandre opened his eyes, then closed them again. He lay
there listening. Voices. The clink of glass. Quick footsteps.
Where was he? He did not care. He sank back into oblivion.

An hour later he opened his eyes again. It took a long
time for him to register what he was seeing. A long room.

Both long walls lines with beds. A hospital, of course. A nurse came over. She looked at him and smiled, then went away. She came back with a doctor.

"Good morning," the doctor said.

"Good morning." The words were a mumble. A tremendous effort.

"You have been ill," the doctor said. "But you are better now. Your fever is gone. You will begin to regain your strength soon." He turned to the nurse. "Try him on a few spoonfuls of broth every half hour."

He fell asleep as the doctor spoke. He was not conscious of the doctor and nurse leaving his bedside. Some time later he woke again. The nurse was sitting beside his bed. Raising his head with one arm, she fed him a spoonful of broth. And another. He tried to turn his head away. He could not swallow more.

"Enough? You have done well," she said encouragingly. "I will be back later." He fell asleep again. The day was a series of brief awakenings when he was fed a few spoonfuls of broth or coaxed to sip water. The next day he ate more. The day after that, the nurse propped him up in bed for a little while. And only then did he ask, "Where am I?"

"You are in Lyons. In the hospital." He nodded. That was enough.

A few days later he was allowed out of bed. First to sit in a chair and then, leaning heavily on the nurse, to walk a few steps down the ward. He was alarmed by his weakness. "What's wrong with me?" he asked. "Why am I so weak?"

"You were very ill," the nurse said. "The doctor will tell you about it. He is going to talk to you tonight after his rounds."

"Do you remember anything?" the doctor asked that evening, pulling a chair up beside his bed.

"Anything?"

"About your illness."

"No, I remember the *Boches* attacked. The fighting went

on night and day. I lost track of time. The wounded—some of them I had to leave to die—'' He coughed. The doctor waited. ''I remember being tired,'' he said slowly. ''Tired. And dirty. The men had lice, you know. So did I. They were everywhere. My hair. My body.''

''Yes,'' the doctor confirmed. ''You were in such a state when they brought you in that I thought you had been in the trenches.''

''And then—'' Alexandre stopped. ''That's all I remember. I was driving. I could not go fast enough. But,'' he looked at the doctor, ''I was not sick. I don't remember being ill. I had a cough. Everyone had a cough.''

''You collapsed with a raving case of influenza after driving night and day for a week,'' the doctor said. ''You must have been sick on your feet for days. If Jean-Luc Chandon had not had you brought to Lyons—'' He did not complete the sentence.

''Chandon.'' Alexandre smiled. ''A good man.''

''And a good friend,'' the doctor said. ''He has been concerned about you.'' He looked at the file he was holding. ''You must have an iron constitution. I don't mind telling you now that I was not at all sure that you would pull through. But you're on the mend,'' he said heartily. ''You're going to be as good as new, but it will take time.''

''How much time?''

''I can't tell. Some weeks. Possibly months. You ran a high fever for over a fortnight. I plan to discharge you in a few days if you continue to improve. Send you back to Paris. You must take it very easy. No climbing stairs. No excitement. Eat and sleep. And when you recover from the trip, walk a little to build up some strength. And when you are a little stronger, go home. Go home to your family. With rest, as I said, you will be as strong as you ever were.''

''I can't do that.''

The doctor misunderstood. ''There'll be no problem. Colonel Chandon has been in touch with the head of the Ambulance Corps in Paris. They will provide transportation to New York for you. You don't have to worry about anything. Just concentrate on resting and getting well.''

Alexandre was silent. What was there to say? This young doctor with the circles under his eyes had no time for the story of a man with no home to go to. He sighed.

"You're tired," the doctor said. "Sleep. It's the best thing for you. You will be in Paris next week." He put his hand on Alexandre's shoulder. "I'll check on you again tomorrow night."

He started to leave and then turned back. "I almost forgot. You have been awarded the Croix de Guerre. For a while there we thought they might have to give it to you posthumously."

The train ride to Paris was slow and exhausting. There had been many long halts as the train was shunted off to sidings to permit military supply trains to go through. Alexandre was not sure he had the strength to walk down the platform and into the station, much less search for a taxi. When he saw Ned Buswell waiting on the platform, tears of relief filled his eyes, even while he cursed himself for his weakness.

Buswell was shocked. Alexandre looked ten years older. There was a streak of gray in his black hair now. He was thin as a rail and hollow-eyed as a caricature of death. Buswell took him by the arm.

"I've got a car waiting. I'm going to take you straight to your hotel."

"No, take me to the house on rue Maubeuge."

"That tenement with the refugees?" Buswell asked in astonishment. "You don't want to go there now. You need to rest. You can see them in another day or two."

"No, I'm going to stay there. They will take care of me."

"You can't," Buswell protested. "They have no facilities. You will be far more comfortable in a hotel."

"Ned, that tenement and those refugees are the closest thing I've got to a home and a family."

Buswell looked at him sharply. Was he feverish? He seemed rational enough except for this last statement. He shrugged and much against his better judgment directed the driver to the rue Maubeuge. He helped Alexandre out. "I'll come by tomorrow to check on you. Get some rest." He looked at the grim facade of the tenement. "If you can," he added.

The door opened. Half a dozen children bounced out onto the sidewalk and were scolded back inside by Madame Soerbijk. "Can I help you—?" she started and then recognized Alexandre. "Monsieur, it is you! Oh! Oh! You must not stand here. Come." She took his arm and led him in. As they went through the door, she turned her head to Buswell. "Never fear, monsieur. We shall take good care of him."

She led him straight into the kitchen. There was the familiar fragrance of soup. She sat him at the table and, exclaiming over how much weight he had lost, put a bowl of soup and some bread in front of him. She smiled. "Do you remember? Soup and bread was the first meal you gave me and my children. Now it is the first meal I give you. Eat. I will be back shortly." She shooed the curious children out of the kitchen in front of her.

Alexandre slumped in the chair, almost too tired to lift the spoon, but he did. The soup was good, although he could not finish it. When she returned, he joked feebly, "If I recall, I also gave you a glass of wine with that first meal."

"You too shall have a glass of wine," she promised, "but first you must go to bed." She helped him up and led him down the narrow hall to a room at the back of the house. It was empty except for a freshly made bed and a wooden table. She took off his shoes and his coat. She untied his tie and unbuttoned his shirt. She took off his trousers, undressing him like a child, and pulled the coarse sheet and rough blanket over him. "Sleep now. Later I will bring you more soup and that glass of wine."

\* \* \*

It had been too much for him. He had a relapse. It was
Christmas before the doctor, hastily summoned by Ned
Buswell when Lucie Soerbijk arrived wild-eyed at his office
on the Place de la Concorde, allowed him to sit up in bed.
And it was New Year's Day when he was allowed to walk
the few steps between his bed and a chair near the window.
It was still longer before he ventured down the narrow
hallway, leaning on Lucie Soerbijk's arm, to sip weak tea in
the kitchen. After that he regained his strength slowly but
surely. He spent hours helping the children with their
homework and drilling them in French. And when the weather
permitted he went out for short walks in the afternoon with
Janine Soerbijk, almost nine, as his companion. She was a
bright and charming child and a revelation to him. He had
never spent time with a child before. He often thought of
Vicky and wished that she was by his side, holding onto his
hand and skipping down the street. Would he recognize her,
he wondered, if he saw her? So much time had passed.

In the evenings he often sat and talked with Lucie. They
had become close during his illness. He had been helpless.
She had fed him and bathed him, cared for him as if he had
been one of her children. It was inevitable as he grew
stronger that they would find themselves together in bed.
And one afternoon when she woke him from his nap with
the tonic prescribed by the doctor, he had held out his arms
to her and she had responded willingly.

"Lucie, Lucie," he murmured later, his head pillowed on
her arm. "I need you so much. What would I do without
you?"

She smiled at him. "You need a woman," she said. "It is
not natural for a man to be alone for so long."

"And I needed a man," she thought to herself. "But not
this one." She still did not understand why this man who
obviously moved in the highest ranks of society and had
maintained that expensive mistress should have concerned
himself with the welfare of a group of Belgian refugees.
Should have spent so much money on providing for them.

What concern was it of his? She was baffled, but nevertheless grateful.

Lying there in the narrow bed, she thought of her husband. She had recently received word that he was safe and well. She had sent word back through the same channels that she and the children were not only well, but prospering in Paris.

It was true, she thought contentedly. With peasant frugality she had squirreled away all her earnings from lace making. Let the other women spend those small earnings on themselves. She scorned such indulgence.

"We will need every *centime* we can scrape together when we go home after the war," she told Janine, who had become her confidante. "The Germans will have taken everything. We will have to start from scratch." She had hidden the slowly accumulating francs of her little hoard in the hiding place she had found far from the rue Maubeuge. When she and her husband were reunited, she would have a nice surprise for him. A second dowry, she thought with placid satisfaction.

Alexandre stretched luxuriously and then burrowed his head between her breasts. "I could stay here forever," he said. After a moment he got up on his elbow and looked at her. "Lucie, what would you think," he asked, "if I were to find a small apartment for us? And the children, of course."

She looked at him. "An apartment!" She was truly astonished. "I have been worrying about asking you for money. I did not want to bother you while you were ill, but the money you left—it has all been spent. Monsieur Buswell gave me some more, but that has gone now too."

"My God!" He was conscience-stricken. "How could I have been so thoughtless? You should have told me before. Don't worry," he reassured her. "If you will give that package I asked you to keep for me when I left last spring, I will take care of everything. Where is it?"

"I don't have it here," she told him. "I did not know

what to do with it. There was no place to hide it in this house.''

His heart leapt within his chest. "You don't have it!" He sat straight up in bed. "For God's sake, what did you do with it?" He had never spoken so harshly to a woman. But he was in a panic. Without the diamonds he had nothing. What an idiot he had been to have entrusted Lucie with the package. Anyone with a grain of common sense would have asked Ned Buswell to keep it in the safe at the Ambulance Corps office for him. But no, he had to play the romantic and entrust all that he had left in the world to this peasant whom he barely knew.

"It is in a safe place," Lucie said, alarmed by his reaction. The blood had drained from his face, leaving him pale as a ghost. "It is just not here."

"Where is it, damn it! And wherever it is, get it for me." She had never dreamed that this gentle man possessed such anger. Intimidated, she whispered, "I buried it."

"Buried it! Where?"

"In the cemetery," she said simply.

Suddenly his anger disappeared and he laughed. "Very suitable," he said. "But now it is time to resurrect it."

When Lucie brought Alexandre his supper that evening, she reached into her apron pocket and handed him the box. It was earth-stained and slightly damp, but intact. He asked her to wait while he opened it.

"I left this with you in case something happened to me. There are a few precious stones." The diamonds tumbled out onto the palm of his hand. "You could have sold these to keep the house going. And then this was a note for you." He crumpled it and tossed it aside. "I gave you my wife's address in New York so that if you had any problems, you could get in touch with her. She would have helped you."

"Fortunately I did not have to open your package. You came back," she said. "And soon, I think, you will be going home to your wife."

He sighed. "I do not think so."

\*   \*   \*

Later that night, after she checked that the kitchen was clean and everything was ready for the morning, she sat down at the table and stared into the distance. After a while she got up and went to the door. "Janine!" she called her daughter.

Janine came running. "Yes, mother."

"Monsieur Alexandre says your French is very good. Is it good enough to write a letter?"

"I think so. If it is an easy letter."

"Very well. You wait here. I will get some paper." She went down the hall to Alexandre's room. He was sleeping. She took the box and the crumpled letter. Back in the kitchen, she tore open the envelope and took out the letter he had written her almost a year earlier. Just as he had said, there was his wife's address.

"I will tell you what to say in Flemish," she told Janine, "and you will write it in your very best French." It was hard to start. She was silent for a long time, thinking of various beginnings and deciding against them all. Finally she spoke:

"Dear Madame de Granville, your husband has been seriously ill. He collapsed while driving an ambulance at the front. It was influenza. He was ill for a long time in the hospital. He is still not strong.

"He should be at home with his family. I believe that is where he wants to be, but for some reason he thinks he cannot go. I do not know your feelings, but if you love him, it is important that you ask him to come home. He is very lonely."

Janine wrote diligently. "Monsieur is lonely?" she asked in amazement as her mother fell silent. "How can he be? We are always with him."

"I know," her mother said. "But he has a little girl of his own. And a wife. I think he misses them very much. Just as your papa misses us."

"Poor monsieur," Janine said understandingly. She looked

at the letter. "I hope she can read it. There may be some mistakes." She looked at her mother anxiously.

"I am sure she will be able to read it," her mother said, smoothing back the child's hair. "Remember, this is our secret."

"I know. I told you I can keep secrets," she said. "May I go play with Gabrielle now?"

"For a few minutes. It is almost time for bed."

Lucie sat there a few more minutes. She folded the letter and put it in an envelope. She brought the box back to Alexandre's room, but before leaving it on the table, she took out the little bag of diamonds and put them in the toe of his shoe. They would be safe there for tonight.

# Nineteen

EARLY ONE RAINY MORNING, soon after Dina had returned to New York that first autumn without Alexandre, the telephone rang while she was supervising the installation of a sandbox in Vicky's third-floor playroom. Anna came running up the stairs to say that Mrs. Schumacher was calling.

"Dina—your father—I think he's had a stroke. I've called Dr. Godfrey." Isabelle's voice was thin and reedy with distress.

"I'll be right there," Dina said. The household was shocked into action. Burns, the chauffeur, ran to bring the car around front. Siddie stationed herself at the door with raincoat, hat, and gloves. Walter was instructed to cancel her luncheon engagement. Vicky was given a quick kiss and a hug. And ten minutes later Dina was running up the front steps of her father's Murray Hill brownstone.

"It was so fast," Isabelle said. "He was sitting at the table. He said he had not slept well and didn't feel like having breakfast. I poured him some coffee. He picked up his cup. And then he dropped it. He looked at me and started to say something and then—oh, Dina, he looked so surprised!—and then he fell off the chair." Isabelle's voice broke into a sob. Dina put her arms around her and let her cry. Tears were running down her own face.

Dr. Godfrey was grave when he joined the two women waiting for him in the upstairs sitting room at the end of the hall. "Your husband has had a severe stroke, Mrs. Schumacher. There is some paralysis. I can't tell how extensive or how permanent at this point. Right now it is in the hands of God. I will come by again this afternoon."

After she had seen the doctor to the door, Isabelle came back and sat beside Dina. She had regained her composure. "You will have to take over," she said. "Your father would want you to. He told me years ago that if anything ever happened to him, you should take his place. He said that you could run the business as well as he could."

Dina was aghast. "Take over from Papa!" she exclaimed. "Never! I could never do it."

"Nonsense," Isabelle said briskly. "Your father has great respect for your capabilities. He has often told me that you've a better brain than most of the men on Wall Street. Besides, it is what he wants," she concluded.

"But I'm so out of touch," Dina said slowly. It was a completely new idea to her. But not *so* new at that. There had been many years before she married Alexandre when she had been deeply engrossed in her father's business. She stood up. "You're right. I was talking nonsense. I'll do my best to keep things going until Papa is better."

"Why don't you tell him so?" Isabelle suggested. "I don't know whether he can understand you or not. But if he can, it will reassure him."

The two women walked down the hall to the bedroom. The nurse whom the doctor had brought was sitting beside the bed. "He is conscious," she whispered. One side of Frederick's face was drawn up in a grimace. His eyes were closed. Dina took his hand. "Don't worry, Papa," she said softly. "Everything is going to be all right. You are going to be fine. I'll take care of things at the office until you are better." His hand was limp. There was no change in his expression. "I'll come back tomorrow, Papa," she said, "after I've been to the office."

It was raining hard when she left. She directed Burns to drive downtown to her father's office. She looked out the window at the rainy city seeing nothing. Papa was ill. Very ill. She had to take charge. Nothing would ever be the same again.

It had been years since she had visited the office. Herbert and Gwillim, her father's two right-hand men, were grayer, a little shrunken. There was a new office boy. But the most striking change was the general shabbiness. The office, which had always seemed to reflect a dignified opulence, looked seedy. The leather upholstery was cracked. The carpeting threadbare. The curtains limp. Only Alexandre's office retained an air of prosperous elegance. It had been newly furnished for him just after they were married, while the rest of the office, she suddenly realized, dated from her father's first days in New York. No wonder it was shabby. Something would have to be done about it.

She sat at her father's huge desk and summoned Herbert to brief her on the current state of affairs. He brought his ledgers and settled down to review each of her father's various interests. There were surprisingly few of them. Frederick was heavily invested in mining ventures as might be expected from a man who had made his first fortune in mining, but most of the rest of his capital was in gold, which was sitting in the vaults doing nothing.

She had always known that her father had been shaken by the Panic of 1907, but just how deeply she only understood now. It was clear that he had resolved to protect himself against the fate so many had suffered then. Herbert quite obviously approved of his employer's defensive position with every cell of his bookkeeping heart, but Dina quietly resolved that her first priority the next morning would be to

check the gold market. Some of this dormant capital had to
be transformed into working assets as rapidly and unobtrusively
as possible. If a significant amount of gold were to be put
on the market, the price would weaken. Nor could she
afford to have rumors spring up that Schumacher & de
Granville was in a cash bind. She would have to find some
way to unload the gold gradually without letting the word
get around about what she was doing. It would be an
interesting maneuver, she thought excitedly, if she could
pull it off. She thanked Herbert and settled down to go over
the books by herself.

It was after ten o'clock that night before she pushed the
high-backed chair away from the desk and rubbed her eyes.
She now had a general grasp of the situation, and it shocked
her, just as the shabbiness of the office had shocked her.

Alexandre had been right when he used to criticize her
father's way of doing business. Papa was old-fashioned. He
had not changed with the times. This giant of a man who
had come roaring out of the West with his new millions,
determined to make a splash on Wall Street, had succeeded
beyond even his own most optimistic fantasies. But in the
past few years he seemed to have lost interest.

Perhaps it was the happiness he had found in his marriage
with Isabelle, Dina thought. He no longer needed to show
the world. Whatever it was, Schumacher & de Granville
had become a pleasant one-man investment firm—a little
slow, a bit idiosyncratic, extremely conservative, safe. If it
was still a force in the marketplace it was simply because it
had been able to coast on its former reputation. And that
was not going to carry it much further.

She stood up and stretched and then sat down at the desk
again. She reviewed the figures she had jotted down during
the evening. There was a lot to do. And the sooner the
better. The office and its staff had to be brought up-to-date.
Herbert and Gwillim were invaluable, but she needed younger
blood, too. Brighter, more aggressive men more tuned in to
the world. And she needed a secretary. Papa's longtime

secretary, Miss Althorpe, was capable and trustworthy, but it had become clear to Dina during the afternoon that the older woman would resent being put under pressure. She would put her in charge of the files. And they would need a stenographer. Probably two. And . . . She smiled. She could hardly wait to get started.

She stood up and stretched again—a long, luxurious stretch—and realized how bone weary she was. It was midnight. She picked up her raincoat from the leather couch where she had dropped it more than twelve hours before. Burns was still waiting in the reception room, half asleep. "I'm ready to leave," she told him as he jumped up and straightened the tunic of his chauffeur's uniform. She switched off the lights and locked the door behind her. She had made a start.

Dina plunged into the world that she loved. It was the talk of the financial community. A woman at the helm! Even one as financially canny as Schumacher's daughter. She would not stay the course, they told each other. Old Frederick would bellow in anger if he only knew what she was doing. But she knew what she was doing and within months the initial flurry of shock and disapproval had subsided and now, over lunch at their clubs, they spoke of her shrewdness and deft sense of timing.

The clubs symbolized the male establishment that was arrayed against her, a Goliath to her David. Her male competitors exchanged tips and gossip over their noontime chops and steaks in the dining rooms of these masculine strongholds. They did business over cigars in the smoking rooms. There was no point in her trying to breach their walls. She would fail. And she did not intend to be linked with failure, at least in the business sphere. It was enough that her husband was carrying on a blatant affair in Paris and that all of New York knew about it. She bided her time, and when the opportunity to restore the balance presented itself, she seized it.

*        *        *

Ephraim Fleming, owner of a Pennsylvania armaments plant, had made an appointment to discuss his expansion plans and his concomitant need for additional capital.

The meeting had gone well. Fleming's initial reservations about doing business with a woman (he had only made the appointment because he had heard a rumor—discreetly circulated by Dina herself—that the firm was floating in an ocean of cash) had disappeared when she showed her understanding of his needs and told him flatly that his expansion plans were too limited.

"You must be bolder," she informed him, her blue eyes wide and earnest. "You are going to have more customers for your guns than you can satisfy with your projected expansion. Not only the Europeans, but our own country as well. It is inevitable that we become involved in the war sooner or later. Your chief problem, as I see it, is to design your expansion so that it can be converted to peacetime needs with minimum delay once the war is over. You don't want to be saddled with an enormous plant and work force and have no markets.

"I have one or two suggestions that you might like to consider . . ." She interrupted herself. "I see that is well after twelve o'clock and I am sure you are hungry. Shall we continue our discussion over lunch?"

This was no casual invitation. The night before she had stopped on her way home to see Louis Sherry at his fashionable Fifth Avenue restaurant and asked his help.

"A man's meal, Mr. Sherry," she had requested. "Simple, but the very best. And wine. And," she smiled at him, "I must also ask you to select the cigars. I put myself completely in your hands."

Sherry returned her smile. "Everything will be as it should be," he promised. "Everything will be superb." Frederick and Isabelle Schumacher were valued clients and he had a feeling that Dina would be, too.

Sherry had chosen wisely and Ephraim Fleming had

relished his meal. Now Dina opened her father's humidor and offered him a choice of cigars. When he hesitated, she laughed. "I am well accustomed to cigar smoke. Both my father and my husband enjoy cigars. Besides, I am a businesswoman."

Once his cigar was lit and he had leaned back in the comfortable wing chair, newly upholstered as was the rest of the furniture in her elegantly refurbished office, Dina outlined her ideas on converting his plant from arms to consumer goods when peace was declared.

Fleming looked at this elegant woman with the gleaming rose-copper hair and alabaster skin with some surprise. He had expected shrewdness, but not the imagination and daring she displayed. He was silent for a moment. Then he spoke. "Interesting," he said. "But what you suggest involves more capital than I . . ."

"Ah, but that's where we can be of use to each other," she said. She leaned forward. He caught the faint scent of her perfume. "Can we speak confidentially?" Her lapis lazuli eyes looked straight into his.

He put his cigar down. "Go ahead."

"I can give you what you need. I am convinced you are a good investment for us. Our firm can handle your needs without outside financing. You will not have a gaggle of stockholders demanding this and that. But things must be done discreetly."

He frowned. "I don't understand."

"Gold." The word rang in the air between them.

"Gold?"

"Gold. We have a large fraction of our assets in gold. If I sell my quantity, the price will be depressed. And it if is known that Schumacher & de Granville is selling gold, there are those who will drive the market down even lower. Our firm would be weakened."

"I understand." He drew on his cigar and let the smoke out slowly, reflectively. "What we are talking about is a private arrangement."

"Exactly. I can deliver gold at today's market price. You can convert it to cash as you need it. If you are careful—and lucky—you may be able to do better than today's price."

"And if I'm not lucky?"

She smiled. "We make our own luck, Mr. Fleming. I would not propose this if I were not sure that you knew how to manipulate the market."

"It's a deal," he told her.

She stood up and held out her hand. "It's a deal," she repeated. "And it is a pleasure doing business with you. I think we will be making money together for many years to come."

"I can return the compliment. It is a pleasure doing business with you. And I hope that the next time I am in New York you will permit me to return your hospitality."

Dina was triumphant. She now had significant participation in Fleming Armaments, and she had made a start in converting that hoard of gold into a profit-making asset. She would recover her original investment in a very short time. And best of all, no one would know that she was a major shareholder of Fleming Armaments until and unless she decided to sell some or all of her holdings.

A few more investments like this and she would have whittled their gold holdings down to a reasonable proportion of their assets.

Her second luncheon included eleven men—businessmen, brokers, bankers, and politicians. The food was superb, the wines equally so, and the conversation, deftly steered by the hostess, was both stimulating and informative. When the waiters from Sherry's cleared the table and poured the coffee, Dina rose and gestured to the sideboard, which held an array of bottles and her father's humidor. She excused herself gracefully. "I will leave you gentlemen to your cigars," she said, and slipped away to dictate notes of what she had learned—and to act upon the more interesting information before the stock market closed, and while her guests dawdled over their cigars.

Invitations to the luncheons soon became coveted. The food was the best in the city. The guest list was highly exclusive, and one way or another the guests found the luncheons profitable. As time went by, however, she began to feel the need for a host—someone who would linger over coffee with her guests and pass the cigars after she had excused herself. Someone who could monitor the all-male conversation after she left. No matter how bright she was, how charming, this was a man's world and she would always be on the outside.

"I need a business partner. A man," she decided. A man who could act as host to her hostess, a man who could smoke with her guests after she left. A man who would attract those investors and firms who steadfastly refused to do business with a woman, even Frederick Schumacher's daughter.

He should be intelligent and energetic. No figurehead. He had to have more than charm. She thought of Ephraim Fleming. What a partner *he* would make. Together they could turn Schumacher & de Granville into the most powerful firm on Wall Street, but he had his hands full with his own concerns.

But he might have some suggestions. She saw Ephraim often now. He was a shrewd and kind man, a good judge of human nature. They had become friends of a sort. Their mutual interest was the world of finance with all its permutations. Ephraim often gave her tips about companies in the Pittsburgh area and she shared her appreciation of trends in the money market with him. She would not mind asking his advice. He, possibly more than anyone else, would understand.

The next time he dropped into her office, she offered him a cigar during the course of their conversation.

"You are a connoisseur of cigars," he remarked. "The first time we met I hesitated to accept one. I thought—what can a woman know about cigars? I discovered that your taste in cigars is flawless. As in most other things."

She laughed. "I can't really take credit for the cigars. Louis Sherry chose them for me. I told him I wanted the best. But I'm happy you approve. I want you in a good mood, because I need advice."

"Ah ha!" He clipped the end of the cigar and lit it, waiting for her to continue.

"I need a partner, Ephraim. I am willing to make the right man a senior partner. In fact, I don't want anyone who does not have the potential to be a senior partner.

"We are doing so much business now that I cannot handle it all. It would be folly even to try. Besides that, I am losing out on business that I should have—just because I am a woman. My weekly luncheons have worked out well, but I am missing the most valuable part because I feel it necessary to excuse myself when the brandy and cigars are passed. I know just how much of my company these men are ready to welcome or tolerate. If I only knew what they were talking about over their brandy, these luncheons would be even more useful, and more profitable. But I don't know. And if I did stay in the dining room, the conversation would be inhibited. I would be no better off. So—"

"I understand." He drew on his cigar and let the smoke out slowly. "I think you're right. The right man though...Do you have anyone in mind?"

"If I didn't have such a profitable investment in Fleming Armaments, I would try to convince you to come in with me. It has to be someone approaching your caliber."

"You'll have to pay, of course."

"I told you. The right man can be a senior partner. And a senior partner of Schumacher & de Granville ...Ephraim, you know how well we're doing."

"I do. And I think I have just the gentleman for you. Whittaker Ames. He's a cold fish, but brilliant. He's a lawyer and vice president of the Broad Street Bank in Philadelphia. Comes from Boston. In his late thirties I would say. Not married. He's a worker. The kind of man who sets goals for himself. You know—promises himself he'll be head of this or that and worth so much by a certain time. And *then* he'll think about marriage.''

"I've met him," she said. "At my father's. He's been there once or twice for dinner. And at the Prentices'. I thought he was quite handsome in a lean, patrician way, but very distant. As a matter of fact, I sat next to him at dinner once. He was a good conversationalist. I rather liked him. And as I recall, he wasn't all that distant once he got started talking.''

"That's Whit," Ephraim said. "He's the original reserved New Englander, but I suspect there's a lot of fire under that cold exterior. He's ambitious.''

"Why should he want to leave the Broad Street Bank?"

"I think he's come to the conclusion it doesn't offer him enough scope. I was talking with him the other day. We're both on the Pittsville board of directors. I got the impression that he was restless, looking for broader fields to conquer. He might suit you.''

"I'll talk to him then," she said. "It can't hurt.''

"He's in town," Ephraim said. "I ran into him at Delmonico's last night. He's staying at the Waldorf-Astoria.''

"Good. I'll make an appointment with him," she said. "And now, tell me, what's your forecast for raw steel production next year? How much of an increase do you expect?''

That night before she went to bed, she thought seriously about Whittaker Ames. He was certainly worth considering. She would get a note off to him first thing in the morning. She would ask him to dinner. That would be best.

She mobilized the household in order to make it a memorable dinner. Céleste was encouraged to pull out all her culinary stops. Walter and Anna were given to understand that the easy ways they had fallen into since she had been alone would not be tolerated on this occasion.

"It is a business dinner, Walter," she instructed. "And although Mr. Ames will be the only guest, the service must be as formal as if we were twelve at table."

"I understand, ma'am."

"We will have coffee and brandy in the library. I may want to offer him champagne later on. Céleste should prepare a plate of small sandwiches and another of petit fours to serve with it. Just in case."

"Very well, ma'am." Walter nodded gravely, but when he was back in the kitchen with Céleste and Anna, he could hardly contain his excitement.

"She calls it a business dinner," he told them. "But Mr. Ames is the only guest. And I am to serve champagne at midnight. Funny business, I call it."

Céleste looked at him disapprovingly. "It is her business, not ours," she said in her French-accented English. "And if she wants to entertain a gentleman, where better than in her own home where everything can be as she wishes?

"I shall prepare a dinner that he will remember." She started going through her dog-eared notebook. "Something light so they will not feel dull. Perhaps my veal roast with the spinach stuffing," she murmured. "And afterwards, a *soufflé surprise*. No, better the chocolate roll with hazelnut cream."

Even Vicky's nanny got in on the act. "Shall I bring Miss Vicky downstairs to say good night?" she asked Dina. "She looks such an angel in that pink-and-white dressing gown."

"I think not, Nanny," Dina said, hiding her amusement. "Mr. Ames is a bachelor and may not be comfortable with children. And this is a business dinner. I don't feel it would be appropriate."

Nanny humphed her way upstairs, feeling that her small charge had somehow been slighted. "I should think she would be happy to have little Vicky come down and make her curtsy and say good night. It would show that she is not like some women I could mention."

"Ah, you don't know Mrs. de Granville," Siddie soothed

her. "When it is a matter of business, she is all business. I remember before she was married, she used to spend hours studying the stock market and reading long reports when other young women were out enjoying themselves."

And when the evening arrived, even Dina felt some of the excitement that she had generated in the others. "Siddie, help me off with this dress," she said with sudden determination. "I'm going to wear the gray silk."

"But you look lovely," Siddie protested. Dina was wearing a low-necked gown of amethyst, all fine pleats that made her look like a Grecian goddess.

"Perhaps, but it's not the right mood. It's too festive. Get the gray out. And please change my hair. Pull it back."

Siddie sighed. The gray was so subdued. And pull her hair back? Did she want to look like a schoolteacher? She said nothing, but accomplished the changes.

"That's better," Dina said, looking at herself half an hour later. "More suitable." She was feeling as edgy as if it were her first dinner party. It was not until she was going downstairs that it dawned on her. "Why, it's like the night I told Papa I wanted to marry Alexandre. I'm buying myself a man again. Only this time I have to make the proposal myself."

Whittaker Ames was startled to find himself the only dinner guest, although nothing in his expression betrayed it. Once they were seated facing each other on either side of the marble fireplace in the drawing room and Walter had served cocktails, Dina said, "I am sure you did not expect to be the solitary guest. Perhaps I should have warned you earlier. The fact is that I want to discuss a business matter with you. More correctly, a business proposition. And I wanted to ensure that it would be in private. I hope you do not mind. Perhaps Céleste's dinner will compensate for the lack of other guests."

"I have heard of Céleste's masterpieces," he said. "And I have been looking forward to this evening. If I had known it was to be a tête-à-tête, even though a business one, I would have looked forward to it even more eagerly.''

"A pretty speech. And thank you." No one would have guessed that she was thirty-one, looking forward to thirty-two. She was ravishing tonight, not at all the schoolteacher Siddie had thought. Her hair was in a chignon low on her neck, and two diamond-studded clips held it smooth at the sides. Her dress of palest gray taffeta with a broad collar and cuffs of Belgian lace from the rue Maubeuge workroom was vaguely Quakerish.

"I would like to tell you what is on my mind now," she said, "and then we can relax during dinner. Afterwards, if you are interested, we can speak more seriously."

"It sounds like a splendidly organized evening. Tell me, what is it you have in mind?"

She folded her hands in her lap and looked straight at him. "I doubt that my father will ever be able to resume direction of his business," she said bluntly. "I intend to carry it on. I have taken a number of steps in the past few months to modernize the firm. We are on a sound financial basis. More than sound. I am ready to expand. But I need a male presence."

He blinked. "A male presence?"

"Let me explain. Two weeks ago the top thirty men in the New York financial community dined with President Wilson. My father would have been invited were he not ill. I was not.

"Every man in my position belongs to at least two downtown clubs where he not only talks business, but does business in a relaxed atmosphere. I will never be invited to join any of these clubs.

"I have done what I could. You may have heard that I give luncheons to which I invite men whom I want to know better, men who are well-informed. But I am the only woman present. If there were a man who held an important position in our firm at these luncheons as well, my guests would be more comfortable. And the luncheons might prove to be even more profitable.

"Beyond that, as I told you, I am ready to expand. I need someone I can count on. Not a figurehead. Someone intelligent. Someone like you. It would be a gamble for you. But I assure you that as a senior partner in the firm, you can have almost unlimited influence and power on Wall Street.

"Now, if you are not at all interested, do tell me and we will spend a pleasant evening. If you would like to consider my proposition, let us have dinner and discuss it later over coffee."

He was taken aback. Certainly he had expected nothing like this. Interested? Of course he was interested. He had heard the talk on Wall Street. She was doing a remarkable job. Her proposal had been honest. She had acknowledged her weaknesses. And she obviously did not want a rubber-stamp executive, but was willing to delegate responsibility. What a challenge, he thought.

"I will be equally open with you," he said. "I am interested. And I look forward to discussing your proposal more fully after dinner."

The dinner was excellent. And Whittaker Ames recognized it. Dina's conversation was amusing and stimulating, and he appreciated it. But all the time in the back of his mind, he was saying, "It's crazy, but I'm going to do it. And the reason I'm going to do it is this woman sitting at the other end of the table. That husband of hers must be an idiot. If there was a chance that she would marry me . . ."

Whittaker Ames was not given to caprice. He had mapped his career carefully and was well on his way to achieving his goals. But tonight he had embraced a new direction, wherever it might take him.

A little after midnight the bell tinkled in the butler's pantry. Walter looked up at the board. It was the library bell. He had removed the coffee tray hours ago. It must be the champagne now. The tray was ready. He filled the silver bucket with fresh ice, uncovered the sandwiches and petit fours Céleste had prepared, and hurried up the stairs to the library.

"Ma'am?"

"Please bring us some champagne, Walter. And perhaps a plate of sandwiches." She was radiant. He bowed. He had been right. She would not look like that if it were simply business. Minutes later he carried the tray into the library, took the bottle from the bucket, wrapped the linen napkin about it, and eased out the cork.

"Thank you, Walter," she dismissed him.

He went back to the pantry somewhat crestfallen. It was business after all, not romance. The floor between their chairs had been littered with sheets of paper covered with scribbled figures.

A year later Whittaker Ames was more than satisfied with the gamble he had taken. Dina had been right. He was making more money and exerting more power already than he would have been if he had continued on his chosen legal track.

And always in the back of his mind was the thought that the elegant, brilliant, and utterly charming Dina de Granville might be a widow one of these days. Or a divorcée. Her husband, she had told him, was driving an ambulance on the Western Front. It was not at all unlikely that he would be a war casualty. The German shells made no distinction between soldiers and civilian volunteers. And if he was not killed, there was cause for reasonable doubt that he would ever return. The gossip was that Kitty had thrown him over in favor of her husband. Dina would certainly not welcome Kitty's reject home.

With luck she would be his. He knew Jack Goddard was her lover and as eager to wed Dina as he was, but Whit was positive she would never marry him. When he had seen Goddard's striking portrait of Dina, however, he realized that the painter was a formidable rival and should not be underestimated. The man understood her. It was not just her likeness he had caught, but her emotions. And there was nothing more seductive to either a man or a woman than being understood.

Dina had no inkling of Whit's feelings. She liked him and enjoyed his company, perhaps even more than she suspected. She had come to rely on him not only for his cool legal mind and competence, but as a friend. It was work, however, that bound them together. Even when he dined alone with her at home, which he did often, it was work that brought him there. It had become routine for him to go home with her several nights a week. They would play with Vicky before dinner and talk of this and that during dinner, but the hours after dinner were devoted to work.

Her relationship with Jack Goddard was quite different. After Duck Island she had fully resolved to stop seeing him, but when her father had fallen ill Jack was there with sympathy and support. Somehow it was impossible to brush him aside, and his lusty lovemaking filled a need. She was sometimes incredulous that she could find so much sexual satisfaction with a man whom she basically did not like. But she did. And she found him amusing, if somewhat grating. She supposed that she would break with him sooner or later, but for the moment it was a very satisfactory arrangement. And a very quiet one. Only someone as acutely tuned in to her as Whit was would have suspected it.

She cared enough about Jack, however, to be concerned that he was not painting. When she asked what he was doing, he always hedged. Finally one Saturday afternoon at the studio after they had made love, she rolled over on the low, wide couch to face him and said, "I haven't seen anything new here for months. I can't believe that you're not working. Especially when I think how feverishly you painted last year on the island."

"I guess I got painted out," he said carelessly. "The creative process is a strange one. There's no governing it. It needs stimulation. On Duck Island I had you. It was the most exciting time of my life as a painter.''

"But don't you want to paint? Doesn't it bother you that you are not working?"

"When I want to paint, I paint," he said. "Right now I don't want to. It's like love." He ran his finger gently around her nipple. It stiffened and he smiled. "You see? That's what I mean by stimulation. Something happens and you can't resist it. But until that something happens, there is no point in my lifting a brush."

He kissed her nipple. "Will you pose for me again?" His smile had disappeared. His face was drawn and intense as he waited for her answer.

"I will not." She caressed his cheek. "Enough is enough. Although," and she stopped to think, "I might ask you to do another portrait. For the office. There is one of Papa that was painted in San Francisco. It might be a good idea to have one of me, too." And some day one of Vicky, she thought. After all, why not? Vicky might very well be the third generation of the firm.

"Mmm," he mused. "Yes, I'll do it. On Wall Street perhaps."

"Wall Street?"

"Not Wall Street itself, but a suggestion of great buildings in the background. A background of power. Something like the view from your office window. That's it," he said excitedly. "The harbor and all the ships and traffic. And you, empress of all you survey.

"I'll do it," he said. "For your wedding present."

"Wedding present?" She sat up in bed. "What do you mean?"

"Marry me, Dina. What are you waiting for? For Alexandre to come back? Will you want him when he comes crawling back? Marry me so we don't have to pretend and hide. I'm tired of being discreet. I want the world to know that you are mine."

Dina was silent. She had dreaded this moment, although

she had hoped it would never come. She had known what was on his mind. Jack was not exactly subtle. But marrying him would be wrong. He was a lover, not a husband. She had to respect the man she married. Just as she respected Whit. The thought startled her momentarily. She had never thought of Whit in connection with marriage. It was simply that he had integrity. And Jack, she feared, had very little.

"No," she said softly. "I can't. I can't divorce Alexandre. I don't know what will happen between us. I don't even know if I will see him again. But he is my husband and Vicky's father. And he is driving an ambulance at the front in France. I am proud of him. If he comes back, he will not have to crawl."

"Proud!" He turned the word into an expletive. "Proud of a man who has betrayed you!"

"Jack!" He had gone too far. "I don't want to hear any more."

He scowled. "You like to keep me dangling, don't you? It amuses you to have me at your beck and call, doesn't it?" His voice was bitter.

"That is enough." Her face was white with shock. She got out of bed and picked her clothes up from the floor. She retreated behind the screen in the studio to dress. It was not a matter of modesty, simply that there was no intimacy between them now.

He was still lying on the low couch when she was ready to leave. "I'm sorry that you are so upset," she said. "It is not like you to be insulting. But if you expect to see me again, an apology is in order." There was no response.

It was the first time that she had left the studio alone. Always before, he had escorted her home, usually trying to coax her into letting him spend the night. She had always refused. Now she wished that Burns was at the curb waiting for her with the car, but she had never asked him to drive her here. She was careful not to flaunt her affairs before the servants. But this was neither a neighborhood nor an hour for a woman to be walking unescorted. She felt uneasy as she made her way toward Fifth Avenue where she hoped to find a hansom cab. It was getting dark. There were men lounging in doorways who looked hard at her as she passed. She realized that no one had any idea where she was. There were footsteps close behind her. She did not turn around, but quickened her pace and as she reached the corner, she collided with a man headed in the opposite direction.

"I beg your—Dina! What are you doing here?"

"Oh, Whit! Never mind what I am doing. The fact is that I was just wishing I had called my chauffeur to come get me."

"It would have been wise," Whittaker Ames agreed. "Let me take you home. I'm on my way to the garage to get my car. It's been in for repairs." A quarter of an hour later he was driving her up Fifth Avenue. When he turned off on the cross street to Madison Avenue, he said, "I don't dare hope that you are free for dinner tonight. If you were, we might go to Delmonico's."

"I'm free," she said, "but why don't you have dinner with me at home? I've been out all day and I promised Vicky I'd spend some time with her. Céleste would love to show off a little. I promise not to talk business for a change."

"You don't have to persuade me," he smiled. "I accept with pleasure."

"Ring Walter and have him bring you the drink tray and the evening papers," Dina said when they reached the house. "I must change and then go up and read Vicky a bedtime story."

Whit was certain she had been with Jack Goddard. There was no other reason for her to have been in that part of town. She had seemed a bit distrait, not her usual confident self. He wondered if something had happened. A quarrel perhaps. Goddard could not be in the habit of letting her make her way home alone, no matter how much of a cad he was.

Whit suddenly felt very protective. The idea of her

needing help endeared her to him even more. It must be hard, he thought, for a woman to run a business as competently as she did and always have to put up a confident front. It was not a woman's nature, he reflected. It had to be a strain on her, a strain he had not recognized before. No wonder she was susceptible to a man like Goddard.

The thought gave him hope. He could protect her. He was not as wealthy as her father, but he was nevertheless very comfortably off and when his father died, he would inherit a substantial fortune. If she would let him, he would devote himself to making her happy. And Vicky too. Vicky was a little charmer. Even if they were to have a child of their own, he would always love Vicky. He smiled, amused at how far his thoughts had carried him.

Dina, coming into the drawing room at that moment, looked at him fondly. The quiet smile was peculiarly appealing. He was an attractive man, she thought. A fine man. She was lucky to have him at her side in the office.

"What are you smiling at?" she asked.

"I was smiling because I was thinking how much I like you and Vicky."

"And we like you, too, Whit. When I told Vicky you were here, she wanted you to tell her a story. She says your stories are more exciting than mine. I promised her that next time, you'll tell her an extra-long, extra-exciting story."

Damnit, he thought. It was a mistake to mention Vicky. And Dina sees me as a friend of the family—not a suitor, a man who wants to marry her. He was the trusted co-worker. The unofficial uncle. "I think I'll have another cocktail if I may," he said getting up. "May I mix one for you?"

Despite Dina's promise of a social evening, they spent it as they had spent so many other evenings, happily engaged in talking shop. They were in the process of transforming Schumacher & de Granville from an investing firm that used its own capital into a brokerage house that would invest the capital of clients. It stood to reason that they would make more money and run less risk by taking a percentage of their clients' purchases and sales than by staking the firm's money as Frederick had always done. "It will free up your capital," Whit had pointed out. "You can afford to be bolder. Even take a gamble or two."

This evening the conversation turned to the kind of clients they should accept. "The safest way," Whit said, "is not to accept clients whose net worth is less than half a million."

"If we really want to grow," Dina argued, "we'll be cutting ourselves off from young men who are on their way up. If we make money for them while they are young, they will be with us for a lifetime."

"You're right," he said. "We'll have to expand the staff faster to take care of them, but it should pay off very rapidly."

"Women too," she said thoughtfully.

"Women?"

"Why not? They have money. Before Isabelle married my father she used to direct her own investments. And I did very well with my own money. But I'm really thinking about what old Mr. Dudley from the Boston Bank said at the luncheon last week. Remember? That it was their women clients who were buying most of the government bonds—even when equally safe, more profitable investments were suggested. He thought it was because the bonds were easy to understand. You lend money to the government and the government pays you interest and eventually returns your money."

"So?" He did not catch her drift.

She lifted her wine glass and studied it as she said, "I think that most women don't understand the stock market or how to invest, so they either buy government bonds or let their husbands manage their money. And when their husbands die, they let their lawyers manage their money."

She took a swallow of the wine. "I want to invite women to our luncheons and explain how they can make more money by investing in companies that are in business to make profits than by lending money to the government, which wouldn't know a profit if it fell over one.'' She emptied her glass.

"And most rich women fall into the second category,'' Whit said. "When I think of the fortunes some women control . . .''

"I can hardly wait to get down to the office on Monday,'' she said, smiling in anticipation. "We have to get started on it right off. Let women know that we want their . . . want their . . .'' She fumbled for the word.

"Their money,'' Whit said, laughing at her.

"It's more than that, Whit. These women manage huge households, often three or four houses and dozens of servants. They entertain on a great scale. They are just as much executives as any man running a business. It's ridiculous that when it comes to money, they are so helpless.''

"Not necessarily helpless,'' he said slowly. "It is more a matter of priorities, I think. There are other things in the world, you know, things that are more important to women than making money.''

She looked at him, her eyes wide and questioning. She was slightly flushed with excitement and a few tendrils had escaped from her smoothly drawn-back hair and curled softly about her face. She had never seemed more adorable. Was it truly only money that made her pulse quicken? Whit tossed aside all his inbred caution as well as his gentlemanly determination not to speak of his feelings until she was free.

"Like friends,'' he said. "And love. Especially love.''

"Love?'' She was completely taken aback. "Whit, are you in love? I never dreamed. Yes, I can see it in your face. You *are* in love. Who is she? Do I know her?''

She was conscious of something like a dull headache. She did not feel right. It was not exactly a headache, more like a heartache. More like jealousy, hurt, betrayal. Whit was in love! She felt as if the bottom were falling out of her world. But that was ridiculous.

He was staring at her. Was it possible that she really had

no idea? Had he been that good an actor? "You know her," he said. "You know her very well."

She thought, her teeth catching her lower lip, her head slightly cocked to the side. "I know her? Well?" She quickly reviewed all the young women at the dinners and receptions where she and Whit often ran into each other. He had never seemed to single out any of them. She shook her head. "I give up. Who is she? Can't you tell me?"

He got up from the table. "I can tell you, but you'll probably think I'm an awful fool." He looked into the fire blazing in the marble fireplace, his back toward her. "I love you, Dina," he said quietly.

He turned toward her and asked almost angrily, "Hadn't you guessed?"

"Me?"

"You. Ever since that first night when you invited me to dinner. You were wearing that gray dress with the white lace collar. You looked like an elegant child dressed up to play teacher—until you smiled. And then you almost broke my heart. I fell in love with you at once. I decided during dinner that night that I wanted you as my wife more than anything else in the world. I've never said anything. I understood your position, but somehow I thought that you knew how I felt.

"Damnit, Dina—" He broke off. "I love you. And sometimes it hurts." He turned back to the fire. "I told you I'd feel an awful fool. I hope you will forgive me."

"Forgive you?" She was standing beside him. "Forgive you?" She took his hand. "Perhaps it is you who should forgive me.

"I am not like other women. The only man I loved," she drew a deep breath, "or thought I loved, married me for my money. It is no secret. I never...I..." She began to stammer. "I n-never thought anyone would l-love me for m-myself."

She felt completely vulnerable. She looked up at him. "I can't play the shy little woman, Whit. It is like magic. As if—what I mean is—can love be born in a moment? Or have I loved you without..." She could not finish. She looked up at him helplessly, tears running down her cheeks.

He took her in his arms and held her close. "Perhaps it is magic," he murmured, "when dreams come true." He held her away from him and looked at her. "So you don't think I'm an awful fool?"

She laughed. "An idiot, perhaps, but never a fool. Oh Whit, I do love you."

When Whit finally let himself out of the sleeping house on Madison Avenue, he was dazed with happiness, drunk with love. Dina was his. He would not pressure her. She would have to untangle herself from her marriage in her own way in her own time. But in the meantime she was his love. His beautiful and beguiling love.

She had feigned sleep when Whit slipped out of her bed. So much had happened so quickly. She did not want to talk. Could not talk. Was this real love? At last? Whittaker Ames was wealthy. He did not need her money, nor the position with her firm. Was this how love grew? Slowly, through the months, suddenly exploding from friendship to the blinding passionate intimacy of the last few hours. She was too tired to think. She did not feel Whit's soft kiss on her forehead as he left.

She woke for a brief moment sometime before daylight to think, "I must have been crazy to have gotten involved with Jack." But then she smiled drowsily. She had made love with two men on the same day. "And both of them want to marry me. If Alexandre only knew." She turned over and went back to sleep.

"Mr. Goddard is calling." Dina's junior secretary poked her head around the office door.

She picked up the telephone. "Jack. I was beginning to wonder what had happened to you." She had not heard from him since that distressing Saturday nearly two months ago.

She had expected him to appear with flowers and an apology, but when he did not, she did not give it a thought. Her life was too full.

"I've been busy," he said. "Putting a show together. It is time that I face the critics. Reggie Hayes has been nagging at me for months to show my work."

"That's wonderful," she said warmly. "When is it going to be?"

"Very soon. It depends on you."

"Oh?"

"I'm calling to ask if you will lend your portrait for the show."

"Of course I will. That was always understood. I'll be proud to be part of your show."

There was a silence and then he said, "I want you to be the first to see it. I want to know what you think of it."

"Just let me know when you're ready. Would you like Isabelle to come too? She's almost as interested in your work as I am."

"Come alone," he ordered. "Isabelle can come another day. Come next Friday. In the late afternoon." He hung up without saying good-bye. She held the receiver for a moment. What was the matter with him? Probably the strain of putting a show together. Or perhaps he was embarrassed by the memory of the last time they had seen each other.

She left the office early that Friday afternoon, directing Burns to the Chelsea studio, way over west by the river. It was truly a terrible neighborhood, she thought. How could she ever have considered it excitingly bohemian when she and Alexandre used to spend evenings there with Jack and Holly, eating spaghetti and talking about this, that, and everything? It was exciting because I was with Alexandre, she decided. He made everything exciting.

Jack met her at the door. He must have been watching at the window. "I knew you would come." His smile was odd. She wondered if he had been drinking. He led her into the studio. Folding screens had been set up to form an entrance hall, hiding the main part of the studio from view.

"I didn't realize," she said, "that you had been painting enough to have a show."

"Judge for yourself," he said, and with a flourish, he folded back one of the screens.

She gasped.

Centered on the wall opposite the door was the huge oil he had painted of her in bed on Duck Island. The rumpled sheets, the languid naked body, the slack expression left no doubt that she had just made love. To the right was the painting of her by the fire, a pale gypsy full of passion.

Stunned, she went from picture to picture. There was the dignified and mysterious portrait he had painted the summer Alexandre had not come home, the portrait he had asked her to lend for the show. Surrounding it were a dozen charcoal sketches of her—naked. Everywhere she looked, there was a sketch, a watercolor, an oil of herself.

She stared at him. "What are you thinking of?" she asked shakily.

"They are remarkable. Don't you agree?" he asked smoothly. "My best work. I'm sure Reggie will confirm that. They are bound to be snatched up the first day of the show."

"You are not going to have a show with these pictures?" She could not believe it.

He smiled.

"Jack, you can't. I forbid it."

"Forbid it? What does that mean? You posed for me. I did not force you."

Dina looked around. She felt trapped. At the same time she realized that she had always known that something like this would happen with Jack. Not this exactly, but something. Her instinct that he was not to be trusted had been right. But she had not heeded it.

"What do you want?" she asked icily.

"You know what I want. I want to marry you." His eyes

were intense. He took her hands in his. "Marry me, Dina. Marry me. If you marry me, the world will never see these pictures. They will be for us alone. Sunny memories. Loving days."

"You seem to forget that I am married."

"Divorce him. He is never going to come back to you."

"You must be mad. I would never marry you. Why are you doing this?"

He looked at her contemptuously. "And you are supposed to be so clever. Why am I doing this? For money, Mrs. de Granville. For money. Something you have a lot of, and of which I have none. But I have these paintings and they will make my fortune."

"This is blackmail!" She was outraged.

"Call it what you want. These pictures will make my fortune," he said coldly. "And they will ruin your reputation. And not just socially. No one will do business with a loose woman."

She closed her eyes. "How much?"

"Five hundred thousand dollars."

She looked at him and suddenly she laughed.

"You find it amusing?"

"Indeed I do." The absurdity of the sum had brought her back to her wits. "My dear Jack, you flatter me. I can assure you that even if you flung your studio open to the public, you would never realize anything close to that figure. The prices might be somewhat inflated because of the element of scandal, but half a million dollars!" She laughed again.

"As for my reputation . . ." She shrugged. "I have never done anything of which I am ashamed. In this instance I have been foolish. I used bad judgment. I was indiscreet. But I did nothing dishonest, hurt nobody. I will survive. Really, Jack, you are not being sensible."

"Go ahead. Laugh. For half a million dollars, you can laugh at me," he blustered, but a tone of uncertainty had crept in.

"Are these all the pictures you have of me?"

"I have a few of you and Vicky. Sentimental mother and daughter things. I'll throw them in."

"All right." She was very matter-of-fact. "I want you to have these wrapped and packed, ready for my chauffeur to pick up tomorrow morning. When they are delivered, I will pay you." She paused. "One hundred thousand dollars."

"It's half a million or nothing." His face was red.

"Then it's nothing." She picked up her fur and settled it around her shoulders and turned to the door.

"Two hundred thousand."

"One hundred fifty thousand," she said firmly.

Silence. Then, "All right. One hundred and fifty thousand dollars. But I want it now."

"Don't be ridiculous. I don't walk around with that kind of money. And I have no intention of paying it until I have all my pictures. I will take the large portrait with me now—it is my property, after all—if you will carry it down to the car. I would ask Burns to do it, but you can hardly expect me to let him come in here. When I have the others tomorrow, I will pay you. In cash." There would be no record of this transaction that he could use to blackmail her later, she thought.

She walked out of the studio and down the bare wooden stairs. She was trembling and her hands were clammy, but she sat erect and expressionless as Jack came down with the portrait and Burns placed it carefully in the trunk.

"I'm going back to the office now," she told the chauffeur. "I'll want you to wait for me. I won't be long and then I'll be going home."

"Are you all right, ma'am?" he asked anxiously.

She was dead white and there were lines bracketing her mouth that had never been there before. "I'm fine, thank you. Just a little tired. The office, please."

She blessed her father for having impressed on her the importance of keeping large sums of cash on hand. "You never know when you might miss the opportunity of a lifetime," he had said, "just for the lack of cash." This was hardly the kind of opportunity Papa had had in mind, but she was thankful that the money was there in the office safe. She sighed tiredly. You pay for everything, she thought. Sometimes in ways you don't expect.

"Tell Anna to bring a glass of white wine to my room," she told Walter as he opened the door for her that evening. She went tiredly up the stairs, not even stopping to glance at her mail.

She kicked off her shoes and rang for Siddie. "Will you brush my hair, Siddie? Perhaps it will calm my mind. My thoughts are chasing each other around like kittens chasing their tails."

The little maid chuckled. "You are working too hard. You should stay home tonight and rest."

"You may be right. But I am a businesswoman and tonight my business is to go to the Andersons' dinner party and look fresh and rested." She leaned back as Siddie brushed her hair with long, practiced strokes as she had ever since Dina had been a wild harum-scarum child. She began to relax. The two fine lines that had bracketed her mouth disappeared. She sipped the wine. "That's good, Siddie. What have you put out for me to wear tonight?"

"I thought your new topaz satin. It will be striking with your hair, but if you are tired..." Siddie considered a moment. "The topaz is demanding. Perhaps the lilac with the green beading, if you are feeling tired."

"No, I'll wear the topaz," she said decisively. "And my yellow diamonds." A little makeup would disguise her fatigue and she had a special reason for wanting to wear the topaz gown that night.

By the time Siddie had dressed her hair and hooked her into the topaz satin and clasped the heavy strand of yellow diamonds about her neck, Dina looked magnificent. It had taken only the slightest touch of makeup. A bit of green shadow to accent her eyes and a hint of beige powder to warm her skin.

She opened the red velvet box and took out the earrings. They were dazzling. Clusters of yellow diamonds dangled at the end of golden chains. Whit had given them to her. "A secret engagement present," he had said. "They will go with your yellow diamond necklace." She had ordered the topaz-colored dress because it set off the diamonds as no other color would. This was the first time Whit would see her wearing his gift. She smiled when she thought of him.

The two of them were working furiously to bring about the changes they had plotted for the firm. When they were not working, they gave themselves up to love, to exploring each other's bodies and thoughts, to marveling at how perfectly suited they were. Without a word being said it had been understood between them that no one was to know. Whit became a more frequent visitor to the house, but the staff thought nothing of it. They had overheard so much business talk between the two of them that the idea of the relationship changing to a more intimate one had never entered their minds. Only Siddie suspected the truth, and she said nothing.

Tonight Dina and Whit would play the familiar charade of business colleagues who, since they were social equals, were often paired at dinner parties. They would smile and chat in the most formal manner, but she knew that Whit would notice the earrings and there would be a special spark between them that no one else would sense.

It was well after midnight when Burns brought her home. She had left orders that no one need wait up for her. The mail was still on the tray on the hall table. She let her short sable cape slip from her shoulders as she riffled through it. Invitations, thank-you notes, and a cheap envelope addressed in a childish scrawl. From Paris. She sat down on the straight-backed hall sofa and ripped it open.

"Alexandre . . . ill . . . influenza . . ." Her heart hurt as she read it. "If you love him . . . ask him to come home." Ask him to come home! She had wanted him home every day for the past two years. But now—

She turned on the lights in the downstairs rooms and wandered around. She ran her fingers over the back of a dining room chair and touched the pale silk damask that covered the wing chair in the drawing room. She sank down into the deep sofa in front of the library fireplace and remembered how she and Alexandre had chosen these furnishings in the hurried months before their wedding and how tactfully he had shaped her taste. She looked at the paintings glowing like jewels against the white walls, just as he had promised they would.

This house was his. His mark was on every room. He did not need to be invited home. It was his home as well as hers. And she was his, too, if he wanted her. He would be far more than welcome. He was desired. Longed for.

She went slowly, wearily up the stairs. Siddie was waiting for her, despite her orders not to wait up. She smiled gratefully. "What would I do without you?"

"I don't know, I'm sure," the maid replied tartly and affectionately. She took off the jewels and locked them away. She undressed Dina and slid a silken nightgown over her head. She took down her hair and brushed it again. She massaged her face lightly with cream to remove the makeup. "There, it's bed for you now," she said.

"Not yet. I have a letter to write. This was in the mail." She indicated the single sheet of paper with the childish handwriting. "It is from Paris. From one of the Belgians he befriended." Siddie did not need to ask who "he" was. "He has been ill," Dina continued. "According to this, a bad case of influenza. I believe he wants to come home."

Siddie beamed. "Of course he wants to come home. Oh, it's about time." She was unreservedly happy. "When is he arriving?"

"Soon, I hope. I have to write and make arrangements. I will leave my letter outside on the table. Please see that it is mailed first thing in the morning."

When Siddie left, she picked up a slim silver penholder and wrote "My dearest Alexandre" on her heavy cream letter paper. Her eyes filled with tears. He was indeed her dearest, and had always been. There was no point in being proud. She wanted him home. In her arms.

Or did she? What about Whit? She sighed heavily. Whit was a wonderful man. They could have a good life together. But Alexandre was part of her. Now that it seemed that he wanted to come home, she could admit it to herself. She no longer had to pretend. Without him she was incomplete.

She took up the pen again and wrote a single sentence. "Come home as fast as you can." She thought a moment and added another sentence. "I love you and need you."

Telling Whit that Alexandre was returning had been hard to face, but she had done it within twelve hours of reading the letter from Lucie Soerbijk. She and Whit were working as usual on Saturday morning. When he came into her office to drop off some papers, she got up and closed the door. "Whit, please sit down a minute. I have something to tell you."

He was struck by her obvious fatigue. Although she was dressed exquisitely as always, she seemed to droop. Something was seriously wrong. But what?

Last night she had been gloriously serene and so beautiful that it had been difficult not to stare at her. She had worn the yellow diamond earrings. He had taken this as a pledge of her love and, during the evening when he caught her eye across the room, her look had confirmed the pledge.

Something had happened to her father, he thought. He must have taken a turn for the worse. That would account for it. But in that case, why would she be in the office and not at his bedside?

He sat in his usual chair by her desk, facing the windows with their panoramic view of New York harbor. His eyes ranged over the harbor traffic as he waited for her to speak. She was stalking about the office like a distraught panther.

The only way to tell Whit was to tell him. She knew that, but it was more difficult than she had imagined. They had lain in each other's arms. They had opened their hearts to each other. It was too cruel. She finally sat at her desk. "I'm sorry. I'm not myself this morning. When I got home from the Andersons' last night, there was a letter. From Paris. From one of the Belgian refugee women." She had told him about the house Alexandre had established for the refugees and of the little lace industry that he had sponsored. "She wrote that Alexandre has been seriously ill. He is better, but still very weak. She said that he wants to come home. That I should ask him to come."

She got up and started stalking about the office again. "Before I went to bed I wrote and asked him to come back. I could not do anything else, Whit. He is my husband. And last night—" Her voice broke and she sat down at the desk again and looked at him with tortured eyes. "Last night I realized that I still love him."

She opened a desk drawer and took out a red velvet jewelry case. He recognized it. It was the box that had held the yellow diamond earrings. She pushed it across the desk to him.

"I can't keep these. But I'm glad I had a chance to wear them. Last night meant a lot to me."

"Keep them," he said huskily. "It would mean the world to me to know that you have them. To see you wearing them some evening. Knowing that they meant something to you."

"They do mean something, my darling. That is why I can't keep them," she said softly. "I don't want to lose you, but I must." Tears were running down her face. "I love you too, but..."

"I know," he said. "I think I always knew. But I had hoped."

It was his turn to get up and pace. He finally stood in front of her and smiled ruefully. "I guess this is our good-bye." He swallowed to keep his voice under control. "If you ever need me, I'll be there for you."

He stood looking down at her for a minute, then picked up the velvet box and stuffed it in his pocket. "I'll see you Monday. We can talk then. But now I . . ." He broke off and left the office.

Back in his own office, he stood looking out the window, seeing nothing. His lean features were stiff in his effort to control his feelings. He had lost her. He took the jewelry box from his pocket and opened it. The earrings flashed their warm fire at him. She had been dazzling last night. He had been impatient for the time when she would be free and they could acknowledge their love to the world. And now this.

He took his hat from the rack. "I'm leaving for the day," he told his secretary, and strode blindly down the hall.

Dina sat at her desk. She felt frozen and utterly desolate. Had she ruined her life on the basis of a letter from a stranger? A stranger who might have been prompted by the most noble of impulses, but was wrong? How could this Lucie Soerbijk know that Alexandre wanted to come home? What if he no longer cared for her? She sat motionless, stone-faced as the questions tumbled through her mind.

There was nothing else she could have done, she decided finally. He might not want to come home, but if he did, if he still loved her, she would have her husband again. As for the Kitty affair, she shrugged. It had been as much her fault as Alexandre's. He had wanted her to accompany him to Brussels, and she had refused. What a stupid mistake! She had paid for it a hundred times over.

She began to pull herself together. An empty Saturday afternoon stretched ahead. For nearly two years her Saturday afternoons had been devoted first to Jack Goddard and later to Whit. Jack was no longer in her life. She was thankful that that affair had been resolved before Jack could learn that Alexandre was coming home. There would have been no bounds to his blackmail if he had known.

And now Whit was out of her life, too. At this thought she stiffened. Out of her life? Out of her heart, yes. But she could not afford to have him leave the firm. She needed him. She could never find another Whittaker Ames.

And there was another consideration. It would seem odd if Whit left just when Alexandre returned. It might give rise to gossip. She would have to convince him to stay. If he truly loved her, he would. There was no reason why they could not work together just as they always had. All it would take was self-control and discipline. Neither of them was a stranger to these qualities.

The switchboard operator rang to say that it was noon and she was closing down the board. Her secretaries were getting ready to leave. She would go home, too, and take a nap. Later she and Vicky would walk down to see Papa and Isabelle. There was nothing more she could do about anything today. She had never dreamed that love could be so complicated.

# Twenty

I<small>T WAS</small> a tired, silent man who moved slowly about the house on Madison Avenue, who took the daily constitutionals that Dr. Godfrey prescribed, who smiled at Vicky and was courteous and attentive to his wife. To Dina, Alexandre seemed like a hollow man going through the motions of living.

Dr. Godfrey had examined him thoroughly and proclaimed that if he exercised patience, took morning walks and afternoon naps, he would eventually be in perfect health again. "It will take time," the doctor told him, "but if you follow the regimen I prescribe, you will be fine in due time."

The doctor, who attended to most of New York's upper crust and was well up on its gossip, thought Alexandre's continued weakness was as much of emotional origin as physical. When Dina consulted him privately, voicing her concern over her husband's lack of energy and interest in life, he tried to indicate this indirectly.

"It's not only the aftereffects of the influenza," he said, "but the aftereffects of the war. He has led a life that has drained him spiritually and emotionally. It will take time, my dear. Time and patience and love. Your love is the best medicine I can prescribe."

She clung to this advice and tried to believe it. Their life together was a fragile thing. There was so much that was not said, so much that was carefully avoided. It was like walking on eggshells. She could see love in his eyes. But she also saw something else—a distance that had not yet been bridged.

He regained strength little by little, but his face was usually gray with fatigue by the end of the day. One night before dinner when he hoisted Vicky onto his knee to tell her a story, Dina saw him turn pale.

"It's nothing," he said in answer to her look. "It's just one more form of physical effort that I'm not quite up to yet." He spoke over Vicky's head. "There are many things I can't do. Not yet." He looked at her meaningfully. It was not quite the truth. Making love with Lucie had been as natural and easy as turning over in bed. But he was not ready to make love with Dina yet. Nor was he able.

She nodded.

"Papa," Vicky claimed his attention. "You said you were going to tell me a story."

New York was too much for him, Dina decided, even with the quiet life that they led. And the summer heat and humidity would be hard on him. "What would you think of spending the summer on the island?" she asked one morning at breakfast. "I can arrange to take the summer off. Whit will hold the fort. I think the salt air and quiet would do you good."

"If you can take the summer off, why don't we go to Newport?" he asked somewhat fretfully. "It's more comfortable. Not as godforsaken."

"Because we can't," she said flatly. "In the first place it would be a burden on Isabelle. Papa has become very demanding since his illness. Besides, there is too much going on in Newport. You would not rest.''

''In other words, I have no choice,'' he said resignedly. ''In that case—yes, let's spend the summer on the island.''

The island air was sweet with the scent of lilacs and crisp with the salt tang of the ocean that June. The hours and days seemed to melt into each other. When Alexandre resumed the walks that Dr. Godfrey had prescribed, Dina accompanied him now. They roamed the island and as they walked, he began to talk about his days at the front.

''I can't believe it now,'' he said one morning. They were sitting on a rock watching the tide ebb and leave small pools behind in the sand. ''But at the time it was very real and I was not prepared for it. Even though I had seen fighting as I made my way out of Belgium. But the front itself . . .'' He fell silent.

Another day he said, ''You know, I hardly remember anything about my collapse. The doctor said I had been hallucinating and thought that death was riding beside me in the ambulance. I'm not so sure it was a hallucination. Death was everywhere during that German attack.

''One night I watched a squad of twelve men go over the top. They carried gas masks and two hundred fifty rounds of ammunition. There was a drenching rain. Those twelve men climbed out of the trenches into the dark and started across no-man's-land toward the German trenches. Only two came back.''

He sighed. ''I don't know why I'm boring you with this.''

''Boring? Quite the opposite. When I listen to you I realize just how little we Americans know about the war. I think you should do something about it.''

''Do something!'' he exclaimed. ''I did my best. And it was nothing. I may have saved a few lives, but I'm not sure. All I did was deliver those young men to the medics who patched them up so they could go back to the front.''

''You don't understand what I mean,'' she said earnestly.

"We are going to get into the war sooner or later. The sooner we do, the sooner it will be over. What I keep thinking as I listen to your stories is that if we don't hurry, Germany will win." The war she had once dismissed as a European aberration an ocean away from her and those she loved had become terrifyingly real. She had confronted it first in business—in the investments she was making for clients and the firm—when she had advised Ephraim Fleming, the munitions manufacturer, that he was not thinking big enough in his plans for expansion. And now the black emotions of horror and fear and anger that Alexandre's stories conjured up brought another kind of reality. Something had to be done before the Germans tore the world apart.

"When we get back to the city, I think you should tell people what you have been telling me. About what happened at St. Hilaire. About the frightening numbers of young men being killed. About supplies being scarce. About the danger that Germany may win. People would listen to you. You were there."

"Listen to me!" he scoffed. "Who would listen to me? A Belgian? We were conquered in a matter of days," he said bitterly.

"Only because Belgium believed the Germans when they swore to respect its neutrality."

He walked along not saying anything, stooping occasionally to pick up a pebble and toss it into the water. "You really think people would listen?" he asked after a while.

"I know they would. Perhaps this is the service you owe your Uncle Albert. When you tell people how he and your poor Aunt Marita were killed so brutally and senselessly, they will understand that something has to be done. Otherwise the same things might happen here one day."

After dinner that night they talked long and eagerly, making plans for a lecture tour. Alexandre's eyes were gleaming. The old spark was back. He had a mission. That day proved to be the turning point. Now they talked ceaselessly.

Not just about the war, but about themselves. About Vicky and their hopes for her. About their future. Their shared future.

And they became lovers again. It was a second honeymoon that neither of them had dared hope for. Alexandre fell in love with Dina all over again. She had changed. There was a new gentleness about her, as if she, too, had been tempered by suffering. Had it been his absence that had wounded her so deeply? Kitty? Her father's illness? Or something he knew nothing about? Certainly not her affair with Jack Goddard. Whatever that had been, it had not involved her heart. He was sure of that. He would have liked to ask her, but there were still silences between them. There were some things that could not be shared, but there was one thing that should be. For some reason, he could not bring himself to do it.

He had never told her about his Aunt Marita's necklace, but let her believe that he had maintained the house on the rue Maubeuge and his apartment on the Left Bank with money from his uncle's business. He had not said this exactly, but intimated it when he told her how, on his last day in Brussels, he had cleaned out the safe in his uncle's office and taken the cash he had found there—a paltry amount in truth, but he had indicated the opposite.

Now he wanted to give her the handful of diamonds that were left. And he wanted to tell her how Wim, his uncle's ancient clerk, had twisted the arm of his uncle's chair and revealed the hiding place of the necklace. How he had hidden it in a sausage when he fled Brussels—and then been so hungry he had eaten the sausage and the necklace had finally ended up wrapped in a dirty sock in his pocket. She would be fascinated by the story. But he hesitated. Who could know what might happen? He thought of the refugees he had seen, homeless and hungry. Without the necklace he would have been one of them. The diamonds were his only security. Why should he give them up?

He argued with himself as the summer went by. There

were times when he decided he would have them made into earrings for her. They would be spectacular—like great star bursts. Or he would give her a glass of champagne with the diamonds sparkling among the bubbles. Or he would simply hand them to her.

There were many loving nights, many peaceful mornings after love when he was on the verge of giving them to her. He even knew what he would say—a few graceful words about these stones being his belated dowry. But he never spoke those graceful words. One night he lay awake in bed, his hand on her hip, happily drained by love, content and grateful. She has given me everything, he thought. Why do I hesitate to give her the only gift I have? No answer came to him in the dark.

One afternoon Dina gathered a huge bouquet of gentian-blue chicory and goldenrod. "The flowers of fall," she said sadly. "We have to think about going back to the city soon."

He stretched lazily. He had been lying on the hammock on the porch, half dozing, half dreaming. Island life was more to his liking than he would have believed. The idea of leaving was so distasteful. "So soon?" he objected. "I thought we might stay through September."

"We could, except that I must get back to work so that Whit can have a vacation. And you, too, you must start arranging your speaking engagements. It's going to be a busy winter."

"Let's give ourselves another ten days," he proposed, "and then we'll put our noses to the grindstone."

He would make up his mind about the diamonds before they left, he promised himself. He had ten days. But the days went by and he still hesitated. One afternoon he went off alone. The decision would be made before he came back. There would be no more of this idiotic wavering.

As he tramped along the shore, his thoughts turned back to Paris and how he had let Kitty lead him about by the nose. He had been docile as a lamb while she spent his money and betrayed him. What an imbecile he had been! And why was it that he had not hesitated to lavish money on grasping little Kitty, but found it impossible to give that handful of precious stones to his wife whom he adored?

It would be no mean gift. The remaining diamonds were the best. The Paris jeweler had counseled him well, advising him to sell the smaller ones first. "They are all fine stones," he had said, "but you may never be able to find the like of the larger diamonds. They are exceptional."

Alexandre had taken his advice. The diamonds that were in the leather pouch at the bottom of his trunk were the largest and best. They represented a fortune, a diminished one to be sure, but still a very substantial one.

He stopped and looked around. He had walked farther than he had realized. The tide was coming in. It was time he turned toward home. Home! Yes. His home was Dina. She was his center, his security. Not the diamonds. He started back, eager to reach the little house. Eager to find Dina, to hold her, to tell her how much he loved her. Tonight he would give her the diamonds.

The sun was setting as he climbed the steep cliff from the beach. He hurried along the path through the fields, clouds of fireflies flickering around him in the early dusk. The lamps were being lit inside the house. One window after another glowed golden and welcoming. He felt lightheaded with happiness and love.

Dina sensed the change in him. He was her own Alexandre again. There was no longer even a hint of distance in his eyes when they sought hers across the dinner table. After they had kissed Vicky good night, he followed her down the narrow stairs and sat at her feet in front of the fire.

There was a chill in the night air—a damp wind blowing off the Atlantic. She had thrown a pale green mohair shawl around her shoulders and as they sat, her fingers tousling his hair, she thought of the night Jack had painted her in this same chair by the fire with the blue-checked tablecloth for a

shawl. He had seen her as a wanton gypsy dreaming of
passion although her thoughts had been far from passionate
that night, but tonight—tonight was different. She wanted
Alexandre as she had never wanted him. And she knew that
he wanted her. The tension grew between them. The fire
died down to a few embers and the house was silent. Only
then did he stand, and smile down at her. "Come, my
darling," he said. And she followed him up the stairs to
bed.

He did not give her the diamonds that night. He had
fallen asleep after making love. In the morning he slept late
and when he woke, he heard her downstairs giving instructions about packing the trunks.

Later that morning when she had gone down to the harbor
with Vicky, he took the small leather pouch of diamonds
from his trunk and buried it near the clump of lilacs by the
old stone wall. He lit a cigar when he finished, and sat on
the porch staring out at the pale line of the horizon. He was
a European with a peasant's conservatism. He felt safer with
a few gold coins hidden under the mattress or buried under
the foundation. Or better still, diamonds. Centuries of wars,
famines, and other disasters had instilled the conviction that
it was foolhardy not to have a secret hoard for the rainy day
that was bound to come. He was not like his father with no
thought for the morrow. He would not die penniless in an
empty room, nor would he die by his own hand because he
had reached the end of what he could beg or borrow.

The diamonds were all he had. Without them he was
dependent on the charity and goodwill of his wife. Perhaps
he would give them to her one day. In the meantime they
were safe where he had buried them and he was secure. It
was not as if Dina would be hurt. She had no idea that he
possessed this treasure. Nor would she be deprived. After
all, as she had told him years ago when he had given her
that pathetic engagement ring, "I have diamonds. Dozens of
them."

He gently knocked the ash from his cigar. He had done

the right thing, the prudent thing. There was no reason for this sneaking feeling of shame, for all this self-justification. Impatiently he threw the cigar over the porch railing. He would go for a swim and get this nonsense out of his head.

# Twenty-one

$A$LEXANDRE PAUSED and looked around the room. Then he bent forward, his hands flat on the table in front of him. "The young men of England and France are being murdered," he said. "In one battle alone, the English lost sixty thousand young men. An entire generation is being killed.

"There is a whole generation of women who will never be wed, of children who will never be born because the men who would have married these women and fathered those children were killed."

Dina looked around the dark-paneled Schumacher & de Granville dining room. It was a handpicked group. She had placed Cornelius Dudley from Boston on Alexandre's right and Whit—dear, dependable Whit—at his left for moral support. Morgan banker Bertie Sutphen, her father's old friend, was on her right and Ephraim Fleming on her left. The other six guests were all luminaries of the New York financial world. She had chosen well.

She smiled as she looked across the table at her husband. He was handsome and distinguished. The white streak over his left temple, the lean tautness of his face gave him an air of dignity and strength. Some men took time to mature. Unlike women, she thought. She had always been mature. It had taken Alexandre to make her young.

She turned her attention back to what he was saying. He had spent the last week working on his speech. The result had been short and factual, suitable for a hardheaded, profit-oriented audience. "We have clients who should hear what you have to say. They have influence," she had said. "It will be a good way to break the ice. You can speak informally." This is exactly what he was doing.

He had pushed aside the pages on which he had worked so hard, and instead talked about how he felt when all Brussels had stayed indoors while the German conquerors marched through the city in their hobnailed boots. He told the story of the massacre in St. Hilaire. How his elderly aunt and uncle had been executed with the villagers. Of the birds pecking at bodies lying in the dust. Of the unmarked graves in a wheat field. He told of life at the front. He told of the men he had driven to the field hospital in his ambulance—of amputations, shell shock, death.

"France and Belgium have been ravaged by the Hun," he concluded passionately. "If we do not come to their aid, Germany will reign supreme over Europe. The Allies need arms, money, ships, and men. We can supply all of these. We cannot afford not to. We must do it before it is too late."

He stopped. He had nothing more to say. He looked at Dina. Her face was grave. Had he been that ridiculous? "I thank you," he said, and sat down.

The dining room was silent. The coffee, in half-full cups, had grown cold. Cigars deposited carefully on ashtrays lay unsmoked, their ashes dropping silently. Alexandre was beginning to feel like a fool when Fleming stood up and clapped. The others joined him, all except Dina, who sat smiling and proud. She glanced down the table at Whit. He looked pinched, his mouth puckered as if he had just bitten into something sour. He was only going through the motions of applause, she noted. His hand claps were carefully muted. "Why, Whit is jealous," she thought. "How ridiculous of him."

As the other men gathered around to shake Alexandre's hand and question him, Whit slipped out. Dina joined the group around her husband. "I promised to give you something to think about today," she said to Cornelius Dudley. "Did I succeed?"

"You did indeed." He turned to Alexandre. "Can I persuade you to address a similar group in Boston? I'd like some friends of mine to hear what you have to say. Perhaps it will convince them that pacifism is poor business."

"Poor business all around," Alexandre said firmly. "If Germany dominates Europe and the seas, we are going to find ourselves cut off from important European markets and sources of raw material in Africa and the Near East. We will have to pay through the nose for our imports. Morally and economically it is our duty to put an end to this conflict."

To Alexandre's half-unbelieving amazement, invitations to speak poured in. Senators and ambassadors, manufacturers and bankers vied for a word with him. It was a hectic time.

Dina worried that the strain would be too much, but he enjoyed it. "I have learned how people react to what I say," he told her one midnight when he returned from a three-day speaking tour. "When I worked for your father, I enjoyed telling people about his new ventures, tantalizing them so they would want to participate. It was like fishing. You dangle expectations and dreams in front of someone and then wait. There comes a moment when he snaps it up." He took a bite of one of the sandwiches Céleste had left ready for him to illustrate how clients had snapped at his bait.

"It's the same with telling people about the war," he went on. "I tell them how devastating it is. How inhuman. Then I pause, just slightly. I let them think for a moment

how terrible it would be if it were happening here—to them.
To their sons and daughters. And then I say that Americans
have the power to put an end to the horror.

"They are happy to hear that. They want to do something
immediately. Americans are wonderful," he said. "They
want to do good. To be good."

Dina was lying in bed propped up on the pillows. Her
hair was like a rosy flame against the linen-cased pillows
with their trimming of heavy Belgian lace from the rue
Maubeuge. Her ivory satin nightgown echoed the creami-
ness of her skin. She laughed. "What about yourself?" she
asked. "I have never seen anyone more intent on doing
good. You've been trotting about the country for months
now telling people that we have a responsibility to put an
end to the war."

"Don't laugh at me, woman." He sat on the bed beside
her and offered her his glass of white wine. "It's not
missionary work I'm interested in at the moment."

"Oh? What is it that interests you?"

He set the glass down on the bedside table. "You," he
answered simply and buried his face in her breasts. "Ah,"
he sighed. "It's good to be home."

It was a good time for both of them. Alexandre shone in a
way he never had before. He was no longer the gallant and
handsome charmer. Another dimension had been added to
his personality. He was a man of integrity and force,
distinguished both in appearance and behavior. "He's every
bit as strong a personality as Papa ever was," Dina told
Isabelle one night when the two women dined together.

"I have the impression that you are happier than ever.
Both of you," Isabelle said.

"We are. Especially now that Alexandre is such a success
on these speaking tours. He's not in anyone's shadow. These
are his own experiences, his own convictions. It has been
wonderful for him. And that makes it wonderful for me. As
for the rest of it . . ." She hesitated.

"The rest of it?"

"You know. Kitty and all that. We've never talked about it, but I've discovered that it doesn't matter. We were a bit awkward with each other at first, but once we got past that . . . well, everything was fine. I only wish he were home more, but I think the time is coming when he will be. There is so much pressure on the President now that the German U-boats are sinking our ships. They are acting as if they were at war with us already. When Alexandre was in Washington last week, the Senator told him that a declaration of war was in the offing. Within the month, he said."

It was early in April 1917 when the United States declared war on Germany, and there were those who believed that Alexandre de Granville had swayed public opinion as much as the German attacks on American shipping had. The morning after Congress responded to President Wilson's appeal to declare war in order to make the world safe for democracy, Dina looked up from the morning paper and said, "I'm so proud of you, darling. If it hadn't been for you, it might have been months more before the President got around to doing what everyone knew he had to do."

"You give me too much credit," he said tiredly. "You should thank the U-boat commanders. If the Germans were not waging submarine warfare on the American merchant fleet, he would not be so concerned about the safety of democracy."

"Perhaps. But you swayed public opinion."

"Possibly. I'd like to think so. I do think that I had some influence with a number of congressmen. At any rate, the step has been taken. And that means victory is in sight."

"Even before a single American soldier lands in France?"

"Absolutely. The Germans will be brought to their knees. It will take a year, possibly two, but there's no doubt about it now that we're in. And the Germans know it. All except the Kaiser perhaps."

She leaned her chin on her hand and looked thoughtfully across the breakfast table. "Do you suppose your Uncle

Albert knows what you have done? If there is such a thing
as consciousness or the like after death, I'm sure he is proud
of you. No one could have done more to avenge his death
than you have. And in the right way. Not by petty retribu-
tion, but by making people understand that they have to
fight against such evils.''

"I don't know." His voice was flat with fatigue this
morning. "It was not just for him," he added. "It was for
myself as well. When I was at the front and understood
what war was like, I would have done anything to rid the
world of it.

"The question now is," he changed the subject, "what
am I going to do?"

"Do."

"Yes, *do*." He emphasized the word. "There is no need
for me to go on telling people we ought to get into the war.
We're in it now. I suppose I ought to get into it myself."

"You'll do no such thing. You know what Dr. Godfrey
said. It'll be another year before you can count yourself
completely recovered. You're not fit to fight."

"A fine thing to tell your husband." He smiled wearily.
"You're going to put me back in a rocking chair, I suppose."

"I think you ought to take it easy for a while. Take a
vacation. You've been working hard. Next fall is time
enough to decide what you will do next."

She did not have to urge him into taking a vacation. The
last few weeks had been difficult and more than a little
frightening, although he had never mentioned it. One night,
speaking to a group in Illinois, he had grown faint and had
felt the familiar heart-flutter, experienced the same breath-
lessness. He had masked it easily. Reaching into his pocket
for the pills Dr. Godfrey had given him, he pretended to
cough, turned his back on the audience, and swallowed the
pill. He had apologized and carried on, and no one was the
wiser.

The same thing had happened a few nights later. He went

through the same charade, but by the time he had finished speaking, he was clutching the lectern for support.

This morning, elated as he was over the declaration of war, he felt fragile, as if any word, any movement might trigger a collapse. He had spoken of finding something to do, because he felt he should, but truth to tell, he had no energy. The very idea of getting up from the breakfast table was almost too much. He had crumbled a roll and drunk half a cup of coffee only because he did not want Dina to comment on his lack of appetite.

"I have letters to write," he said, pushing back his chair. "I must cancel the rest of my speaking engagements." He started to stand, but thought better of it.

"What's wrong?" She was at his side, alarmed.

"I don't know," he said. "I think I'm ill."

"Exhaustion, nothing more," Dr. Godfrey told her an hour later. "I can't be absolutely sure. I'll have to observe him. He's been pushing himself too hard. Traveling too much. Not sleeping enough. I don't think it's anything serious, but he's going to need rest. This influenza is a treacherous disease. It weakens the body more than one suspects. He has had a relapse, but he will bounce back if he takes care of himself."

Ned Buswell visited him toward the end of May. Alexandre received him upstairs in the den, wearing a paisley dressing gown with dark green silk lapels. He was elegantly groomed, but the hollows in his cheeks and the circles under his eyes testified to his fragility.

The Ambulance Corps had been absorbed into the American army and Buswell had transferred his energies to the Red Cross. He had planned to ask Alexandre to come work with him in Paris, but when he saw the pale man who steadied himself holding onto the back of a chair as he shook hands, he felt awkward. It was obvious that Alexandre was far from fit, but Buswell plowed ahead, regardless. "We need a liaison man to work with the civilian population in the villages behind the front," he said. "Someone who can talk with them and understand their needs. When I mentioned your name, the French agreed you were the right man for the job. They remember how smoothly everything went when you were liaison for the Ambulance Corps."

"I can't, Ned," he said. "I don't have the energy. They say all I need is rest, but I get awfully tired. Even if I were in tip-top condition, my place is at home right now. There is nothing I can do in France that someone else can't do better. My wife and daughter need me."

Buswell patted him on the shoulder. "Good man. I think you're making the right decision. I know you are. It's a shame though. We could use you."

After Buswell left, Alexandre sank into his favorite chair by the window, his feet up on the ottoman, resting as Dr. Godfrey had prescribed. As he looked over the back garden, his features were relaxed. There was a touch of color in his face. Buswell's visit had done a lot for him. He was not a weak and forgotten man. There were people who thought him competent, who wanted to put him to work. Well, when he was stronger . . .

Alexandre was still a listless convalescent, although greatly improved, when Frederick had his second stroke. This time it was in the evening. And this time Alexandre waited with Isabelle and Dina in the upstairs sitting room for Dr. Godfrey to emerge from the sickroom.

He was brusque when he came to them shortly before midnight. "There's no hope," he said. "He can't recover from this one. He's never going to talk again. Nor walk." He took Isabelle's hand. "I don't think he has much time, my dear."

"You forget how strong he is, what a fighter," she protested. "He's going to be with us for a long time yet."

"That's the spirit," he encouraged her. There was no point in telling her that Frederick would probably never be aware of how helpless he was. The brain damage was extensive this time.

Alexandre could not believe it. That vigorous bear of a man, boisterous and charming, shrewd and gallant. He could never die. He had too much life in him. But as the days passed, he came to recognize the extent of the damage inflicted by the stroke. It was almost too much for him to bear. Frederick had been more of a father to him in many ways than his own father. Alexandre would have done anything to make him well. But there was nothing he could do. So he sat at Frederick's bedside for hours every day and kept him company.

He arrived in the morning with the newspapers and read Frederick the items he thought would interest him. He told him who said what at whose dinner party and related the latest gossip, but mostly he talked about himself without knowing whether Frederick understood him, or even heard what he said.

It was like a confessional. The room was dim, the light filtered through the pale summer curtains. There was only the sound of Alexandre's voice. He told Frederick everything. About Kitty. About Paris. Lucie Soerbijk. How grateful he had been to Dina for welcoming him back as if nothing had happened. He told Frederick how he had planned to give her the rest of his Aunt Marita's diamonds.

"I don't know why I didn't," he told the older man, holding his hand and looking straight into his eyes. "I've thought about it a thousand times. How surprised she would be when she opened the pouch and the diamonds tumbled out. I've lived that scene over and over in my mind," he said. "I wish you could tell me why I haven't been able to make it come true."

He would leave Frederick in the early afternoon and walk home up Madison Avenue to take the nap that Dr. Godfrey still prescribed. Afterwards he prowled restlessly through the house. He reviewed the contents of his wine cellar and congratulated himself on having stocked it so generously, since French wines were a casualty of the war. He visited the kitchen to chat with Céleste. Sometime she would bring out her tattered notebook of recipes and they would work out menus for the week. He spent hours in the nursery suite on the top floor, reading to Vicky and teaching her the children's songs he remembered from his Belgian childhood.

One afternoon he went up to the attic and poked about idly at the odds and ends stored there. Wedding presents they had found no use for. Vicky's old crib. Trunks and packing cases. A flat, rectangular package caught his eyes. It was obviously a painting. Probably something Dina had bought and then rejected, but was too kindhearted to return to the artist, he guessed. Mildly curious, he undid the wrappings, carefully rolling back layers of brown paper. When he finally extracted the canvas, he gasped. He had been aware that it was a nude, but that was all. His concentration had been on the wrappings, not the contents.

It was a magnificent nude, all tousled hair and glowing skin, asleep in a disheveled bed. He recognized Goddard's brushwork immediately even without the signature in the corner. Dina! Jack! For a moment he thought he was choking.

He had known it, known it ever since Kitty had made sure he knew that night in Paris. He had been invaded by an anger that had driven him back into her arms in wild retaliation. With the anger had come a black and gripping jealousy and a loneliness so deep that even his mad pursuit of pleasure with Kitty could not make him forget it.

Time had been the healer, bringing the slow realization that he was in no position to be angry with his wife. In the end he had been able to dismiss her affair with Goddard as unimportant. But this afternoon in the hot stuffy attic the anger grew in him again until he thought his head would split. The blood was throbbing in his veins. He pounded on the wall until, suddenly weak, he had to lean against it for support. He had no idea how long he stood there, but it was long enough for the anger to subside and the agony to begin.

Dina had been unfaithful.

It was one thing to know it abstractly, but this painting tore him apart until he was a mass of raw, quivering nerve endings. It showed a woman exhausted from love, surfeited with love, languid with love.

He started to replace the canvas in its wrappings. There was more. A large portfolio. Inside were sketch after sketch of Dina. On the beach. In the bedroom. Nude. He bundled them hastily back into the portfolio. He could not stand any more. But as he started to rewrap, he saw another large package. He could not stop himself. Slowly, meticulously, he peeled away the wrappings. There were several canvases in this one. Dina again. Dina by the fireplace on the island. Ah, that look of the wanton. That pale face and fiery hair and the passion just below the surface. A masterpiece. Only a man in love, a man besotted, could have seen it in her. He looked at the others. Laughing Dina. Tender Dina. A proud wild Dina facing the wind. Oh God, it was a nightmare!

He rewrapped everything. When he was through he went downstairs slowly, holding onto the banister for support, and took a bath. He had to wash away everything that he had seen and felt before she came home. How could he face her tonight?

It was a silent evening. "Are you all right?" Dina asked, eventually putting down the folder of reports she was studying. He had barely spoken during dinner, which he had left untouched. Now he was sitting in the big wing chair, his face pale as a martyr's.

He pulled himself back from the vivid scenes his jealousy was painting for him. "What? All right? Of course I'm all right. A bit tired perhaps." His voice was carefully neutral, but his knuckles were white against the arms of the chair. "I think I may go to bed."

"Why don't you?" she encouraged him. "I'll have Walter bring you a brandy eggnog. It will help you sleep."

He did not answer. He pushed himself out of the chair with a visible effort and left the room. She looked after him. What was wrong? Should she try to pry it out of him? She would leave him alone, she decided. He had probably tried to do too much today. She rang for Walter.

"Please make one of your brandy eggnogs for Mr. de Granville. He has gone to bed. And make it rich, Walter. He ate practically nothing tonight."

"I'll put an extra egg yolk in," he promised. The whole kitchen staff had exclaimed over Alexandre's lack of appetite.

Alexandre pretended to be asleep with Dina came to bed. If he were to speak, it would all spill out, and that would open too many doors. The whole past that they had so discreetly buried without even acknowledging it would confront them. And how could *he* accuse *her* of infidelity? God! He had been such a fool! From the very first moment on the *Lusitania* when he had let Kitty into his cabin, he had done everything he could to ruin his life and betray Dina's trust. Whenever a wrong turn had presented itself, he had taken it. If he loved Dina, and he did—loved her so much it hurt sometimes—it was up to him to be silent. To forgive. And—hardest of all—to forget.

He spilled the whole thing out to Frederick. There were tears in his eyes as he sat at the old man's bedside and poured out his misery. Sometimes Frederick blinked. He did not know whether it was in sympathy or a meaningless reflex. "I would like to shoot Goddard," he said fiercely. Frederick blinked. Did it mean anything? He had no idea.

Frederick died that August on a hot, humid day on which there seemed to be no breath of air to be had. Alexandre was with him, holding his hand and telling him about the new Mary Pickford film he and Dina had seen. Frederick had sighed. And then he had gone.

The funeral was at the Fifth Avenue Presbyterian Church where Dina and Alexandre had been married. Angus Buchan, who had presided over that ceremony, presided over this one, too. The church was packed. To many it was the passing of an era. J. P. Morgan had died. Edward Harriman had died. And now Frederick Schumacher, the man who had come out of the West and made himself a vital part of the New York establishment, was gone. As Angus Buchan told the assembled mourners, "Frederick Schumacher was a good man, and all of us are the poorer for his passing."

Only half listening to the service, Dina grieved, "I never thanked Papa." Even though she knew how ill he had been, she had never thought of life without him. And now, for the first time in her life, he had gone away and left her. And he was never coming back. There was so much for which she had not thanked him. "Papa wanted me to be happy," she thought. "Most of all he wanted me to be strong. And he helped me to be both."

Late that night, after they had finally said good night to Isabelle, Dina leaned back in the car and looked at Alexandre sitting beside her in his somber dark suit, his head bent in sorrow. She took his hand. "Don't grieve for Papa," she said. "It is better this way. If he had been himself, he would have hated his existence. He is free now." Her voice broke. "And I'm going to miss him so terribly."

He put his arm around her. "I know. We both will." And for the moment, they were at peace.

A few weeks after the funeral Alexandre wandered into Dina's dressing room. "I'm lunching with Ned Buswell today." He spoke to her reflection in the mirror. Siddie was doing her hair while she riffled through pages full of figures, preparing for the first meeting of her day at the office.

"He's back in New York? We should ask him to dinner. How long will he be here this time?"

"Not long enough for a dinner. He's sailing for France tomorrow. He's been in Washington looking for someone to fill that liaison post. I've half a mind to tell him I'll do it after all."

"You'll do no such thing." She was alarmed. She turned

and looked at him, making Siddie gesture in despair as the
smooth plait she had been working on for the last five
minutes came undone. "You know what Dr. Godfrey said.
If you go off to France and travel from village to village in
the dead of winter . . ." She was almost sputtering.

"I've got to do something," he said, sinking into an
armchair, his legs stretched out in front of him. "I've no
intention of resuming the life of an interesting invalid.
Anyway, Godfrey's just being cautious. I'm fine." It was
true. He looked well. The long summer of rest and carefully
monitored activity had restored him. He was erect and
energetic, his amber-flecked eyes gleaming with vitality.

"I quite understand that you want to do something," she
said. "But does it have to be in France?"

He shrugged. "What else is there? I would go back
downtown, but you've got Whittaker now—although I don't
see how you can stand that cold drink of water. I suppose
he's competent."

"Yes, he is," she said slowly. "Very. But there's no
reason why you shouldn't come back. After all, Papa made
it Schumacher & de Granville. Your office is empty, waiting
for you. It's just that—well, I didn't think you wanted to
come back."

"I'd like to," he said simply.

"Wonderful!" She blew a kiss to him in the mirror. "I
can't think of anything I would like more. Now do run away
or Siddie will never get my hair done and I'll be late for my
meeting. We can talk tonight."

Alone with Siddie, she sighed and laid down the papers
she had been studying. Alexandre had no head for business.
True, he had recognized that Papa was behind the times, but
anyone with half an eye could have seen that. She would
have to find a niche for him. Perhaps Whit would have an
idea. She frowned. No, she could not discuss her husband
with Whit. But—and now she smiled—there was no problem. Alexandre should simply do what he did best. He was
far better with people than Whit. Whit was too cold with

clients. Alexandre could charm and cosset them while Whit concentrated on analysis and planning.

"And so that's the way it would work," she concluded. They had finished dinner and were sitting in the drawing room. A fire had been lit in the marble fireplace against the unexpected chill of the early October evening. "You will bring in new clients and watch over the interests of the old ones. Whit will expand his research staff and do more in-depth analysis of the areas I feel we should move into."

"No," he said flatly. "No."

"No? What do you mean, no?"

"I'd be a laughingstock," he said bitterly. "The man who goes downtown and works for his wife. Like your favorite mechanical toy. It would be the same as telling the world that no one had any use for me and so you sweetly made a place for me. No!" His face was cold with anger and hurt.

Shocked by his outburst, she opened her mouth and then closed it. Nothing she could say would convince him he was wrong. And it might be that he was right. Finally she broke the silence. "Oh," she said.

"Oh! Is that all you've got to say?" he demanded. He got up and poured himself a whiskey.

"You might give me one too." He poured a second glass and handed it to her wordlessly.

She sipped her whiskey. "Why not? Why not stay home? As long as Whit is there, nothing can go very wrong. I will have more time for Vicky. I've missed so much of her growing up. And I'll have more time for Alexandre too."

She smiled with a sudden radiance that astonished him. "You are right," she said. "You should take over. I just had not thought of asking you. You have been ill for so long. But you are well now. It's a good time to make the change. And I," she swallowed hard, "I will enjoy being a wife and mother again."

"Are you sure?" he asked, watching her keenly.

"As sure as I am that I love you, darling. It makes good sense."

"Then that is settled," he said and, smiling now, asked, "You know what the best part will be?"

She shook her head.

"Coming home to you every night." He sat beside her on the primrose silk-covered sofa and turned her face toward his. "Coming home to this." As he kissed her he suddenly thought of the day he had sat at his uncle's desk in Brussels and gone through his papers—and understood nothing.

# Twenty-two

$B$Y SPRING Dina was restless and bored. "What did I do before?" she asked Isabelle one afternoon when they were having tea at the Marlborough. "The days used to fly by, but what did I do?"

Isabelle poured the tea—"Lemon?" she asked—before she addressed herself to the younger woman's question. "Do? You were dizzyingly busy. You were still buying things for the house. You spent hours at the dressmaker's. You gave dinner parties. You were always dashing about."

"It's not enough now. I'm used to doing more. And don't tell me I should do war work. I'm not the type to roll bandages." She chose a small cake from the three-tiered dish in the center of the table. "I can't tell you how much I miss running the firm," she confessed.

Isabelle nodded sympathetically. "Your father always said that if you were a man, you would take Wall Street by storm. From what I heard, you did just that." She hesitated. "I admire the way you have managed with Alexandre," she said tentatively, not wanting to intrude where she might not be welcome. "I believe he has no idea of what you accomplished."

"No, I don't think he has. And it is just as well," Dina said frankly. "He would feel he had to surpass it. And when he didn't, he would decide he was a failure. I couldn't stand that. He has been hurt enough. Whatever happened in France left its mark."

"He's a good man, Dina. When I think of the hours he spent with Freddy. I leaned on him for courage and he never failed me."

"Yes, he is a good man." Her face was tender. "That's why he wants to run Schumacher and de Granville. He wants to take care of me and to make me proud of him. But I do miss all the excitement downtown. It was like a wonderful game. What worries me is that Alexandre doesn't really know how to play it. His talents are in organization and handling people. He's superb at both. Oh, well," she handed her empty cup to Isabelle, "I suppose I should be thankful. It's just that I'm so bored I could scream."

"Tell me," Isabelle said, her attention on the tea she was pouring, "who is managing your personal investments? Whit?"

"Whit! For heaven's sake, no! He is much too conservative. He is just what I needed for the firm, but he would never suit me. Once I have an assured return on seventy-five percent of my holdings, I gamble madly with the rest." Her eyes were sparkling. "And I usually win."

"Like your gamble on Alexandre," Isabelle teased.

"Isabelle!" Dina was shocked, then with the old gleam in her eyes, she said, "Yes, he was the best investment I ever made. Papa used to say that you pay for what you get and you get what you pay for. What I've learned is that you keep on paying—and Alexandre's price has been high at times. But I love him. And he loves me. That is more than even the gambler in me had dared hope for when we got married."

"You know," Isabelle said casually, "at one point I was

afraid that you and Whit—how shall I put it?—I thought
that if Alexandre did not come home soon, you would be
Mrs. Whittaker Ames."

"What nonsense!" Dina scoffed, hoping that she would
not blush. "Whit is so single-minded it is almost alarming.
All he thinks about is making money. I understand he even
put his wife's stables on a paying basis."

Isabelle was satisfied. She had been quite aware of their
affair despite Dina's discretion, and concerned lest smoldering
ashes remained ready to be fanned into a fresh blaze. Her
suspicions were closer to the truth than she knew.

There had been times in the first weeks after Dina had
handed over the reins of Schumacher & de Granville when
she had seriously considered resuming her affair with Whit.
She would never leave Alexandre, never stop loving him,
but giving Whit up when Alexandre returned from France
had been a wrench. Working with him had kept the attrac-
tion alive, and after Alexandre took over, she missed the
daily contact and the pleasurable inner flutter it gave her.
Missed the meaningful glances, the ostensibly accidental
touch of his hand. She was tempted. But she could not be
unfaithful to Alexandre. Oh yes, there had been smoldering
ashes, but they were dead long before this tête-à-tête over
tea; they had been dead ever since the February day when
Whit had telephoned and asked permission to call on her.

"Permission!" she laughed. "You are always welcome.
Come by this afternoon. Walter will mix his famous Orange
Blossoms." She was conscious of a certain excitement. As
she talked, she was thinking of what she would wear.

"I would prefer to see you before the cocktail hour," he
said stiffly. "To be sure that we will not be interrupted."

She lifted her eyebrows. What could be on his mind?
"By all means come earlier. We will simply move the
cocktail hour ahead."

Tall and elegant, he arrived as the hall clock struck four.
The discreet herringbone of his dark gray suit, the starched
white collar, the dark blue club tie, the English shoes with

the muted glow that testified to his valet's conscientious attention made him a figure of quiet distinction.

"Come into the little sitting room," she invited him. "It's cozier there." They sat in the chintz-covered armchairs in front of the fire and Dina made small talk. The weather. The heatless and meatless days. The epidemic of Spanish influenza. He dismissed each topic with a few words. Surely conversation had not always been so difficult between them, she thought. What was prompting this visit?

Finally he set his glass on the silver tray and leaned toward her, hitching himself to the edge of the chair. "I've come to say good-bye, my dearest. I wanted you to be the first to know. I will present a formal letter of resignation to your husband tomorrow."

"Good-bye! Resignation! What is going on?"

He leaned forward even more and took her hands. His were cold and just slightly damp. "The firm is not the same now that you have left," he said. "I no longer feel I have anything to contribute. Your husband and I do not think along the same lines. I have deemed it best to make other plans."

"I'm sorry to hear this. Your leaving will be a great loss. I am sure Alexandre will tell you the same thing. And I will miss you." As she said this last, she realized that she did not care whether he stayed or went. It was strange. Renouncing him had been so difficult. The hidden flirtation that had followed had been a bittersweet delight compounded by equal parts of guilt and pleasure at knowing that she was desired and desirable. There had also been an element of secret revenge. And now—her only regret was that he would be a loss to the firm. Nothing more.

"I want you to know how much I have admired your loyalty to your husband," he went on. How ridiculously pompous, she thought. How presumptuous. "It cannot have been easy for you. I also have something else to tell you." He paused. "I myself am planning to marry."

"Why, Whit! How lovely! This is a pleasant surprise. I am so happy for you. Who is she?"

"It will represent a great change in my life," he said, getting up and standing in front of the fire. "I am marrying Miss Althea Morris Quentin of Baltimore. Directly after our marriage," he barely suppressed a smile, "my appointment as president of Quentin and Quentin will be announced."

"Oh, she's one of the chemical Quentins. Well, Whit, this is wonderful news. Except that you are leaving. I am sure Baltimore is a very pleasant place to live."

"It is," he agreed, "although we are planning to live outside the city. Althea is a great horsewoman."

Dina sighed with relief half an hour later as the door closed behind him, grateful that it was not she who was marrying him. How had she ever convinced herself that she loved him?


"It's amazing what a little distance will do," she told Alexandre that evening as she recounted the details of the visit. "I had never realized how pompous he was. How boring. He is such a brilliant financial thinker. I suppose that blinded me to the rest. And he was always so helpful, so stalwart. I think I pity Miss Althea Morris Quentin."

"I told you he was a long drink of water. I'm not going to miss him for a moment," Alexandre said with heartfelt satisfaction. "But don't waste your pity on Miss Quentin. The word downtown is that she is a forty-five-year-old spinster who will inherit fifty-one percent of Quentin and Quentin. She is considered a very shrewd woman. Old Mr. Quentin has one foot in the grave, and she wants a manager she can trust so that she can devote her time to her horses. While Whit," Alexandre laughed, "Whit wants a woman with a substantial fortune who will let him manage it. I have been expecting his resignation for some time."

"Whit marrying for money! You can't mean it!"

"Let's just say—how does that ridiculous saying go—he knows how to get his bread buttered on the right side." He looked at her sharply. "Hadn't it ever occurred to you that Whit was so stalwart and helpful because he thought you might—he might . . ."

"Never!" She said firmly. "No," she said, hoping she had not been overly emphatic, "my impression was that he was ambitious for power and I made it clear that if he came to work for me, he would have power." But as she dismissed Alexandre's suggestion, she knew he was right. What an idiot she had been! To Whit she had represented the possibility of a rich layer of butter on his financial bread. She smiled mischievously at Alexandre. "I rather think I might send them two dozen butter knives for their wedding present."

As Isabelle, getting ready to leave, drew on her white kid gloves she looked across the tea table and said, "My thought was that you might find your own investments as much of a challenge as those of Schumacher & de Granville.

"And something else. I don't like to criticize, my dear, but you must know that ever since you took over for your father, your household has become just a trifle slack. It has not improved since you have been at home. Anna's apron was wrinkled the other day. And the new maid had a spot on her uniform. When we were driving here this afternoon, I noticed the metal work on the Packard wasn't what it should be. Burns should polish the cars every morning. I imagine the household accounts might bear looking into as well. When the mistress's mind is elsewhere, the servants tend to cut all kinds of corners."

Dina stood up, fastening the clasp of the sable fur piece draped about her shoulders. "You make me ashamed of myself. I've been moping about wishing I was sitting behind that desk in the office and I haven't been tending to my job at home. It's time I stopped acting like a sulky child."

"You are not hurt that I made those suggestions?" Isabelle asked a few minutes later as Burns drove them up Fifth Avenue.

"Hurt? How could I be. I am thankful. When I was living with Papa I would not have tolerated the things that I now tolerate in my own house. I am the one who has become slack."

After dropping Isabelle off in Murray Hill, she turned a cold eye on her domestic domain. Notebook in hand, she went from room to room on the first floor. The yellow damask on the sofa in the little downstairs sitting room was faded. The velvet swags above the windows were dusty. The pale silk seats of the dining room chairs were disgraceful. There was a stain on one of the marble mantels in the drawing room. Scratches on the leather sofa in the library. Dust on a table top. A bouquet of fading flowers on the hall table. This was too much! She rang for Anna.

"What are these flowers doing here?"

Anna looked at her, not comprehending.

"They are dead," Dina said sharply. "Why were they left here?"

"I'm sorry, ma'am. I'll take them away immediately." She picked up the vase and dusted underneath it with a corner of her apron.

"Since when have you used your apron as a duster, Anna?" she rebuked her. "If there are any more dead flowers about the house, please dispose of them." Isabelle was right. Things were not as they should be. Everything needed sprucing up. The furnishings, the staff—and herself.

Upstairs in her dressing room, she rang for Siddie. It was time to dress for dinner. For the first time in months she felt alive. She was looking forward to tomorrow. She had work to do.

She tied the ribbons of Vicky's school hat under her chin and gave her a kiss. She then kissed Alexandre. She looked enchanting in a flower-sprigged wrapper. Her hair was done, but now that she was staying home, she breakfasted in a morning gown instead of getting dressed and ready for the office. Alexandre liked seeing her, soft and feminine, across the table. She stood at the door waving as Burns pulled away from the curb. They would drop Vicky at school and then continue on downtown to the office.

She was going to have a lovely day, too. Siddie had laid out her clothes—a gray silk shirtwaist and a black skirt. "I'll wear the single strand of pearls today," she decided, "and the pearl-and-diamond earrings. The small ones."

She twirled in front of the mirror, pleased with what she saw. "Ask Walter to come see me," she asked and crossed the hall into the small sitting room that she planned to use as an office. She would need files and a desk, but for the moment, the mahogany gate-legged table between the windows would serve.

There was a knock on the door. "Come in, Walter."

He entered, slightly puzzled about the summons, but suspecting it had something to do with the faded flowers she had commanded Anna to remove the previous afternoon.

She came straight to the point. "I am distressed about the way the house looks. And the staff. I confess that I have not given you much supervision lately, but I thought I had a competent and conscientious staff.

"Yesterday I walked around the house for less than an hour, and look." She showed him her notebook with page after page of specifics.

"There is dust on the moldings. Fingerprints on the service door to the dining room. The silver in the cabinet is tarnished. Curtains need to be laundered. Draperies need to be cleaned. I filled six pages in this notebook yesterday afternoon and that is only the first floor.

"Walter, I am shocked. Starting this morning things must be different or I will be forced to make some changes. I want you to call everyone together—except Siddie and Céleste—and tell them their work is not up to my standards. I want to see an immediate improvement."

He stood rigid in front of her, pale with dismay, angry at his own negligence. Little by little the staff had been cutting corners. It was his responsibility.

"Yes, ma'am. I will see to it that things improve. You will have no further cause for complaint."

"I'm counting on you," she said. "I want no more dead flowers or dust or fingerprints or tarnish. I want starched aprons, polished shoes. I will not tolerate anything less than perfection."

As the door closed behind him, she turned her attention to her investment portfolio. Hours later, she raised her head. It had been too long since she had reviewed her holdings. She was encouraged by the strength of her stocks. She had made no serious mistakes, but she would have done better if she had been paying attention to business.

She leaned back and began to think. What should she sell? What should she buy? What did the future hold? The war would be over soon. Everyone was agreed on that. Ever since the opening of the Allied offensive on the Western Front, the German armies had been crumbling. She had to look ahead. What next? The overheated war economy was bound to cool down. Years ago she had advised Ephraim Fleming to plan his expansion so his plant could be retooled easily for the peacetime market. But what was the market going to be like?

She got up and stood at the window. The factories that were now turning out uniforms and boots, rifles and gas masks, and all the rest of war's paraphernalia would be closing down. There would be unemployment, probably high unemployment, for a while. Not only the factory workers. The homebound soldiers would swell the ranks of those out of work. They were also going to create a market, she thought. They would be getting married, starting families. Yes, they would need homes and furniture, radios, automobiles. Hmmm. Automobiles.

She sat at the makeshift desk and jotted down the ideas as they came to her. Automobiles meant highways. Towns and cities would be building roads. Automobiles need gasoline. Along those new roads would be places to buy gas. Oil would be in great demand. And steel. And rubber for tires.

There was going to be a phenomenal economic boom centered around the automobile alone. Good Lord! She must talk to Alexandre. They had to be in a position to take advantage of it. She stuck her pencil in her hair and walked about the room excitedly. What else would change? The time was coming when everyone would have electric lights. Electric power would be needed not only for lights, but a hundred uses. The opportunity for growth there was unlimited.

The important question, though, was not so much *what* to buy as *when*. There would be a recession before the boom. It was inevitable. It was vital that Schumacher & de Granville put itself in a strong cash position.

I'm as security-minded as Papa ever was, she thought. It was not a bad way to be. She had vivid memories of the Panic of 1907. She had never forgotten the morning Papa had sat slumped at the breakfast table after an all-night session with J. P. Morgan and the top financiers of New York. "You can't let the country fall into a depression," Papa had said. "The price is too terrible. The human tragedy unimaginable."

She would do anything to keep Alexandre and Vicky safe. Papa had guarded against future economic cataclysms with that hoard of gold. She had been right, she told herself, to use the gold to modernize and expand the firm, but now it was necessary to think about preserving what she had built, to make sure that Alexandre and Vicky would never want for anything. Schumacher & de Granville must achieve a strong cash position before the end of the war.

She leaned back and stretched. It had been a long time since she had worked so hard, concentrated so intently, thought so creatively. It was tiring, but exhilarating. She straightened up and made a few notes for the next day, stacked the folders neatly, and stood up. It was almost four o'clock. She had been working for nearly seven hours. It was the most satisfying day she had spent in a long time.

*      *      *

Alexandre could hear laughter floating down from the nursery floor—Vicky's high-pitched giggle and Dina's low,
silvery tone. He smiled. It was good for Dina to be home
and good for Vicky to have her mother at home. He handed
his umbrella and hat to Walter, then ran up the stairs, two at
a time. When the hugs and kisses were over, Dina told him,
"We don't have much time with Vicky tonight, darling. We
are going to the Doughboy's Ball and dinner before at the
Schiffs'."

All week Dina had been trying to find the right moment
to talk with Alexandre about the firm's future, to discuss
what holdings should be liquidated in anticipation of the
future recession and boom, but their social schedule had
been so hectic there had been no time. And there was no
time now. "I'll leave you two together," she said. "I must
start to dress. There is time for one game of Parcheesi
before Vicky has her supper. No more."

She was wearing a new gown that evening—a daring
innovation in gold-lamé chiffon. It was cut slim and straight,
so simple it could have been mistaken for an undergarment
except for the luxurious fabric. There was a matching wrap
in the same gold-lamé chiffon bordered with sable, designed
to be worn with one end tossed over her shoulder and
trailing to the floor behind her. The whole ensemble was so
light she felt undressed. It was a new silhouette—quite
startling, and very sophisticated. She hoped Alexandre would
approve.

She watched carefully as Siddie did her hair. "I wonder if
I should have it cut short," she said.

"Nobody has short hair." Siddie was appalled at the idea.
"You would not cut your beautiful hair. Would you?"

"I don't know. I'm ready for a change."

"You'll be wearing the yellow diamonds tonight, I
suppose?"

"I—no—I think something else." She had not worn the
yellow diamond necklace since the day she had given the
earrings back to Whit. She was in no mood to parry Siddie's

questions about what had happened to them. "Let's look through the boxes."

Siddie opened the safe and brought out the trays containing her jewelry cases. The women opened one box after another and considered the contents. Dina scrabbled through the jewelry cases. "Here! My black pearls." She looped the long strand of caviar-colored pearls around her neck. "Not important enough," she finally decided. Then she picked up the yellow diamond and emerald necklaces and began twisting them together with the pearls. "Look. They are marvelous together."

"The stones will scratch the pearls," Siddie warned.

"Not if I don't tug at them. Here, fasten them for me." She watched intently as Siddie fastened the triple strand about her neck. "That's it." She gathered the feather-light wrap around her and turned slowly. "Yes," she confirmed. "And the emerald earrings." She gazed at herself and frowned. "I need more makeup."

"Will there be no end to it?" Siddie exclaimed, her smile denying any intention of sting. She set to work eagerly, tying a crepe de Chine makeup apron around Dina's neck like a huge bib. She darkened her eyelashes so they were almost black. She deepened the green eye shadow and brushed a tracing of gold over it. Then she stood back and examined her work.

"More rouge. But darker." She rummaged through the makeup cupboard until she found a pot of rouge that was almost brick-colored and smoothed it over the lighter rouge she had applied earlier. She stood back again. This time she nodded. This was a Dina no one had seen, a creature of golden fire and flame.

"You are a true artist," Dina said seriously. Siddie had transformed her in minutes. She glanced in the mirror again as she drew the sable-trimmed wrap around her. "No, I don't think I will cut my hair."

When she joined Alexandre in the drawing room, he

stared, then kissed her hand. "Congratulations, Madame de Granville. You are magnificent!"

She looked at him almost shyly. "What do you think, really?"

"It's fantastic. You look like someone out of a dream. Golden and strange—and very desirable. Like the flame that attracts moths. Move around and let me see you."

She let the wrap slide off her shoulders and walked the length of the drawing room, then came back and turned around for his closer inspection.

"A triumph! Every man is going to be jealous of me, my darling."

Siddie was waiting up to help her undress when they came home. "Thank goodness we left early," Dina said when she finally joined Alexandre in bed. "It takes almost as long to get undressed as it does to get dressed."

"We *had* to leave early." He smiled lazily. "If we had stayed five more minutes, some woman would have clawed your eyes out. You were dazzling."

"You do exaggerate, but I like it," she said. "Tell me, what did Mr. Fessenden want with you? He had you in a corner most of the night."

"Business, what else? He's asked me to go in with him on a big project. It will take a lot of capital, but it's worth it. He's a shrewd old bird, you know."

"But darling," she began and then stopped.

"But darling what?" he asked good-humoredly.

"Oh, nothing. But you know he's made mistakes. Big ones. Papa had to bail him out a couple of times."

"Nobody will have to bail anyone out of this deal," he said confidently. "It can't fail. But what are we spending the best part of the night talking business for? We have something better to do before we go to sleep."

"How do you suppose it happens that lovemaking always gets better?" she asked some time later. "I would think one would reach a plateau and that would be it, but we never do. At least I never do.''

He leaned on his elbow and smiled down at her. ''It's because we are two extraordinarily gifted people.'' He smiled mischievously and whipped the sheet off her.

''Wretch!'' She grabbed for it.

''I want to see you. All of you.''

''Idiot!'' She rolled toward him and kissed him, then got out of bed. He lay there admiring her long-legged grace. She was truly a goddess. The slim waist, the swelling hips, those marvelous breasts. She slipped into her nightgown and he groaned. ''Cruel,'' he accused her. ''Cruel. You keep hiding.''

''You call this hiding?'' The nightgown was cut low in front and back and tied at the shoulders with ribbons that fluttered as she crossed the room to the dressing table. Her body, silhouetted against the lamplight, was even more seductive behind the transparent veil of the nightgown. She tied her hair back with a ribbon.

''Come here,'' he ordered in mock command. ''I haven't finished with you.''

''You're insatiable. It's late.'' As she moved around the large bedroom turning off the shaded lamps, her eye fell on the stock charts she had been working on that afternoon. They were on the table by the chaise longue. ''Darling, there's something I've been meaning to tell you for days.''

''Ah ha! Let me guess. You are in love with another man and you are going to leave me. No, no, that couldn't be it. You have decided to learn how to fly. I forbid it. Or is it that you have accepted an invitation to the Catlings?'' He put on a fierce face. ''I tell you I will not go. They are the dullest people in the world. How can you do such a thing to me?''

''Such silliness.'' She sat beside him and ruffled his hair. ''No, it's something serious. I've been working on my investments and it has made me realize that we must start to prepare for the end of the war. The firm has to be in a liquid position so that we can take advantage of the boom that is sure to come. That's why I think this business with Holcombe Fessenden . . .''

She stopped in midsentence. There was a look in his eyes that went straight to her heart, that combination of pride and insecurity that she had first seen the day he had slipped the little makeshift engagement ring on her finger. She glanced down at it now. It was her most cherished possession.

She berated herself silently for her stupidity. She was on the verge of taking away all his confidence in his ability to run the business and the pride he felt in providing for her and Vicky.

She bent down and kissed him. "Forgive me, darling. It's just that I started thinking about stocks and bonds for the first time in months. It's probably been obvious to you all along, but it struck me as a revelation and I got all excited. You know I wouldn't dream of telling you what to do. I'm too far away from things now."

He drew her down beside him. "I know," he said softly. "You don't have to explain. You had so much on your shoulders for so long. Worrying gets to be a habit. Now you have to make a habit of leaving the worrying to me. That's what a husband is for."

"No," she contradicted, putting her arms around him. "Husbands are to love."

Later when his breathing told her he was asleep, she pulled herself up on her pillows and stared into the dark. He was going to destroy the firm. Sooner or later, it was inevitable. But if she intervened, she would wreck their marriage.

It was as simple as that—the firm or their marriage. She had no choice. She had to follow her heart. She had almost lost Alexandre once because she had thought it more important to stay home than to go to Brussels with him. Her priorities had been wrong then. She could not make the same kind of mistake again. He came first. So what if he should run Schumacher & de Granville into the ground? She loved him and she needed him. He had made life wonderful for her. And anyway, she had plenty of money. They would still be rich no matter what happened. When the postwar boom comes, she told herself, I'm going to be richer than Papa ever was.

She yawned and snuggled down close to Alexandre. A minute later, she was asleep.

# Twenty-three

THE DE GRANVILLES were richer than ever. The postwar recession had been short-lived and the boom that followed, hectic. More than five million automobiles were rolling off the assembly lines every year and the growth of the electric power industry was spectacular. The twenties were golden.

Alexandre sparkled with confidence. Where he had once been accepted as Frederick Schumacher's son-in-law, he was now welcomed as a man of status in his own right. His highly effective speaking tours that had helped sway public opinion in favor of joining in the war had gained him respect. He was considered "one of us" by the Wall Street insiders now.

When the "sure things" that his friends touted him on, offering him a chance to get in on the ground floor, never rose from the ground floor but sunk right through the basement, he took it with equanimity. He could afford the losses. The suspicion that he was being tapped as a source of capital for undertakings that wiser heads had refused to touch never entered his mind. As far as he was concerned, his Wall Street colleagues were a bunch of fine fellows.

The most flamboyant aspects of the postwar prosperity left the de Granvilles untouched. The radicals, the smart set, the cocaine users, the apostles of free love, the social and political changes that were part of the jazz age did not touch their lives. Their only contact with the speakeasy culture was the bootlegger who kept Alexandre's wine cellar well stocked and preserved them from bathtub gin and whiskey of dubious pedigree. Their social life was the same round of dinner parties and receptions and periodic appearances at the opera and theater that it had always been; their summers were divided between Duck Island and Newport. It was a quiet and sedate life, varying little from year to year.

The greatest change was their new house—or rather the expansion of the old one. With Vicky growing up, the house was suddenly much too small. They discussed building a larger place farther uptown, but their sentimental attachment to the house where they had begun married life held them back. When the house next door came on the market unexpectedly, they snapped it up and engaged an architect to turn the two houses into one.

The result was a mansion with its own art gallery, a drawing room sixty feet long, and a dining room that sat thirty. There were twenty-seven rooms altogether. Vicky had her own suite. The third floor was given over to a ballroom with all the necessary appurtenances, cloakrooms, a splendid entrance hall, and two small salons for those who preferred bridge or gossip to dancing.

"A ballroom!" Alexandre had exclaimed when Dina showed him the blueprints. "My dearest wife, what do you have in mind? Vicky's dancing class could not fill one corner of this room. And I have no intention of inviting the world to foxtrot on our third floor. Do we really need a ballroom?"

"No one *needs* a ballroom, but don't forget that Vicky will be making her debut soon. I would much prefer we have her coming-out ball at home than at a club or a hotel."

"You must be feverish. Vicky is a child!"

She smiled at him fondly. "Your daughter will be seventeen in 1929, my love. That is only two years away. I am planning her debut for that May."

"I see," he said cheerfully. "It is a necessity after all. By all means let us have a ballroom." He was already seeing himself leading Vicky out onto the floor for the first dance of her debutante ball.

Dina and Alexandre stood at the side of the ballroom watching their daughter. She was as fresh and as devastatingly pretty at two in the morning as she had been at the start of the evening. With a circlet of white orchids twined with pearls crowning her coppery hair, she was a princess out of a fairy tale. The orchestra was playing a waltz, and as she whirled around the room, yards of white chiffon floated and swirled about her giving the illusion that she was dancing in a cloud. By the expression on her face she might have been. Her huge sea-colored eyes were fixed on her partner's eyes, her face tilted up to his. She was only seventeen, but to her parents she had the absorbed look of a woman in love.

"Who is that she's dancing with?"

"I don't know. It must be one of the young men from out of town. He looks familiar though." Her gaze followed the couple across the floor. He was smiling at Vicky with a mixture of joy and incredulity as if he had just discovered the lost city of Atlantis.

"I'm going to tell that young man that I want to dance with my daughter." Alexandre walked across the floor to the bedazzled couple. He said a few words and then Vicky was in his arms. The young man stood against the wall watching them. Dina studied him. He was handsome with black hair and emerald eyes. His lips were sensuously full.

She caught her breath. Familiar! Of course he looked familiar. She looked around for Isabelle and found her holding court among New York's most eligible widowers. "Isabelle, may I kidnap you for a few minutes?"

Isabelle rose. "It is a lovely party, my dear. A great success."

Dina disregarded this. "Isabelle, who is that boy?" she demanded. "Over there by the wall. Do you see the one I mean?"

"The one who looks like Alexandre?"

"You see it too. Who is he?" Her voice was strained.

"Come, let's sit over there where we can talk." Isabelle led her to a loveseat shielded by potted palms and banks of flowers. "I heard that Sam Parseval insisted that he wanted to see his grandson before he lost his sight completely," she said once they were seated.

"Then he is *Kitty's* son?"

"He must be."

"He is not her husband's son," Dina stated.

"I didn't say that."

"You didn't have to. He is Alexandre's son," she whispered. "Alexandre's."

The music stopped and Alexandre and Vicky joined them. Vicky beckoned to the young man. "This is Sam Milraven-Peake," she said, introducing him to her parents and Isabelle. "He has just come from England to visit his grandfather, Mr. Parseval." Her eyes were gleaming almost mischievously.

"Milraven-Peake," Alexandre said. "You must be Kitty's son."

"Yes, sir."

"How is she these days?"

"Very well, sir. She is living in Paris now." He had a pronounced English accent. "She has remarried. My father died when I was six."

"I am sorry to hear that." Alexandre was white-faced.

Vicky took Sam's arm. "Let's ask them to play another waltz," she proposed, and they set off toward the orchestra at the other end of the room. Isabelle slipped away. Dina and Alexandre looked at each other.

"This is an awkward little surprise." She tried to keep her voice light, but it broke with a suspicion of a sob.

"I don't suppose you will believe me." He was still pale with shock. "It is just as much a surprise to me as to you."

"I'm glad you're not trying to deny it anyway."

"How could I? There is no possible doubt." His face hardened. "That bitch. She must have known it all these years. And that poor fellow she married. I wonder if he ever suspected."

Holcombe Fessenden and his wife came up to them. "A grand party," he said. "You've launched your daughter well."

"She's such a pretty girl," Mrs. Fessenden said.

"Pretty! She's a raving beauty. And I told her so. You're not going to have her much longer, Alexandre. Some young man is going to carry her off one of these days."

"I think we'll have her for a few more years," Dina said. "She's planning to go to Radcliffe next year."

"What! That adorable creature! You're not going to make a bluestocking out of her!"

"It's her choice. I see nothing wrong with it."

"Well. Hmmph." He was at a loss for words, then he cheered up. "She may think she wants to go to college," he said, "but once she has embarked on the debutante whirl, mark my words she is going to find men more interesting that musty old books."

"You may be right," she responded. "We shall have to wait and see."

It was obvious they could not talk now. They still had work to do as host and hostess—smiles to smile and compliments to receive. "I must go say a few words to the Edingtons," she said. She looked at him soberly. "Sometime very soon you and I must have the conversation we have been avoiding all these years."

It was dawn before the last guests left, trailing out to the automobiles with sleepy chauffeurs lined up along the avenue. The orchestra had packed up its instruments and gone.

The caterers had disappeared. Just the wilting flowers and the three de Granvilles remained. Dina looked around and sighed. "It was so beautiful a few hours ago and now it's just a room that needs to be cleaned. And we need to go to bed and get some sleep."

"Bed!" exclaimed Vicky. "I have no time for bed. I told Sam that I would go riding with him in the park this morning."

"I promise you that Sam will not present himself before noon," her father said. "I suggest you try to sleep."

"I'll try, but I don't know if I can. I'm still so excited. It was the most wonderful ball anyone ever had. Thank you." She kissed them and, holding her chiffon skirts high, ran downstairs.

"A bombshell," he said wearily when she was out of earshot.

"Miss Parmenter, who handled the invitations, told me that Mr. Parseval had asked if a young relative of his could be invited and I said that of course he could and that she should add him to the list. But I had no idea." Dina frowned. "How could he do such a thing to us? Without any warning. Without saying a word?"

"I doubt that he knows. He is practically blind."

"I suppose that's the explanation. But what are we going to do?" she said despairingly.

"After we get some sleep, I suggest we sit down and have that talk that you claim we have been postponing."

"Yes, we should. But right now I need to be alone. This has been a shock. I'd appreciate it if you would sleep in your dressing room."

"If that's what you want." The hurt showed in his face.

I don't care, she thought. It is too much to expect me to take this in my stride. I'm sorry his feelings are hurt. But he doesn't seem to consider I might be hurt by discovering that he has a bastard son. She turned without saying anything and went down the stairs slowly.

Once in her own dressing room with Siddie helping her

undress, Dina looked at herself in the mirror. A forty-four-year-old woman looked back at her. A woman with circles under her eyes and fine lines around her mouth. She was too old to be acting like a melodramatic ninny. What did it matter what had happened all those years ago? Why should the existence of this boy affect her feelings for Alexandre?

"Just a moment, Siddie." She crossed the bedroom swiftly and knocked on the door to his study. Without waiting for an answer, she opened it. He was standing at the window in his dressing gown. He turned to look at her, his face expressionless. She embraced him. "Forgive me, darling. I don't know what got into me. I was just upset. Do come to bed. I need you." The words came spilling out.

"I need you too," he said holding her tight.

Half an hour later they were asleep in each other's arms.

They approached their confrontation late that afternoon as if it were a meeting of the League of Nations. Dina had ordered the tea tray brought up to the new second-floor conservatory, a serene room overlooking the garden where the trees were in fresh spring leaf.

This was the moment they had dreaded ever since Alexandre had returned from Paris all those years ago. Where to begin? How to begin? What would be the outcome of this afternoon's talk?

It was Dina who broke the silence. Unexpectedly, shocking Alexandre, she laughed. "Now that we are here," she said, "I don't know that we really have anything to talk about." Her voice was dryly amused. "There is a reason why we have never discussed this, you know."

He lifted an eyebrow.

"We didn't have to. I have always known about your relationship with Kitty. It was no secret. Everyone was gossiping about it. I consider myself partly to blame, as a matter of fact. I should have gone to Brussels with you as you wanted. But it's ancient history. There is nothing to be gained by raking up the past."

"There is one thing I must tell you," he said, "and that is I had absolutely no idea. None whatsoever. I did not know Kitty was pregnant. When she got word that her husband was wounded and was being invalided home, she left me on the same day. I never spoke to her again."

"I believe you. The only thing we really have to talk about is what we are going to do." She was deeply concerned. "What in the world are we to do?"

"I don't understand."

"Vicky is falling in love with your son." She was agitated now. "Didn't you see the way she looked at him? The way he looked at her? And now they are spending the afternoon together. What are we going to do?"

"I suggest we simply wait and see what happens."

"Wait! Wait until she comes to us and says she wants to marry him? Or do you mean wait until somebody points out the resemblance and tells her of your old affair with his mother?"

He lifted his hand. "I think I hear her."

She came into the conservatory, still in riding clothes, looking as fresh as if she had slept the night away instead of dancing it away. "Sam is every bit as nice as I thought he would be," she said, sinking down on the couch. "We discovered that we agree on practically everything. I think we should ask him to the island this summer."

"Isn't that a bit precipitous?" Now Alexandre was alarmed. "You may not be as interested in him by July."

"Not interested in my own brother?"

"What?" they exclaimed with one voice.

"Did you think I didn't know? You can't keep it a secret. Sam and I talked about it this afternoon. I'm not shocked." She smiled at them. "I'm grown now. I've made my debut. I'm delighted to discover that I have a brother. And besides, it's so romantic."

"Romantic!" her mother exclaimed. "What is so romantic about it?"

"It's like a film. There was Papa all alone in France,

helping those Belgian refugees and driving ambulances and all that. He must have missed you terribly, Mama, and been awfully lonely. And there was Sam's mother working for the Red Cross while her husband was fighting at the front and she didn't know whether he was alive or dead. And when she and Papa ran into each other one night in Paris—well, it was inevitable. They comforted each other. I think it's romantic.''

"Er, yes. I suppose you could think of it that way,'' her father said. "But tell me, how did you learn all this?''

"Why, I knew the minute I saw him last night. He looks just like you, Papa. Doesn't he, Mama? When he asked me to dance I said—'I think my papa is your papa too.' And he said—'That's what Mother told me.' And then he told me the whole story.''

"How do you feel about it?'' her mother asked.

"About what?''

"About everything. His mother. Your father.'' Dina could not bring herself to be more explicit.

"I know that Papa never stopped loving you. It was just one of those things. And I know you never stopped loving Papa. So I don't see that it really matters to us.''

"I was thinking about the gossip. With his looks, it's inevitable.''

"I don't think we should pay any attention to it. Do you, Papa? Sam is a very nice boy. He is going back to England in a few weeks. If anyone should say anything, I will simply say he is my half-brother. And if they want to know more, I will say that I do not discuss my family's personal affairs.''

"Bravo!'' Alexandre bent over and kissed her cheek. "You are indeed a sensible girl. I agree with you that we should ask him to the island. I'd like to get to know him better. That is,'' he looked at Dina, "if it is all right with you?''

"It is all right with me, darling. He is your son.'' She smiled ruefully and told Vicky, "You know, your father and I were sitting here worried out of our wits that you might be falling in love with Sam. We didn't know how to tell you the truth. We didn't want you to be hurt.''

"In love with Sam!" Vicky shrieked. "But he's only fourteen years old!"

Dina and Alexandre looked at each other and burst into uncontrollable laughter. "We are such idiots," Dina said when she was finally able to speak. "Of course. If we had only thought. It is just that he looks so mature."

"We de Granvilles have always been quite mature for our age," Alexandre said. "I remember myself at fourteen. I was . . .''

"Not now, dearest," she interrupted him. "I cannot cope with any more disclosures." Her eyes were amused and her face relaxed. "I suppose this is what one calls a tempest in a teapot.''

Vicky yawned. The excitement that had buoyed her up all day had dissipated. She was no longer the unshockable young woman of the world, but a tired girl who needed to sleep. "It's time you have a bath and get to bed," her mother said. "I'll have Céleste prepare a tray for you and you can have your supper in bed.''

Vicky struggled to her feet. "I am tired," she admitted. She kissed them and seconds later they heard the hum of the ascending elevator. "I think we should follow suit," Dina said. "Supper on trays upstairs.''

An hour later they were eating one of Céleste's soufflés in front of the fire in Alexandre's study. The May evening had turned cool and the fire felt good. "This reminds me of our wedding night," she told him, "except that I wasn't as tired then as I am now. And I think I prefer this chablis to the champagne we had then.''

"I agree. It is a far better wine." He leaned over and refilled her glass. "I think I was more tired on our wedding night. Or," he smiled, "now that I look back on it, possibly I was just plain scared.''

"So much has happened since then. But this has been the most unexpected. I still can't believe it.''

"I know. It's an odd feeling to suddenly discover that I have a son." He poured the last of the wine. "It's the end of an era," he said with a tinge of amusement. "Our daughter is a young woman now, launched into society. In another year she will be going to college. And here we are, you and I by the fire talking about things that would have torn our marriage apart at one time, and all I can think of is that if I have another glass of wine, I'll probably fall asleep in my chair just the way I did on our wedding night."

Sam joined them on the island for a week in July. He slipped easily into their casual barefoot life. Dina found herself becoming fond of him, but when Alexandre asked if he had any plans for his future and Sam answered that he considered England his home and that his future lay there, she was relieved. And so, she discovered, was Alexandre.

As they stood on the dock waving to Sam as the ferry bore him toward the mainland, Alexandre sighed heavily. "You're going to miss him," she sympathized.

"No, I'm not. That's why I sighed. He's a nice young chap, but I don't feel like his father. I have little more feeling for him than I do for Tim Prentice's boy. He is a stranger to me. A son only by accident of conception."

The ferry was out of sight. She took his hand as they turned to walk home down the dirt road. "I'm sure that Sam feels much the same way. He probably feels a little guilty that he does not have the same feeling for you that he did for Bucky."

"I suppose you're right. We may not have seen the end of him, you know. He is going to tell his English grandparents that he is not Bucky's son. There is always the chance they might send him packing. I would want him to come to us in that event."

"I doubt that they will. I am sure they are as devoted to him as he is to them." She hoped she was speaking the truth. Sam was a charming boy, but he was Kitty's son as well as Alexandre's. She had had enough of Kitty in her life.

Two weeks later Alexandre left Dina and Vicky with Isabelle in Newport and returned to the city. The stock market was higher during the dog days of August than he had ever seen it. He was eager to get back.

Newport had hardly changed since Dina had been Vicky's age. Now the debutantes wore their hair bobbed short, the champagne was bootleg, and the young people danced to new popular songs like "Stardust" and "My Blue Heaven" and "You're the Cream in My Coffee." But these were mere details. Newport was still Newport. This year Vicky was the center of the young group that danced the nights away and gathered at the beach club in the afternoons to gossip and flirt. She loved it all. Her happiness delighted Dina. "I can't help but remember how miserable I was when I was seventeen," she told Isabelle one afternoon when the two of them sat in the shade of an umbrella and watched Vicky with her friends. "I was such an outsider. And so gauche." She sighed reminiscently. "It is almost unbelievable that I should have a daughter who is so attractive and popular."

But Dina soon had had enough. The Newport scene had bored her when she was young and it bored her now. She refused most invitations and spent her days on the shady porch working on her investments. She was concerned. Things were going too well.

"Papa would never have believed what is going on," she told Isabelle at lunch. "There seems to be no end to the money to be made, but this boom has gone on too long. It's no longer a boom, it's a bubble that is bound to burst. I have decided to sell everything as fast as I sensibly can." She hesitated. "I hope you're not overinvested."

"No, I'm not," Isabelle said frankly. "You know what your father used to say: 'Put your faith in gold and cold cash.' I've followed his advice."

Dina hoped that Alexandre was being equally cautious,

but there was nothing she could, or would, do about it. He
was happy. That was all that mattered. If worst came to
worst, she had plenty of money. He might run the firm into
the ground, but it would make no real difference in their
lives.

She decided to cut short her stay in Newport. Isabelle was
only too happy to assume responsibility for Vicky, and Dina
returned to New York. It was not only boredom. She
yearned to be with her husband.

Their reunion was the high point of her summer. It was
good to be alone, just the two of them. "I would never have
thought we could grow closer after all these years of
marriage," she said one night. She was wearing a periwinkle-
blue gown of gossamer-light silk and her hair was piled high
on her head because of the August heat. She looked enchanting, he thought, as she leaned toward him with love in
her eyes. "But I feel we have this summer. Perhaps because
of Sam. It rattled me—knowing that he existed—and made
me realize how good a life we have together. And now we
have this lovely private time all to ourselves. No dinner
engagements, no parties. Not even Vicky. I am loving it."

He smiled at her as he lit his cigar. "I suppose the answer
is that marriages don't just happen, they take time to
develop. Like a good wine."

Early in September the stock market hit an all-time high, a
dizzying peak. Dina decided to step up the pace of her
selling. She sensed trouble ahead. She could not resist
cautioning Alexandre. "It's too high," she said. "It's
bound to go down. And when it does, it will go down fast."

"It's not going to fall for a long time," he said comfortably. "Tim Prentice expects it to keep rising at least until
the new year. And Peckham says it is good for another ten
months."

Prentice! Peckham! Neither of them ever matched my
investment record, she stormed to herself. Why does he
listen to them and not to me? But she said nothing.

"I'm out of the market," she said at dinner a week later.

"You are? Why? Have you lost interest?"

"I've lost faith."

"You may be right," he said thoughtfully. "It may be time to take some profits." The next morning he started selling. He turned the proceeds into cash, packet after packet of hundred-dollar bills that he stored in the office vault.

On the twenty-fourth of October, a day that came to be known as Black Thursday, the bottom fell out of the market. Brokers, speculators, large and small investors sold and sold until there were no buyers at any price. The panic was on. Overnight, many of the richest men in America found themselves penniless. In the months that followed, millions upon millions of ordinary Americans found themselves out of work. There were suicides, broken families, hopeless young people, despairing old people. Squatters' shanties covered New York's Central Park. Several of the Fifth Avenue apartment buildings facing the park had mounted machine guns on their roofs, fearful of an attack by the maddened poor.

Dina counted her blessings every morning the way another woman might say her rosary. She was grateful for the solid assets that would see them through no matter what. The gold. The cash. The paintings. Her jewelry, especially the diamond-and-sapphire parure that Papa had given her. Her family was safe. They would be able to live as they had always lived.

Thanks to its strong cash position, achieved hurriedly by Alexandre in the weeks before the crash, Schumacher & de Granville survived. It was a triumph for Alexandre. He resolved to take advantage of his position. He remembered Dina's strategy at the end of the war. She had sold when the wartime economy was still hot and taken her profits. During the postwar recession she had bought stock at the lowest prices in a decade. He would do the same, only he would be even more canny. He would buy on margin. It was impossi-

ble that the market would sink any lower. The only way it
could go was up, and then he could sell at a profit.

He was acutely aware that not everyone was as fortunate:
He was generous to those in trouble. When Tim Prentice
told him that he would go under within the week unless
there was a miracle, Alexandre had simply asked, "How
much of a miracle do you need?" and given him the money.

Todd Winship had come to him like a scared little boy. "I
can't tell Flossie that we haven't a penny," he had said.
"I'd rather kill myself." Looking into his eyes, Alexandre
understood that he was his friend's last hope. "It's a loan,"
he assured Todd. "A business transaction. Don't think of it
as a favor. I'm charging you interest. You're a good investment." But they both knew that the chances of the interest
being paid were remote, let alone the capital sum.

And so it went in the years immediately after the crash.
When Herbert, once Frederick's bookkeeper and now trea-
surer of the firm, warned him that he was skating on thin ice,
Alexandre paid no attention. It was true that he had been
wrong about the market. It kept sinking and Herbert kept
saying, "We can't go on," when the margin calls came in.
But somehow they did until one Friday afternoon. It was the
cumulative effect of unwise decisions and misguided generosity that finally brought the firm down. But the last straw,
the infinitesimal weight that brought the whole structure
tumbling down, had been the Holcombe Fessenden note.

There had been no time to tell Dina before they went out
that night. Alexandre found it difficult to play the gallant
and charming dinner partner. His conversation was abstracted,
his smile forced. The dinner seemed endless, but finally the
men were alone at the table with their cigars and brandy.

"There's going to be a revolution," one guest declared.
"Things can't go on this way." Alexandre nodded agreement. Tonight he was ready to join a revolution against most
of the men in the room. He had been an utter fool. He had
believed them and their promises and their rosy forecasts. I

thought they knew what they were talking about, he thought bitterly. I suppose they did. They bled me of hundreds of thousands of dollars without my even feeling it.

It was little comfort to think that Schumacher & de Granville's cash reserves had staved off the hour of reckoning for several Wall Street firms. It had been money down the drain. Eventually they had gone under. As he was going to go under. Why had he cast himself in the role of altruist? That was for the Mellons and the Rockefellers. He was simply Alexandre de Granville, custodian of the Schumacher fortune. And he had been flattered into making a bloody fool of himself.

"Shall we move to the drawing room and join the ladies?" their host suggested, cutting in on Alexandre's musings.

He stood up smiling. "Why have we stayed away from them so long? They are prettier than we are. And far more cheerful." He trusted that no one had noticed his abstraction. They would be sure to read the worst into it. But what if they did? It was true. He was ruined.

He had signed a note for Frederick's old friend Holcombe Fessenden a long time ago. It was due in a few days. That morning a gray-faced Fessenden had called on him to say that he could not meet his obligation. Alexandre had called Herbert into his office. "We will have to make good on the Fessenden note," Alexandre told him. "He can't meet it."

Herbert stared at him. "Neither can you," he said. "Haven't you listened to what I've been telling you for the past six months?" It would have been insolence if it had not been for the utterly sincere shock in his eyes. "We don't have a penny. And margin calls are coming in every day."

Alexandre had spent the day reviewing the situation with Herbert. It was worse than he could grasp. He had been using money he did not have. The firm was deeply, inextricably in debt. He did not understand how it had happened, but Herbert did. And there was no way out. Now he knew why men had committed suicide in the nightmare weeks after the crash. He would almost rather die than face Dina with this news. He had to tell her tonight.

He put down his cigar and followed the other men into the drawing room.

# Twenty-four

It was a disaster. He had been living in a fool's paradise. Dina leaned back in the chair and shook her head. She was sitting at the desk in Whit's former office going over the books. How could Alexandre have been so naive?

There was a knock at the door. The two auditors, Casper Keyes and Henry Suffolk, came in. Gray-faced men in black suits, their expressions were somber. They could have been pallbearers. Keyes was carrying a slim folder. "We have completed the audit. The full report will be ready by the end of the week," he said. "In the meantime we have prepared this brief summary of the situation." He placed the folder on the desk.

Suffolk coughed. "We recommend that the firm go into bankruptcy," he said. "This would leave your personal assets untouched. As individuals you are not responsible for the debts of the firm."

"I shall read your report carefully." She did not ask them to sit down.

"It's a shame," Keyes said. "But it's the sensible solution. It is not as if you were the only ones. Nearly twenty-six thousand businesses went into bankruptcy last year." He wanted to offer her his sympathy—he had known and respected Frederick Schumacher—and her stony face deterred him. "You'll have the full report by the end of the week," he repeated, and they left.

She bent over the ledger again. Others were piled on the corner of the desk. Unbelieving she turned the pages. Incredible! It was as if a child had been playing store—buying high and selling low. Alexandre had been buying on margin, putting down only ten percent in cash. And every time the market went down a fraction of a point, he had had to put up more money. Dina pressed her lips together in a thin line. He had ruined Papa's business. Papa had built it up himself, and Alexandre had torn it down, blissfully unconscious of what he had done until he was confronted by stark ruin.

She slammed the ledger shut, picked up her coat, and left the office. She had to get some air. She was fuming. Her husband was an idiot. It was impossible for anyone to have been so stupid. She strode along Trinity Place toward the Battery as if the devil were pursuing her. At the harbor's edge, she stood looking over the water. She lifted her face to the October wind, welcoming the brisk chill. Bankruptcy. The very word horrified her. Thank God she had had the sense to concentrate on increasing her own fortune while Alexandre was frittering away the one Papa had made.

"No!" She shouted it into the wind. She would not allow it. Better to have to scrub floors for a living than have such a stigma attached to her name. She turned back to the office after a while. Burns was waiting in front with the new Packard they had bought that spring. When she stopped, he sprang out. "Take me to Mrs. Schumacher's, please," she told him as she settled herself in the back seat. She had to talk to someone. Isabelle was the only person she could trust.

Burns looked worried. "Mr. de Granville will be wanting me to drive him to his club for lunch."

"He can walk," she said dryly.

*     *     *

"What do you think?" Dina demanded.

For the last hour, she had been pacing the floor of the library while she told Isabelle what the auditors recommended and how incredibly incompetent Alexandre had been. "I can't face going through bankruptcy," she said. "I'd never be able to hold my head up again. I'm going to pay back every penny that the firm owes. The Fessenden note and all the rest. I'll clear up those margin accounts if it takes every penny I have.

"What do you think?" she asked again.

"I think you should have a whiskey. It's what I used to prescribe for your father when he got into this kind of state." Isabelle got up and went to the big drink tray on the library table. Dina stood looking out of the window. The faint splash of whiskey into the glass and the muted jangle of ice shards in the silver pitcher were the only sounds in the room. Isabelle handed the drink to Dina and settled herself again in the plumply cushioned arm-chair.

"What do I think? I think it's dreadful. Simply dreadful," she said, sounding unexpectedly old.

"You loved Papa as much as I did. What do you think he would do?" Dina asked.

"Your father would never have allowed himself to be in such a position," Isabelle said. "But if he had been I am certain he would have considered it a matter of honor to pay every cent he owed if it took him the rest of his life. He would have done what you are going to do."

She twisted the rings on her fingers, looking worried. "But what about Alexandre?" she asked, looking directly at Dina.

"What about him?"

"Your father is dead. It is Alexandre you must consider now. How is he going to feel if you—"

"I don't care how he feels," Dina broke in angrily. "If he had only had the sense to ask for advice . . . He didn't

even know he needed advice. He followed the herd. Just
another one of the sheep.'' She was red-faced with anger.
''Who cares how he feels?'' She gulped down the whiskey
and started pacing back and forth again.

Isabelle had never seen Dina like this, but she had seen
Frederick in similar tempers. Like father, like daughter, she
thought. There was nothing to do but wait for the passion to
die down and for reason to return. She watched Dina stalk
about the room until finally she flung herself in a chair.

''I know, I know,'' she said tiredly. ''You will say that
I've always known this was bound to happen eventually.
We've talked about it, you and I. I just never dreamed it
would be quite the total disaster it is.'' She stared at the
floor moodily. The room was quiet. The sun came in
through the west windows and glinted off the brass pendu-
lum of the grandfather clock. Isabelle waited.

At last Dina looked up. ''That was a shameful performance. I'm sorry,'' she apologized. ''My tantrum is finished. I'm going to pay those debts. And then we'll see. I
may not have a husband when it is over. He certainly will
not have a rich wife. But we will be able to face the world
without shame.''

''*You* will,'' Isabelle corrected. ''It will be different for
Alexandre. He will have to come to terms with the fact that
in paying the debts he has incurred, you will have put up a
considerable amount of your fortune. He may not be able to
accept that. He is a proud man, you know.

''Dina,'' she urged, ''let me help you. I have far more
money than I will ever need. It will be yours when I die, so
why not make use of it now? It would be our secret. He
need never know.''

''No, no, no!'' Dina smiled at her and shook her head. ''I
must do this myself. You hold on to your money. Heaven
only knows what is going to happen in the next few years.
This depression is brutal. You know how much I appreciate
everything you have done for me over the years. But I can't
let you do this.''

She stood up. "I must go. I'll walk home. The exercise will chase away the rest of my evil temper. I'm really more angry with myself than with Alexandre. I knew this would happen one way or another. So why am I so upset when the inevitable finally happens?"

She answered her own question. "I suppose it was because I was so happy. I thought it made me immune from trouble. Well," she bent down and kissed Isabelle, "we expect you for dinner tomorrow night as usual. We'll try not to be too dismal."

It was like an earthquake. Or a tidal wave. Their lives were turned inside out. The auctioneer and his staff took over the house, appraising and categorizing. The movers transferred the contents of the house to the auction rooms. The staff was dismissed. All except Siddie. "Where would I go?" she had asked. "My home has been with you for almost as long as I can remember. And what would you do without me?" Dina had hugged her. "You have a home with us as long as you want, but it will be a humble one after this." Céleste had saved her wages, and had enough to retire to her native village outside Lyons. The others unhappily joined the ranks of the unemployed. They had little to look forward to. More than a quarter of the work force had been unemployed for the last couple of years.

Every day another part of their lives disappeared. Then suddenly it was all over. The house had been sold. The furniture. The automobiles. Dina's furs. Her jewels. Everything. It had been miserably depressing. Nothing had brought anywhere near its true value except for the contents of Alexandre's wine cellar, which in a discreet bow to Prohibition had been auctioned off secretly for a surprisingly substantial amount.

It was the Depression. When no one had money, you could not expect to get a fair price. They had been fortunate to find buyers, Dina assured herself. But it stung. The house had been sold for less than it had cost to create the third-floor ballroom. Her sables had brought less than a hundred dollars. The jewels had been particularly disappointing. Even the magnificent diamond-and-sapphire parure had gone for the metaphorical song. She had been so complacent, assuring herself that she had enough money to shelter her husband and daughter from the effects of any conceivable financial disaster. Now it seemed they would lose every last penny that she was able to scrape up.

The paintings had done poorly for the most part. In later years she was to see many of them hanging in museums, and others bought and sold by private collectors for enormous sums of money, but in the autumn of 1932, no one was spending money on art. Jack Goddard's paintings were the only exceptions. They had brought surprisingly high prices. Not as much as the blackmail Jack had extracted from her in the first place, but far more than she had hoped.

She had agonized over the Goddards. When she unwrapped the paintings and sketches that she had hidden in the attic nearly twenty years before, she had been struck by their energy and vibrancy. She spent a long morning looking at them and worrying about how to dispose of them. In the end, the decision was unexpectedly easy. *Dina in the Wind* and *Dina by the Fire* could be auctioned along with the formal portrait he had painted of her. There was nothing incriminatingly intimate about them. But the nude sketches and the large painting of the *Nude in Bed*—never! It would be as if she were standing on the auction block herself, stark naked.

She took the sketches down to her bedroom and fed them to the fire one by one. When the last had gone up in a brief flame, she had stirred the ashes with a poker and added another log, then returned to the attic. She could not burn the nude. It was a masterful piece of work. She rewrapped it and packed it in a crate of linens that she was sending to Duck Island. The little house there was all they would have left. She had not even considered putting it up for sale. It would bring nothing—a few hundred dollars, possibly not even that.

The painting would be safe from discovery there, buried among the bed linens and bureau scarves. Perhaps some day after her death and Alexandre's, it could be shown.

It was harrowing. When it was over all they had left was each other and Vicky and the little house on the island, but Dina had met every obligation, paid every debt. Schumacher & de Granville had not had to suffer the disgrace of bankruptcy. And thanks to Isabelle, they had a roof over their heads. She had invited them to share the Murray Hill house. "You must consider it your home," she told Dina. "You father would want it this way."

It was strange being back in the old house, in her old rooms. She sat in her small sitting room late one afternoon thinking of the bewildered and often miserable, yet determined girl she used to be. It was unbelievable that she and Alexandre would be celebrating their twenty-second wedding anniversary in a couple of weeks, that a marriage founded solely on the need for money on the one hand and passionate determination on the other could have succeeded as well as it had.

He found her there, sitting in the dark. "You are sad?" he asked, turning on the light.

"No, I was just thinking about the past. Pleasant memories."

"Ah yes, when the present is bleak, one has to take refuge in memories," he said bitterly. His failure had cut deep. Worst of all was the knowledge that everything Dina possessed had gone to pay for his failure. He lay awake nights going over his mistakes, cursing himself for his blindness. He thought of suicide. And then he thrust the thought away in disgust. It was a weakling's way out. It had been his father's way out. It would not be his.

There was another way and he was prepared to take it. It would not be easy, facing life alone, but it would be best for all of them. Dina and Vicky would be all right, he assured himself. Isabelle would see to that. As for himself, a fresh start would help him recover his honor.

"I don't see the present as bleak," Dina said. She took his hand and pressed it against her cheek. "We are poor, that's true. But now—now there is no longer any barrier between us. I have no money. You have no money. It is better this way, I think."

"You cannot be happy about being plunged into poverty." His voice was harsh. He could not believe what he was hearing. There was no scorn in her voice. No anger. Only the sound of love.

"I *am* happy." She smiled up at him. "I have no money—and I think you still love me."

"I always have," he told her. "I always will." His voice was deep with emotion now. She means it, he told himself. She really means it. It was as if a soothing poultice had been applied to a wound. For the first time in weeks a little of the hurt disappeared. Perhaps he would not need to take that other way.

That night the four of them sat at the table a long time after dinner, too tired to move. The reaction from the weeks of strain had suddenly set in. They were almost too tired to talk until Vicky said, "I wish there was something I could do to help. Get a job or something."

"Your job is to go back to Radcliffe tomorrow," Dina said. Isabelle had insisted on paying for Vicky's college expenses and Dina had been happy to accept her generosity. "That is the way you can help us most. After you graduate, you can think about a job."

"Or marriage," her father added. "Cambridge is a good place to meet wealthy young men of good family. Perhaps even better than New York. I understand Harvard is full of them. You can always do what I did. Marry for money."

Dina was rigid with shock. How could he say such a thing? She looked at Vicky. How was she going to react? This was something she had never wanted her daughter to know.

Vicky smiled. "I would, Papa. I'd do it in a minute if there was someone who loved me the way Mama loves you. And if I loved him the way you love Mama."

Was that all? No questions? No horror? No tears? Had Vicky understood what her father had said? "You mean you would marry for money?" Her voice reflected her shock.

"Grandpa told me that it is as easy to love someone with money as someone without," Vicky replied. "The impor-. tant thing, he said, is love. Not money."

Vicky remembered that day very well. She could not have been more than seven or eight. She and her grandfather had been playing Parcheesi on the porch one rainy afternoon in Newport.

"Did I ever tell you how your mama and papa happened to get married?" he asked.

The little girl shook her head.

"Your mama had a mind of her own. Just like you. When she met your papa, she decided that he was exactly the right husband for her. She did not wait for him to ask her to marry him, because she was afraid he might not ask her because she had a lot of money and he had no money at all. Do you know what she did?"

Vicky looked at her grandfather, her eyes wide and questioning.

"She asked me to ask him if he would like to marry her. So I did. I asked him right in this very house. Your papa thought it was a good idea. And that's how they got married.

"They have lived happily ever after," her grandfather said. "I want you to remember this in case any old Newport biddies start gossiping. What you have to remember is that they don't know what they're talking about." He paused for emphasis. "But you do.

"And I'll tell you something else," he said. "I think you are every bit as smart as your mama. You've beaten me again at Parcheesi."

Vicky had beamed.

Tears were streaming down Dina's face. Alexandre jumped up and rushed to her side. "What's the matter?"

"Nothing," she sobbed. "It's just that I'm so happy."

He shook his head and looked at Isabelle and Vicky. "I married a very strange woman," he said. "All it takes to make her cry with happiness is to find herself without a penny in the world."

# Twenty-five

ALEXANDRE RETREATED behind the morning paper and Dina picked up a book. Ten minutes later she had not turned the page. The words were a blur. She could not stop going over the events of the past week like a dog worrying at a cut paw. Alexandre observed her from behind his paper, then put it down.

"A good book?" he asked.

"What? Oh, it's all right."

"You haven't read one word," he said. "I've been watching you. We've got to get out of here. We can't skulk around as if we were criminals."

It had been easy to be brave, even to smile in the midst of the debacle. But now that it was over, they were disoriented. The world they knew had collapsed about them. They wandered about the Murray Hill house like country-weekend guests during a spell of bad weather, not knowing what to do with themselves, longing to leave.

"There's nothing I'd like more, but where would we go?"

"What about the island? Our wedding anniversary is next week. Why don't we celebrate it there? Just the two of us."

"The island? In December?" She looked at him as if he had taken leave of his senses, then she sighed. "Well, why not? At least we'll be able to go out of the house without knowing that everyone we meet is feeling sorry for us."

"We could stay through the holidays."

"That might not be a bad idea. In fact," she sat up straight, warming to the idea, "I think it is exactly what we ought to do." She had been dreading the holiday season. On the island they would not have to put up a brave front and pretend to be cheerful.

"You mean it?" he asked. "You'd really like to go?"

"I'd love to," she said emphatically. "The more I think of it, the better I like it. Let's go."

And so they found themselves on the island late one December afternoon. It was almost dark. The wind, howling with a fury they had never experienced in summer, swept clouds of sand along the harbor road. They climbed into the battered truck that was the island's taxi and delivery van, and minutes later they were at the house. A damp cold rushed out to meet them when Alexandre opened the door. Dina looked at the truck's red taillight disappearing up the sandy track, and her heart fell. What were they doing here? In the middle of nowhere?

Alexandre looked at her anxiously. She smiled at him. She could not let him feel that coming here had been a mistake. "Once the fire is going, it will be more cheerful," she said. It had been laid just before they left in the summer, ready for a match to be touched to it.

In seconds it flared up, brightening the room and giving an illusion of warmth. "I'll light the lamps," she told him, "while you bring in our bags." She lit a candle in the fire, placed it in a holder, and went to the kitchen where a fire had also been laid in the big black stove, ready to be lit. When it was going, she added more wood and then set about filling the oil lamps. Sheets and blankets warmed in front of the kitchen stove while they ate scrambled eggs by the fire in the big room. Afterwards they made the bed together, laughing at their awkwardness. That night they slept like lost children, too exhausted to dream.

They woke to the glitter of frost on the meadows. Their spirits were high as they made plans for the day. They gathered driftwood on the beach and walked to the harbor to buy fish. Alexandre inspected the root cellar that he had converted into a wine cellar and brought in an armful of bottles. That night he pronounced their meal of island fish and potatoes accompanied by a chalky Chablis better than anything he had eaten in the past two months. They smiled at each other across the table. It had been a good day. "I'm glad we came," he said. There was a kind of triumph in his face.

They went outside for a few minutes before they went to bed. The night was crisp and the stars bright. They could hear the waves crashing against the cliff. He put his arm around her shoulder. "This is real," he said quietly. "Not the world we were living in this fall."

She was surprised at how happily he settled in. He seemed to have put his failure behind him as if the clean sea winds had blown defeat away. He was himself again. He coped with the chores as if he were a born islander, carrying in wood, cleaning out ashes, repairing a shutter that banged in the night. He pruned the old apple tree near the well and stacked driftwood in high piles close to the kitchen door.

One morning she looked out to find him raking leaves around the lilacs. She almost called to him that the lilacs had survived many a winter without a blanket of leaves over their roots, but she stopped herself. He was enjoying his role as responsible householder. Why should she diminish his contributions?

She was less content with island life. After a few days she was bored. She found the domestic tasks, which had always been taken care of by servants on previous visits, distaste-

ful. And yet she did not want to go back to Isabelle's. Nor
to her old life. She had outgrown it. As for the island, she
loved it, but as an occasional retreat from the world, not as
a way of life.

She walked along the beach one afternoon, restless and
frustrated. For the first time since she had left Miss Caldwell's
School for Young Ladies, she was not in command of her
life. She had never fully understood the power of money
before. No wonder Alexandre's Uncle Albert had wanted
him to marry an heiress. With money one could do anything.

The years when she had been at the helm of Schumacher
& de Granville had possessed a heady excitement that had
been missing from her life ever since. She loved Alexandre.
But marriage was not enough. She wanted more.

"I would sell my soul for some capital," she said,
through gritted teeth. The wind tore the words away as soon
as they were uttered. It dried the tears of frustration running
down her cheeks. "I can do it." She spoke into the wind
again. "I know I can." If she had not invested so shrewdly
in the postwar period, they would not have been able to
come out of the maelstrom with honor. "But I have nothing.
Nothing!" she cried desperately.

She walked along, careless of the incoming tide that wet
her heavy shoes from time to time. She could borrow from
Isabelle, of course. But she wouldn't. It would be like
betraying Papa. "Don't borrow," he had always said. "Lend.
Only gamblers and weaklings borrow." There must be a
way she could get her hands on some capital. There was the
little house. The cache of wine Alexandre had here on the
island. Her engagement and wedding rings. Lumped all
together they would bring practically nothing, she thought
hopelessly. She had nothing of real value.

But she did! She stood still, a slim straight figure on the
empty beach, her hair whipped by the wind. The Goddard.
The sleeping nude. It was in one of the crates piled up in the
servants' quarters at the back of the house. The Goddard
paintings had brought more at the auction than the Picassos

and the Bonnards. She bit her lip. Did she dare? It would bring a substantial sum, there was no doubt about it. In the first place it was a superb painting. And in the second, the scandal that it would provoke when it was put up for sale would send the price sky high. To possess such a painting of Dina de Granville . . . and a Goddard! People would pay for that, she told herself. They might pay enough so that Schumacher & de Granville could start up again. On a very small scale. It was a possibility.

She started walking again. How could she do it to Alexandre? What man could accept that another man had painted his wife in such intimacy? And, on top of that, accept that it was public knowledge? If he saw the painting, it was possible he would leave her. If she told him she was going to sell it . . . Impossible. She must put it out of her mind. She turned back and began retracing her steps toward the house.

She was in the kitchen preparing their anniversary dinner. It was a major undertaking. She had gone through the recipes that Céleste had written out for her before she left, recipes she had claimed were so simple a child could prepare them, and decided on coq au vin. That morning she had negotiated with one of the island women for a chicken. The woman had grabbed one that was running around the yard, twisted its neck, and asked, "Would you want me to pluck it for you?"

"Oh, please," she had said. She had left carrying the plucked chicken by its feet. Now she stared at it. How did one turn this obscene carcass into something to eat? Isabelle had given her *The Boston Cooking School Cookbook* before they left. "You will need it," she said, "if you are doing your own cooking."

Dina turned to the pages on poultry. "Cut off the head," she read, ". . . Snap the bone and pull off the foot. . . . with the hand remove entrails, gizzard, heart, and liver. . . . The windpipe may easily be found and withdrawn . . ." It was too revolting. She threw the book across the room and then picked it up, found her place again, and started working. When she was through, she looked at the result dubiously. She wiped her forehead with the back of her hand. How did women do this day after day?

She pumped water into a basin in the sink and washed her hands. This life was not for her. At that moment she made up her mind. She would sell the Goddard, come what may.

Later when she was upstairs getting ready for dinner, brushing her hair by lamp light, her hand stopped in midair. Was she risking too much? Alexandre would be hurt, jealous, angry. Her face softened with concern. And then her old grittiness surfaced. If he loves me, we can use this relic of that old affair to become independent again. If he doesn't . . . She examined her reflection as if it held the answer. But the answer came from within. If he does not love me enough, well, I have been hurt before, unhappy before, and I have survived.

She dressed carefully in a long dress of black silk with a frill of jade-green lace forming a Pierrot collar. It was much too elegant for dinner in this small house, but she wore it as a gesture to let Alexandre know how important he and their anniversary were to her. Without Siddie to do her hair, she brushed it back smoothly and twisted it in a knot at the nape of her neck. She turned in front of the mirror and nodded, satisfied with her efforts. Surely he would understand, she thought worriedly. If he did not, this might be their last anniversary.

She went down the steep stairs that wound about the chimney to the big room where Alexandre was waiting in front of the blazing fire.

The coq au vin was a success. "Céleste would have approved," he complimented her.

"Oh, how I miss her." Dina was dismayed. It had taken so little time to eat what had taken so much time to prepare. The revelation strengthened her resolve to go through with her plan.

He smiled at her. "Twenty-two years. It is a long time to be as happy as you have made me. Happy anniversary, my dear." He reached into his pocket. "I have something . . ."

"Oh, please. I want to give you your present first." She was unaccountably flustered. He wondered what it was. Under the circumstances he doubted that she would have spent money on a present. Could she have tried to make something? Knit a scarf perhaps? His Dina who was so unhandy in the domestic arts. He braced himself to exclaim with pleasure over whatever it was.

She looked sharply at him as if assessing him, then eased the large package out from behind the sofa. Good God in heaven! He knew exactly what it was. Why was she giving it to him? He hesitated to open it. It was a moment he could have postponed forever, but she was hovering over him, so palpably and uncharacteristically nervous that there was no possibility of delay or diversion.

He unwrapped it carefully, folding back the heavy brown paper layer by layer just as he had so many years ago. He propped the painting against a chair and stepped back to look at it. He might have been in a Manhattan art gallery for his quiet self-possession and the slight tilt of his head as he considered it. "Beautiful," he said finally. "A major work of art. It is time it saw the light of day."

"You . . . you have seen it? How . . . are you angry?" She had been prepared for almost anything but this matter-of-fact acceptance.

"Yes, I have seen it. And no, my darling, I am not angry. I was once, but that was long ago. Now I think we should drink to it—and to you." He opened the door to the porch and brought in the bottle of Pol Roger that he had left there to chill. He busied himself for the next few minutes easing out the cork and pouring the champagne. He placed the glasses on the low table in front of the sofa.

"Come," he pulled her down beside him. "I will tell you the story." And he told her about the afternoon he had discovered the paintings in the attic. "I, too, had heard gossip. I knew about your affair just as you knew about me and Kitty. But when I saw the paintings and the sketches, they made it too real." His face darkened at the memory. "I think I almost wanted to die from jealousy. If I had seen Goddard I would have strangled him, weak as I was. But that was years ago. Now I can look at his painting and admire it. But tell me," he took her face between his hands. "Why are you giving it to me?" His green eyes searched her face.

"Because I am desperate." She took his hands away from her face and moved away from him, looking at him directly. "I do not want to live this kind of life, exiled from everything and everybody because we do not have a penny. Nor do I want to accept money from Isabelle. I can't and I won't." Her face had been stern, but now she put out her hand and looked at him pleadingly. "I want to run Schumacher & de Granville again. Those were the most exhilarating years of my life. I want that life again. And this," she nodded at the painting, "is my only chance to have it.

"If we sell it, there will be gossip. I don't have to tell you that. But the gossip will increase its value. If it brings enough to buy a few blocks of stock, that is all I need to start. Alexandre," her face was alight with eagerness now, "I know I can do it. We can be rich again. But I need capital to get started."

"I see. And I understand." Instead of anger or shock, he radiated a happy serenity that startled her. How could he react to the painting and her proposal so calmly? "It is a magnificent gift. I thank you." He kissed her forehead. "And it was brave of you," he said, putting his hand on her cheek lovingly. "You are not simply giving me the painting, you are giving me truth. There are no more secrets between us."

She lowered her eyes. She had a twinge of guilt as she thought of Whit. Should she confess? But to what end? Honesty was admirable, but enough was enough.

"May I give you my present now?" His eyes were

gleaming with anticipation. He reached into his pocket again and as he handed her a small rectangular box, he said, "This is the last secret." His eyes did not leave her face as she opened it.

"Alexandre!" His name caught in her throat as she looked at the eleven perfectly matched diamonds sparkling up at her. "What . . . what are these? Where did you get them? What is this?" Her eyes were almost purple with shock.

"It is my Aunt Marita's diamond necklace that my Uncle Albert gave her on their wedding day," he said. "Or what was left of the necklace after Paris. I used some of the stones to set up the house for Belgian refugees. Others went—well, you know how they went. But these are the largest and best stones. And they are for you."

"You have had them all these years?"

"I planned to give them to you when I came back from Paris. But I knew you knew about Kitty. I was afraid that once I got my health back, you would tell me to get out of your life and then I would need the diamonds. They were all I had in the world. So that summer when we came here, I buried them under the lilacs. I knew they would be safe there. And I told myself that, after all, you had no need for diamonds. You had a safe full of precious jewels.

"Many times since then I have wanted to give them to you. But then I discovered the Goddard paintings. And later I didn't know how to explain why I hadn't given them to you before. Last month I decided to give them to you for the auction. It would be a dramatic last-minute presentation." His smile was self-mocking. "You would be grateful, and I would be contributing something toward the debts I had incurred for the firm. But I could not do it."

He was silent. A muscle twitched in his jaw. "You are sure you love me?"

She brought his hands up to her lips and kissed them. "I am sure. Why didn't you give them to me then?"

"It was the Goddard paintings. I was devoured by jealou-

sy all over again when you put them in with the other
paintings to be auctioned. The worst of it was that I did not
know what you had done with this one. I tortured myself
that you had sold it privately, and that the owner was
laughing at me for a cuckold all the time his eyes were
wandering over your body. Why should I give her the
diamonds? I asked myself.

"Once I started thinking that way—this is damnably
hard. Tell me now if you despise me so I can stop this
ridiculous confession."

She shook her head. "Go on," she urged gently.

"Well, I convinced myself that once the auction was over
and everything was settled, you would leave me. I was sure
you scorned me as a failure." He covered his face with his
hands for a moment. "I told myself that before you threw
me out of your life, I would leave. I would take the
diamonds and make a new start in life. Go to South
America where no one knew me. And then there was the
miracle."

"Miracle?"

"That evening I found you sitting alone in the dark. Do
you remember? When you said you were happy that neither
of us had any money, because now there were no barriers
between us. Suddenly the jealously and shame started to
disappear. It was a miracle. You loved me. You *still* loved
me. Despite everything. If you had asked for the blood in
my veins, you could have had it, but it was too late to give
you the diamonds for the auction. But perhaps it is better
this way." He paused, and then he asked, "Do you remember when I gave you the engagement ring that afternoon
under the wisteria? I told you I wished it was a diamond
ring."

"And I told you I had dozens of diamonds." She laughed
through her tears, crying because she was so happy.

"Now I can give you diamonds. A little late, but they are
yours. To use as you please. Will you accept them?" There
was a world of love and trepidation in his eyes.

She looked down at the diamonds glittering in her lap and then at him. She could not speak. Finally she gasped, "Oh yes! Yes!" She threw her arms around him, the diamonds spilling onto the floor. "I will never be able to thank you. You have given me back my life." For a long time the only sound in the room was the crackling of the fire, then she pulled away from his embrace and said, "But what will we do with the painting?"

"It is mine now," he said cheerfully. "I propose to wrap it up and put it away. It is said that every family has a skeleton in the closet. Why should we not have a nude in the safe? Much more attractive to my way of thinking.

"So it is settled," he turned serious. "We will be back in business."

We? Her heart plunged. What did he mean? Hadn't he been listening to what she said? Didn't he understand that she intended to run the firm? He could never cope with this depression market.

He smiled at her. "No, my love, this time we will do it right." He had understood what was going through her mind. "I will not try to pretend that I am a great financier this time. You will run the firm and I will charm the clients. Your father always said I had a way with clients."

"It's true. You do know how to handle people."

"Well then, shall we do it? Sell the diamonds and start up again?"

"No, no!" She was shocked. He would never learn. "That would be a mistake. We must not sell them. We will use them for collateral."

"Ah, the diamonds will feel at home that way," he said. "Aunt Marita rarely had a chance to wear her diamonds because Uncle Albert kept using them for collateral."

Dina did not respond to his smile. She was absorbed. After a few moments she asked, "Are you sure you want to give me the diamonds? Perhaps you should keep some of them for yourself."

"Why in heaven's name should I do that?"

"I was thinking of what you said before. That the diamonds were all you had in the world. You are—"

He laid a finger across her lips. "My dearest wife." He was very serious. "I promised you something twenty-two years ago today. If I remember the words . . ." He paused and then said quietly, "With all my worldly goods, I thee endow. That was my wedding vow. These are all my worldly goods and they are yours. Along with my heart."

With the firelight on her face, Dina looked like a girl again. Her hair was paler now—the rosy copper color had faded. But her eyes were as loving a blue as they had ever been, and her smile as enchanting. She was smiling at him now through a mist of tears.

"You will still have me?" he asked, knowing the answer, but wanting to hear it.

"For richer or poorer," she whispered. "In sickness and in health." She drew his face toward hers. "Until death do us part," she promised.

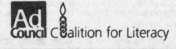